DRAGON HAVEN

ALSO BY ROBIN HOBB

THE RAIN WILDS CHRONICLES
Dragon Keeper

THE SOLDIER SON TRILOGY
Shaman's Crossing
Forest Mage
Renegade's Magic

THE FARSEER TRILOGY
Assassin's Apprentice
Royal Assassin
Assassin's Quest

THE LIVESHIP TRADERS TRILOGY
Ship of Magic
Mad Ship
Ship of Destiny

THE TAWNY MAN TRILOGY
Fool's Errand
Golden Fool
Fool's Fate

WRITING AS MEGAN LINDHOLM

Harpy's Flight
The Limbreth Gate
The Windsingers
Luck of the Wheels
Wizard of the Pigeons
Reindeer People
Wolf's Brother
Alien Earth
Cloven Hooves
The Gypsy (with Steven Burst)

Dragon Haven

Volume Two of
the Rain Wilds Chronicles

Robin Hobb

An Imprint of HarperCollinsPublishers

DRAGON HAVEN. Copyright © 2010 by Robin Hobb. All rights reserved. Printed in the United States of America. No part of this book may be used or reproduced in any manner whatsoever without written permission except in the case of brief quotations embodied in critical articles and reviews. For information address HarperCollins Publishers, 10 East 53rd Street, New York, NY 10022.

HarperCollins books may be purchased for educational, business, or sales promotional use. For information please write: Special Markets Department, Harper-Collins Publishers, 10 East 53rd Street, New York, NY 10022.

Design by Paula Russell Szafranski

Eos is a federally registered trademark of HarperCollins Publishers.

ISBN 978-0-06-193141-3

CONTENTS

CAST OF CHARACTERS

THE RAIN WILDS CHRONICLES

KEEPERS AND DRAGONS

ALUM: Pale skin, silvery gray eyes. Very small ears. Nose almost flat. His dragon is ARBUC, a silver-green male.

BOXTER: Cousin to Kase. Coppery-eyed, short, stoutly built. His dragon is an orange male SKRIM.

COPPER: An unclaimed, sickly brown dragon.

GREFT: Eldest of the keepers, and most heavily marked by the Rain Wilds. His dragon is blue-black KALO, the largest male.

GRESOK: Large red dragon, first to leave the cocooning grounds.

HARRIKIN: Long and slim as a lizard, at twenty, he is older than most of the other keepers. Lecter is his foster brother. His dragon is RANCULOS, a red male with silver eyes.

JERD: A blond female keeper, heavily marked by the Rain Wilds. Her dragon is VERAS, a queen, dark green with gold stippling.

KASE: Boxter's cousin. He has copper eyes and is short, wide, and muscular. His dragon is the orange male DORTEAN.

LECTER: Orphaned at seven, raised by Harrikin's family. His dragon is SESTICAN, a large blue male, with orange scaling and small spikes on his neck.

NORTEL: A competent and ambitious keeper. His dragon is the lavender male TINDER.

RAPSKAL: A heavily marked keeper. His dragon is the small red queen HEEBY.

SILVER: Has an injured tail and no keeper.

SYLVE: A twelve-year-old girl, youngest of the keepers. Her dragon is the golden MERCOR.

TATS: The only keeper to have been born a slave. He is tattooed on the face with a small horse and a spiderweb. His dragon is the smallest queen, green FENTE.

THYMARA: Sixteen years old; has black claws instead of nails and is at home in the trees. Her dragon is a blue queen, SINTARA, also known as SKYMAW.

TINTAGLIA: An adult queen dragon, she assisted the serpents on their journey up the river to cocoon. It has been years since she has been seen in the Rain Wilds.

WARKEN: A tall, long-limbed keeper. He is devoted to his dragon BALIPER, a scarlet male.

THE BINGTOWNERS

ALISE KINCARRON FINBOK: Comes from a poor but respectable Bingtown Trader family. The dragon expert. Married to Hest Finbok. Gray eyes, red hair, many freckles.

HEST FINBOK: A handsome, well-established, and wealthy Bingtown Trader.

SEDRIC MELDAR: Secretary to Hest Finbok, and friends with Alise since childhood.

THE CREW OF THE *TARMAN*

BELLIN: Deckhand. Married to Swarge.

BIG EIDER: Deckhand.

CARSON LUPSKIP: Hunter for the expedition. Leftrin's old friend.

DAVVIE: Apprentice hunter and nephew of Carson Lupskip. About fifteen years old.

GRIGSBY: Ship's cat. Orange.

HENNESEY: First mate.

JESS: Hired hunter for the expedition.

LEFTRIN: Captain. Robust build, gray eyes, brown hair.

SKELLY: Deckhand. Leftrin's niece.

SWARGE: Tillerman. He has been with the *Tarman* for more than fifteen years.

TARMAN: A river barge, long and low. Oldest existing liveship. Home port Trehaug.

MISCELLANEOUS CHARACTERS

ALTHEA VESTRIT: First mate, *Paragon* out of Bingtown. Aunt to Malta Khuprus.

BEGASTI CORED: Chalcedean merchant; bald, rich trading partner of Hest Finbok.

BRASHEN TRELL: Captain of the *Paragon* out of Bingtown.

CLEF: Ship's boy on the *Paragon*, former slave.

DETOZI: Keeper of the messenger birds at Trehaug.

DUKE OF CHALCED: Chalced's dictator, elderly and ailing.

EREK: Keeper of the messenger birds at Bingtown.

MALTA KHUPRUS: The Elderling "queen," resides in Trehaug. Married to Reyn Khuprus.

PARAGON: A liveship. Helped escort the sea serpents up the river to the cocooning grounds.

SELDEN VESTRIT: A young Elderling; Malta's brother and Althea's nephew.

SINAD ARICH: Chalcedean merchant who strikes a deal with Leftrin.

✧ ✧ ✧

Day the 5th of the Prayer Moon

Year the 6th of the Independent Alliance of Traders

From Erek, Keeper of the Birds, Bingtown
To Detozi, Keeper of the Birds, Trehaug

A message from Trader Jurden to be delivered to the Trehaug Rain Wild Traders' Council, regarding an order for Sevirian cutlery and the unfortunate shortage that has caused an unexpected and substantial increase in the price for it.

Detozi,

Greetings! The king pigeons have proven disappointing for speed and homing ability, but their swift breeding habits and quick growth to size make me wonder if there is an opportunity to create a supply of food birds that might be especially suitable to raising in the Rain Wilds. Your thoughts on this?

Erek

✧ ✧ ✧

PROLOGUE

T he humans were agitated. Sintara sensed their darting, stinging thoughts, as annoying as a swarm of biting insects. The dragon wondered how humans had ever managed to survive when they could not keep their thoughts to themselves. The irony was that despite spraying out every fancy that passed through their small minds, they didn't have the strength of intellect to sense what their fellows were thinking. They tottered through their brief lives, misunderstanding one another and almost every other creature in the world. It had shocked her the first time she realized that the only way they could communicate with one another was to make noises with their mouths and then to guess what the other human meant by the noises it made in response. "Talking" they called it.

For a moment, she stopped blocking the barrage of squeaking and tried to determine what had agitated the dragon keepers today. As usual, there was no coherence to their concerns. Several were worried about the copper dragon who had fallen ill. It was not as if they could do much about it; she wondered why they were flapping about it instead of tending to their duties for the other dragons. She was hungry, and no one had brought her anything today, not even a fish.

She strolled listlessly down the riverbank. There was little to see here, only a strip of gravel and mud, reeds and a few scrawny saplings. Thin sunlight touched her back but gave small warmth. No game of any size lived here. There might be fish in the river, but the effort of catching one was scarcely worth the small pleasure of eating it. Now, if someone else brought it to her . . .

She thought about summoning Thymara and insisting the girl go hunting for her. From what she had overheard from the keepers, they'd remain on this forsaken strip of beach until the copper dragon either recovered or died. She considered that for a moment. If the copper died, that would make a substantial meal for whichever dragon got there first. And that, she decided bitterly, would be Mercor. The gold dragon was keeping watch. She sensed that he suspected some danger to the copper, but he was guarding his thoughts now, not letting dragons or keepers know what he was thinking. That alone made her feel wary.

She would have asked him outright what danger he feared if she hadn't been so angry at him. With no provocation at all, he had given her true name to the keepers. Not just to Thymara and Alise, her own keepers. That would have been bad enough. But no, he had trumpeted her true name out as if it were his to share. That he and most of the other dragons had chosen to share their true names with their keepers meant nothing to her; if they wanted to be foolishly trusting, it was up to them. She didn't interfere between him and *his* keeper. Why had he felt so free about unbalancing her relationship with Thymara? Now that the girl knew her true name, Sintara could only hope that she had no idea of how to use it. No dragon could lie to someone who demanded the truth with her true name or used it properly when asking a question. Refuse to answer, of course, but not lie. Nor could a dragon break an agreement if she entered into it under her true name. It was an unconscionable amount of power that he had given to a human with the life span of a fish.

She found an open place on the beach and lowered her body onto the sun-warmed river stones, closed her eyes, and sighed. Should she sleep? No. Resting on the chilly ground did not appeal to her.

Reluctantly, she opened her mind again, to try to get some idea of what the humans had planned. Someone else was whining about blood on his hands. The elder of her keepers was in an emotional storm as to whether she should return home to live in boredom with her husband or mate with the captain of the ship. Sintara made a grumble of disgust. There was not even a decision to ponder there. Alise was agonizing over trivialities. It didn't matter what she did, any more than it mattered where a fly landed. Humans lived and died in a ridiculously short amount of time. Perhaps that was why they made so much noise when they were alive. Perhaps it was the only way they could convince one another of their significance.

Dragons made sounds, it was true, but they did not depend on those sounds to convey their thoughts. Sound and utterances were useful when one had to blast through the clutter of human thought and attract the attention of another dragon. Sound was useful to make humans in general focus on what a dragon was trying to convey to it. She would not have minded human sounds so much if they did not persist in spouting out their thoughts at the same time they tried to convey them with their squeaking. The dual annoyance sometimes made her wish she could just eat them and be done with them.

She released her frustration as a low rumble. The humans were useless annoyances, and yet fate had forced the dragons to rely on them. When the dragons had hatched from their cases, emerging from their metamorphosis from sea serpent to dragon, they had wakened to a world that did not match their memories of it. Not decades but centuries had passed since dragons had last walked this world. Instead of emerging able to fly, they had come out as badly formed parodies of what a dragon was supposed to be, trapped on a swampy riverbank beside an impenetrable forested wet land. The humans had grudgingly aided them, bringing them carcasses to feed on and tolerating their presence as they waited for them to die off or muster the strength to leave. For years, they had starved and suffered, fed barely enough to keep them alive, trapped between the forest and the river.

And then Mercor conceived of a plan. The golden dragon concocted the tale of a half-remembered city of an ancient race, and the vast treasures that surely resided there still, waiting to be rediscovered. It did not particularly bother any of the dragons that only the memory of Kelsingra, an Elderling city built to a scale that welcomed dragons, was a true memory. If a treasure of glittering riches was the false bait it took to encourage the humans to help them, so be it.

And so the trap was set, the rumor spread, and when sufficient time had passed, the humans had offered to assist the dragons as they sought to rediscover the Elderling city of Kelsingra. An expedition was mounted, with a barge and boats, hunters to kill for the dragons, and keepers to see to the needs of the dragons as they escorted them upriver and back to a city they recalled clearly only when they dreamed. The grubby little merchants who held power in the city did not give them their best, of course. Only two real hunters were hired to provide for over a dozen dragons. The "keepers" the Traders had selected for them were mostly adolescent humans, the misfits of their population, those they preferred would not survive and breed. The youngsters were marked with scales and growths, changes the other Rain Wilders wished not to see. The best that could be said of them was that they were mostly tractable and diligent in caring for the dragons. But they had no memories from their forebears, and skittered through their lives with only the minimal knowledge of the world that they could gather in their own brief existence. It was hard to converse with one, even when she had no intent of seeking intelligent dialogue. As simple a command as "go bring me meat" was usually met with whining about how difficult it was to find game and queries such as, "Did not you eat but a few hours ago?" as if such words would somehow change her mind about her needs.

Sintara alone of the dragons had had the foresight to claim two keepers as her servants instead of one. The older human, Alise, was of little use as a hunter, but she was a willing if not adept groomer and had a correct and respectful attitude. Her younger keeper, Thymara, was the best of the hunters among the keepers, but suffered from an unruly and impertinent nature. Still, having two keepers assured her that one was almost always available for her needs, at least for as long as their brief lives lasted. She hoped that would be long enough.

For most of a moon cycle, the dragons had trudged up the river, staying to the shallows near the densely grown riverbank. The banks of the river were too thickly forested, too twined with vines and creepers, too tangled with reaching roots to provide walking space for the dragons. Their hunters ranged ahead of them, their keepers followed in their small boats, and last of all came the liveship *Tarman,* a long, low river barge that smelled much of dragon and magic. Mercor was intrigued with the so-called liveship. Most of the dragons, including Sintara, found the ship unsettling and almost offensive. The hull of the ship had been carved from "wizardwood," which was not wood at all but the remains of a dead sea serpent's cocoon. The timber that such "wood" yielded was very hard and impervious to rain and weather. The humans valued it highly. But to dragons, it smelled of dragon flesh and memories. When a sea serpent wove its case to protect it while it changed into a dragon, it contributed saliva and memories to the special clay and sand it regurgitated. Such wood was, in its own way, sentient. The painted eyes of the ship were far too knowing for Sintara's liking, and Tarman moved upriver against the current far more easily than any ordinary ship should. She avoided the barge and spoke little to his captain. The man had never seemed to wish to interact with the dragons much. For a moment, that thought lodged in Sintara's mind. Was there a reason he avoided them? He did not seem cowed by dragons, as some humans did.

Or repulsed. Sintara thought of Sedric and snorted disdainfully. The fussy Bingtown man trailed after her keeper Alise, carrying her pens and paper, sketching dragons and writing down snippets of information as Alise passed it on to him. He was so dull of brain that he could not even understand the dragons when they spoke to him. He heard her speech as "animal sounds" and had rudely compared it to the mooing of a cow! No. Captain Leftrin was nothing like Sedric. He was not deaf to the dragons, and obviously he did not consider them unworthy of his attention. So why did he avoid them? Was he hiding something?

Well, he was a fool if he thought he could conceal anything from a dragon. She dismissed her brief concern. Dragons could sort through a human's mind as easily as a crow could peck apart a pile of dung. If Leftrin or any other human had a secret, they were welcome to keep it. Human lives were so short that knowing a human was scarcely worth the effort. At one time, Elderlings had been worthy companions for dragons. They had lived much longer than humans and been clever enough to compose songs and poetry that honored dragons. In their wisdom, they had made their public buildings and even some of their more palatial homes hospitable to dragon guests. Her ancestral memories informed her of fatted cattle, of warm shelters that welcomed dragons during the wintry season, of scented oil baths that soothed itching scales and other thoughtful amenities the Elderlings had contrived for them. It was a shame they were gone from the world. A shame.

She tried to imagine Thymara as an Elderling, but it was impossible. Her young keeper lacked the proper attitude toward dragons. She was disrespectful, sullen, and far too fascinated with her own firefly existence. She had spirit but employed it poorly. Her older keeper, Alise, was even more unsuitable. Even now, she could sense the woman's underlying uncertainty and misery. An Elderling female had to share something of a dragon queen's decisiveness and fire. Did either of her tenders have the potential for them? she wondered. What would it take to put spurs to them, to test their mettle? Was it worth the effort of challenging them to see what they were made of?

Something was poking her. Reluctantly, she opened her eyes and lifted her head. She rolled to her feet, shook herself, and then lay down again. As she began to lower her head, movement in the tall rushes caught her eyes. Game? She fixed her gaze. No. Nothing more than two of the keepers leaving the beach and heading into the forest. She recognized them. One was a female, Jerd, keeper to Veras. The green dragon's keeper was tall for a human female, with a brush of blond hair cresting her head. Thymara didn't like her. Sintara knew that without precisely knowing why. With her was Greft. She blew out softly through her nostrils. She had little use for Kalo's keeper. Greft might tend the huge blue-black dragon and keep him gleaming, but not even Kalo trusted him. All of the dragons had misgivings about him. Thymara regarded him with both interest and fear. He fascinated her, and Thymara resented that fascination.

Sintara snuffed the wind, caught the scents of the retreating keepers, and half closed her eyes. She knew where they were bound.

An intriguing thought came to her. She suddenly glimpsed a way to measure her keeper, but would it be worth the effort? Perhaps. Perhaps not. She stretched out on the warmed rocks again, vainly wishing they were sun-scorched banks of sand. She waited.

Day the 5th of the Prayer Moon

Year the 6th of the Independent Alliance of Traders

From Erek, Keeper of the Birds, Bingtown
To Detozi, Keeper of the Birds, Trehaug

Enclosed, a missive from Trader Polon Meldar to Sedric Meldar, to ascertain that all is well and ask his date of return.

Detozi,

There seems to be some concern over the well-being of some Bingtown residents who were scheduled to visit Cassarick, but now seem to have moved beyond it. Two anxious parents have separately visited me today, promising a bonus if news returns swiftly. I know you are not on the best of terms with the Keeper of the Birds in Cassarick, but perhaps this once, you might use that connection to see if there are any tidings of either Sedric Meldar or Alise Kincarron Finbok. The Finbok woman comes from a wealthy family. Good tidings of reassurance might be amply rewarded.

Erek

CHAPTER ONE

POISONED

The sucking gray mud pulled at her boots and slowed her down. Alise watched Leftrin walking away from her toward the huddled dragon keepers as she struggled to break free of the earth's grip and go after him. "Metaphor for my life," she muttered savagely and resolutely stepped up her pace. A moment later, it occurred to her that just a few weeks ago, she would have regarded crossing the riverbank as not only a bit adventurous but as a taxing walk. Today, it was only a muddy patch to get across, and one that was not particularly difficult. "I'm changing," she said to herself, and was jolted when she sensed Skymaw's assent.

Do you listen in on all my thoughts? She queried the dragon and received no acknowledgment at all. She wondered uneasily if the dragon was aware of her attraction to Leftrin and of the details of her unhappy marriage. Almost immediately, she resolved to protect her privacy by not thinking of such things. And then recognized the futility of that. *No wonder dragons think so poorly of us, if they are privy to every one of our thoughts.*

I assure you, most of what you think about we find so uninteresting that we don't even bother having opinions about it. Skymaw's response floated into her mind. Bitterly, the dragon added, *My true name is Sintara. You may as well have it; all the others know it now that Mercor has flung it to the wind.*

It was exciting to communicate, mind to mind, with such a fabulous creature. Alise ventured a compliment. *I am overjoyed to finally hear your true name. Sintara. Its glory is fitting to your beauty.*

A stony silence met her thought. Sintara did not ignore her; she offered her only emptiness. Alise attempted to smooth things over with a question. *What happened to the brown dragon? Is he ill?*

The copper dragon hatched from her case as she is, and she has survived too long, Sintara replied callously.

She?

Stop thinking at me!

Alise stopped herself before she could think an apology. She judged it would only annoy the dragon more. And she had nearly caught up to Leftrin. The crowd of keepers that had clustered around the brown dragon was dispersing. The big gold dragon and his small pink-scaled keeper were the lone guardians by the time she arrived at Leftrin's side. As she approached, the gold dragon lifted his head and fixed his gleaming black eyes on her. She felt the "push" of his regard. Leftrin abruptly turned to her.

"Mercor wants us to leave the brown alone," he told her.

"But, but, the poor thing may need our help. Has anyone found out what is wrong with him? Or her, perhaps?" She wondered if Sintara had been mistaken or was mocking her.

The gold dragon spoke directly to her then, the first time he had done so. His deep bell-like voice resonated in her lungs as his thoughts filled her head. "Relpda has parasites eating her from the inside, and a predator has attacked her. I stand watch over her, to be sure that all remember that dragons are dragons' business."

"A predator?" Alise was horrified.

"Go away," Mercor told her, ungently. "It is not your concern."

"Walk with me," Leftrin suggested strongly. The captain started to take her arm, and then abruptly withdrew his hand. Her heart sank. Sedric's words had worked their mischief. Doubtless Sedric had thought it his duty to remind Captain Leftrin that Alise was a married woman. Well, his rebuke had done its damage. Nothing would ever be easy and relaxed between them again. Both of them would always be thinking of propriety. If her husband, Hest, himself had suddenly appeared and stood between them, she could not have felt his presence more strongly.

Nor hated him more.

That shocked her. She hated her husband?

She had known that he hurt her feelings, that he neglected her and humiliated her, that she disliked his manner with her. But she hated him? She'd never allowed herself to think of him in such a way, she realized.

Hest was handsome and educated, charming and well mannered. To others. She was allowed to spend his wealth as she pleased, as long as she did not bother him. Her parents thought she had married well, and most of the women of her acquaintance envied her.

And she hated him. That was that. She had walked some way in silence at Leftrin's side before he cleared his throat, breaking in on her thoughts. "I'm sorry," she apologized reflexively. "I was preoccupied."

"I don't think there's much we can do to change things," he said sadly, and she nodded, attaching his words to her inner turmoil before he changed their significance by adding, "I don't think anyone can help the brown dragon. She will live or she'll die. And we'll be stuck here until she decides she's doing one or the other."

"It's so hard to think of her as female. It makes me doubly sad that she is so ill. There are so few female dragons left. So I don't mind. I don't mind being stuck here, I mean." She wished he would offer her his arm. She'd decided she'd take it.

There was no clear dividing line between the shore and the river's flow. The mud got sloppier and wetter and then it was the river. They both stopped well short of the moving water. She could feel her boots sinking. "Nowhere for us to go, is there?" Leftrin offered.

She glanced behind them. There was the low riverbank of trampled grasses and beyond that a snaggled forest edge of old driftwood and brush before the real forest began. From where she stood, it looked impenetrable and forbidding. "We could try the forest," she began.

Leftrin gave a low laugh. There was no humor in it. "That wasn't what I meant. I was talking about you and me."

Her eyes locked with his. She was startled that he had spoken so bluntly, and then decided that honesty might be the only good thing that could come from Sedric's meddling. There was no reason now for either of them to deny the attraction they felt. She wished she had the courage to take his hand. Instead, she just looked up at him and hoped he could read her eyes. He could. He sighed heavily.

"Alise. What are we going to do?" The question was rhetorical, but she decided she would answer it anyway.

They walked a score of paces before she found the words she truly wanted to say. He was watching the ground as he walked; she spoke to his profile, surrendering all control of her world as she did so. "I want to do whatever you want to do."

She saw those words settle on him. She had thought they would be like a blessing, but he received them as a burden. His face grew very still. He lifted his eyes. His barge rested on the bank before them and he seemed to meet its sympathetic stare. When he spoke, perhaps he spoke to his ship as much as to her. "I have to do what is right," he said regretfully. "For both of us," he added, and there was finality in his words.

"I won't be packed off back to Bingtown!"

A smile twisted half his mouth. "Oh, I'm well aware of that, my dear. No one will be packing you off to anywhere. Where you go, you'll go of your free will or not at all."

"Just so you understand that," she said and tried to sound

strong and free. She reached out and took his calloused hand in hers, gripping it tight, feeling the roughness and the strength of it. He squeezed her hand carefully in response. Then he released it.

THE DAY SEEMED DIM. Sedric closed his eyes tightly and then opened them again. It didn't help. Vertigo spun him, and he found himself groping for the wall of his compartment. The barge seemed to rock under his feet, but he knew it to be drawn up on the riverbank. Where was the handle to the damn door? He couldn't see. He leaned against the wall, breathing shallowly and fighting not to vomit.

"Are you all right?" A deep voice at his elbow, one that was not unfamiliar. He fought to put his thoughts in order. Carson, the hunter. The one with the full ginger beard. That was who was talking to him.

Sedric took a careful breath. "I'm not sure. Is the light odd? It seems so dim to me."

"It's bright today, man. The kind of light where I can't look at the water for too long." Concern in the man's voice. Why? He scarcely knew the hunter.

"It seems dim to me." Sedric tried to speak normally, but his own voice seemed far away and faint.

"Your pupils are like pinheads. Here. Take my arm. Let's ease you down on the deck."

"I don't want to sit on the deck," he said faintly, but if Carson heard him, he didn't pay any attention. The big man took him by the shoulders and gently but firmly sat him down on the dirty deck. He hated to think what the rough boards would do to his trousers. Yet the world did seem to rock a little less. He leaned his head back against the wall and closed his eyes.

"You look like you've been poisoned. Or drugged. You're pale as white river water. I'll be right back. I'm going to get you a drink."

"Very well," Sedric said faintly. The man was just a darker shadow in a dim world. He felt the man's footsteps on the deck, and even those faint vibrations seemed sickening. Then he was gone and Sedric felt other vibrations, fainter and not as rhythmic as the footsteps had been. They weren't even really vibrations, he thought sickly. But they were something—something bad—and they were directed toward him. Something knew what he had done to the brown dragon and hated him for it. Something old and powerful and dark was judging him. He closed his eyes tighter, but that only made the malevolence seem closer.

The footsteps returned and then grew louder. He sensed the hunter crouch down by him. "Here. Drink this. It'll buck you up."

He took the warm mug in his hands, smelling the dreadful coffee. He raised it to his lips, took a sip, and found the bite of harsh rum hidden in the coffee. He tried to keep from spitting it on himself, choked, swallowed it, and then coughed. He wheezed in a breath and then opened his watering eyes.

"Is that better?" the sadistic bastard asked him.

"Better?" Sedric demanded furiously, and heard his voice more strongly. He blinked away tears and could see Carson crouched on the deck in front of him. His ginger beard was lighter than his unruly mop of hair. His eyes were not brown, but that much rarer black. He was smiling at Sedric, his head cocked a little to one side. *Like a cocker spaniel,* Sedric thought viciously. He moved his boots against the deck, trying to get his feet under him.

"Let's walk you into the galley, shall we?" Carson took the mug from Sedric's hands, then with apparent ease seized him by the upper arm and hauled him to his feet.

Sedric's head felt wobbly on his neck. "What's wrong with me?"

"How should I know?" the man asked him affably. "You drink too much last night? You might have bought bad liquor in Trehaug. And if you bought any liquor in Cassarick, then it's almost definitely rotgut. They'll ferment anything there—roots, peelings from fruit. Lean on me, don't fight me now. I knew one fellow tried to ferment fish skins. Not even the whole fish, just the skins. He was convinced it would work. Here. Mind your head. Sit down at the galley table. Could be if you eat something, it'll absorb whatever you drank and you'll be able to pass it."

Carson, he realized, stood a head taller than he did. And was a lot stronger. The hunter moved him along the deck and into the deckhouse and sat him down at the galley table as if he were a mother harrying a recalcitrant child to his place. The man's voice was deep and rumbling, almost soothing if one overlooked his uncouth way of putting things. Sedric braced his elbows on the sticky galley table and lowered his face into his hands. The smells of grease, smoke, and old food were making him feel worse.

Carson busied himself in the galley, putting something in a bowl and then pouring hot water from the kettle over it. He stood for a time, jabbing at it with a spoon, before he brought it to the table. Sedric lifted his head, looked at the mess in the bowl, and belched suddenly. The dark red taste of dragon blood rose up in his mouth and flooded his nose again. He thought again that he might faint.

"You got to feel better after that," Carson observed approvingly. "Here. Eat some of this. It will settle your gut."

"What is it?"

"Hardtack softened with hot water. Works like a sponge in the gut, if you got a man with a sour belly or one you got to sober up fast for a day's work."

"It looks disgusting."

"Yes, it does. Eat it."

He hadn't had any food, and the aftertaste of the dragon blood still lingered in his mouth and nose. Anything, he reasoned, had to be better than that. He took up the wide spoon and stirred the muck.

The hunter's boy Davvie entered the deckhouse. "What's going on?" he demanded. There was a note of urgency in his voice that puzzled Sedric. He put a spoonful of soggy hardtack in his mouth. It was all texture and no taste.

"Nothing you need to worry about, Davvie." Carson was firm with the boy. "And you have work to do. Get after mending those nets. I'm betting we won't be moving from here for most of the day. We set a net out in the current, we may get a haul of fish, maybe two. But only if the net is mended. So get to it."

"What about him? What's the matter with him?" The boy's voice sounded almost accusing.

"He's sick, not that it's any of your business. You get about your work and leave your elders and your betters to their own. Out."

Davvie didn't quite slam the door but shut it more firmly than he needed to. "Boys!" Carson exclaimed in disgust. "They think they know what they want, but if I gave it to him . . . well. He'd find out that he just wasn't ready for it. But I'm sure you know what I mean."

Sedric swallowed the sticky mass in his mouth. It had absorbed the dragon blood taste. He ate another spoonful, and then realized that Carson was looking at him, waiting for a response. "I don't have any children. I'm not married," he said, and took another spoonful. Carson had been right. His stomach was settling, and his head was clearing.

"I didn't think you did." Carson smiled as if at a shared joke. "I don't either. But you look to me like someone who would have had some experience of boys like Davvie."

"No. I haven't." He was grateful for the man's rustic remedy, but he wished he'd stop talking to him and go away. His own whirling thoughts filled his head and he felt he needed time to sort them rather than filling his brain with polite conversation. Carson's words about poison had unsettled him. Whatever had he been thinking, to put dragon blood in his mouth? He couldn't remember the impulse to do so, only that he'd done it. His only intention had been to take blood and scales from the beast. Dragon parts were worth a fortune, and a fortune was what he was after. He wasn't proud of what he'd done, but he'd had to do it. He had no choice. The only way that he and Hest would ever leave Bingtown together would be if Sedric could amass the wealth to finance it. Dragon blood and dragon scales would buy him the life he'd always dreamed of.

It had seemed so simple, when he'd crept away from the boat

to harvest what he needed from the sickly dragon. The creature was obviously dying. What would it matter to anyone if Sedric took a few scales? The glass vials had weighed heavy in his hands as he filled them with blood. He'd meant to sell it to the Duke of Chalced as a remedy for his aches and pains and advancing age. He'd never even considered drinking it himself. He could not even remember wanting to drink it, let alone deciding that he would.

Dragon blood was reputed to have extraordinary healing powers, but perhaps like other medicines, it could be toxic, too. Had he truly poisoned himself? Was he going to be all right? He wished he could ask someone; it came to him abruptly that Alise might know. She'd done so much research on dragons, surely she must know something about the effects their blood could have on a man. But how could he ask such a question? Was there any way to frame it that didn't incriminate him?

"That pudding helping your stomach at all?"

Sedric looked up suddenly, and regretted it. Vertigo rocked him briefly and then cleared. "Yes. Yes, it is." The hunter sat down across from him and kept looking at him. Those black eyes locked with his own, as if they wished to see inside Sedric's head. He looked down at his bowl and forced himself to take another mouthful of the stuff. It was helping his stomach, but he didn't enjoy the experience of eating it. He glanced up again at the watchful hunter. "Thank you for your help. I don't mean to keep you from your duties. I'm sure I'll be fine now. As you say, it was probably something I drank or ate. So you needn't bother about me."

"It's no bother."

Again the man waited, as if there was something he expected Sedric to say. He was at a loss. He looked down at his "food" again. "I'm fine, then. Thank you."

And still the man lingered, but now Sedric refused to look up from his bowl. He ate steadily in small bites, trying to seem as if it demanded all his attention. The hunter's attention flustered him. When he rose from his seat across the table, Sedric repressed a sigh of relief. As Carson passed behind Sedric, he put a heavy hand on his shoulder and leaned down to speak right next to his ear. "We should talk some time," he said quietly. "I suspect we have far more in common than you know. Perhaps we should trust each other."

He knows. The thought sliced through Sedric's aplomb and he nearly choked on his mouthful of sodden bread. "Perhaps," he managed to say and felt the grip on his shoulder tighten briefly. The hunter chuckled as he lifted his hand and left the deck-house. As the door shut firmly behind him, Sedric pushed the bowl away and cradled his head on his arms. *Now what?* He asked the enclosed darkness. *Now what?*

THE BROWN DRAGON looked dead. Thymara longed to go closer and have a better look at her, but the golden dragon standing over her intimidated her. Mercor had scarcely moved since the last time she had walked past them. His gleaming black eyes fixed on her now. He did not speak, but she felt the mental push he gave her. "I'm only worried about her," she said aloud. Sylve had been dozing, leaned back against her dragon's front leg. She opened her eyes at the sound of Thymara's voice. She gave Mercor an apologetic glance and then came over to Thymara.

"He's suspicious," she said. "He thinks someone hurt the brown dragon on purpose. So he's standing watch to protect her."

"To protect her, or to be first to eat her when she dies?" Thymara managed to keep all accusation out of her voice.

Sylve did not take offense. "To protect her. He has seen too many of the dragons die since they came out of their cocoons. There are so few females that even one who is stunted and dull-witted must be protected." She laughed in an odd way and added, "Rather like us."

"What?"

"Like us keepers. Only four of us are females and all the rest males. Mercor says that no matter how deformed we are, the males must protect us."

The statement left Thymara speechless. Without thinking,

she lifted her hand to her face, touching the scales that traced her jawline and cheekbones. She considered the ramifications of it and then said bluntly, "We can't marry or mate, Sylve. We all know the rules, even if Mercor does not. The Rain Wilds marked most of us from the day we were born, and we all know what it means. A shorter life span. If we do conceive, most of our children aren't viable. By custom, most of us should have been exposed at birth. We all know why we were chosen for this expedition, and it wasn't just so we could care for the dragons. It was to get rid of us as well."

Sylve stared at her for a long moment. Then she said quietly, "What you say is true, or used to be true for us. But Greft says we can change the rules. He says that when we get to Kelsingra, it will become our city where we will live with our dragons. And we will make our own rules. About everything."

Thymara was appalled at the girl's gullibility. "Sylve, we don't even know if Kelsingra still exists. It's probably buried in the mud like the other Elderling cities. I never really believed we'd get to Kelsingra. I think the best we can really hope for is to find a place suitable for the dragons to live."

"And then what?" Sylve demanded. "We leave them there and go back home, back to Trehaug? And do what? Go back to living in shadows and shame, apologizing for existing? I won't do it, Thymara. A lot of the keepers have said they won't do it. Wherever our dragons settle, that's where we're staying, too. So there will be a new place for us. And new rules."

A loud snapping sound distracted Thymara. She and Sylve both turned to see Mercor stretching. He had lifted his golden wings and extended them to their full length. Thymara was surprised to see not only the size of them but that they were marked with eyes like a peacock's feathers. As she watched, he flapped them again, sharply, gusting wind and the scent of dragon at her. She watched him refold them awkwardly, as if moving them were an unfamiliar task. He snugged them firmly to his back again and resumed his watchful stance over the brown dragon.

Thymara was suddenly aware that a communication had passed between Mercor and Sylve. The dragon had not made a sound, but Thymara had sensed something even if she was not a party to it. Sylve gave her an apologetic look and asked, "Are you going hunting today?"

"I might. It doesn't look as if we're going to do any traveling today." She tried not to think of the obvious—that until the brown died they were all stuck here.

"If you do and you get fresh meat . . ."

"I'll share what I can," Thymara replied instantly. She tried not to regret the promise. Meat for Sintara, and meat for the sickly copper and the dim-witted silver dragon. Why had she ever volunteered to help care for them? She couldn't even keep Sintara well fed. And now she had just said she'd try to bring meat for Sylve's golden dragon, Mercor. She hoped the hunters were going out as well.

In the days since the dragons had made their first kill, they had learned to do some hunting and fishing for themselves. None of them was an exceptional predator. Dragons were meant to hunt on the wing, not lumber after prey on the ground. Nonetheless, all of them had enjoyed some success. The change in diet to freshly killed meat and fish seemed to have affected almost all of them. They were thinner, but more muscular. As Thymara strode past some of the dragons, she looked at them critically. With surprise, she realized that they now more closely resembled the depictions of dragons she had seen in various Elderling artifacts. She halted where she was to watch them for a moment.

Arbuc, a silver-green male, was splashing along in the shallows. Every now and then he thrust his whole head into the water, much to the amusement of Alum, his keeper. Alum waded alongside, fish spear at the ready, even as his frolicking dragon drove off any possible game. As she watched, Arbuc spread his wings. They were ridiculously long for him, but he beat them anyway, battering water up and showering Alum with it. His keeper yelled his disapproval and the dragon stopped and stood puzzled, his arched wings dripping. She looked at him and wondered.

Abruptly, she turned her steps and went looking for Sintara. *Sintara, not Skymaw,* she reminded herself moodily. Why had it injured her pride so much to learn that some of the dragons had never concealed their true names from their keepers? Jerd had probably known her dragon's name since the first day. Sylve had. She clenched her teeth. Sintara was more beautiful than any of them. Why did she have to have such a difficult temperament?

She found the blue dragon sprawled disconsolately on a patch of muddy reeds and grasses. The dragon rested her head on her front paws and stared out at the moving water. She didn't lift her head or give any indication she was aware of Thymara until she spoke. "We should be moving, not waiting here. There are not many days left before the winter rains, and when they come, the river will run deeper and swifter. We should be using this time to seek for Kelsingra."

"Then you think we should leave the brown dragon?"

"Relpda," Sintara replied, a vindictive note creeping into her thoughts. "Why should her true name remain unknown while mine is not?" Sintara lifted her head and suddenly stretched out her front feet and extended her claws. "And she would be copper, not brown, if proper care were given to her. Look here. I've split a claw end. It's from too much walking in the water over rock. I want you to get twine and bind it for me. Coat it with some of that tar you used on the silver's tail."

"Let me see." The claw was frayed and softened from too much time in water. It had begun to split at the end, but luckily it hadn't reached the quick yet. "I'll go ask Captain Leftrin if he has twine and tar to spare. While we're at it, let's look at the rest of you. Are your other claws all right?"

"They're all getting a bit soft," Sintara admitted. She stretched her other front foot toward Thymara and spread her toes, extending her claws. Thymara bit her lip as she checked them; they were all slightly frayed at the ends, like hard driftwood finally surrendering to damp. Thinking of wood gave her a possible solution. "I wonder if we could oil them. Or varnish them to keep the water away."

The dragon twitched her foot back, very nearly knocking Thymara over. She examined her claws herself and then responded with a reserved, "Perhaps."

"Stand up and stretch out, please. I need to check you for dirt and parasites."

The dragon rumbled a protest but slowly obeyed. Thymara walked slowly around her. She hadn't imagined the changes. Sintara had lost weight but gained muscle. The constant immersion in river water was not good for her scales, but walking against the current was strengthening the dragon. "Open your wings, please," Thymara requested.

"I'd rather not," Sintara replied primly.

"Do you want to shelter parasites in their folds?"

The dragon rumbled again but gave her wings a shudder and then unfolded them. The skin clung together like a parasol stored too long in the damp, and it smelled unpleasant. Her scales looked unhealthy, the feathery edges showing white, like layers of leaves going to mold.

"This is not good," Thymara exclaimed in dismay. "Don't you ever wash them? Or shake them out and exercise them? Your skin needs sunlight. And a good scrubbing."

"They're not so bad," the dragon hissed.

"No. They're damp in the folds and smelly. At least leave them unfolded to air while I go get something to help your claws." Heedless of Sintara's dignity, Thymara seized the tip of one of the dragon's finger-ribs and pulled the wing out straight. The dragon tried to close her wing but Thymara held on stubbornly. It was entirely too easy for her to hold the wing open. The dragon's muscles should have been stronger. She tried to think of the right word for it. Atrophy. Sintara's wing muscles were atrophying from disuse. "Sintara, if you don't listen to me and take care of your wings, soon you won't be able to move them at all."

"Don't even think such a thing!" the dragon hissed at her. She gave a violent flap and Thymara lost her grip and fell to her knees in the mud. She looked up at the dragon as Sintara began indignantly to fold her wings again.

"Wait. Wait, what's that? Sintara, open your wing again. Let me look under it. That looked like a rasp snake under there!"

The dragon halted. "What's a rasp snake?"

"They live in the canopy. They're skinny as twigs but long. They're really fast when they strike, and they have a tooth, like an egg tooth, on their snouts. They bite and hold on, and dig their heads in. And then they just hang there and feed. I've seen monkeys with so many on them that they look like they have a hundred tails. Usually the animal gets an infection around the head and dies from that. They're nasty. Unfold your wing. Let me look."

It hung from high under the wing, a long nasty snakelike body. When Thymara braved herself to touch it, the dangling thing suddenly lashed about angrily and Sintara gave a startled chirp of pain. "What is it? Get it off me!" the dragon exclaimed and thrust her head under her wing and seized the parasite.

"Stop! Don't bite it, don't pull on it. If you rip it off you, the head will tear free and stay inside and make a terrible infection. Let go, Sintara. Let go of it and let me deal with it!"

Sintara's eyes glittered, copper disks whirling, but she obeyed. "Get it off me." The dragon spoke in a tight, furious voice, and Thymara was jolted to feel, beneath Sintara's anger, her fear. An instant later, Sintara added in a low hiss. "Hurry. I can feel it moving. It's trying to dig deeper into me. To hide inside my body."

"Sa save us all!" Thymara exclaimed. Her gorge rose in revulsion, and she tried to recall how her father had said one got rid of a little rasp snake. "Not fire, no. They dig deeper if you put fire to them. There was something else." She searched her memory desperately, and then had it. "Whisky. I have to go see if Captain Leftrin has whisky. Don't move."

"Hurry," Sintara pleaded.

Thymara ran toward the barge, then caught sight of the captain and Alise strolling together. She changed her course and raced toward them, shouting, "Captain Leftrin! Captain Leftrin, I need your help!"

At her cries, both the captain and Alise turned and hurried toward her. She was out of breath by the time they reached each other, and to Leftrin's worried, "What's wrong, girl?" she could only reply, "Rasp snake. On Sintara. Biggest I've ever seen. Going into her chest, under her wing."

"Those damned things!" he exclaimed, and Thymara could only feel gratitude that she didn't have to explain it.

She caught a gasping breath. "My father used liquor to make them back out."

"Yes, well, tereben oil works better. Trust me on that. Had to get one out of my own leg once. Come on, girl. I've got some on board. Alise! If one dragon has a rasp snake, chances are the others do, too. Tell the keepers to check their animals. And that brown one, the one that's down? Check her, too. Look on her underbelly. They'll go for a soft place for an easy bite and then dig in."

Alise felt a surge of purpose as Leftrin turned away from her and headed back toward the barge. She hastened down the beach, going from keeper to keeper, giving the warning. Greft almost immediately found one dangling from Kalo's belly, concealed by one of his hind legs. There were three fastened to Sestican; she'd thought for a moment that his keeper, Lecter, was going to faint when he discovered three short ends of snakes poking out from his dragon's nether regions. She spoke to him sharply to jolt him from his panic, directing him to take his dragon over to where Sintara was and to wait for Leftrin there. The boy seemed shocked that she could speak so severely. He gave a gulp, recovered himself, and obeyed her.

She swallowed her own shock at that and hurried on. When she came to Sylve and the golden dragon guarding the dirty brown one, she had to pause and rebuild her courage for a moment. She did not want to confront him; she wanted nothing more than to turn and hasten away. It took her a moment to convince herself that what she felt was not her own cowardice, but the dragon's efforts to repulse her. She squared her shoulders and marched up to him and his keeper.

"I'm here to check the brown dragon for parasites. Some of the other dragons have been attacked by rasp snakes. Your keeper should check you over while I look at the brown dragon."

For a time the gold just stared at her. How could solid black eyes glitter so bleakly?

"Rasp snakes?"

"A parasitic burrowing creature. Thymara says she knows of them from the canopy. But these, she thinks, come from the river. They are much larger. It's a snake that bites and eats its way in, to live off your flesh."

"Disgusting!" Mercor declared. The gold immediately stood and spread his wings. "It makes me itch to think of it. Sylve, check me for those creatures immediately."

"I groomed you completely today, Mercor. I do not think I would have missed such a thing. But I will check you."

"And I must look at the brown dragon to see if she has any," Alise asserted firmly.

She had expected Mercor to oppose her. Instead, he seemed completely distracted by the thought that he himself might have such a parasite.

Alise ventured toward the impassive copper dragon. She was crumpled on the ground in a way that was going to make inspecting her underbelly difficult if not impossible. And Sylve was right. The coating of mud on the dragon was so even that it almost looked deliberate. It was going to have to come off before she could tell much of anything about the creature.

She glanced helplessly toward Sylve, but the small girl had her hands full with Mercor. An instant later, her first impulse shamed her. What had she thought to do? Summon the Rain Wild child to have her clean the dragon so that Alise could inspect her without getting her hands dirty? How arrogant a thought was that? For years, she had been claiming she was an expert on dragons, yet at her first opportunity to tend to one, she quailed at a bit of mud? No. Not Alise Kincarron.

Not far from where the copper dragon sprawled, part of a bank of coarse reeds remained untrampled, their tasseled heads standing half as tall as Alise. She drew her little belt knife, cut half a dozen of them, folded them into a coarse cushion of reeds, and, returning to the dragon, began to give her a good scrubbing with it, starting at the creature's upper shoulder.

The dried mud was river silt and it came away surprisingly easily. Alise's coarse brush bared coppery scales that quickly took on a lovely sheen as she worked on the poor creature. Relpda did not make a sound, yet Alise thought she sensed a dim gratitude from the prostrate dragon. She redoubled her efforts, moving her scrubbing rushes down the dragon's spine. As she worked, the size of a dragon was forcibly impressed on, not just her mind, but her muscles. The area of skin to be cleaned suddenly reminded her of the routine work of the crew scrubbing the barge's deck. And this was a small dragon. She glanced over her shoulder at the gleaming gold of Mercor's scaled hide and mentally compared it to the small pink-scalped girl who tended him. How much of each evening did the girl devote to her task?

As if Sylve had sensed her gaze, she turned to Alise. "He's clean, every inch of him. No snakes on him. I'll help you with Relpda now."

Her pride made Alise want to say she had her task well in hand. Instead she heard herself say "Thank you" with utter gratitude. The girl smiled at her, and for an instant her lips caught a glint of light from the sun. Was her mouth scaled, too? Alise jerked her stare away and renewed her scrubbing efforts, sending a cascade of fine silt from Relpda's hip to the damp earth below her. Sylve had not seemed so scaly when she'd first seen the girl. Was she changing as much as the dragons were?

Sylve came to join her, carrying a coarse reed "brush" of her own. "This is a really good idea. I've been using evergreen boughs when I can get them, and handfuls of leaves when I can't. But this works much better."

"If I'd had the time to weave the stems and leaves together, I think it would work even better. But this will get the job done, I think." Alise had a hard time speaking and scrubbing at the same time. Her years in Hest's house had softened her. As a girl, she'd always helped with the household cleaning; her family had not been able to afford many servants. Now she could feel sweat damping her back and blisters starting to form on her hands. Her shoulder already ached. Well, so be it! A little hard work never hurt anyone. And when she looked back over the area of dragon that she had cleaned, she felt a rush of pride.

"What's this? What's this? Is this a snake hole?" The fear and distress in Sylve's voice seemed to infect her dragon. Mercor came lumbering over and swung his large head down to snort at a spot on the copper dragon's neck.

"What does it look like?" Alise asked, leery of coming closer while the golden was so intent.

"A raw spot. The dirt around it was damp, maybe with blood. She's not bleeding now, but . . ."

"Something jabbed her there," Mercor opined. "But it's not a 'snake hole' my dear. Still, the blood smell is strong, so she bled quite a bit."

Alise found her wits. "I don't think the snakes make a hole and crawl inside. I think they only stick their heads in and drink blood."

Mercor stood absolutely still, his head still hanging over the copper dragon. His eyes were black on shining black; still Alise had a sense of that color slowly swirling in them. He seemed to go away from them for a time. Then he shuddered his coat, rippling his scales in a way that reminded her more of a cat than a reptile. An instant later, she felt again the presence of his mind, and marveled. If he had not briefly left them, she would never have recognized how strongly he affected her when he was focused on them.

"I do not know about snakes called rasp snakes. These things you describe, I have heard of, long ago, and then they were called burrowers. They dug in deep. They may be more dangerous than the rasp snakes the other keeper spoke about."

"Sa have mercy," Sylve said quietly. She stood silently a moment, her rush scrubber still in her hands. Then she abruptly walked around the dragon and pushed her. "Relpda!" she shouted, as if to penetrate the dragon's stupor. "Roll over. I want to see your belly. Roll over!"

To Alise's astonishment, the sickly dragon stirred. She moved her hind legs feebly against the mud she sprawled in. She lifted a wobbly head, unlidded her eyes, and then let her head drop back to the earth. "Move away," Mercor directed them roughly, and both women obeyed him promptly, jumping back to be clear of the prone dragon. Mercor lowered his head, thrust his muzzle under Relpda, and tried to turn her over. She rumbled a feeble protest and scrabbled her legs as if the motion pained her.

"Is he eating her? I don't think she's dead!" The protest came from another dragon keeper who had suddenly joined him. *Rapskal,* Alise thought. Was that his name? He was a handsome lad, despite his Rain Wild strangeness. His thick dark hair and black clawed hands contrasted oddly with his pale blue eyes and angelic smile. His dragon was with him, a dumpy red creature with stumpy legs and a brilliant sheen to her scales. When Rapskal stopped to stare, the small dragon leaned her head affectionately against her young keeper, nearly knocking him over. "Stop it, Heeby. You're bigger and stronger than you know! Stand up on your own feet." There was more affection than rebuke in his voice. He gave his dragon a shove, and she playfully nudged him back.

"Mercor's not trying to eat her," Sylve explained indignantly. "He's trying to turn her over so we can check her belly for parasites. There's a snake kind of creature—"

"I know. I was just over watching them get them out of Sestican. Just about made me puke to see them back out, and Lecter was almost crying and blaming himself. I've never seen him so broken up before."

"But they got them out?"

"Yes, indeed they did. Must have hurt, though. That big blue dragon was squeaking like a mouse as they came out. I don't know what Captain Leftrin had mixed up, but they put it around the hole where the snake went in and pretty soon it started thrashing its tail, and then it started backing out. Lots of blood and goop come with it, and hoo, what a stink! And then when it finally dropped to the ground, Tats jumped on it and chopped it up with an ax. Made me glad I check my Heeby from top to toe every day. Right, Heeby?"

The red dragon gave a snort in response and shoved Rapskal

again, sending the boy staggering. His account had made Alise feel a bit queasy, but Sylve had other things on her mind. "Rapskal, can you get Heeby to help Mercor? We're trying to turn the copper dragon onto her back."

"Well, sure I can. All I got to do is ask her. Hey, Heeby! Heeby, look here, look at me. Heeby, listen. Listen, girl. Help Mercor turn the copper dragon onto her back. Understand? Help him turn her over? Can you do it? Can my big strong dragon do that for me? Sure she can. Come on, Heeby. Put your nose under here, right here, just like Mercor. That's my girl. Now lift and push, Heeby, lift and push!"

The little red dragon dug her feet in. As Alise watched, the muscles in her short thick neck bulged. She made a rumbling noise of great effort, and suddenly Relpda began to move. She gave a squeal of pain, but both Mercor and Heeby ignored it. Pushing and grunting, they turned her onto her back. Her legs waved feebly in the air. "Hold her there, Heeby. That's my girl. Hold her there!" And in response to Rapskal's cries, the small red dragon braced herself and stood with her head butted up against the copper. Her neck muscles bulged, but her golden eyes spun in pleasure to her keeper's loud praises.

"Look there!" Mercor said, and Alise stared in horror. The copper dragon's muddy belly was studded with snake tails. There were at least a dozen, the exposed stubs twitching and writhing because their victim had been moved. Sylve covered her mouth with both her hands and stepped back. She rocked her head from side to side and spoke breathlessly through her fingers.

"She never let me groom her belly. I tried. I did try! She always pulled away from me and rubbed it in the mud. She was trying to get rid of them, wasn't she, Mercor? She wouldn't let me groom her belly because it hurt."

"Her mind was not clear enough for her to know that you could help her," Mercor said heavily. "No one blames you, Sylve. You did what you could for her."

"Is she dead?" The call reached them, and all heads turned. Thymara and Tats were coming at a trot. Captain Leftrin was close behind them. Sintara was following at a more dignified pace. Behind them, half a dozen other keepers and dragons were converging.

"No! But she's infested with them. I don't know if we can save her." Sylve's voice broke on the words.

"Try," Mercor commanded her sternly, but then he leaned over the girl and gently blew his breath down on her. At most, it could have been a gentle breeze, but Sylve swayed in it. To Alise, the sudden change in the girl's countenance was stunning. And frightening. Sylve went from a near-hysterical child to a calm woman. She drew herself up taller, glanced up at her dragon, and smiled at him.

"We will." She looked over at Alise and said, "First, we will use our reed brushes to clean away as much of the mud as we can. Heeby, you will have to hold her in this position, on her back. She will not like what we do, but I think we must clear the mud from her injuries before we can treat them."

"That makes sense to me," Alise concurred, and wondered where the poise had come from. Was she seeing Sylve as she was when her own doubts didn't taunt her, or was this, somehow, an overlay of the dragon Mercor? Alise took up her reed scrubber and turned it to a fresh spot. She approached the dragon cautiously. The copper might be small and weak for a dragon, but a kick from any of her gently waving legs would send a human flying. And if she struggled and rolled over onto a keeper, serious injuries would result.

THYMARA HALTED AND stared at Alise. For a moment, the Bingtown woman looked like a different person. She was scrubbing away at the belly of the copper dragon, heedless of dust and mud that cascaded onto her trousers and boots. Dust coated her face, and her blouse was filthy to the elbows. Even her pale eyelashes were laden with dust. Yet her expression was one of determination, and almost pleasure in her task. When had she changed from being an elegant Bingtown lady, impeccably dressed and with manners to match? A grudging admiration stirred in Thymara.

Heeby stood, her scarlet head lowered and braced against the copper dragon, pinning her in an ungainly belly-up posture. Rapskal stood at her shoulder, proudly patting his dragon and murmuring praise of her. Mercor hovered over the group, while Sylve appeared to be in charge of the operation. The girl also looked different, Thymara thought, though she could not quite put her finger on what it was.

She took two steps closer and felt ill. Barely exposed snake tails dotted the dragon's belly. She swallowed hard. It had been awful to watch the writhing parasite exit from Sintara's body. The snake had not been in her long, and most of its body had still been outside the dragon's. Once Leftrin had daubed the strong smelling tereben oil around the injury, the snake had gone limp, and then suddenly began to lash wildly. The dragon had trumpeted her distress. Thymara had stepped forward hastily and seized the lashing snake by the tail. "Hold on. I'm applying more oil!" Leftrin had warned her.

At the second application, the snake had become frantic. It had begun to writhe backward out of the dragon, and as the length of bloody snake emerged, Thymara had forced herself to seize it and hold on lest it try to reenter the dragon. It had slithered and slipped in her grip. Sintara had blasted news of her pain and the other dragons and keepers had begun to gather around her. As the final length of the snake had emerged, the animal had whipped its head about, splattering Thymara's face with blood as it tried to attack the creature who gripped it. She had shrieked as the blood hit her and flung the animal to the ground. Tats had been ready and waiting with a hatchet. It hadn't got far. She'd stood numbly, shaking with her dragon's shared pain. She'd dragged her sleeve across her face, but it only smeared the thick blood more. It had smelled and tasted of dragon, and even now, after she'd washed it off, the clinging scent of it filled her nose, and she could not be rid of the taste of it. Afterward, Leftrin had swabbed the injury with rum and then sealed it over with a daub of tar lest the acid river water ulcerate it. The captain spoke as he worked. "After this, you'll have to do nightly checks of your dragons. Those snakes got something in their mouths that numbs the flesh. You don't even feel one burrowing in. I got a little one in my leg once, didn't even know it was there until I got out of the water."

As Alise and Sylve worked, the copper dragon made small sounds of pain. Thymara squatted down beside her to look into her face, but the dragon's eyes were closed. She wondered if Relpda was even conscious. She stood up again slowly. "Well, at least we know what's wrong with her now. If we can get them out of her, clean her wounds, and seal them against the river water, maybe she'll have a chance."

"We've cleaned away enough dirt. Let's get them out of her," Sylve decided.

Thymara stood with the circle of watchers, staring in sick fascination. As Leftrin stepped forward with his pot and brush, she turned aside. Ever since Sintara's blood had hit her face, it was all she could smell or taste. She had no desire to see more of it tonight. When she saw Sintara waiting on the outskirts of the gathering, Thymara pushed through the other onlookers to get to her dragon. "I don't want to watch this," she told her in a low voice. "It was hard to see one snake removed from you, and you hadn't carried it long. I can't watch this."

Sintara turned her head to regard her keeper. Her copper eyes whirled, and suddenly they appeared molten to Thymara, pools of liquid copper whirling against the gleaming backdrop of her lapis lazuli scales. Dragon glamour, she tried to warn herself, but couldn't care. She let herself be drawn into that gaze, let herself become important because of the dragon's regard for her. A tiny cynical part of her snidely asked if a dragon's regard truly made her important. She ignored it.

"You should go hunting," Sintara suggested to her.

She was reluctant to leave the dragon. Moving away from her glorious copper gaze would be like leaving the warmth of a cheery fire on a cold and stormy night. She clung to the dragon's gaze, refusing to believe her dragon might wish her to leave.

"I'm hungry," Sintara said softly. "Won't you go and find food for me?"

"Of course," Thymara responded promptly, overcome by Sintara's will.

Sintara's voice grew very soft, as if it were no more than a breath blowing past Thymara's ear. "Greft and Jerd went into the forest not so long ago. Perhaps they know where the hunting is good. Perhaps you should follow them."

That stung. "I am a better hunter than Greft will ever be," she told her dragon. "I've no need to follow him."

"Nonetheless, I think you should," Sintara insisted, and suddenly it did not seem like a bad idea. A thought teased at the edge of Thymara's mind; if Greft had already made a kill, perhaps she could help herself to a share, just as he had with hers. She still had not paid him back for that trespass.

"Go on," Sintara urged her, and she went.

EACH OF THE keepers had formed the habit of keeping their gear in their boats. Dealing with Rapskal's untidiness was a daily trial for Thymara. When she thought about it, it seemed unfair that a random choice on the first day had doomed her to be his partner. The others regularly rotated partners, but Rapskal had no interest in such swaps. And she doubted she would find anyone willing to take him on, even if she could persuade him to try it. His strangeness was too great. Yet he was handsome, and adept on the river. And always optimistic. She tried to recall him speaking crossly, and could not. She smiled to herself. So he was strange. It was a strangeness that she could get used to. She pushed his gear bag to one side and rummaged in her own for her hunting items.

Away from Sintara's gaze, it was easier to think about what she was doing and why. She recognized that the dragon had exerted some sort of glamour over her. Yet even being aware of it did not disperse it entirely. She had nothing more pressing to do, and certainly they could use the meat; they could always use the meat. The copper would benefit from a meal after they'd cleared the snakes off her, and certainly Mercor could do with some meat. But as she slung her bag over her shoulder, she wondered if she were merely trying to find a more acceptable reason to let herself follow the dragon's suggestion. She shrugged at the uselessness of wondering about it and set off for the forest eaves.

The shores of the Rain Wild River were never the same and never different. Some days, they passed ranks of needled and lacy fronded evergreens. The next day those dark green ranks might give way gradually to endless columns of white-trunked trees with reaching pale-green leaves, and all their branches festooned with dangling vines and creepers heavy with late blossoms and ripening fruit. Today there was a wide and reedy bank, with ranks of rushes topped with tufts of fluffy seedheads. The bank was only silt and sand, temporary land that might vanish in the next flood. Beyond it and only slightly elevated above it a forest of gray-barked giants with wide spreading branches chilled the earth with their eternal shade. Vines as thick as her waist dropped down from those spreading branches, creating an undergrowth as restrictive as the bars of a cage.

It was easy enough to follow Greft's trail through the marsh grasses. Water was already welling up in some places to fill his boot tracks. The prints of Jerd's bare feet were less visible. Thymara scarcely gave her mind to her tracking, thinking instead of the dragon. The more time and distance she acquired from Sintara, the clearer became her own thoughts. Why Sintara had sent her hunting was an easy question to answer; the dragon was always hungry. Thymara had intended to hunt today anyway; she did not mind her errand. More puzzling was why the dragon had suddenly decided to make the effort to charm her. She never had before. Did that mean that she now considered Thymara more important than she had previously?

A thought light as wafting bulrush down floated into her mind. "Perhaps she could not use her glamour before. Perhaps she grows stronger in many ways, not just physically, as she challenges herself."

She had whispered the words aloud. Was the thought hers, or had she, briefly, touched minds with one of the other dragons? That question was as disturbing as the thought itself. Was Sintara acquiring more of the powers that legends associated with dragons? Were the other dragons? And if so, how would they use them? Would their keepers be blinded by glamours, to become little more than fawning slaves?

"It doesn't work that way. It's more like a mother loves a wayward child." Again she spoke the words aloud. She stopped, just beneath the eaves of the forest, and shook her head wildly, making her black braids whip against her neck. The small charms and beads that adorned them snapped against her neck. "Stop it!" she hissed at whoever was invading her thoughts. "Leave me alone."

Not a wise choice, but the choice is yours, human.

And like a gauzy mantle lifting from her head and shoulders, the presence was gone. "Who are you?" she demanded, but whoever it had been was gone. Mercor? She wondered. "I should have asked that question first," she muttered to herself as she entered the thick shade of the forest. In the dimmer light, Greft's trail was not as easy to follow, but he had still left plenty of signs. And she had not gone far before she no longer needed to bother with tracking him. She heard his voice, his words indistinct, and then another voice in reply to his. *Jerd,* she thought. They must be hunting together. She went more slowly and quietly, and then came to a complete halt.

Sintara had all but insisted she follow them. Why? She suddenly felt very awkward. How would it seem to them if she suddenly came up on them? What would Jerd think? Would Greft see it as her admitting he was a better hunter than she was? She moved up into a tree and began to traverse from branch to branch. She was curious to see if he'd made a kill yet and if so, what he'd taken down, but she had no desire for them to know she was there. Their voices came more clearly, a scattering of words. Jerd said she "didn't understand" and there was anger in her voice. Greft's voice was deeper and harder to follow. She heard him say, "Jess isn't a bad man, even if he" and then his words were too soft to follow. She edged closer, thanking Sa for the black claws she dug in to the slippery bark. She changed trees again, moving from one thick branch to another, and then she was suddenly looking down on Jerd and Greft.

They weren't hunting. She doubted they had been hunting. It took a long moment for her mind to make sense of what her eyes saw. They were naked and lying next to each other on a blanket. Their discarded clothing was draped on nearby bushes. Greft's scaling was blue and covered far more of his body than Thymara had ever suspected. He was turned away from her as he reclined. In the dim light of the forest, he looked like a large lizard trying to find a sunning spot. What little light there was touched the long line of his hip and thigh down to his knee.

Jerd faced him. She lay on her belly, her chin propped on her elbows. Her bushy blond hair was even more disorderly than usual. Greft's hand was on her bare shoulder. Her body was long and slender, and the line of greenish scaling down her spine suddenly seemed beautiful to Thymara. It gleamed in the dim light, a rivulet of emerald shining down her back. Her legs were bent at the knee, and her heavily scaled calves and feet gently waved in the air as she replied to Greft. "How could you even suggest it? It is exactly the opposite of what we promised to do."

He shrugged one naked shoulder, making the light move in a sapphire line on his back. "I don't see it that way. No keeper claimed that dragon. No one is bonded to her. She's nearly dead. The other dragons can eat her when she dies and get some nourishment and a few memories. Dumb as that copper dragon is, chances are she doesn't have many memories at all. But, if we can persuade the dragons to let us have her carcass, or even part of it, Jess could turn it into some solid wealth that would benefit all of us."

"But that's not—"

"Wait. Let me speak." He set a finger to her lips to quench her protest. She bridled, turning her head away from his touch, but he only chuckled. Thymara, watching them, could not decide what was more shocking: their nakedness or the topic of their conversation. They could only have been doing one thing. One forbidden thing. But Jerd seemed irritated, almost angry with him, and yet she so casually stayed next to him. Greft caught Jerd's jaw in his fingers, turned her face back to him. She bared her teeth at him and he laughed outright.

"You are such a child sometimes."

"You didn't treat me like a child a little while ago!"

"I know." His hand moved down the side of her neck and he slipped it under her body. He was touching her breast. Jerd's bared teeth changed to a very peculiar smile and she stretched, moving herself against Greft's hand. Shock and a strange thrill ran through Thymara. Her breath caught in her throat. Was that what it was like? She had thought of sex as something that belonged only to adults, and only to those fortunate enough to have normal bodies. Now as she watched Jerd rub herself against Greft's touch, a peculiar envy awoke in her. Jerd had obviously just taken this for herself. Or perhaps Greft had begun it, tricking her or forcing her? No. The look she was giving him now was all too knowing. An unsettling warmth was infusing Thymara's own body. She couldn't look away.

Greft seemed to have forgotten entirely that he had been speaking. Jerd suddenly wiggled aside from his touch and demanded, "You were saying? You were trying to justify selling dragon parts to the filthy Chalcedeans, I believe."

He made a small noise in his throat, and then pulled his hand back to his side. His voice was husky when he spoke. "I was trying to explain that we will need money if my dream for us is to come true. I don't really care where it comes from. I know where it won't come from. Neither the Bingtown Traders nor the Rain Wild Traders will want to help us establish a town of our own. Both groups see us as abominations. They were glad to see us leave Trehaug and even gladder that we took the dragons with us. They don't expect us to return; they don't expect us to survive.

"And if we do find Kelsingra do you think they'll respect it as ours? No, Jerd. If we find Kelsingra and there are any Elderling artifacts left there, you can bet the Traders will claim them for themselves. I've seen Captain Leftrin at work, charting the path we've taken. There's only one reason for him to do that. It's so that if we find something valuable, he can return to Trehaug and tell the Traders. And they'll know how to come back and find us and take it away from us. And we'll be on the outside again, the leftovers, the rejects. Even if all we find is a piece of land large enough for dragons to survive on, we won't be safe. How long have the Traders been looking for arable land? Even that they would take from us. So we have to think ahead. We all know that Cassarick and Trehaug depend on outside trade for survival. They dig up Elderling treasure and sell it through the Bingtown Traders. They can't feed themselves. Without Elderling stuff to sell, it would all have fallen apart years ago. But what will we have? Nothing. Maybe, if we find solid ground, we can build something for ourselves and our children. But even if all we plan to do is grow crops, we'll still need seed and tools. We'll need to build homes for ourselves. And we'll need money, solid coin, to buy what we need."

Thymara's head was whirling. Was Greft speaking of a town for the keepers and their dragons? A future for them, a future separate from Trehaug or Cassarick? A future with children? With husbands, wives? It was unthinkable, unimaginable. Without consciously making the decision, she stretched out flat on the tree limb and wormed her way closer.

"It won't work," Jerd responded scornfully. "Any town site you find will be too far up the river. And who would trade with us?"

"Jerd, you are such a child sometimes! Now wait, don't glare at me. It's not your fault. You've never known anything but the Rain Wilds. I myself have only ventured out once or twice, but at least I've read of what the outside world is like. And the hunter is an educated man. He has ideas, Jerd, and he sees things so clearly. When he talks, everything just makes so much sense. I always knew that there had to be a way to have a different life, but I just couldn't see it. Jess says it was because for so long I'd been told what the rules were that I couldn't see they were just rules made by men. And if men can make rules, then other men can change them. *We* can change them. We don't have to be bound by the 'way things have always been.' We can break out of it, if we just have the courage.

"Look how we are with the dragons. They remember how the world was, back when they dominated, and they think that's how it's going to be again. But we don't have to give them that power. None of the dragons needs to have that dragon's body when it dies. It's just meat to them, and we've given them plenty of meat. So, in a sense, they owe it to us, especially when you think what it could mean to us. With the kind of wealth we could get for the dragon's corpse, we could make a foundation for a better life for all of us, including the other dragons! If we have the courage to change the rules and do what is best for us for a change." Thymara could almost see Greft's imagination soaring on what could be. The grim smile on his face promised triumph over old humiliations and wrongs. "Jess says that if you have money, anyone will trade with you. And if, from time to time, we have rare merchandise, unique merchandise that no one else anywhere can get, then there will always be people willing to come to you, no matter the difficulties. They'll come, and they'll meet your price."

Jerd had rolled slightly to face him. In the dimness, the touches of silver in her eyes gleamed more sharply. She looked uneasy. "Wait. Are you talking about selling dragon body parts again? Not just now, maybe, if the copper dies, but in the future? That's just wrong, Greft. What if I were talking about selling your blood or bone? What if the dragons were thinking of raising your children for meat?"

"It won't be like that! It doesn't have to be like that. You're thinking of this in the worst possible way." His hand came back, gentle, soothing. He traced her arm from shoulder to elbow and back again. Then his touch slipped to her neck, and his hand wandered slowly down her rib cage. Thymara saw Jerd's breasts move with her indrawn breath. "The dragons will come to understand. A few scales, a bit of blood, the tip of a claw. Nothing that harms them. Sometimes but not often, something more than that, a tooth perhaps or an eye, taken from a dragon who will die anyway . . . Never often, or what is rare becomes commonplace. That would do no one any good."

"I don't like it." She spoke flatly and pulled away from his exploring hand. "And I don't think any of the dragons will like it. How about Kalo? Have you shared your plan with your own dragon? How did he take it?"

He shrugged, and then admitted, "He didn't like it. Said he would kill me before he allowed that to happen. But he threatens to kill me several times a day. It's just what he says when things don't go his way. He knows he has the best keeper. So he threatens me, but he puts up with me. In time, I think even he would see the wisdom of the idea."

"I don't. I think he'd kill you." Her voice was flat. She meant it. She stretched as she spoke and then glancing down at her own breasts, brushed at her left nipple as if dislodging something. Greft's eyes followed her hand, and his voice went deeper.

"Maybe it won't ever come to that," he conceded. "Maybe we will find Kelsingra and maybe it will be rich with Elderling artifacts. If we do find our fortune there, then we must be sure that all recognize it is *ours*. Trehaug will try to claim it; be sure of that. Bingtown will want to be the sole marketplace for it. We'll hear it all again from them. 'This is the way it has always been.' But you and I, we know it doesn't always have to be that way. We must be very ready to defend our future from grasping hands."

Jerd pushed blond hair back from her face. "Greft, you spin such wonderful webs of dreams. You speak as if we were hundreds of people in search of a haven, instead of just over a dozen. 'Defend our future' you say. What future? There are too few of us. The best we can think of would be finding a better life just for ourselves. I like how you think, most of the time, with your talk of new rules for a new life. But sometimes you sound like a little child playing with wooden toys and claiming them as your kingdom."

"Is that wrong? That I'd like to be a king?" He cocked his head at her and smiled his tight-lipped smile. "A king might need a queen."

She sounded scornful of him as she told him sternly, "You will never be a king." But her deprecation of him was a lie, her hands said. Thymara watched in amazement as Jerd caught Greft's shoulders in both her hands, twisted onto her back, and then drew him down on top of her. "Enough talk," she announced. One of her hands moved to the back of Greft's neck. She pulled his face down to hers.

Thymara watched.

She didn't mean to. There was no moment when she decided to stay. Instead, her claws dug deep into bark and held her there. Her brow furrowed and she stared, heedless of the biting insects that found her and hummed around her.

She had seen animals mate, a male bird mounting a female. With a flutter and a shudder, it was soon done and sometimes the female scarcely seemed to notice it. Her parents had never spoken to her of mating, for it was forbidden to her and to those like her. Any curiosity about it had been firmly discouraged. Even her beloved father had warned her, "You may encounter men who will try to take advantage of you, well knowing that what they seek is forbidden. Trust no man who tries to do more than touch your hand in greeting. Leave his company at once, and tell me of it."

And she had believed him. He was her father, with her best interests at heart. No one would make a marriage offer for her. Everyone knew that if those the Rain Wilds touched heavily had children, the children were born either completely monstrous or not viable at all. It made no sense for such as her to mate. The food she would eat during a pregnancy while she was unable to hunt or gather, the difficulty her body would endure in bringing forth a child that would most likely die . . . no. Resources in the Rain Wilds were always scarce; life was always difficult. No one had a right to consume and not produce. It was not the Trader way.

Except that her father had broken that rule. He'd taken a chance on her, taken a chance that she would pull her own weight. And she had. So perhaps the rules were not always right . . . Was Greft right? Could it be that any rules that men made, other men could change? Were the rules not so absolute as she has always believed them?

The couple below her didn't seem to be thinking of the rules at all. It also seemed to be taking them substantially longer than when birds mated. They made sounds, small sounds of approval that sent shivers up Thymara's back. When Jerd arched her back and Greft put lingering kisses on her breasts, Thymara's whole body reacted in a way that embarrassed and astonished her. Light flowed in glittering waves on the scaled bodies that moved in rhythm. Greft pounded his body against Jerd's in a way that looked punishing, but the woman below him only writhed and then suddenly gripped his buttocks and pulled him tight and still against her. She gave a muffled moan.

An instant later, Greft collapsed upon her. For a long time, they sprawled there. Greft's heaving breath gradually calmed. He raised his head and lifted himself slightly from her body. A moment later, Jerd reached a lazy hand to push her sweaty strands of hair from her eyes. A slow smile spread across her face as she looked up at him. Then her eyes widened, and suddenly her gaze shot past Greft and met Thymara's stare. She gave a shriek and snatched uselessly at her discarded clothes.

"What is it?" Greft demanded, rolling off her and turning his gaze skyward. But by then, Thymara was two trees away and moving fast. She leaped from branch to branch, scurrying like a lizard. Behind her, she heard Jerd's voice raised in an angry complaint, and then Greft's laughter scalded her. "Probably the most she'll ever dare to do is watch," he said in a carrying voice, and she knew that he meant her to hear the words. Tears stung her eyes, and her heart hammered against her ribs as she fled.

SEDRIC STOOD ALONE on the deck of the *Tarman*. He gazed toward the shore. There was no sign that anyone intended to travel today. Instead, Leftrin was hurrying about with a steaming bucket, doing some sort of doctoring on the dragons. It made Sedric anxious to see that the major gathering of people and dragons was now clustered around the prone copper dragon. It wasn't his fault. The animal had been sick when he first visited it. Uneasily he wondered if he had left any sign of his passage there. He hadn't meant to hurt it, only to take what he so desperately needed. "I'm sorry," he said quietly, not sure to whom he apologized. Leftrin joined the keepers clustered around the prone dragon. He could not see what they were doing now. Was it dead? Keepers and other dragons formed a wall. What were they doing down there?

Sedric gave a sudden low cry and curled forward over his belly. Terrible tearing cramps uncoiled inside him. He sank to his knees, then fell over on his side. The pain was such that he couldn't even call for help. It wouldn't have done him any good anyway. Everyone else had gone ashore to help with the dragons. His bowels were being torn from his body. He clutched at his gut but could not shield himself from the agony. He closed his eyes as the world seemed to swirl around him and abruptly surrendered his consciousness.

✦ ✦ ✦

Day the 7th of the Prayer Moon

Year the 6th of the Independent Alliance of Traders
From Detozi, Keeper of the Birds, Trehaug
To Erek, Keeper of the Birds, Bingtown

Dispatched today, three birds bearing wedding invitations from the family of Trader Delfin. Enclosed, a list of the intended recipients in Bingtown. If any bird fail, please see that a duplicate of the invitation is still delivered to each addressee.

As the wedding is to be celebrated soon, promptness in delivery is essential.

Erek,

Be certain these invitations reach their destinations promptly, or I fear the families will be invited to celebrate the child's birth before they have time to arrive for the wedding! Customs are not observed in Trehaug as they once were. Some blame it on the Tattooed, but this couple is Rain Wild born and bred!

Detozi

✦ ✦ ✦

CHAPTER TWO

TRICKY CURRENTS

est stood over Sedric, looking down on him, a sneer distorting his handsome face. He shook his head in disappointment. "You fail because you don't try hard enough. When it comes right down to it, you always back down from the challenge." In the gloom of the small cabin, Hest seemed larger than life. He was bare chested, and his broad shoulders and the musculature of his well-kept body framed the black triangle of thick curly hair on his chest. His belly was flat and hard over the waistband of his trim trousers. Sedric looked at him with longing. Hest knew it. He laughed, short, low, and ugly, and shook his head. "You're lazy and soft. You've never been able to keep up with me. I really don't know why I took up with you in the first place. Probably out of pity. There you stood, all mawkish and shy, bottom lip trembling at the thought of what you'd never have. What you didn't even dare ask for! So, I was tempted to give you a taste of it." He laughed harshly. "What a waste of my time you were. There's no challenge left in you, Sedric. Nothing left to teach you and there's never been anything for me to learn from you. You always knew this day would come, didn't you? And here it is. I'm tired of you. Bored with you and your whimpering. Tired of paying you wages you scarcely earn, tired of you living off me like a leech. You despise Redding, don't you? But tell me, how are you better than he is? At least he has his own fortune. At least he can pay his own way."

Sedric moved his mouth, trying to make words come. Trying to tell him that he'd done something significant, that the dragon blood and scales would make a fortune for him, one he'd be happy to share with Hest. *Don't give up on me,* he tried to say. *Don't end it now and take up with someone else when I'm not even there to try to change your mind.* His lips moved, his throat strained, but not a sound emerged. Only drops of dragon blood dripped from his lips.

And it was too late. Redding was there; Redding with his plump little whore's mouth and his stubby-fingered hands and greasy gold ringlets. Redding was there, standing beside Hest, running the back of one finger lightly up and down Hest's bared arm. Hest turned to him, smiling. His eyelids drooped suddenly in a way that Sedric knew well, and then like a stooping hawk he swooped in to kiss Redding. He could no longer see Hest's face, but he saw Redding's hands starfish on Hest's muscular back, pulling him closer.

Sedric tried to shout, strained until his throat hurt, but no sound came out.

They hurt you? Shall I kill them?

"No!" The sound suddenly burst from him in a shout. He jerked awake to find himself sprawled on his sweaty bedding in his small, smelly cabin. Around him, all was murkiness. No Hest, no Redding. Only himself. And a small copper dragon who pushed insistently at the walls of his thoughts. Dimly he felt her inquiry, her dull-witted concern for him. He pushed the contact away, shut his eyes tightly, and buried his face in the bundle that served him as a pillow. *Just a bad dream,* he told himself. *Only a nightmare.*

But it was one that was all too possibly real.

When he was morose, he thought that perhaps Hest had wanted to be rid of him for some time. Perhaps his defending of Alise had given Hest the excuse he was looking for to send Sedric away.

He could, by an effort of will, recall how it had been when they first began. Hest's calmness and strength had drawn him. In moments alone, in Hest's strong embrace, he felt like he had finally found safe harbor. Knowing that shelter existed for him had made him stronger and bolder. Even his father had seen the change in him and told him that he took pride in the man his son was becoming.

If he'd only known!

When had Hest's strength stopped being a shelter and become a prison wall? When had it become, not the comfort of protection, but the threat of that strength turned against him? How could he have continued unaware of how things had changed, of how Hest was changing him? He hadn't, he admitted now. He'd known. But he'd stumbled on blindly, excusing Hest's cruelty and slights, blaming the discord on himself, pretending that somehow, things would go back to the way they had once been.

Had it ever really been that good? Or was it all a dream he had manufactured for himself?

He rolled over, pushing his face into the pillow and closing his eyes. He would not think about Hest or how things had once been between them. He would not dwell on what their relationship had become. Right now, he did not even have the heart to try to imagine something better for them. There had to be a better dream somewhere. He wished he could imagine what it was.

"ARE YOU AWAKE?"

He hadn't been but now he was. A slice of light was falling into Sedric's room from the open door. The silhouette standing in it had to be Alise. Of course. He sighed.

As if that were an invitation, she ventured into the room.

She didn't close the door behind her. The rectangle of light fell mostly on the floor, illuminating dropped clothing. "It's so dark in here," she said apologetically. "And close."

She meant smelly. He'd scarcely stirred out of the room for three days, and when he did, he spoke to no one and returned to his bed as soon as he could. Davvie, the hunter's apprentice, had been bringing him meals and then taking them away again. At first, he'd been in too much pain to be hungry. And now he was too despondent to eat.

"Davvie said he thought you were feeling better."

"I'm not." Couldn't she just go away? He didn't want to talk to her, didn't want to confide his problems to anyone. Davvie was bad enough, with his pestering, prying questions and his voluntary biography of his own unremarkable life. At fifteen years old, how could the boy imagine he had done anything that could possibly interest anyone other than himself? All of the boy's meandering stories seemed to be leading up to some point that Sedric couldn't grasp and the boy couldn't seem to make. He suspected that Carson was using the boy to spy on him. He'd woken twice to find the hunter sitting quietly beside his bed. And once, he'd struggled out of a nightmare and opened his eyes to that other hunter, Jess, crouched on the floor nearby. Why all three of them were so fascinated with him, he didn't know. Not unless they had guessed his secret.

At least he could order the boy out of his room and he obeyed. He doubted that tactic would work on Alise, but abruptly decided to try it. "Just go away, Alise. When I feel well enough to deal with people, I'll come out."

Instead, Alise came into the room and sat down on his shoe trunk. "I don't think it's a good idea for you to be alone so much, especially when we still don't know what made you so ill." Her fingers tangled in her lap like writhing serpents. He looked away from them.

"Carson said it was something I ate. Or drank."

"That makes sense, except that we've all had the same food and drink that you've had, and no one else was affected."

There was one drink she hadn't shared. He pushed the thought aside. *Don't think about anything that could incriminate you, or bring those alien thoughts back into your mind.*

He hadn't answered her. She was looking down at her hands. She spoke as if the words were teeth she were spitting out. "I'm sorry I dragged you along on this, Sedric. I'm sorry I ran off to help the dragons that day and wouldn't listen to what you had to say. You're a friend; you've been my friend for a very long time. Now you're ill and we're so far from any real healers." She halted for a moment, and he could tell she was trying to hold back tears. Strange, how little he cared about that. Perhaps if she knew the real danger he faced and was moved by it, he would feel more sympathy for how she struggled with her guilt.

"I've talked to Leftrin and he says it's not too late. He said that even though we've traveled farther upriver, he thinks Carson could still take one of the smaller boats and get us safely back to Cassarick before autumn closes in. It wouldn't be easy, and we'd be camping out along the way. But I've persuaded him." She paused, choking on emotion, and then went on in a voice so tight that her words almost squeaked. "If you want me to take you back, I'll do it. We'll leave today if you say so."

If he said so.

It was too late now. Too late even on that morning when he'd demanded she go back with him, though he hadn't known it then. "Too late." He hadn't realized he'd whispered the words until he saw her reaction.

"Sa's mercy, Sedric. Are you that ill?"

"No." He spoke quickly to stop her words. He truly had no idea how ill he was, or if "ill" was a way to describe it. "No, nothing like that, Alise. I only mean it's too late for us to attempt to make our way back to Cassarick in one of the small boats. Davvie has warned me, numerous times, that the autumn rains will soon be falling, and that when they start to come down, our journey upstream is going to be more difficult. Perhaps then Captain Leftrin will recognize how foolish our mission is and turn back with the barge. In any case, I don't wish to be in a small boat on a torrential river with rain pouring down all around us. Not my idea of camping weather."

He'd almost managed to find his normal tone and voice. Maybe if he seemed normal, she'd go away. "I'm very tired, if you don't mind," he said abruptly.

Alise stood up, looking remarkably unattractive in trousers that only emphasized the female swell of her hips. The shirt she wore was beginning to show signs of hard use. He could tell she had washed it, but the water she had used had left it gray rather than snowy white. The sun was taking a toll on her, bleaching her red hair to a carroty orange that frayed out around her pins, and making her freckles darker. She'd never been a beauty by Bingtown standards. Much more of the sun and water, and he wondered if Hest would take her back at all. It was one thing to have a mousy wife, and another to have one who was simply a fright. He wondered if she ever thought of the possibility that when she returned, Hest might not take her back. Probably not. She had been raised to believe that life was meant to be a certain way, and even when all evidence was to the contrary, she couldn't see it differently. She'd never suspected that he and Hest were more than excellent friends. To Alise, he was still her childhood friend, erstwhile secretary to her husband and temporarily serving as her assistant. She so firmly believed that the world was determined by her rules that she could not see what was right in front of her.

And so she smiled gently at him. "Get some rest, dear friend," she said, closing the door quietly behind her, shutting him into his oversized packing crate and leaving him in the dark with his thoughts.

He rolled to face the wall. The back of his neck itched. He scratched it furiously, feeling dry skin under his nails. She wasn't the only one whose appearance was being ruined. His skin was dry, his hair as coarse as a horse's tail now.

He wished he could blame everything on Alise. He couldn't. Once Hest had banned him, dooming him to be her companion, Sedric had done all he could to seize any opportunity the trip might present. He was the one who had schemed to take advantage of every opportunity to take a scrap of dragon flesh, a scale, a drop of blood. He'd planned so carefully how he would preserve his collection; Begasti Cored would be waiting to hear from him, anticipating that his own fortune would be founded on being the man to facilitate supplying such forbidden merchandise to the Duke of Chalced.

In some of his daydreams, Sedric returned to Bingtown to show Hest his loot, and Hest helped him to get the best prices for his wares. In those dreams, they sold the goods and never returned to Bingtown, establishing themselves as wealthy men in Chalced, or Jamaillia, or the Pirate Isles, perhaps even beyond, in the near-mythical Spice Islands. In others, he kept his newly gained wealth a secret until he had established a luxurious hideaway in a distant place. In those dreams, he and Hest took ship by night in secret and sailed off to a new life together, free of lies and deceptions.

And, of late, he'd had other daydreams. They had been bitter but sharp-edged with sweetness, too. He'd imagined returning to Bingtown to discover that Hest had replaced him with that damn Redding. In those dreams he took his wealth and established himself in Chalced, only to reveal to Hest later all that he might have had, if only he'd valued Sedric more, if only he'd been true of heart.

Now all of those dreams seemed silly and shallow, the stuff of adolescent fancy. He pulled the itchy wool blanket up over his shoulders and closed his eyes more tightly. "I may never go back to Bingtown," he said aloud. He tried to force himself to confront that. "Even if I do, I may never be completely sane again."

For a moment, he let go his grip on himself as Sedric. Instantly, she was hip deep in chill river water, wading against the cold current. On her belly, he felt the tar plugs that Leftrin had smeared over her injuries. He felt her dim groping toward him, a plea for companionship and comfort. He didn't want to give it. But he had never been a hard-hearted man. When she invaded his mind, pleading, he had to reach back. *You are stronger than you know,* he told her. *Keep moving. Follow the other ones, my copper beauty. Soon there will be better days for you, but for now you must be strong.*

A flow of warm gratitude engulfed him. It would have been so easy to drown in it. Instead, he let it ebb past him and encouraged her to focus what little mind she had on keeping up the grueling pace. In the small corner of his mind that still belonged solely to himself, he wondered, Was there any way to be free of this unwanted sharing? If the copper dragon died, would he feel her pain? Or only the sweet release of freedom?

ALISE WENT BACK to the galley table. She sat down opposite Leftrin and his perpetual mug of black coffee. All around them, the work of moving the barge went on, like the busy comings and goings of an insect hive. The tillerman was at his tiller, the pole crew moved up and down the decks in their steady rhythm. From the deckhouse window, she watched the endless circuit of Hennesey and Bellin on the starboard side of the barge. Grigsby, the orange ship's cat, perched on the railing and watched the water. Carson had risen before dawn and set off up the river to do his day's hunting for the dragons. Davvie had stayed aboard. The boy had developed a peculiar fixation on Sedric and his well-being. He could not tolerate anyone else preparing the sick man's meals or waiting on him. Alise found it both endearing and annoying that a lad from such a rough background would be so fascinated by an elegant young Trader. Leftrin had twice muttered against it, but she could not grasp the nature of his complaint, and so had ignored it.

Usually by this hour, she and Leftrin would be left in relative peace and isolation. Today, the hunter Jess had lingered, a near-silent yet very annoying presence on the barge. No matter where she went, he was nearby. Yesterday, twice she had looked up to find him staring at her. He'd met her gaze and nodded meaningfully, as if there were something they agreed upon. For the life of her, she couldn't work out what he was about. She'd have discussed it with Leftrin, except that Jess always seemed to be lurking just within earshot.

The hunter made her uncomfortable. She'd become accustomed to how the Rain Wilds had marked Leftrin. She accepted it as a part of him now and scarcely noticed it except for the moments when a flash of sunlight would strike a gleam from the scaling in his brows. Then it seemed exotic, not repulsive. But Jess was marked in less flattering ways. He reminded her, not of a dragon or even a lizard, but of a snake. His nose was flattening into his face, his nostrils becoming slitlike in the process. His eyes seemed set too far apart, as if they were seeking to be on the sides of his head instead of the front. She'd always taken pride that she didn't judge folk by their appearances. But she could not look at Jess and feel comfortable, let alone have a real conversation with him.

So in the man's presence, she kept her discussion to generalities and expected topics. She said brightly, "Well, Sedric seems a bit better today. I did ask him if he'd like to return to Cassarick in one of the small boats, but he said he didn't. I think he feels the trip would be too dangerous, with the autumn rains coming on."

Leftrin lifted his eyes to hers. "So you'll both be continuing with the expedition, no matter how long it takes?" She heard a hundred questions in his voice and tried to answer them all.

"I think we will. I know I want to see this through to the end."

Jess laughed. He was leaning against the frame of the galley door, apparently looking out over the river. He didn't turn to either of them and made no other comment. Her glance sought Leftrin's again. He met her gaze, but gave no sign of a reaction to the man's odd behavior. Perhaps she was overreacting. She changed the subject.

"You know, until I came for this visit, I never truly understood what the Rain Wilders faced in trying to build settlements here. I suppose I always imagined that in all this vast valley, somewhere they would have found some truly dry ground. But there isn't, is there?"

"Bog and slough and marsh," Leftrin confirmed for her. "No other place in the world like it, as far as I know. There are a few charts from the old days when settlers first came here. They tried to explore. Some show a big lake upriver of us, one that is said to spread as far as the eye can see. Others charted over a hundred tributaries that feed the Rain Wild River, some big, some small. They all wander back and forth in their beds. Some years two become one, and a year later, there are three streams where one tributary used to dump into the river. Two years after that, it's just all marsh, no defined streams or river at all.

"The forest ground sometimes looks solid, and sometimes folk have found a patch they think is dry and tried to settle on it. But the more traffic there is, the sooner the 'dry ground' starts to give way. Pretty soon the groundwater breaks through to the surface and from there, well, it goes marshy pretty fast."

"But you do think that somewhere upriver there will be an area of truly dry land for the dragons to settle on?"

"Your guess is as good as mine. But I think there must be. Water flows downhill, and all this water comes from somewhere. Trouble is, can we navigate that far, or does it all turn into marsh before we get there? I think we're about as far upriver as anyone has ever come by ship. Tarman can go where others can't. But if we hit a place that's too shallow for Tarman, well, that's where our journey will end."

"Well, I hope we at least find a better beach to camp on tonight. Thymara has said that she is worried about the dragons' feet and claws. The constant immersion is bad for them. She said that one of Sintara's claws cracked and she had to trim and bind it for her. She said she treated it with tar. Perhaps we should do all the dragons' claws, to prevent damage."

Leftrin scowled at the idea. "I don't have that much tar to spare. I think we'll just have to hope for a drier camping spot tonight."

"We should trim their claws," Jess abruptly announced, pushing his way into both the room and the conversation. He shoved the end bench out from the table and sat down heavily on it. "Think about it, Cap. We dull the dragons' claws down for them. Cut them a bit, tar them up. Do everybody a world of good, you take my drift." He looked from Leftrin to Alise and back again, grinning at both of them. He had small teeth, set wide in a generous mouth. It looked like a baby's innocent smile set in a man's face; it was disconcerting, even unsettling to her. So was Leftrin's reaction to it.

"No." He spoke the word flatly. "No, Jess. And that's my last word. Don't push it. Not here, not now. Not with the keepers, either." He narrowed his eyes meaningfully.

Jess leaned back, bracing his back against the wall and swinging his boots up onto the bench in front of him. "Superstitious?" he asked Leftrin with a knowing grin. "I'd have pegged you for a man of the world, Cap. Not someone trapped in all those old Rain Wild notions. It's awfully provincial of you. Those keepers, some of them recognize that sometimes we need to make new rules to make the best of a situation."

Leftrin slowly stood, leaned both his fists on the table, knuckles down and shoulders tensed as he put his face close to the hunter's. He spoke in a low voice. "You're an ass, Jess. An ass and a fool. You don't even know what you're suggesting. Why don't you go do what you were paid to do?"

The way Leftrin's body blocked Jess's access to her suggested he was protecting her. She wasn't sure from what but felt profoundly grateful he was there. Alise had never seen the captain so clearly enraged and yet so controlled. It frightened her, and at the same time it spurred a powerful surge of attraction toward him. This, she suddenly knew, was the sort of man she wanted in her life.

Yet despite Leftrin's intensity, Jess seemed unfazed. "Go do what I was 'paid' to do? Isn't that exactly what we're talking about here, Captain? Getting paid. And sooner rather than later. Perhaps we should all sit down and have a chat about the best way to make that happen." He leaned around Leftrin to shoot Alise a knowing grin. She was appalled. What was he talking about?

"There is nothing to discuss!" Leftrin's voice rattled the windows.

Jess's gaze went back to Leftrin. His voice lowered suddenly, taking the note of a warning snarl. "I'm not going to be cheated out of this, Leftrin. If she wants a share, she'll have to go through me. I'm not going to stand by and watch you take a new partner and cut me out for the sake of making a sweet little deal for yourself."

"Get out." From a roar, Leftrin's voice had dropped to a near whisper. "Get out now, Jess. Go hunting."

Perhaps he knew he'd pushed Leftrin to his limit. The captain hadn't verbalized a threat, but killing hung in the air. Every beat of her thundering heart seemed to shake Alise. She couldn't draw a breath. She was terrified of what might happen next.

Jess swung his feet to the floor so that his boots landed on the deck with a thump. He stood, taking his time, like a cat that stretches before it turns its back on a slavering dog. "I'll go," he offered lightly. "Until another time," he said as he walked out the door. Around the corner but still within hearing, he added, "We all know there will be another time."

Leftrin leaned across the table to reach the door's edge. He slammed it so hard that every cup on the table jumped. "That bastard," he snarled. "That traitorous bastard."

Alise found she was hugging herself and trembling. Her voice shook as she said, "I don't understand. What was he talking about? What does he want to discuss with me?"

LEFTRIN WAS AS angry as he'd ever been in his life, and by his fury, he knew that the damn hunter had woken fear in him as well. It wasn't just that the man was misjudging Alise in such a base way. It was that his assumptions threatened to ruin Leftrin's good image in her eyes.

The questions he didn't dare answer hung in the air between them, razor-edged knives that would cut them both to pieces. He took the only safe course. He lied to her. "It's all right, Alise. Everything will be fine."

Then, before she could ask what was all right and what would be fine, he silenced her in the only way he could, drawing her to her feet and folding her into his arms. He held her firm against him, his head bent over hers. Everything about it was wrong; he could see her small fine hands against the rough, grimy weave of his shirt. Her hair smelled like perfume, and it was so fine and soft it tangled against his unshaven chin. He could feel how small she was, how delicate. Her blouse was soft under his hands, and the warmth of her skin seeped right through it. She was the opposite of him in every way, and he had no right to touch her, none at all. Even if she hadn't been a married lady, even if she hadn't been educated and refined, it still would have been wrong for two such different people to come together.

And yet she did not struggle or shriek for help. Her hands didn't pound against his chest; instead they gripped the rough fabric of his shirt and pulled him tighter, fitting herself against him, and again, they were opposite of each other in every way, and each way was wonderful. For a long moment he just held her in silence, and in that brief instant he forgot Jess's treachery, and his vulnerability and the danger awaiting all of them. No matter how complicated the rest of it was, this was simple and perfect. He wished he could stay in this moment, not moving on, not even thinking of all the complications that threatened him.

"Leftrin." She spoke his name against his chest.

In another time and another place, it would have been permission. In this time and place, it broke the spell. That simple moment, their brief embrace, was over. It was as much as he would ever taste of that other life. He tipped his head just slightly and let his mouth brush her hair. Then, with a heavy sigh, he set her back from him. "Sorry," he muttered, even though he was not. "Sorry, Alise. I don't know what came over me. Guess I should not let Jess rile me up like that."

She gripped his shirt still, two small tight handfuls of fabric. Her brow pressed against his chest. He knew she didn't want him to step away from her. She didn't want him to stop what had begun. It was like peeling a clingy kitten from himself to ease free of her grip, and all the harder because he didn't want to do so. He had never imagined that he would be the one to gently push a woman away "for her own good." But he'd never imagined that he would find himself in such a precarious position. Until he could deal with Jess in a way that solved his problem permanently, he couldn't allow Alise to do anything that might make her more of a weapon to be used against him.

"Feels like the current is getting tricky. I need a word with Swarge," he lied. It would take him out of the galley and away from her so she couldn't ask the questions that Jess had stirred up. And it would give him a chance to make sure that Jess had actually left the barge and gone hunting.

As he set her gently away from him, she looked up at him with utter bewilderment. "Leftrin, I—"

"I won't be gone long," he promised and turned away from her.

"But—" he heard her say, and then he closed the door gently on her words and hurried aft. Out of sight of the galley windows, he halted and walked to the railing. He didn't need to talk to Swarge or anyone else. He didn't want any of his crew to know what a situation he'd put them all in. Damn Jess and his sly threats, and damn that Chalcedean merchant and damn the wood carvers who couldn't keep their mouths shut. And damn himself for getting them all into this mess. When he had first found the wizardwood, he had known it could bring him trouble. Why hadn't he left it alone? Or spoken of it to the dragons and the Council and let them worry about it? He knew it was now forbidden for anyone to take it and make use of it. But he had. Because he loved his ship.

He felt a thrum of anxiety through Tarman's railing. He gripped the wood soothingly and spoke aloud but softly to the liveship. "No. I regret nothing. It was no less than you deserved. I took what you needed, and I don't really care if anyone else can understand or excuse that. I just wish it hadn't brought trouble down on us. That's all. But I'll find a way to solve it. You can count on that."

As if to confirm both gratitude and loyalty, he felt the ship pick up speed. Back on the tiller, he heard Swarge chortle and mutter, "Well, what's the hurry now?" as the polemen picked up their pace to match the ship's. Leftrin took his hands from the railing and leaned back against the deckhouse, hands in pockets, to give his crew room to work. He said nothing to any of them, and they knew better than to speak to the captain when he stood thus, deep in thought. He had a problem. He'd settle it without help from any of them. That was what captains did.

Leftrin dug his pipe out of one pocket and his tobacco out of the other, and then stuffed them both back as he realized he couldn't go back into the galley to light it. He sighed. He was a Trader in the tradition of the Rain Wild Traders. Profit was all-important. But so was loyalty. And humanity. The Chalcedeans had approached him with a scheme that could make him a wealthy man. As long as he was willing to betray the Rain Wilds and butcher a sentient creature as if it were an animal, he could have a fortune. They'd made their offer in the guise of a threat; such a typically Chalcedean way to invite a man to do business. First there had been the "grain merchant," bullying his way aboard the *Tarman* at the mouth of the Rain Wild River. Sinad Arich had spoken as plainly as a Chalcedean could. The Duke of Chalced was holding his family hostage; the merchant would do whatever he had to do to obtain dragon parts for the ailing old man.

Leftrin had thought he'd seen the last of the man when he set him ashore in Trehaug, thought that the threat to himself and his ship was over. But it wasn't. Once a Chalcedean had a hold on you, he never let go. Back in Cassarick, right before they left, someone had come on board and left a tiny scroll outside his door. The clandestine note told him to expect a collaborator on board his ship. If he complied with their agent, they'd pay him well. If he didn't, they'd betray what he had done with the wizardwood. That would ruin him, as a man, as a ship owner, as a Trader. He was not sure if it would lower him in Alise's esteem.

That final doubt was more powerful than the first three certainties. He'd never been tempted to take the bait, though he had wondered if he might surrender to the duress. Now he knew he would not. The moment he'd heard the scandalized whispers of the dragon keepers over what Greft had proposed, he'd known who his traitor was. Not Greft; the youngster might claim to be educated and radical in his thinking, but Leftrin had seen his ilk before. The boy's political ideas and "new" thoughts were skin-shallow. The keeper had only fallen in with an older man's persuasive cant. And not Carson, he thought with relief. And there was that to be grateful for. It wasn't an old friend he'd have to confront over this.

It was Jess. The hunter had come aboard at Cassarick, ostensibly hired by the Cassarick Rain Wild Traders' Council to help provide for the dragons on their journey. Either the Council had no knowledge of Jess's other employer or the corruption ran deeper than he wanted to think about. He couldn't worry about that now. The hunter was his focus. Jess was the one who had seemed to be befriending Greft, talking with him at the campfire each night, offering to teach him to be better with his hunter's tools. Leftrin had seen him building up the young man's opinion of himself, involving him in sophisticated philosophical conversations and persuading him that Greft understood what his fellow keepers were too rural and naive to grasp. He was the one who had convinced the boy that leadership meant stepping forward to do the unthinkable for the "greater good" of those too tenderhearted to see the necessity. Jess had been reinforcing Greft's belief that he was the leader of the dragon keepers. *Not so likely, my friend,* he thought. Leftrin had seen the faces of the other keepers when they had spoken of what Greft had proposed. One and all, they'd been shocked. Not even his no-necked sidekicks, Kase and Boxter, had followed him into that quicksand. They'd looked at each other, as bewildered as puppies. So he hadn't talked it over with them previously.

Therefore, Leftrin knew the source of that toxic idea. Jess. Jess would have made it sound logical and pragmatic. Jess would have introduced the idea that a real leader would sometimes have to make hard decisions. True leaders sometimes had to do dangerous and distasteful, even immoral, things for the sake of those who followed them.

Such as carving up a dragon and selling the bits to a foreign power to line your own pockets.

And the young man had been gullible enough to listen to the wise old hunter and had put the idea out as his own. When it had fallen flat, only Greft had been touched with the ignominy of it. Jess was unscathed in his friendship with some of the other keepers, and much more aware now of how they felt about the idea of butchering dragons for profit. And that was a shame, for privately Leftrin thought that Greft had the potential to captain the group, once he'd had his share of hard knocks on the way up. He supposed that his misstep with the other keepers would be one of them. If the young man had grit, he'd learn from it and keep on going. If not, well, some sailors grew up to be captains and others never even rose to be mate.

Be that as it would be, Greft's mishap had lifted the lantern high for Leftrin. He had suspected Jess before, but on that day, he'd known. When Leftrin had first confronted Jess privately and accused him of being the Chalcedean merchant's man, Jess had not even flinched. He'd admitted it and promptly suggested that now that things were out in the open between them, their task would be much easier. Even now, Leftrin gritted his teeth to think of how the slimy bastard had smiled at him, suggesting that if he slowed the barge down and let the keepers and dragons and the other hunters range far ahead of him, it would be easy for them to pick off the last lagging dragon. "And once we've put the poor suffering creature down and butchered it up proper, we can turn right around and head back for the open water. No need to stop by Trehaug or Cassarick, or even to pass by them during daylight hours. We could just head for the coast with our cargo. Once we're there, I've a special signal powder— puts up a bright red smoke from even a tiny fire. Your galley stove would do it. A ship comes right to meet us, and off we go to Chalced and money such as you and your crew can't even imagine how to spend."

"Me and my crew aren't the only ones aboard the *Tarman*," Leftrin had pointed out coldly to him.

"That hasn't escaped my notice. But between the two of us, I think the woman fancies you. Take a forceful hand with her. Tell her you're swooping her off to Chalced and the life of a princess. She'll go. And the fancy lad who's with her, all he wants to do is get back to civilization. I don't think he'll much care where you take him, as long as it isn't the Rain Wilds. Or cut him in on the deal, if you want." He'd grinned wider and added, "Or just be rid of him. It makes small difference to me."

"I'd never abandon the *Tarman*. My barge isn't suited to a trip to Chalced."

"Isn't it?" The traitor had cocked his head and said, "It seems to me that your barge is better suited to many things than it would appear. If your share of the money from the dragon parts didn't sate you, I'd wager you'd get near the same amount for the barge, 'specially modified' as it is. In one piece. Or as parts."

And there it was. The man met his outraged gaze squarely, never losing his nasty little smile. He knew. He knew what Tarman was, and he knew what Leftrin had found, and what he'd done with it. Leftrin, that smile said, was no better than he was. There was no difference between them. Leftrin had already trafficked in dragon parts for his own benefit.

And if Leftrin did anything to betray Jess for what he was, Jess would return the favor. He felt Tarman quest toward him. He stepped quickly to the railing and put his hand on the silvery wood. "It will be all right," he assured his ship. "Trust me. I'll think of something. I always do."

Then he took his hands off the railing and walked back to talk to Swarge, just in case Alise happened to come out on deck.

Swarge, taciturn as ever, was leaning on his tiller, his eyes fixed on the river, distant and dreaming. He wasn't a young man anymore, Leftrin suddenly realized. Well, he supposed he wasn't a young fellow himself anymore. He totted up the years they'd been together, and thought of all they'd been through, good days and bad. Swarge had never questioned Leftrin's decision when his captain had revealed the trove of wizardwood and outlined his use for it. Swarge could have talked, but he hadn't. Swarge could have held him up, demanded a chunk of the wood to keep his silence, gone off and sold it and been a wealthy man. But he hadn't. He'd made only one request, a simple one he should have made long ago. "There's a woman," he'd said slowly. "A good river woman, can do a good day's work on a ship. If I stay aboard for this, I know I'm staying aboard forever. She's the kind of woman who's easy to live with. Could be part of the crew on this boat forever. You'd like her, Cap. I know you would."

So Bellin had been part of Swarge's deal, and no one had ever regretted it. She'd come aboard and hung up her duffel bag and sewn a curtain to give them a bit of privacy. Tarman had liked her, right from the start. Tarman was her home and his life. She and Swarge had lost their shoreside ties long ago, and Swarge was a man content with his life. Now he stood, his broad hands gripping the handle of the tiller, doing what he did all day long. Gripping the wood like that, Leftrin reckoned that Swarge knew Tarman almost as well as he did. Knew the boat and loved him.

"How's he going today?" he asked the man, as if he didn't know himself.

Swarge looked at him, a bit surprised by such a useless question. "He goes well, Captain," he said. As always, the man's voice was so deep it took a trained ear to make out his words. "He goes with a will. Bottom's good here. Not all sink-silt like yesterday. We're on our way. No doubt about it. Making good time, too."

"Good to hear you say it, Swarge," Leftrin said and let him go back to his dreaming and staring.

Tarman had made a hard transition that year. Leftrin had let most of his crew go, confiding his discovery of the wizardwood and his plans for it only to the people he felt could keep a secret and would stay. No poleman would ever work aboard Tarman and not know the difference in the barge. Every member of this crew was handpicked now and likely to remain aboard for life. Hennesey was devoted to the ship, Bellin loved her life aboard, and Eider was as conversational as the anchor. As for Skelly, the ship was her fortune. The secret should have been safe.

But it wasn't. And now they were all at risk, his ship included. What would the Council do if it knew what he had done? How would the dragons react? He clenched his teeth and fists. Too late to turn back.

He took a slow turn around the deck, checking things that didn't need checking and finding all exactly as it should be. Jess and his canoe were gone. Good. He considered for a moment, then took out his rum flask and upended it over the side of the barge and into the water below. "That he may not come back," he offered El savagely. It was well known that that particular god wasn't moved by prayer but sometimes succumbed to bribery. Ordinarily, Leftrin worshipped Sa, when he worshipped anything. But sometimes the harshness of a pagan god was a man's last resort.

Well, not quite his last resort. He could always murder Jess himself . . .

He didn't like to think about it, and not just because he was pretty certain the man would be hard to kill. He didn't like to think of himself as a man who killed inconvenient people. But Jess had indicated that he was going to be much worse than inconvenient.

There were, he reflected, lots of ways to kill a man on the water, and many of them could be made to look accidental. He considered it coldly. Jess was tough and sagacious. Leftrin had been foolish to growl at him today. He should have pretended interest in his offer, should have chummed him in close. He should have invited him to make a midnight raid on the sleeping dragons. That would have been the prime opportunity to do him in. But the man had irritated him beyond any sort of strategic thinking. He hated how Jess snickered around Alise. The rat knew how Leftrin felt about her. Leftrin had a feeling that Jess would be happy to ruin all that simply because he could. And he'd seen Jess's face when Alise had come back on board with the dragon scale and so delightedly exhibited it to all of them. He'd seen the fires of greed kindle in the man's eyes and worried for her then. Leftrin walked a few more steps down the deck and then stooped to tidy a coil of line that was already tidy enough.

Two nights ago, Jess had come to Leftrin with his new scheme. He'd maddened Leftrin with his insistence that Sedric would be amenable to "their" plans. He refused to say what he based that opinion on, but twice Leftrin had caught him lurking around the sick man's room. He only smiled that sneery smile; it was plain that he thought Leftrin and Alise and Sedric were conspiring together about the dragons. He thought it was an alliance he could break into and use for himself. Sooner or later, he'd talk to Sedric. Sedric would easily believe that Leftrin was complicit with Jess's plotting. He could just imagine the Bingtown man's reaction to Jess's suggestion that Leftrin could kidnap Alise and carry her off to Chalced, with the understanding that, given enough money, Sedric would also be happy to go to Chalced. Or Alise's reaction to the idea that Leftrin was just waiting for an opportunity to butcher up a dragon.

The man was a loose cannon. Leftrin had to do away with him. A cold certainty welled up in him; he could feel Tarman accede to the decision. Almost, it was a relief to reach it.

There would be consequences to killing Jess, he supposed, even if he made it look like an accident. The Chalcedean merchant Sinad Arich would wonder what had become of his hireling when Jess failed to contact him. Well, let him wonder! The Rain Wild River was a dangerous place. Men just as competent as Jess and a lot nicer had died there. He felt the decision settle in him and sink down to his bones. Jess was going to die.

But he'd have to set him up for it. And that would mean trying to convince him that he'd had a change of heart. He wondered if he could make him believe that he'd lost interest in Alise as well. If Jess didn't see her as a weapon he could use against Leftrin, he might stop haunting her. After that, it would be a matter of waiting for the right opportunity.

Tarman nudged him. "What?" he demanded of his ship and stood. A quick scan around betrayed no perceptible danger. Despite his excuse to Alise, this part of the river was a fairly easy stretch. It was edged with reed beds that ventured out into the channel, so that the barge moved through them. The fishing would be good, and he suspected that the dragons would feed fairly well along today's path.

Then he saw a shivering in the trees behind the reed banks. Every tree shook, and a few dropped yellowed leaves and small twigs. An instant later, the reed bank rippled like a wave, a wave that moved out into the river, trembling water and grasses. The motion slapped the barge's hull and then moved past it, almost vanishing in the deeper water.

"Quake!" Swarge raised the cry from the stern.

"Quake!" Big Eider bellowed the warning to the keepers in their small boats.

"So it is!" Leftrin shouted back. "Move Tarman away from the banks as much as you can, but don't lose our grip on the bottom. "Ware, now!"

"Ware!" his polemen cried him back.

As Tarman edged away from the bank, Leftrin watched another rippling move the trees. On the shore, small debris of leaves, twigs, and old birds' nests showered down. An instant later, rank after rank of reeds bowed to the river, followed by a wavelet that rocked the boat. Leftrin scowled but kept his eyes on the trees. Quakes were frequent in the Rain Wilds, and for the most part, little tremors were ignored by everyone. Larger ones endangered not only the underground workers in the buried Elderling cities, but could also bring down old or rotten trees. Even if a tree didn't hit the barge directly, he'd heard of falling trees that swamped boats. In his grandfather's time, supposedly a tree had fallen that was so large it had actually stopped all traffic on the river and had taken workers nearly six months to clear away. Leftrin was a bit skeptical about the full truth of that tale, but every legend had a grain of truth. Doubtless a very big tree had come down somewhere to spark that one.

"What's going on?" Alise sounded apprehensive. She'd heard the shouts and come out on the deck.

He answered without looking at her. "We've had a quake, and a pretty good one. No problem for us right now, and it looks like it didn't do much more than give the trees a good shake. None fell. Unless we get a second bigger shake, we'll be just fine."

To her credit, Alise simply nodded. Quakes were common all along the Cursed Shores. No Bingtown resident would be surprised by one, but he doubted she'd ever experienced one on the water, nor had to worry about a big tree coming down. And it came to him that the next warning would probably be new to her as well. "Sometimes a quake will wake up the acid in the river. But it doesn't happen right away. The theory is that it does something way upriver, releases the white somehow. In a couple or three days, we may suddenly find the river is running white again. Or it may not. A really bad quake may warn of a dirty rain to follow."

She realized the danger instantly. "If the river runs acid, what will the dragons do? And can the small boats the keepers use withstand it?"

He took a deep breath and exhaled it through his nose. "Well, an acid run is always a danger on the river. The small boats could probably stand up to it for a time, but for safety's sake, if the acid was strong, we'd bring the small boats on deck, stack them, and have the keepers ride with us."

"And the dragons?"

He shook his head. "From what I've seen, they've got tough hides. Some of the animals, fish, and birds in the Wilds can deal with the acid. Some creatures avoid the river when it runs white; others don't seem to notice the difference. If the river runs white, a lot will depend on how white it is, and how long the run lasts. If it's only a day or so, my guess is that the dragons will be able to take it. Much longer than that, and I'd be concerned. But maybe we'll be lucky and find ourselves near a fairly solid bank where the dragons could haul out and wait for the worst to pass."

"What if there isn't a bank?" Alise asked in a low voice.

"You know the answer to that," Leftrin replied. So far in their journey, that had only happened once. One night, evening had come with no resting place in sight. There had been only marshlands as far as the eye could see, nowhere for the dragons to get out of the water. Despite their grumbling, the dragons had had to stand overnight in the water, while the keepers had taken refuge on Tarman's deck. The dragons hadn't enjoyed the experience, but they had survived. But the water had been mild then, and the weather kind. "They'd have to endure it," Leftrin said, and neither one spoke of how the acid might eat at injuries and tender tissue.

After a few moments of silence, Leftrin added, "That's always been a danger to this journey, Alise. The most obvious danger, actually, and one we've always had to live with. The first 'settlers' in the Rain Wilds were actually abandoned here; no one in their right mind would come here of their own accord."

"I know my history," Alise interrupted a bit brusquely, but then added with a small smile, "and I definitely came here of my own accord."

"Well, it's so that Bingtown's history is the Rain Wilds's history. But I think we live it here a bit more than you folks do." He leaned on the railing, feeling Tarman sturdy beneath him. He glanced up and down the current of his world. "Strangeness flows with the water in this river, and it affects us all, one way or another. Trehaug might not be the easiest place in the world to live, and Cassarick is no better. But without those cities, Bingtown wouldn't have Elderling magic to sell. So, no Rain Wilds, no Bingtown is how I see it. But what I'm trying to say is that generation after generation, decade after decade, young explorers have set out vowing they're going to find a better place to settle. Some don't come back. And those who do report the same thing. Nothing but an immense wide valley, with lots of trees and lots of wet ground. And the deeper you go into the forest, the stranger it gets. All the expeditions that have gone up this river have come back saying that they either ran out of navigable waterway, or that the river just flattened out, wider and wider, until it seemed there were no real banks to it anywhere."

"But they just didn't go far enough, did they? I've seen enough references to Kelsingra to know that the city existed. And somewhere, it still does."

"The sad truth is that it could be under our hull right now, and we'd never know. Or it could be half a day's journey away from us, back there in the trees, cloaked in moss and mud. Or it could have been up one of the tributaries we've passed. Two other Elderling cities either sank or were buried. No one is sure just exactly what befell them, but we know they're underground now. The same thing could have happened to Kelsingra. Probably did happen. We know that something big and bad happened here a long time ago. It ended the Elderlings and nearly ended the dragons. It changed everything. All we're really doing right now is following the dragons up the most navigable waterway, and hoping we come to something."

He glanced at her, saw her face pale under her freckles and her set mouth. He tried to speak more gently. "It only makes sense, Alise. If Kelsingra had survived, wouldn't the Elderlings have lived? And if the Elderlings had survived, wouldn't they have kept dragons alive somehow? In all the tapestries, they're always together."

"But . . . if you don't believe we can find Kelsingra, if you never believed we could find Kelsingra, why did you undertake this expedition?"

He looked at her then, full in her gray-green eyes. "You wanted to go. You wanted me to go. It was a way to be with you, even if only for a time." Her heart was in her eyes as he spoke those words. He looked aside from her. "That was what decided me. Before, when I first heard of it, I thought to myself, 'Well, there's a mission for a madman. Small chance of success, and so I'll bet they pay accordingly.' A chunk of money up front, and a big promise of lots more 'when all is done.' And a good adventure along the way. There isn't a man on the river who doesn't wonder where it comes from. Here was a chance to find out. And I've always been a bit of a gambler. Everyone who works the river plays the odds one way or another. So I took the bet."

He dared himself and took his own wager. Her hands were resting on the railing next to his. He lifted his hand and set it down gently upon hers. The effect on him was almost convulsive. A shiver ran over his body. Her hand was trapped under his and beneath her touch, there was Tarman. A thought floated through his mind. *The whole of everything I want in this world is right here, under my hand.*

The thought echoed through him, to his very bones and out to Tarman's timbers and back again until he couldn't define where it had originated.

✦ ✦ ✦

Day the 12th of the Prayer Moon

Year the 6th of the Independent Alliance of Traders

From Erek, Keeper of the Birds, Bingtown

To Detozi, Keeper of the Birds, Trehaug

Enclosure in sealed tube, highly confidential, to be delivered to Trader Newf. An extra fee has been paid to assure that this message is delivered with the stamped seal intact.

Detozi,

My apprentice continues to do his tasks very well. My compliments to your family on a young man well raised. There will soon be a vote of the bird keepers, but it is likely he will be raised to the status of journeyman. I tell you this in confidence, of course, knowing that no word of it will reach him until the finding is official.

He has excelled at his tasks so well that I am considering taking some time to myself. I've long considered a trip to the Rain Wilds and its wonders. I would not, of course, presume upon your family's hospitality, but I would greatly enjoy meeting you in person. Would you be amenable to this?

Erek

✦ ✦ ✦

CHAPTER THREE

FIRST KILL

Every one of the keepers had instantly recognized the danger when the shuddering water had rippled against their small boats. Ahead of them, the dragons had suddenly halted, spreading their legs wide and digging their feet into the riverbed as the wave of motion passed. The silver dragon had trumpeted wildly, flinging his head about as he tried to look in every direction simultaneously. Dislodged birds burst upward from the trees and flew out over the river, croaking and squawking their distress.

When the second quake hit and branches and leaves showered down in the forest and on the shallows, Rapskal had exclaimed, "Good thing we didn't run for the shore. Think any of the trees will fall on us?"

Thymara hadn't worried about it until he mentioned it. She had been caught up in comparing how a quake felt on water to how it felt when one lived high in a treetop. She wondered if her parents had felt it; up high in the canopy of Trehaug, in the flimsy cheap houses known as the Cricket Cages, a quake would make everything dance. People would shout and grip a tree limb if they could. Sometimes houses fell during quakes, heavy ones as well as flimsy ones. The thought had filled her with both worry for her parents and homesickness. But Rapskal's wondering snapped her out of that as she realized that being crushed under a falling tree might be just as dangerous as tumbling out of one. "Move away from the shore," she directed him, digging her own paddle into the water more vigorously. They had nearly caught up with the waiting dragons. Around them, the scattered flotilla of keeper boats moved chaotically.

"No. It's all over now. Look at the dragons. They know. They're moving on again."

He was right. Ahead of them, the dragons made small trumpeting sounds to one another as they resumed their slogging march through muck and water. They had bunched up around Mercor when they first halted. Now they spread out again. Mercor led the way and the others fell in behind him. Thymara had almost become accustomed to the daily sight of dragons wading upriver in front of her. At that moment, as they resumed their trek, she saw them afresh. There were fifteen of the creatures, varying in size from Kalo, who was almost the size of a proper dragon now, down to the copper, who was barely taller than Thymara at the shoulder. The sun glinted on the river's face and on their scales. Gold and red, lavender and orange, gleaming blue black to azure, their hides threw the glory of the sun back up into the day. It made her realize that their colors had deepened and brightened. It was not just that the immense dragons were cleaner now; it was that they were healthier. Some of them were developing secondary colors. Sintara's deep blue wings were laced with silver, and the "fringes" on her neck were turning a different shade of blue.

All of them moved with ponderous grace. Kalo and Sestican followed behind Mercor. Their heads wove back and forth as they moved, and as she watched them, Sestican darted his head into the water and brought up a fat, dangling river snake. He gave his head a sharp shake and the writhing creature suddenly hung limp in his jaws. He ate it as he walked, tilting his head back and swallowing it as if he were a bird with a worm.

"I hope my little Heeby finds something to eat on the way. She's hungry. I can feel it."

"If she doesn't, we'll do our best tonight to come up with something for her." She spoke the words almost without thinking. She was becoming resigned, she suddenly realized, to sharing whatever she could bring back from her evening hunt. Most often it went to whichever dragon was hungriest. That did not endear her to Sintara, but the blue queen had not been exactly generous with Thymara. Let her find out that loyalty was supposed to run both ways.

The rest of that day, Thymara expected to feel echoing quakes, but if they came, they were so small that she didn't notice them. When they camped that night on a mud bank, the main topic of discussion had been the quake, and whether a rush of acid water would follow it. After spending the meal hour chewing over the potential threat to all of them, Greft had suddenly stood and dismissed the topic. "Whatever will happen is going to happen," he said sternly as if expecting them to argue. "It's useless to worry and impossible to prepare. So just be ready."

He stalked away from their firelit circle into the darkness. No one spoke for a few minutes after he left. Thymara sensed awkwardness; doubtless Greft was still smarting from his misspoken words about the copper dragon. His pronouncement of the obvious seemed a feeble attempt to assert his leadership over them. Even his closest followers had seemed embarrassed for him. Neither Kase nor Boxter followed him or even looked in the direction he had gone. Thymara had kept her eyes on the flames, but from the corner of her eyes, she marked how shortly after that Jerd stood up, made a show of stretching, and then likewise wandered away from their company. As she passed behind Thymara, she bid her "Good night" in a small catty voice. Thymara gritted her teeth and made no response.

"What's bothering her lately?" Rapskal, to Thymara's right, wondered aloud.

"She's just like that," Tats said in a low, sour voice.

"I'm sure I don't know what's bothering her. And I'm off to bed now," Thymara replied. She wanted to get away from the firelight, lest anyone notice how embarrassed she was.

"Good night, then," Tats muttered, a bit stiffly, as if her brusque reply was a rebuke to him.

"I'll be along shortly," Rapskal informed her cheerfully. She had not found a way to tell him that she didn't really want him to sleep against her back each night. Once, when she'd gently told him that she didn't need anyone to guard her, he'd replied cheerfully that he liked sleeping against her back.

"It's warmer, and if danger does come, I think you'll probably wake up faster than me. And you've got a bigger knife, too." And so, to the veiled amusement of the others, he had become her constant night companion as well as her boat partner by day. In a way, she was fond of him but could not help but be annoyed by his constant presence. Ever since she had observed Greft and Jerd, she'd been troubled. She'd pondered it deeply on her own and found no satisfying answers to her questions.

Could Greft just make new rules for himself? Could Jerd? If they could, what about the rest of them? She desperately wanted to find a quiet time to talk with Tats, but Rapskal was almost always present. And when he wasn't following her about, Sylve was trailing after Tats. She wasn't sure that she would actually tell Tats what she had seen, but she knew she did want to talk with someone about it.

When she had first returned to camp that night, she'd actually wondered if she should go to Captain Leftrin and let him know what was going on, as captain of the vessel that supported their expedition. Yet the more she thought about it, the more reluctant she felt to go to him. It would, she decided, fall somewhere between tattling and betrayal. No. What Jerd and Greft were doing was a matter that concerned the dragon keepers, and no others. They were the ones who had always been bound by those rules. It was a rule that had been imposed on them by others, others like Captain Leftrin, ones who were marked but did not restrict their own lives because of it. Was that fair? Was it right that someone else could make a decision like that and bind her and the other keepers with it?

Every time she thought of what she had seen, her cheeks still burned. It was uncomfortable enough that she had seen them and was now aware of what they were doing. It was even worse to know that they knew of her spying. She felt unable to face them and felt almost as uncomfortable in how she avoided them. Worse, Jerd's little barbed remarks and Greft's complacent stares made her feel as if she were the one in the wrong. That couldn't be so. Could it?

What Greft and Jerd were doing ran counter to everything she'd ever been taught. Even if they had been wed, it would still have been wrong . . . not that they would have been allowed to wed. When the Rain Wilds marked a child heavily from birth, all knew that it was best to expose the baby and try again. Such children seldom lived past their fifth birthdays. In a place where scarcity was the norm, it was foolish for parents to pour effort and resources into such a child. Better to give it up at birth, and try for another baby as soon as possible. Those like Thymara who, by fluke or stubbornness, survived were forbidden to take mates, let alone have children.

So if what they were doing was wrong, why was she the one who felt not only guilty but foolish? She wrapped her blanket more tightly around herself and stared off into the darkness. She could still hear the others talking and sometimes laughing around the fire. She wished she were with them, wished she could still enjoy the companionship of their journey. Somehow Jerd and Greft had spoiled that for her. Did the others know about it, and not care? What would they think of her if she told them? Would they turn on Greft and Jerd? Would they turn on her and laugh at her, for thinking she was still bound? Not knowing the answers made her feel childish.

She was still awake when Rapskal came to take his blanket from their boat. She watched him from under her lashes as he came to her cloaked in his blanket. He stepped over her, sat down with his back to her, and then snugged himself up against her back. He heaved a great sigh and within a few moments fell into a deep sleep.

His weight was warm against her back. She thought how she could just roll over to face him, and how that would wake him. She wondered what would happen next? Rapskal, for all his oddness, was physically handsome. His pale blue eyes were at once unsettling and strangely attractive. Despite his scaling, he'd kept his long dark eyelashes. She didn't love him, well, not that way, but he was undeniably an attractive male. She caught her lower lip between her teeth, thinking about what she had seen Jerd and Greft doing. She doubted that Jerd loved Greft, or that he cared deeply for her. They'd been arguing right before they'd done it. What did that mean? Rapskal's back was warm against hers through the blankets, but a sudden shiver ran over her. It was a quiver, not of chill, but of possibility.

Moving very slowly, she edged her body away from his. No. Not tonight. Not by impulse, not without thought. No. It did not matter what others did. She had to think for herself about such things.

DAWN CAME TOO soon and brought no answers with it. Thymara sat up stiffly, unable to tell if she had slept or not. Rapskal slept on, as did most of the others. The dragons were not early risers. Many of the keepers had taken to sleeping in almost as late as the dragons did. But for Thymara, old habits died hard. Light had always wakened her, and she'd always known from her father that the early hours were the best for hunting or for gathering. So despite her weariness, she rose. She stood a time looking thoughtfully down on Rapskal. His dark lashes curled on his cheeks; his mouth was relaxed, full and soft. His hands were curled in loose fists under his chin. His nails were pinker than they had been. She bent closer for a better look. Yes, they were changing. Scarlet to match his little dragon. She found herself smiling about that and realized that she could smell him, a male musk that was not at all repellent. She straightened up and drew back from him. What was she thinking? That he smelled good? How had Jerd chosen Greft, she wondered, and why? Then she folded her blanket and restored it to her boat.

Part of the camp routine each night was to dig a sand well. The hole was dug some distance away from the water's edge and then lined with canvas. The water that seeped up in the shallow hole and filtered through the canvas was always less acidic than the river water. Even so, she approached it with caution. She saw with relief that this morning the river was still running almost clear, so she judged it safe to wash her face and hands, and drank deeply. The cold water shocked the last vestiges of sleep from her mind. Time to face the day.

Most of the others were still bundled in their blankets around the smoldering embers of last night's fire. They looked, she thought, rather like blue cocoons. Or dragon cases. She yawned again and decided to take a walk along the water's edge with her pole spear. With a bit of luck, she'd find either breakfast for herself or a snack for Sintara.

Fish would be nice. Meat would be better. The sleepy thought from the dragon confirmed her impulse.

"Fish," Thymara replied firmly, speaking aloud as she shared her thoughts with the dragon. "Unless I happen to encounter small game at the river's edge. But I'm not going into the forest at the beginning of the day. I don't want to be late when everyone else wakes up and is ready for travel."

Are you sure that you don't fear what you might see back there? The dragon's question had a small barb to it.

"I don't fear it. I just don't want to see it," Thymara retorted. She tried, with limited success, to close her mind to the dragon's touch. She could refuse to hear Sintara's words, but not evade her presence.

Thymara had had time to think of Sintara's role in her discovery. She was sure that the dragon had deliberately sent her after Greft and Jerd, that she had been aware of what they were doing, and had used every means at her disposal to be sure that

Thymara witnessed it. It still stung when she thought of how Sintara had used her glamour to compel her to follow Greft's trail into the forest.

What she didn't know was *why* the dragon had sent her after them, and she hadn't asked directly. She'd already learned that the fastest way to make Sintara lie to her was to ask her a direct question. She'd learn more by waiting and listening. *Not so different from dealing with my mother,* she thought, and smiled grimly to herself.

She pushed the thought out of her mind and immersed herself in her hunting. She could find peace in this hour. Few of the other keepers roused so early. The dragons might stir but were not active, preferring to let the sun grow strong and warm them before they exerted themselves. She had the riverbank to herself as she quietly stalked the water's edge, spear poised. She forgot everything else but herself and her prey as the world balanced perfectly around her. The sky was a blue stripe above the river's wide channel. Along the river's edge, knee-high reeds shivered in water that was almost clear. The smooth mudbank of the river had recorded every creature that had come and gone in the night. While the dragon keepers had slumbered, at least two swamp elk had come down to the water's edge and then retreated. Something with webbed feet had clambered out on the bank, eaten freshwater clams and discarded the shells, and then slid back in.

She saw a large whiskered fish come groping into the shallows. He did not seem to see her. His barbels stirred the silt, and with a snap he gobbled some small creature he had ousted. He ventured closer to where she stood, spear poised, but the instant she jabbed with her weapon, he was gone with a flick of his tail, leaving only a haze of silt floating around her spear.

"Damn the luck," she muttered and pulled her spear back out of the silt.

"That doesn't sound like a prayer," Alise rebuked her gently.

Thymara tried not to be startled. She brought her spear back to the ready, glanced at the woman over her shoulder, and resumed her slow patrol of the riverbank. "I'm hunting. I missed."

"I know. I saw."

Thymara kept walking, her eyes on the river, hoping the Bingtown woman would take the hint and leave her alone. She didn't hear Alise following her, but from the corner of her eye, she was aware of Alise's shadow keeping pace with her. After holding her silence for a time, Thymara defiantly decided she wasn't afraid of the woman. She spoke to her. "It's early for you to be out and about."

"I couldn't sleep. I've been up since before dawn. And I confess that a deserted riverbank can be lonely after an hour or so. I was relieved to see you."

The comment was far friendlier than she had expected. Why was the woman even speaking to her? Could she truly be that lonely? Without pausing to think she said, "But you have Sedric to keep you company. How can you be lonely?"

"He still isn't well. And, well, he has not been as friendly to me of late. Not without cause, I'm ashamed to say."

Thymara stared into the river, glad that the Bingtown woman could not see her expression of astonishment. Was she confiding in her? Why? What could she possibly think they had in common? Curiosity dug its claws into her and hung on until she asked, in what she hoped was a casual voice, "What cause has he to be unfriendly to you?"

Alise sighed heavily. "Well, you know he hasn't been well. Sedric usually has excellent health, so it would be hard for him to be ill at any time. But it is especially hard for him when he is in what he regards as very uncomfortable living circumstances. His bed is narrow and hard, he doesn't like the smell of the boat or the river, the food either bores or disgusts him, his room is dim, there is no entertainment for him. He's miserable. And it's my fault that he's here. He didn't want to come to the Rain Wilds, let alone embark on this expedition."

Another big lunker had come into the shallows, investigating the silt. For an instant, he seemed to see her. Thymara stood perfectly still. Then, as he began to sift the silt with his whiskers, she struck. She was so sure that she had hit him, it was a surprise to have the silt clear and find that her spear was simply dug into the mud. She pulled it out.

"You missed again," the Bingtown woman said, but there was genuine sympathy in her voice. "I was so sure you got that one. But they're very quick to react, aren't they? I don't think I could ever manage to spear one."

"Oh, it just takes practice," Thymara assured her, keeping her eyes on the water. No, it was gone, long gone. That one wouldn't be back.

"Have you been doing this since you were a child?"

"Fishing? Not so much." Thymara continued her slow patrol along the water's edge. Alise kept pace with her. She kept her voice soft. "I hunted in the canopy mainly. Birds and small mammals up there, some lizards and some pretty big snakes. Fishing isn't that different from hunting birds when it comes to the stalking part."

"Do you think I could learn?"

Thymara halted in her tracks and turned around to face Alise. "Why would you want to?" she asked in honest confusion.

Alise blushed and looked down. "It would be nice to be able to do something real. You're so much younger than I am, but you're so competent at taking care of yourself. I envy you that. Sometimes I watch you and the other keepers, and I feel so useless. Like a pampered little house cat watching hunting cats at work. Lately I've been trying to justify why I came along, why I dragged poor Sedric along with me. I said I was going to be collecting information about dragons. I said I'd be needed here to help people deal with the dragons. I told my husband and Sedric that this was a priceless opportunity for me to learn, and to share what I'd learn. I told the Elderling Malta that I knew about the lost city and could possibly help the dragons find their way back. But I've done none of those things."

Her voice dropped on her last words and she sounded ashamed.

Thymara was silent. Was this grand Bingtown lady looking to her for comfort and reassurance? That seemed all wrong. Just when the silence would have become too obvious, she found her tongue. "You have helped with the dragons, I think. You were there when Captain Leftrin was helping us get the snakes off

them, and before, when we were bandaging up the silver's tail. I
was surprised, I'll admit. I thought you were too fine a lady for
messy work like that—"

"Fine a lady?" Alise interrupted her. She laughed in an odd
shrill way. "You think me a fine lady?"

"Well . . . of course. Look at how you dress. And you are
from Bingtown, and you are a scholar. You write scrolls about
dragons and you know all about the Elderlings." She ran out of
reasons and just stood looking at Alise. Even today, to walk on
the beach at dawn, the woman had dressed her hair and pinned
it up. She wore a hat to protect her hair and face from the sun.
She wore a shirt and trousers, but they were clean and pressed.
The tops of her boots were gleaming black even if fresh river
mud clung to her feet. Thymara glanced at herself. The mud that
caked her boots and laces was days, not hours, old. Her shirt and
her trousers both bore the signs of hard use and little washing.
And her hair? Without thinking, she reached up to touch her
dark braids. When had she last washed her hair and smoothed it
and rebraided it? When had she last washed her entire body?

"I married a wealthy man. My family is, well, our fortune is
humbler. I suppose that I am a lady, when I am in Bingtown, and
perhaps it is a fine thing to be. But here, well, here in the Rain
Wilds I've begun to see myself a bit differently. To wish for different things than I did before." Her voice died away. Then she
said suddenly, "If you wanted, Thymara, you could come to my
cabin this evening. I could show you a different way to do your
hair. And you'd have some privacy if you wished to take a bath,
even if the tub is scarcely big enough to stand in."

"I know how to wash myself!" Thymara retorted, stung.

"I'm sorry," Alise said immediately. Her cheeks had gone
very red. She blushed more scarlet than anyone Thymara had
ever known. "My words were not . . . I didn't express what I was
trying to say. I saw you look at yourself, and thought how selfish I've been, to have privacy to bathe and dress while you and
Sylve and Jerd have had to live rough and in the open among the
boys and men. I didn't mean—"

"I know." Were they the hardest words Thymara had ever

had to say? Probably not, but they were hard enough. She didn't meet Alise's eyes. She forced out other words. "I know you meant it kindly. My father often told me that I take offense too easily. That not everyone wants to insult me." Her throat was getting smaller and tighter. The pain of unsheddable tears was building at the inner corners of her eyes. From forcing words, suddenly she couldn't stop them. "I don't expect people to like me or be nice to me. It's the opposite. I expect—"

"You don't have to explain," Alise said suddenly. "We're more alike than you think we are." She gave a shaky laugh. "Sometimes, do you find reasons to disdain people you haven't met yet, just so you can dislike them before they dislike you?"

"Well, of course," Thymara admitted, and the laughter they shared had a brittle edge. A bird flew up from the river's edge, startling them both, and then their laughter became more natural, ending as they both drew breath.

Alise wiped a tear from the corner of her eye. "I wonder if this is what Sintara wanted me to learn from you. She strongly suggested this morning that I seek you out. Do you think she wanted us to discover that we are not so different?" The woman's voice was warm when she spoke of the dragon, but a chill went up Thymara's back at her words.

"No," she said quietly. She tried to form her thought carefully, so as not to hurt Alise's feelings. She wasn't sure, just yet, if she wanted to be as friendly as the Bingtown woman seemed inclined to be, but she didn't want to put her on her guard again. "No, I think Sintara was manipulating you, well, us. A couple of days ago, she pushed me to do something, and well, it didn't turn out nicely at all." She glanced at Alise, fearing what she'd see, but the Bingtown woman looked thoughtful, not affronted. "I think she may be trying to see just how much power she has over us. I've felt her glamour. Have you?"

"Of course. It's a part of her. I don't know if a dragon can completely control the effect she has on humans. It's her nature. Just as a human dominates a pet dog."

"I'm not her pet," Thymara retorted. Fear sharpened her words. Did Sintara dominate her more than she realized?

"No. You're not, and neither am I. Though I suspect she considers me more her pet than anything else. I think she respects you, because you can hunt. But she has told me, more than once, that I fail to assert myself as a female. I'm not sure why, but I think I disappoint her."

"She pushed me to go hunting his morning. I told her I preferred to fish."

"She told me to follow you when you hunted. I saw you here on the riverbank."

Thymara was quiet. She lifted her fish spear again and walked slowly along the river's edge, thinking. Was it betrayal? Then she spoke. "I know what she wanted you to see. The same thing I saw. I think she wanted you to know that Jerd and Greft have been mating."

She waited for a response. When none came, she looked back at Alise. The Bingtown woman's cheeks were pink again, but she tried to speak calmly. "Well. I suppose that, living like this, with no privacy and little supervision, it is easy for a young girl to give in to a young man's urging. They would not be the first to sample the dinner before the table is set. Do you know if they intend to marry?"

Thymara stared at her. She put her words together carefully. "Alise, people like me, like them, people who are already so heavily touched by the Rain Wilds, we are not allowed to marry. Or to mate. They are breaking one of the oldest rules of the Rain Wilds."

"It's a law, then?" Alise looked puzzled.

"I . . . I don't know if it's a law. It's a custom. It's something everyone knows and does. If a baby is born and it's already changed so much from pure human, then its parents don't raise it. They 'give it to the night'; they expose it and try again. Only for some of us, like me, well, my father took me back. He brought me home and kept me."

"There's a fish there, a really big one. He's in the shadow of that driftwood log. See him? He looks like he's part of the shadow."

Alise sounded excited. Thymara was jolted at the change of

subject. On an impulse, she handed her spear to Alise. "You get him. You saw him first. Remember, don't try to jab the fish. Stab it in like you want to stick it into the ground beyond the fish. Push hard."

"You should do it," Alise said as she took the spear. "I'll miss. He'll get away. And he's a very big fish."

"Then he's a good big target for your first try. Go on. Try it." Thymara stepped slowly back and away from the river.

Alise's pale eyes widened. Her glance went from Thymara to the fish and back again. Then she took two deep shuddering breaths and then suddenly sprang at the fish, spear in hand. She landed with a splash and a shout in ankle-deep water as she stabbed the spear down with far more force than she needed to use. Thymara stared openmouthed as the Bingtown woman used both hands to drive the spear in even deeper. Surely the fish was long gone. But no, Alise stood in the water, holding the spear tightly as a long, thick fish thrashed out its death throes.

When it finally stilled, she turned to Thymara and cried breathlessly, "I did it! I did it! I speared a fish! I killed it!"

"Yes, you did. And you should get out of the water before you ruin your boots."

"I don't care about them. I got a fish. Can I try again? Can I kill another?"

"I suppose you can. Alise, let's get the first one ashore, shall we?"

"Don't lose it! Don't let it get away!" This she cried as Thymara waded out and put a hand on the spear.

"It won't get away. It's very dead. We have to pull the spear out of the ground so we can get the fish to shore. Don't worry. We won't lose it."

"I really did it, didn't I? I killed a fish."

"You did."

It took some effort to free the spear from the mud. The fish was bigger than Thymara had expected. It took both of them to drag it back to shore. It was an ugly creature, black and finely scaled with long teeth in its blunt face. When they flipped it up onto the shore, it had a brilliant scarlet belly. Thymara had never seen anything like it. "I'm not sure if this is something we can eat," she said hesitantly. "Sometimes animals that are brightly colored are poisonous."

"We should ask Mercor. He'll know. He remembers a great deal." Alise crouched down to examine her prize. She reached out a curious finger and then pulled it back. "It's strange. All of the dragons seem to have different levels of recall. Sometimes I think Sintara refuses to answer my questions because she cannot. But with Mercor, I always feel like he knows things but won't share them. When he talks to me, he talks about everything except dragons and Elderlings."

"I'm not sure we should touch it before we know." Thymara had remained crouched by the fish. Alise nodded. She rose, took up the spear, and began prowling along the river's edge. Her excitement was palpable.

"Let's see what else we can kill. Then we'll ask Mercor about that one."

Thymara stood up. She felt a bit naked without her spear. It was odd to be the one trailing after someone else who was hunting. She didn't much like the feeling. She found herself talking, as if it would restore her sense of importance. "Mercor seems older than the other dragons, doesn't he? Older and more tired."

"He does." Alise spoke quietly. She didn't move as smoothly as Thymara did, but she was trying. Thymara realized that her tiptoeing and hunched stance was an exaggerated imitation of Thymara's prowl. She couldn't decide if she was flattered or insulted. "It's because he remembers so much more than the others. I sometimes think that age is based more on what you've done and what you remember than how old you are. And I think Mercor remembers a lot, even about being a serpent."

"He always seems sad to me. And gentler, in a way that the other dragons are not gentle at all."

Alise hunkered down on her heels, peering under a tangle of branches and fallen leaves. She sounded both intent and distracted as she replied. "I think he remembers more than the others. I had one good evening of talking to him. When he spoke to me, he was far more open and direct than any of the other dragons had been. Even so, he only spoke in generalities rather than of his specific ancestral memories. But he expressed things I've never heard the other dragons say." She extended the spear and tried to lift some of the weed mass out of her way. As she did so, a fish darted out. She lunged at it with a splash and a shout, but it was gone.

"Next time, if you think a fish might be there, just stab down. If you move the water anywhere near a fish looking for it, it's gone. Might as well risk a jab and maybe get something."

"Right." Alise expended an exasperated breath and continued to stalk down the shore.

Thymara followed. "Mercor said unusual things?" she prompted Alise.

"Oh. Yes, he did. He spoke quite a bit about Kelsingra. He said it was a significant city for both dragons and Elderlings. There was a special kind of silvery water there that the dragons especially enjoyed. He couldn't or wouldn't explain that to me. But he said it was an important place because it was where the Elderlings and dragons came together and made agreements. The way he spoke, it gave me a different view of how Elderlings and dragons interacted. Almost like adjacent kingdoms making treaties and having accords. When I mentioned that to him, he said it was more like symbiosis."

"Symbiosis?"

"They lived together in a way that benefited both. But more than benefited. He did not say it directly, but I think he believes that if Elderlings had survived, dragons would not have vanished from this world for as long as they did. I think he feels that restoring Elderlings will be key to the dragons continuing to survive in this world."

"Well, there is Malta and Reyn. And Selden."

"But none of them is here," Alise pointed out. She started to step into the water and halted. "Do you see that speckled place? Is that a shadow on the river bottom or a fish?" She tilted her head the other way. "So the dragons now depend on their keepers for what Elderlings did for them, once upon a time." She cocked her head. "Hmm. I wonder if that was why they insisted on having keepers accompanying them, as well as the hunters? I've wondered about that. Why did they want so many keepers but were content with only three hunters? What could all of you do for them that the hunters didn't do?"

"Well, we groom them. And we pay a lot of attention to them. You know how much they love to be flattered." Thymara paused, thinking. Why had the dragons demanded keepers? She saw Alise's intent stare. "If you think it might be a fish, jab it! If it's only a shadow, no harm done. If it's a fish, you'll kill it."

"Very well." Alise took a deep breath.

"Don't scream this time. Or jump in the water. You don't want to scare other nearby game or fish."

Alise froze. "Did I scream last time?"

Thymara tried to laugh quietly. "Yes. And you jumped in the water. Just use the spear this time. Farther back. Pull your arm farther back. There. Now look at where you want to hit it and jab for it." *I sound like my father,* she realized abruptly. And just as suddenly discovered that she was enjoying teaching Alise.

Alise was a good student. She listened. She took her breath, focused on whatever she was seeing, and plunged the spear in. Thymara had not believed there was a fish there, but the spear went into something alive, for a very large patch of water suddenly erupted into furious thrashing. "Hold the spear firm, hold the spear firm!" she shouted at Alise and then leaped forward to add her weight to the Bingtown woman's. Whatever she had jabbed was large, and possibly not a fish at all. The thrust had pinned something to the river bottom. It was large and flat bodied and had a lashlike tail that suddenly began snapping about below the water. "It might have barbs or a sting! Watch out!" Thymara warned her. She thought Alise would let go her grip on the spear; instead she hung on doggedly.

"Get . . . another spear . . . or something!" Alise gasped.

For a moment, Thymara froze. Then she dashed off back to the boats. Tats's was closest and his gear was inside it. He was sitting on the ground next to it, just waking up. "Borrowing your spear!" she barked at him, and as he began to stir, she snatched it up and ran back with it.

"It's getting away!" Alise was shouting as Thymara dashed back. Someone followed her. She glanced back and saw Rapskal and Sylve coming at a run, with Captain Leftrin behind them. The camp had awakened while she and Alise were fishing. Heedless of the animal's lashing tail, Alise had waded out into the water to lean more heavily on the spear. Thymara gritted her teeth and plunged in. She jabbed her spear into the murky water where she judged the main part of the fish's body to be. It went deep into something muscular; the spear pole was all but snatched out of her hands by the creature's furious reaction. It moved, dragging her and Alise into deeper water in its efforts to escape.

"We'll have to let it go!" she gasped, but behind her Rapskal shouted, "No!" and waded in with a will. Heedless of the tail that wildly lashed through the water, he proceeded to jab the thing half a dozen times with his own fish spear. Dark blood tendriled through the murky water and the fish only redoubled its efforts.

"Pull out my spear! Don't let it carry it off!" Thymara shouted at Alise. She was soaked to the waist and grimly clinging to the spear.

"Nor mine!" Tats shouted. "Thymara, that's my last one!"

"Out of the way!" Sintara trumpeted, but gave no one time to obey her. The dragon lumbered into the water as Rapskal frantically tried to avoid her.

"Thymara!" Tats shouted, and then Sintara's unfolding wing hit her. The water seemed to leap up and seize her; the spear was jerked from her hands. Then something large, flat, and alive struck her, rasping fabric and skin from her left arm before propelling her into deeper water. She opened her mouth to shout a protest and silty water filled it. She blew it out, but had no air to replace it. She held her breath desperately. She had never learned to swim; she was a climber, made for the canopy, and she floundered in this foreign element that had seized her and was hurrying her along to somewhere.

Light broke over her face suddenly, but before she could take a breath, she sank again. Someone, she thought, had shouted something. Her eyes stung and her arm burned. Something seized her, engulfing her torso and squeezing. She beat at the scaly thing with her fists, and her mouth burst open in an airless scream. It dragged her through the water and then out of it. A thought penetrated her mind. *I have her! I have her!*

Then she was hanging from Mercor's jaws. She could feel his teeth through her clothes. He held her gingerly, but still they scratched her. Before she could react to being in a dragon's mouth, he dropped her on the muddy riverbank. A circle of shouting people closed around her as she gagged up river water and sand. It ran in gritty streams from her nose. She wiped at her face and someone pushed a blanket into her hands. She dried her face on a corner of it and blinked her eyes. Her vision was blurry, but it slowly cleared.

"Are you all right? Are you all right?" It was Tats, kneeling next to her, soaking wet, and asking the same question over and over.

"It's my fault! I didn't want to let the fish go. Oh, Sa forgive me, it's all my fault! Is she going to be all right? She's bleeding! Oh, someone get some bandaging!" Alise was pale, her red hair hanging in wet streamers down her face.

Rapskal was fussing over her, trying to hold her down. Thymara pushed him aside and sat up, to belch and spit out more sandy water. "Please, give me some space," she said. It was only when a shadow moved away that she became aware that a dragon had been standing over her also. She spat more grit out of her mouth. Her eyes were sore and tears could not come. She wiped at them lightly with her fingers, and silt came away.

"Tip your head back," Tats ordered her gruffly, and when she did, he poured clean water over her face. "Doing your arm now," he warned her, and the cool flow made her gasp as it eased the burning she'd been trying to ignore. She sneezed abruptly, and water and mucus flew everywhere. She wiped her face with the blanket, earning a cry of "Hey, that's my blanket!" from Rapskal.

"You can use mine," she said hoarsely. She suddenly realized she wasn't dead or dying, only strangely humiliated by everyone's attention. She struggled to get to her feet. When Tats helped her, she managed not to jerk her arm away from him, though she didn't like to appear weak in front of everyone. An instant later, it was even worse when Alise enveloped her in a hug.

"Oh, Thymara, I'm so sorry! I nearly killed you and all for a fish!"

She managed to disentangle herself from Alise. "What sort of a fish was it?" she asked, trying to divert attention away from herself. Her abraded arm stung and her clothes were wet. She slung the blanket around her shoulders as Alise said, "Come and see. I've never seen anything like it."

Neither had Thymara. In shape, it was like an inverted dinner plate, but a plate twice the size of Thymara's blanket. It had two bulbous eyes on top of its body, and a long, whiplike tail with a series of barbs on the end. The top of it was speckled light and dark, like the river bottom, but its underside was white. It bore the wounds of spears in a dozen places, and gashes where Sintara had dragged it ashore. "Is it a fish?" she asked incredulously.

"Looks a bit like a ray; yes, a fish," Leftrin commented. "But I've never seen anything like this in the river, only in salt water. And I've never seen one this size."

"And it's mine to eat," Sintara asserted. "But for me, it would have been lost."

"Your greed nearly killed me," Thymara said. She did not speak loudly but firmly. She was surprised she could say the words so calmly. "You knocked me into the river. I nearly drowned." She looked at the dragon and Sintara looked back. She sensed nothing from her, no sense of remorse, or justification. They'd come so far together. The dragon had grown stronger and larger and definitely more beautiful. But unlike the other dragons, she had not grown closer to her keeper. A terrible regret welled up in Thymara. Sintara grew more beautiful daily; she was, without doubt, the most glorious creature that Thymara had ever seen. She had dreamed of being companion to such a wonderful being, dreamed of basking in her reflected glory. She'd fed the dragon to the best of her ability, groomed her daily, doctored her when she thought she could help her, and praised her and flattered her through every step of their day. She'd seen her grow in health and strength.

And today the dragon had nearly killed her. By carelessness, not temper. And did not express even a moment of regret. Her earlier question came back to her. Why had the dragons wanted keepers? The answer seemed clear to her now. To be their servants. Nothing more.

She had heard people speak of "heartbreak." She had not known that it actually caused a pain in the chest, as if, indeed, her heart were torn. She looked at her dragon and struggled to find words. She could have said, "You are no longer my dragon, and I am not your keeper." But she didn't, because it suddenly seemed as if that had never been true at all. She shook her head slowly at the beautiful sapphire creature and then turned aside from her. She looked around at the circle of gathered keepers and dragons. Alise was looking at her, her gray eyes wide. She was soaking wet; Captain Leftrin had put his coat around her shoulders. The Bingtown woman stared at her wordlessly, and Thymara knew that she alone grasped what she was feeling. That was unbearable. She turned and walked away. A stone-faced Tats stepped aside and let her pass.

She hadn't gone a dozen steps before Sylve fell in beside her. Mercor moved slowly along beside her. The girl spoke quietly. "Mercor found you in the water and pulled you out."

Thymara stopped. Mercor had been the dragon overshadowing her when she was recovering. Reflexively, she touched her ribs where his teeth had torn her clothes and scraped her skin. "Thank you," she said. She looked up into the golden dragon's gently swirling eyes. "You saved my life." Sylve's dragon had saved her after her own had shoved her into the water and left her there. She could not bear the contrast. She turned and walked away from both of them.

ALISE COULD SCARCELY bear to watch Thymara go. Pain seemed to emanate from her in a cloud as she trudged away. She swung her gaze back to Sintara. But before she could find words to speak, the dragon suddenly threw up her head, wheeled around, and stalked off, lashing her tail as she went. She opened her wings and gave them a violent shake, heedless that she spattered the gathered humans and dragons with water and sand.

One of the younger keepers spoke into the silence. "If she isn't going to eat that, can Heeby have it? She's pretty hungry. Well, she's always hungry."

"Is it safe for any of the dragons to eat? Is it edible?" Alise asked anxiously. "These fish look strange to me. I think we should be cautious of them."

"Those are fish from the Great Blue Lake. I know them of old. The one with the red belly is safe for dragons, but poisons humans. The flatfish, any may eat."

Alise turned to Mercor's voice. The golden dragon approached the gathered humans. He moved with ponderous grace and dignity. Perhaps he was not the largest of the dragons, but he was certainly the most imposing. She lifted her voice to address him. "The Great Blue Lake?"

"It is a lake fed by several rivers, and the mother of what you call the Rain Wild River. It was a very large lake that swelled even larger during the rainy seasons. The fishing in it was excellent. These fish you have killed today would have been regarded as small in the days that I recall." His voice went distant as he reminisced. "The Elderlings fished in boats with brightly colored sails. Seen from above, it was a very pretty sight, the wide blue lake and the sails of the fishing vessels scattered across it. There were few permanent Elderling settlements near the lake's shores, because the flooding was chronic, but wealthy Elderlings built homes on piers or brought houseboats down to the Great Blue Lake for the summers."

"How close was the Great Blue Lake to Kelsingra?" She waited breathlessly for the answer.

"As a dragon flies? Not far." There was humor in his voice. "It was no difficulty for us to cross the wide lake, and then we flew straight rather than follow the winding of the river. But I do not think you can look at these fish and say that we are close to the Great Blue Lake or Kelsingra. Fish do not stay in one place." He lifted his head and looked around as if surveying the day. "And neither should dragons. Our day is escaping us. It is time we all ate, and then left this place."

With no more ado, he strolled over to the red-bellied fish, bent his head, and matter-of-factly claimed it as his own. Several of the dragons moved in on the flatfish. Little red Heeby was the first to sink her teeth into it. The tenders moved back and allowed them room. None of them seemed inclined to want a share of the fish.

As they dispersed back to their abandoned bedding and cook fires, Leftrin offered Alise his arm. She took it. He said, "You should get out of those wet clothes as soon as you can. The river water is mild today, but the longer it's against your skin, the more likely you are to get a reaction to it."

As if his words had prompted it, she became aware of how her collar itched against her neck and the waistband of her trousers rubbed her. "I think that would be a good idea."

"It would. Whatever possessed you to get involved in Thymara's fishing anyway?"

She bristled a bit at the amusement in his voice. "I wanted to learn to do something useful," she said stiffly.

"More useful than learning about the dragons?" His tone was conciliatory, and that almost offended her more.

"I think what I'm learning is important, but I'm not certain it's useful to the expedition. If I had a more solid skill, such as providing food or—"

"Don't you think the knowledge you just got out of Mercor is useful? I'm not sure that any of us would have been able to provoke that information out of him."

"I'm not sure it's that useful to know," Alise said. She tried to keep her edge, but Leftrin knew too well how to calm her. And his view of her conversation with the dragon intrigued her.

"Well, Mercor is right in that fish don't have to stay in one spot. They move. But you're right in that we haven't seen any of these kinds of fish before. So I'd guess that we're closer to where they used to live than we were. If their ancestors came from a lake that used to be on the water system before one got to Kelsingra, then we're still going in the right direction. There's still hope of finding it. I'd begun to fear that we'd passed by where it used to be and there'd been no sign of it."

She was flabbergasted. "I'd never even considered such a thing."

"Well, it's been on my mind quite a bit of late. With your friend Sedric so sick and you so downhearted, I'd begun to ask myself if there was any point to going any farther. Maybe it was a pointless expedition to nowhere. But I'm going to take those fish as a sign that we're on the right track, and push on."

"For how much longer?"

He paused before he answered that. "Until we give up, I suppose," he said.

"And what would determine that?" The itching was starting to burn. She began to walk faster. He didn't comment on it, but accommodated his stride to hers.

"When it was clearly hopeless," he said in a low voice. "Until the river gets spread so shallow that not even Tarman can stay afloat. Or until the rains of winter come and make the water so deep and the current so strong that we can't make any headway against it. That was what I told myself at first. To be honest with you, Alise, this has turned out very differently from what I expected. I thought we'd have dead and dying dragons by now, not to mention keepers that either got hurt or sick or ran off. We've had none of that. And I've come to like these youngsters more than I care to admit, and even to admire some of the dragons. That Mercor, for instance. He's got courage and heart. He went right after Thymara, when I thought she was dead and gone for sure." He chuckled and shook his head. "Now she's a tough one. No tears or whining. Just got up and shook it off. They're all growing up as each day passes, keepers and dragons alike."

"In more ways than you might guess," she confirmed. She tugged her collar loose. "Leftrin, I'm going to run for the boat. My skin is starting to burn."

"What did you mean by what you just said?" he called after her, but she didn't reply. She darted away from him, easily outdistancing his more ponderous stride. "I'll haul some clean water for you," he shouted after her, and she fled, skin burning, toward Tarman.

SINTARA STALKED AWAY down the beach, away from the fish that she had rightfully brought to shore when the others were in danger of losing it. She hadn't even had a bite of it. And it was all Thymara's fault, for not getting out of the way when the dragon entered the water.

Humans were stupid in a way that Sintara found intolerable. What did the girl expect of her? That she was to be her coddling, enamored pet? That she would endeavor to fill every gap in her gnat's life? She should take a mate if she wished for that sort of companionship. She did not understand why humans longed for so much intense contact. Were their own thoughts never sufficient for them? Why did they look for others to fulfill their needs instead of simply taking care of themselves?

Thymara's unhappiness was like a buzzing mosquito in her ear. Ever since her blood had spattered on Thymara's face and lips, she'd been aware of the girl in a very uncomfortable way. It wasn't her fault; she hadn't intended to share her blood with her, or to create the awareness of each other that would always exist now. And it certainly had not been her decision to accelerate the changes that Thymara was undergoing. She had no desire to create an Elderling, let alone devote the thought and time that molding one required. Let the others contemplate such an old-fashioned pastime. Humans were ridiculously short-lived. Even when a dragon modified one to extend its lifetime several times over, they still lived only a fraction of a dragon's life. Why bother to create one and become attached to it when it was only going to die soon anyway?

Now Thymara had gone off on her own, to sulk. Or to grieve. Sometimes the distinction between the two seemed very insignificant to Sintara. There, now, the girl was crying, as if crying were a thing one did to fix something rather than a messy reaction that humans had to anything difficult. Sintara hated sharing Thymara's sensation of painful tears and dribbling nose and sore throat. She wanted to snap at the girl, but she knew that would only make her wail more. So, with great restraint, she reached out to her gently.

Thymara. Please stop this nonsense. It only makes both of us uncomfortable.

Rejection. That was all she sensed from the girl. Not even a coherent thought, only a futile effort to push the dragon out of her thoughts. How dare she be so rude! As if Sintara had wanted to be aware of her at all!

The dragon found a sunny spot on the mudbank and stretched out. *Stay out of my mind,* she warned the girl and resolutely turned her thoughts away from her. But she could not quite quench a small sense of desolation and sorrow.

Day the 14th of the Prayer Moon

Year the 6th of the Independent Alliance of Traders
From Detozi, Keeper of the Birds, Trehaug
To Erek, Keeper of the Birds, Bingtown

Shipped this day twenty-five of my birds on the liveship *Goldendown*. The captain of that vessel bears for you a payment from the Trehaug Rain Wild Traders' Council sufficient for three hundredweight sacks of the yellow peas for pigeon feed.

Erek,

I have finally persuaded the Council of the value of a good diet for the birds. I also showed them several of the king pigeons, including two half-grown squabs, and told them that the birds could lay two eggs every sixteen days, and that a good pair frequently laid another set of eggs as soon as the first hatched, so that a steady stream of squabs suitable for the table could be produced by free-ranging birds. They seemed very amenable to the idea.

Of Meldar and Finbok, I can tell you only what I have heard from Cassarick. The woman was very eager to depart with the expedition and signed on as a contracted member of the crew. Meldar appears to have simply gone along. The ship did not take any message birds with it, a foolish oversight in my opinion. Until they return or do not return, we shall not know what has become of them. I am sorry I do not have more details for the families.

Detozi

CHAPTER FOUR

BLUE INK, BLACK RAIN

Alise sat stiffly at the galley table. Outside the windows, evening was venturing toward night. She was attired modestly, if exotically, in a long robe of soft fabric. She could not, by touch, tell what it had been made from. Bellin ghosted through the room in her quiet, private way. She raised her dark brows in surprised approval, gave her a conspiratorial smile that made Alise blush, and continued on her way. Alise dipped her head and smiled.

Bellin had become a friend, of a type she'd never had before. Their conversations were brief but cogent. Once, she had come upon Alise leaning on the railing, looking at the night sky. She'd paused by her and said, "We of the Rain Wilds do not have long lives. We have to seize our opportunities, or we have to recognize we cannot have them, and let them go by and seek out others. But a Rain Wild man cannot wait forever, unless he is willing to let his life go by him."

She had not waited for a response from Alise. Bellin seemed to know when Alise needed time to think over what she had said. But tonight, her smile hinted that Alise was closer to a decision that she approved of. Alise took a breath and sighed it out. Was she?

Leftrin had produced the silky, clinging gown after her mishap in the river had left her skin so enflamed that she could scarcely bear the touch of cloth against it. Even two days after her dip in the river, she was still sore. The robe was of Elderling make; of that she was certain. It was a scintillant copper and reminded her more of a fine mesh than a woven garment. It whispered lightly against her skin when she moved, as if it would divulge the secrets of whatever Elderling princess had worn it in days long past remembering. It soothed the rash wherever it touched her skin. She had been astonished to discover that a simple river captain could possess such a treasure.

"Trade goods," Leftrin had said dismissively. "I'd like you to keep it," he added gruffly, as if he did not know how to offer a gift. He'd blushed darkly at her effusive thanks, his skin reddening so that the scaling on his upper cheeks and along his brow stood out like silver mail. At one time, such a sight might have repulsed her. Now she had felt an erotic thrill as she imagined tracing that scaling with her fingertips. She had turned from him, heart thumping.

She smoothed the sleek copper fabric over her thighs. This was her second day of wearing it. It felt both cool and warm to her, soothing the myriad tiny blisters that her river immersion had inflicted on her skin. She knew the garment clung to her more closely than was seemly. Even staid Swarge had given her an admiring glance as she passed him on the deck. It had made her feel girlish and giddy. She was almost relieved that Sedric still kept to his bed. She was certain he would not approve of her wearing it.

The door banged as Leftrin came in from the deck. "Still writing? You amaze me, woman! I can't hold a pen in my paw for more than half a dozen lines before feeling a cramp. What are you recording there?"

"Oh, what a story! I've seen all the notes you take and the sketches you make of the river. You're as much a documentarian as I am. As for what I'm writing, I'm filling in the detail on a conversation that I had with Ranculos last night. Without Sedric to help me, I'm forced to take my own notes as I go along and then fill in afterward. Finally, finally, the dragons have begun to share some of their memories with me. Not many, and some are disjointed, but every bit of information is useful. It all adds up to a very exciting whole." She patted her leather-bound journal. It and her portfolio case had been new and gleaming when she left Bingtown. Now both looked battered and scarred, the leather darkening with scuffs. She smiled. They looked like an adventurer's companions rather than the diary of a dotty matron.

"So, read me a bit of what you've written, then," he requested. He moved efficiently about the small galley as he spoke. Lifting the heavy pot off the small cookstove, he poured himself a cup of thick coffee before taking a seat across from her.

She suddenly felt as shy as a child. She did not want to read her scholarly embellished treatise aloud. She feared it would sound ponderous and vain. "Let me summarize it," she offered hastily. "Ranculos was speaking of the blisters on my hands and face. He told me that if they were scales, I would be truly lovely. I asked if that was because it would be more like dragon skin, and he told me 'Of course. For nothing can be lovelier than dragon skin.' And then he told me, well, he implied, that the more a human was around dragons, the greater the chance that she or he might begin the changes to become an Elderling. He hinted that in ancient times, a dragon could choose to hasten those changes for a worthy human. He did not say how. But from his words, I deduced that there were ordinary humans as well as Elderlings inhabiting the ancient cities. He admitted this was so, but said that humans had their own quarters on the outskirts of the city. Some of the farmers and tradesmen lived across the river, away from both dragons and Elderlings."

"And that's important to know?" he asked.

She smiled. "Every small fact I gather is important, Captain."

He tapped her thick portfolio. "And what's this, then? I see you write in your journal all the time, but this you just seem to lug about."

"Oh, that's my treasure, sir! It's all my gleaned knowledge from my years of study. I've been very fortunate to have had access to a number of rare scrolls, tapestries, and even maps from the Elderling era." She laughed as she made her announcement, fearful of sounding self-aggrandizing.

Leftrin raised his bushy eyebrows. It was ridiculously endearing. "And you've brought them all with you, in there?"

"Oh, of course not! Many are too fragile, and all are too valuable to subject them to travel. No, these are only my copies and translations. And my notes, of course. My conjectures on what missing parts might have said, my tentative translations of unknown characters. All of that." She patted the bulging leather case affectionately.

"May I see?"

She was surprised he'd ask. "Of course. Though I wonder if you'll be able to read my chicken-scratch writing." She unbuckled the wide leather straps from the sturdy brass buckles and opened the portfolio. As always, it gave her a small thrill of pleasure to open it and see the thick stack of creamy pages. Leftrin leaned over her shoulder, looking curiously as she turned over leaf after leaf of transcription. His warm breath near her ear was a shivery distraction, one she treasured.

Here was her painstaking copy of the Trehaug Level Seven scroll. She had traced each Elderling character meticulously, and reproduced, as well as she was able, the mysterious spidery drawings that had framed it. The next sheet, on excellent paper and in good black ink, was her copy of the Klimer translations of six Elderling scrolls. In red ink she had marked her own additions and corrections. In deep blue she had inserted notes and references to other scrolls.

"It's very detailed," her captain exclaimed with an awe that warmed her.

"It is the work of years," she replied demurely. She turned a handful of pages to reveal her copy of an Elderling wall hanging. Decorative leaves, shells, and fish framed an abstract work done in blues and greens. "This one, well, no one quite understands. Perhaps it was damaged or is unfinished in some way."

His brows arched again. "Well, it seems clear enough to me. It's an anchorage chart for a river mouth." He touched it carefully, tracing it with a scaled forefinger. "See, here's the best channel. It has different blues to show high and low tidelines. And this black might be the channel for deep-hulled ships. Or an indication of a strong current or tide rip."

She peered down at it, and then looked up at him in surprise. "Yes, I see it now. Do you recognize this place?" Excitement coursed through her.

"No. It's nowhere I've ever been. But it's a river chart, one that focuses all on water and ignores land details. On that, I'd wager."

"Will you sit with me and explain it?" Alise invited him. "What might these wavy lines here be?"

He shook his head regretfully. "Not now, I'm afraid. I only came in for a quick cup of coffee and to be out of the wind and rain for a time. It's getting dark outside, but the dragons show no signs of settling for the night. I'd best be out there. Can't have too many eyes on the river if you must run at night."

"Do you still fear white water then?"

Leftrin scratched his beard, then shook his head. "I think the danger has passed. It's hard to say. The rain is dirty and smells sooty. It's black when it hits the deck. So, somewhere, something is happening. I've only seen a true white flood happen twice in my life, and each time it was only a day or so after the quake. It's common enough to have the acid in the river vary. But my feeling is that if we were going to be hit with white water, it would have happened by now."

"Well. That's a relief then." She groped for something more to say, words that would keep him in the galley, talking to her. But she knew he had his work, and she closed her mouth on such silliness.

"I'd best be about my work," he said reluctantly, and with a girlish lurch of her heart, she was abruptly certain that he, too, wished he could stay. Such knowledge made it easier to let him go.

"Yes. Tarman needs you."

"Well, some days I'm not sure Tarman needs any of us. But I'd best get out there and put my eyes on the river." He paused and daringly added, "Though I'd just as soon be keeping them on you."

She ducked her head, flustered by his compliment, and he laughed. Then he was out of the door, and the river wind banged it shut behind him. She sighed, and then smiled at how foolish she had become about him.

She went to dip her pen, then decided she needed the blue ink if she were to make a note on the page of Leftrin's interpretation. Yes, she decided, she wanted blue, and she'd credit him for the theory as well. It pleased her to think that scores of years hence, scholars would read his name and know that a common river captain had deduced what had eluded others. She found the small ink bottle, uncorked it, and dipped her pen. It came up dry.

She held the bottle to the light. Had she written that much on her journey? She supposed she had. She'd seen so much that had given her ideas or made her revise old thoughts. She thought of adding water to the pigment that remained and scowled. No. That would be her last resort. Sedric, she recalled, had plenty of ink in his portable desk. And she hadn't visited him since morning. It was as good an excuse to check on him as any.

SEDRIC CAME AWAKE, not suddenly, but as if he were surfacing from a deep dive into black water. Sleep sleeked away from his mind like water draining from his hair and skin. He opened his eyes to the familiar dimness of his cabin. But it was different. The air was slightly cooler and fresher. Someone had recently opened the door. And entered.

He became aware of a figure hunched on the deck by his pallet. He heard the stealthy pawing of thieving hands on his wardrobe chest. Moving by tiny increments, he shifted so he could peer over the edge of his bed. The compartment was dim. Outside the light was fading and he had not lit a lamp. The only

illumination came from the small "windows" that also venti-
lated his room.

Yet the creature on the floor beside his bed gleamed a warm
copper and seemed to cast back light that had not struck it. As
he watched, it shifted and brilliance ran over a scaled back. She
scrabbled at the wardrobe chest, seeking for the hidden drawer
that held the vials of her stolen blood.

Terror flooded him and he nearly wet himself. "I'm sorry!"
he cried aloud. "I'm so, so sorry. I did not know what you were.
Please. Please, just let me be. Let go of my mind. Please."

"Sedric?" The copper dragon reared up and abruptly took
Alise's shape. "Sedric! Are you all right? Do you have a fever or
are you dreaming?" She put a warm hand on his damp brow.
He pulled back from her touch convulsively. It was Alise. It was
only Alise.

"Why are you wearing a dragon's skin? And why are you
rummaging through my possessions?" Shock made him both
indignant and accusing.

"I'm . . . a dragon's skin? Oh, no, it's a robe. Captain Leftrin
loaned it to me. It's of Elderling make and completely lovely.
And it doesn't irritate my skin. Here. Feel the sleeve." She offered her arm to him.

He didn't try to touch the shimmering fabric. Elderling made.
Dragon stuff. "That still doesn't explain why you've sneaked
into my room to dig through my things," he complained petu-
lantly.

"I haven't! I didn't 'sneak'! I tapped on your door and when
you didn't answer, I let myself in. The door wasn't latched. You
were asleep. You've looked so weary lately that I didn't want to
wake you. That's all. The only thing I want from you is some
ink, some blue ink. Don't you keep it in your little lap desk? Ah.
Here it is. I'll take some and leave you in peace."

"No! Don't open that! Give it to me!"

She froze in the act of working the catch. Stonily silent, she
handed the lap desk to him. He tried not to snatch it from her,
but his relief at keeping it out of her clutches was too evident.
He swung it onto the bed beside him so he could conceal it

with his body. She didn't say a word as he opened it and slid his hand in to grope for the ink bottles. Fortune favored him. He pulled out a blue one. As he offered it to her, he ventured a halfhearted apology. "I was asleep when you came in. And I am out of sorts."

"Indeed you are," she replied coolly. "This is all I need from you. Thank you." She snatched it from his hand. As she went out the door, she muttered for him to hear, "Sneaked, indeed!"

"I'm sorry!" he called, but she shut the door on his words.

The moment she was gone, he rolled from his bed to latch the door tight, then dropped to his knees beside the hidden drawer. "It was just Alise," he said to himself. Yes, but who knew what the copper dragon might have told her? He worked it open clumsily, the drawer jamming, then forced himself to calm as he carefully lifted the flask of the copper dragon's blood. It was safe. He still had it.

And she still had him.

He'd lost count of how many days had passed since he'd tasted the dragon's blood. His dual awareness came and went like double vision after a blow to the head. He'd be almost himself; morose and despondent, but Sedric. Then that overlay of physical sensation and confused memory would wash through him as her baffled impressions mingled with his thoughts. Sometimes he tried to make sense of the world for her. *You are wading through water, not flying. Sometimes the water lifts you almost off your feet, but this is not flying. Your wings are too weak to fly.*

Sometimes he encouraged her. *The others are almost out of sight. You have to try to move faster. You can do it. Move to your left, where the water is shallower. See? It's easier to walk now, isn't it? That's a girl. Keep going. I know you're hungry. Watch for fish. Maybe you could catch a fish and eat it.*

Sometimes he felt vaguely proud of himself for being kind to her. But at other times, he felt his life had become an eternity of caring for a rather stupid child. By dint of effort he could sometimes block most of his awareness of her. But if she felt pain or her hunger grew too strong or if she were frightened, her dim thoughts burst through into his. Even when he could avoid sharing her dull mental processes, he could not escape her constant weariness and hunger. Her desolate *Why?* echoed through every moment of his day. It did not help that he shared that same question about his own fate. Worse was when she tried to make sense of his thoughts. She did not understand that sometimes he was asleep and dreaming. She broke into his dreams, offering to kill Hest or trying to comfort him with her company. It was all too strange. He was weary, doubly exhausted from his interrupted sleep and by his sharing of her dismal endless struggle.

Life aboard the barge had become very strange for him. He kept to his compartment as much as he could. Yet there was no solitude for him. Even when the dragon was not intruding into his thoughts, he had too much company. Alise was racked with guilt and could not seem to leave him alone. Every morning, every afternoon, and every evening before she retired, she came to call on him. Her visits were brief and uncomfortable. He didn't want to hear her chatter enthusiastically about her day, and there was nothing that he dared share with her, yet there was no graceful way to shut her up and send her out of his room.

The boy was the second worst. Sedric could not understand Davvie's fascination with him. Why couldn't he just bring his meal tray and then leave? Instead, the boy watched him avidly, eager to perform the most menial service, even offering to wash his shirts and socks, an offer that made him cringe. Twice he'd been rude to the boy, not because he enjoyed it, but because it was the only way to get the lad to leave. Each time, Davvie had been so obviously crushed by Sedric's rejection that Sedric had felt like a beast.

He turned the vial of dragon blood that he held, watching again how it swirled and gleamed even in the dim cabin. Even when the vial was still in his hand, the red liquid inside it shifted in a slow dance. It held its own light, and red on red, the threads of crimson inside the glass twined and twirled about each other. Temptation or obsession? he asked himself, and had no answer. The blood drew him. He held a king's ransom in his hand, if he could but get it to Chalced. Yet the possessing of it seemed

very important to him now. Did he want to taste it again? He
wasn't sure. He didn't think he wanted to experience that again.
He feared that if he gave in to his reluctant compulsion, he
would find himself even more tightly joined to the dragon. Or
dragons.

In late afternoon, when he'd ventured out on the deck for
a short breath of cool air, he had heard Mercor calling to the
other dragons. He called two of them by name. "Sestican. Ranculos. Stop your quarreling. Save your strength to battle the
river. Tomorrow is another day's journey." He'd stood there,
the dragon's words shimmering through his mind. He'd heard
the words, as clear as could be. He tried to remember if he'd
heard the dragon's trumpeting or whuffling that carried the
thought, but he couldn't. The dragons spoke to one another,
reasoned with one another, just as men did. He'd felt a whirl of
vertigo that combined with his guilt. Heartsick and dizzy, he'd
staggered back to his cabin and shut the door tight. "I can't
go on like this. I can't," he'd said aloud to his tiny space. And
almost immediately, he'd felt a worried query from the copper
dragon. She sensed his agitation. And was concerned for him.

No, I'm fine. Go away. Leave me alone! He'd pushed at her and
she'd retreated, saddened by his harshness. "I can't go on like
this," he'd repeated, and longed for a day when he had known
that no one else shared his thoughts. He tipped the vial of blood
again. If he drank it all, would it kill him?

If he killed the dragon, would his mind be his own private
territory again?

There was a heavy knock at his door. "Wait!" he shouted,
terror and anger making his voice louder than he'd intended.
There was no time to hide the blood properly. He wrapped it in
a sweaty shirt and stuffed it under his blanket. "Who is it?" he
called belatedly.

"It's Carson. I'd like a word with you, please."

Carson. He was the other person who seemed unable to leave
Sedric alone. The hunters were gone during the day, doing
what they were paid to do. But if Sedric arose early or ventured
into the galley in the evening, Carson always seemed to appear.

Twice he'd come to Sedric's room when Davvie was there, to remind the boy that he wasn't to bother Sedric. Each time, the boy had left, but not graciously. And each time, Carson had lingered. He'd tried to engage Sedric in conversation, asking him what it was like to live in a civilized place like Bingtown and if he'd ever traveled to other cities. Sedric had answered each of his queries briefly, but Carson hadn't seemed to realize he was being brusque. The hunter continued to treat him with gentle courtesy that was very at odds with the man's rough clothing and harsh vocation.

The last time he had come and shooed the boy away, Carson had taken the boy's seat on the end of Sedric's trunk and proceeded to tell him about himself. He lived a lonely life. No wife, no children, just a man on his own, taking care of himself and living as he pleased. He'd taken on Davvie, his nephew, because he foresaw the same sort of life for him, if Sedric took his drift. Sedric hadn't. He'd finished eating and then made a great show of yawning.

"I suppose you're still tired from being ill. I'd hoped you were feeling better by now," Carson had commented. "I'll leave you to rest." Then, with the precision of a man accustomed to caring for himself, Carson had tidied Sedric's supper things back onto the tray and whisked them away. As he folded up the square of cotton that passed for a napkin on the barge, he'd looked at Sedric and given him an odd smile. "Sit still," he'd warned him and then, with the corner of the napkin, he'd dabbed something off the edge of Sedric's mouth. "It's plain you're not used to having a bit of a beard. They take caring for. I think you should go back to shaving, myself." He'd paused and glanced meaningfully around the untidy room. "And bathing. And caring for your things. I know you're not happy to be here. I don't blame you. But that doesn't mean you should stop being who you are."

Then he'd departed, leaving Sedric feeling both shocked and affronted. He'd found his small mirror and leaned closer to his candle to inspect his face. Yes. There had been soup at the corner of his mouth, caught in the short whiskers that had sprouted there. It had been some days since he'd shaved, or washed thoroughly. He studied himself in the mirror, noting that he looked haggard. There were dark circles under his eyes above his unshaven cheeks. His hair was lank and uncombed. The mere thought of going to the galley to heat some water and shave and wash wearied him. How shocked Hest would be to see him in such a state!

But somehow that thought had not spurred him to clean himself up, but to sit back on his bed and stare up into the darkness. It didn't matter what Hest would think if he saw him like this, sweaty and unshaven, in a room littered with laundry. It was becoming more and more unlikely that Hest would ever see him again at all. And that was something that Hest had caused, with his stupid vengeance in sending him off to nursemaid Alise. Did Hest even think of him? Wonder what had delayed their return? He doubted it.

He had begun to doubt many things about Hest.

He'd crawled onto his pallet, a bed more fit for a dog than a man, and slept the rest of the day away.

Another bang on his door jerked his mind back to the present. "Sedric? Are you all right? Answer, or I'm coming in."

"I'm fine." Sedric took the one step he needed to cross the room and flipped the hook on the door clear. "You may come in, if you must."

Either the man didn't hear the lack of a welcome in his voice or he ignored it. Carson opened the door and looked about the dim cabin. "Seems to me that light and air might make you feel better than lying about in the close dark," he observed.

"Neither light nor air will cure what ails me," Sedric muttered. He glanced at the tall, bearded hunter and then away. Carson seemed to fill the small cabin with his presence. He had a broad forehead that sheltered wide dark eyes beneath heavy brows. His close-cropped beard was the same ginger as his rough hair. His cheeks were wind reddened, and his lips were ruddy and well-defined. He seemed to feel Sedric appraising him, for he smoothed his hair self-consciously.

"Did you need something?" Sedric asked. The words came

out more abrupt than he intended. The friendliness in Carson's eyes suddenly became more guarded.

"Actually, yes, yes I do." He shut the door behind him, dimming the room again, cast about for something to sit down on, and perched, uninvited, on the end of the trunk. "Look, I'll say this bluntly and then be out of your way. I think you'll understand; well, I'll make you understand, one way or another. Davvie is just a boy. I won't have him hurt, and I won't have him used. His dad and I were like brothers, and I could see the way Davvie was going a long time before his mother did. If she does even now, which I doubt." The man gave a short bark of laughter and glanced over at Sedric as if expecting a response. When he said nothing, Carson looked back down at his big hands. He rubbed them together as if his knuckles pained him. "So, you take my drift?" he asked Sedric.

"You're like a father to Davvie?" Sedric hazarded.

Carson barked another laugh at that. "As much as I'm ever likely to be a father to anyone!" he declared, and again, he looked at Sedric as if expecting some sort of response. Sedric just looked back at him.

"I see," the hunter said, and his voice went softer and more serious. "I understand. It goes no further, I promise you that. I'll speak my piece plain and then be gone. Davvie's just a youngster. You're probably the handsomest man he's ever seen, and the boy is infatuated. I've tried to make him see that he's much too young and that you're way above his social class. But puppy love can blind a boy. I'll be doing my best to keep him clear of you, and I'd appreciate it if you kept him at a distance. Once he realizes that there's nothing here for him, he'll get over it quick enough. Might even hate you a bit, but you know how that is. But if you mock him, or belittle him to the other men aboard, I'll take issue with you."

Sedric stared at him, his face like stone. His mind raced, filling in the meaning behind his words.

Carson met Sedric's eyes flatly. "And if I've misjudged you, and you're the kind who would take advantage of a boy, I'll come after you. Do you understand me?"

"Very well," Sedric replied. Carson's meaning finally penetrated to his mind, and he was torn between shock and embarrassment. His cheeks burned; he was glad of the dimness of the room. The hunter's eyes were still fixed on his. He looked aside. "What you said about belittling the boy to the crew. I would never do that. I ask the same of you. As for Davvie's . . . infatuation, well." He swallowed. "I didn't even see it. Even if I had, I wouldn't take advantage of it. He's so young. Almost a child still."

Carson was nodding. A sad smile edged his mouth. "I'm glad I didn't read you wrong. You didn't look the type to take advantage of a youngster, but you never know. Especially a boy like Davvie who seems to put himself in harm's way. A few months ago, in Trehaug, he read a young man the wrong way and said the wrong thing. And just for the offer, the fellow hit him twice in the face before the boy could even stand up. And that left me no choice but to get involved, and I've a temper. I'm afraid that we won't be welcome back in that tavern for a long time. It's one reason I signed us up for this expedition. I thought to get him away from town and temptation for a few months. Let him grow a bit of discretion and self-control. Thought it might keep him out of trouble, but as soon as he set eyes on you, he was gone. And who could blame him? Well . . ." He stood up abruptly. "I'll be going now. The boy won't be bringing your meals anymore. I thought that was a bad idea from the start, but it was hard to give a reason why he shouldn't. Now I'll tell Leftrin that I need him up earlier and at my side if we're to keep the dragons fed. I'll be taking him out of here earlier than usual. You may have to fetch your own grub. Or maybe Alise will bring it to you." He turned and put his hand on the door. "You work for her husband, right? That's what she told us at dinner the first night I met her. That usually you go everywhere he does, and she can't imagine why he sent you off with her, or how he's managing without you. She feels real bad about that, you know? That you're here and so unhappy about it."

"I know."

"But my guess is that there's a lot she doesn't know, and another reason that you're unhappy. Am I right?"

Sedric couldn't quite get his breath. "I don't think that's any of your concern."

Carson risked a glance over his shoulder. "Maybe not. But I've known Leftrin a long, long time. Never seen him gone on a woman like he is on Alise. And she looks pretty gone to me, too. Seems to me that if her husband has been able to find a bit of joy in his life, maybe she deserves the same. And maybe Leftrin does, too. They might find that, if she felt free to look for it."

He lifted the catch and began to ease the door open. Sedric found his voice. "Are you going to tell her?"

The big man didn't reply at first. He remained with the door ajar, staring out. Evening was deepening toward night. Finally he shook his bushy head. "No," he said with a sigh. "It's not my place. But I think you should." He moved like a large cat as he slipped out of the door and shut it firmly behind him, leaving Sedric alone with his thoughts.

THEY HAD TRAVELED longer than usual that day, through a misty, dirty rain that made her skin gritty and itchy. For the latter half of the day, the banks of the river had been unwelcoming, thick with a prickly vine. The upper reaches of the dangling lianas, held up to the sunlight by the stretching tree branches, had been thick with scarlet fruit. The incessant rain jeweled the leaves and fruit and freckled the river's face. Harrikin had pulled his boat in to shore to try to harvest some of the fruit but had got only scratches and mud for his efforts. Thymara hadn't even attempted it. She knew from experience that the only way to win that fruit was to come at it from above, climbing down to it. Even then, it was a scratchy, precarious business. She decided that the time it would take her to find a pathway to the tops of the trees would put her and Rapskal far behind the other boats. "Perhaps tonight, when we stop," she suggested to him in response to his longing glances at the dangling orbs.

But as the light faded from the sky and the shores continued to be inhospitable, she resigned herself to a night aboard the *Tar-*

man, with hard bread and a bit of salt fish as her only guaranteed meal. The dragons with their scaled skin could push close to the base of the trees and spend a drier but uncomfortable night if they must. She and the other keepers did not have that option. Her latest experience had proven that to her. The scaling on her skin might be increasing, but it was not the mail the dragons wore. Mercor's teeth had left their marks despite his efforts to be gentle. It had been embarrassing to have Sylve see how scaled she had become as the girl helped her dress the scratches his fangs had left on her and the large scrape on her left arm. Most of her injuries had been superficial, but one score at the top of her back was still sore and hot to the touch. It ached and she longed to pull her boat in to shore and rest for the night. But the dragons plainly hoped to find a better landing, for they continued their migration, and the keepers had no choice but to follow.

The dragons were darker silhouettes against the gleaming water when she and Rapskal caught up with them that night. They were scattered on a long broad wash of silty mud that curved out into the river. The sandbar was a relatively young one, bereft of trees. A few bushes and scrolls of grass banks grew down its spine. It offered a plentiful supply of firewood in the form of an immense beached log and a tangle of lesser driftwood banked against it. It would do.

A hard push with her paddle drove the nose of her boat onto the muddy shore. Rapskal shipped his paddle and jumped out to seize the painter and drag the boat farther ashore. With a groan, Thymara stored her own paddle and unfolded herself stiffly. The constant paddling had strengthened her and built her endurance, but she was still weary and aching at the end of each day.

Rapskal seemed almost unscathed by the extralong exertion. "Time to get a fire going," he announced cheerily. "And dry off. I hope the hunters got some meat. I'm awful sick of fish."

"Meat would be good," she agreed. "And a good fire." All around her, the other keepers were pulling their boats ashore and climbing wearily out.

"Let's hope," he replied, and without a backward glance he scampered off into the darkness.

She sighed as she watched him go. His unfailing optimism and energy wearied her almost as much as they cheered her. With a sigh of annoyance, she busied herself with tidying Rapskal's scattered gear from the bottom of the boat. She arranged her own pack so that her blanket and eating gear were on top and then followed him. A fire was being constructed in the lee of the big log. The log would provide fuel as well as trap and reflect the heat. Small flames were already starting to blossom. Rapskal excelled at setting fires and never seemed to tire of it. His fire-starting kit was always in a small pouch at his throat. The endless misting rain sizzled as it met the reaching flames.

"Tired?" Tats's voice came from the darkness to her left.

"Beyond tired," she replied. "Will this journey never be over? I've forgotten what it is like to be in one place for more than a night or two."

"It's worse than that. Once we get wherever we're going with the dragons, eventually we'll have to make the trip back downriver."

She was still for a moment. "You'd leave your dragon?" she asked him quietly. She had still not made amends with Sintara, still ached when she thought of the dragon. She cared for the dragon as she always had, grooming her and finding extra food for her, but they spoke little now. It made the contrast sharper when she saw the fondness that some of the other keepers shared with their dragons. Tats and Fente were close. Or she had thought they were.

He put his hands on her shoulders and squeezed gently. "I don't know. It depends, I suppose. Sometimes she seems to need me, to even be fond of me. Other times, well—"

Even as she shrugged away from his hands, her body registered how good it felt to have his warm touch on her sore muscles. He stepped back from her, acknowledging her rebuke. Like a rising flood of warm water, the image of Greft's and Jerd's tangled bodies washed through her. For a blink of time, she thought of turning to face him, dared to imagine running her hands down his warm, bare back. But the next image that jolted her was the thought of his hands sliding over her scaled skin.

Like petting a warm lizard, she mocked herself, and folded her lips tightly to keep from crying out at the unfairness of it. Greft and Jerd might be able to indulge in the forbidden, but perhaps it was only because each had found a fellow outcast as a partner. Neither would be repelled by how the Rain Wilds had touched the other. That would not be the case with someone like Tats. He came from the Tattooed folk; he had not been born here. His skin was as smooth as a Bingtown girl's, unmarked by wattles or scaling. Unlike her own.

"A long day," Tats said into her silence.

His tentative tone wondered if he had angered her by taking a liberty. She swallowed her fury at fate and evened her voice. "A long day, and I'm still sore from being 'rescued' by Mercor. I'll be glad of a warm fire and a bit of hot food tonight."

As if in answer, the fire suddenly climbed up the heaped driftwood. The glowing light outlined her friends gathering around the fire. Slight Sylve was there, standing next to narrow Harrikin. They were laughing, for long-limbed Warken was doing a frenzied dance to shake a shower of sparks from his wild hair and worn shirt.

Boxter and Kase were twin blocks of darkness, the cousins together as always. Lecter stalked past them, the spines on his neck and back clearly limned against the fire's light. He'd had to cut the neck of his shirt to allow for their growth. That sight somehow reassured her. *Those are my friends,* she thought and smiled. They were just as marked as she was. Then she caught a glimpse of Jerd's seated profile. She was perched on a piece of driftwood, and Greft stood behind her, powerful and protective. As Thymara watched, Jerd leaned back so that the top of her head touched his thigh as she spoke up to him. Greft bent to answer her and for an instant they formed a closed shape, the two of them becoming a single entity that shut out the rest of the world.

Jealousy cut her. It was not that she wanted Greft, merely that she wanted what they had simply taken for themselves. Jerd laughed aloud and Greft's shoulders moved in a way that echoed her amusement. The others either ignored or accepted their closeness. Was she the only one who still felt a twinge of outrage and unease at what they were proclaiming?

Without thinking about it, she was following Tats toward the fire. "What do you make of Jerd and Greft?" she asked him and then was shocked she had spoken the words aloud. She regretted the question instantly, for when Tats turned his head to glance back at her, he was plainly surprised by her query.

"Jerd and Greft?" he said.

"They're sleeping together. Mating." She heard the bluntness of her own words, the anger behind them. "She's with Greft every chance she gets."

"For now," Tats said as he dismissed her comment. And he seemed to be replying to something else as he went on, "Jerd will go with anyone. Greft will discover that soon enough. Or perhaps he knows and doesn't care. I could well imagine him taking what he could get, while he could get it, and planning to have something better later." The meaningful look he gave her as he added those last words confused her and made her uncomfortable. Her thoughts hopped like a flea through his words. What was he saying? She tried to lighten the tone of the conversation. "Jerd will go with anyone? Even you?" She started to laugh as she teased her old friend, but the smile froze on her lips as Tats hunched his shoulders and turned slightly away from her.

"Me? Perhaps," he said roughly. "Is that so unthinkable?"

She suddenly recalled the night that Greft's words had driven Tats from the fire, and how Jerd had risen and left shortly after that. And the next day, the two had shared a boat, and for several days after that . . . Understanding suddenly stilled her. Tats spreading his blankets near Jerd's, sitting by her during the evening meals. How could she not have seen what it meant? Jealousy flared in her, but before its heat could scorch her heart, ice chilled and broke it. What a fool she was! Of course that would be how it was, probably from the very first night they'd left Trehaug. Jerd, Greft, Tats, all of them had discarded the rules. Only stiff, stupid Thymara had assumed they still applied.

"Me, too!" Rapskal announced, materializing from the dark to make an unwelcome addition to their conversation.

"You too what?" Tats asked him unwillingly.

Rapskal looked at him as if he were stupid. "Me with Jerd. Before you, I was. Though she didn't like much how I did it. She said it wasn't funny and when I laughed at how messy it was, she said that only proved I was a boy and not a man. 'Never with you again!' she told me after that one time. 'I don't care,' I told her. And I don't. Why do that with someone who takes it so seriously? I think it would be more fun with someone like you, Thymara. You can take a joke. I mean, look at us. We get along. You never take offense just because a fellow has a sense of humor."

"Shut up, Rapskal!" she snarled at him, proving him very wrong. She stormed off into the darkness, leaving them both gawking after her. Behind her, she heard Tats berating Rapskal and his protests of innocence. Rapskal? Even Rapskal? Hot tears squeezed from her eyes and left salt tracks on her lightly scaled cheeks. Her face burned. Was she blushing? Could she still blush or was it the flush of anger?

She'd been blind to all of it. Blind and stupid and trusting, simple as a child. It was so mortifying. She'd had some doltish idea that because she secretly cared for Tats, he felt the same for her. She'd known she was condemned by what she was to leading a life bereft of human passion. Had she believed that he would deny himself simply because he knew he couldn't have her? Idiot.

And Rapskal? She was suddenly outraged in so many ways she almost choked. How could Jerd do that with simple, unassuming Rapskal? Somehow what she had led him to do spoiled him for Thymara. His sassy optimism and endless good nature seemed something else now. She thought suddenly of how he slept beside her each night, sometimes warm against her back. She had thought it a childish affection. Now a squeak of indignation escaped her. What had he been dreaming on those nights? What did the others think of their closeness? Did they imagine that she and Rapskal were tangling their bodies at night as Jerd and Greft did?

Did Tats think such a thing of her?

A fresh wave of outrage flooded her. She looked at the fire and knew, despite her wet clothes and empty belly, she would not join her fellows there tonight. Nor would she allow Rapskal to sleep anywhere near her. She whirled about suddenly and went back to her beached boat. She'd take her blanket and sleep near Sintara tonight. Not that she cared about the stupid dragon anymore, but even as uncaring as Sintara was, she was better than her so-called friends. At least she made her lack of feelings about Thymara obvious.

In her absence, Tarman had been driven up onto the shore beside the beached boats. The barge watched her with sympathetic eyes as she angrily pulled her blanket from her pack and took out her stored supply of dried meat. She didn't want to share a meal with anyone tonight. The temptation of hot food suddenly threatened her resolution. She glanced at Tarman and wondered if Leftrin would allow her aboard to warm herself at the galley stove and perhaps have a hot cup of tea? She ventured closer, looking up at the ship. The captain was strict in maintaining his authority on his deck. None of the keepers boarded without an express invitation. Perhaps she might obtain one from Alise? She hadn't had much chance for conversation with her since their mishap.

As the thought crossed her mind, she saw the silhouette of a man lower himself over the bow railing and climb awkwardly down the ship's ladder to the shore. He was thin and did not move like any of the crew members she knew. He stumbled as he stepped away from the ladder and swore softly. She knew him.

"Sedric!" she exclaimed in surprise. "I had heard you were very ill. I'm surprised to see you. Are you better now?" Privately she thought that a silly question. The man looked terrible, gaunt and ravaged. His lovely clothes hung on him, and she could smell that he had not washed himself.

The man turned toward her with a shuffling step very different from the grace she recalled. He looked irritated to see her, but replied anyway. "Better? No, Thymara, not better. But soon perhaps I shall be." His voice sounded thick as if his throat were very dry. She wondered if he were slightly drunk, then rebuked herself for thinking such a thing. He had been very ill; that was all.

As he turned away from her without any farewell, she saw that he carried a heavy wooden case. That burden was what had made him awkward on the ladder. He walked leaning to one side as if it were almost too heavy for him. She nearly ran after him to offer to help him with it, but she stopped herself. Surely a man would be humiliated for her to see how weakened he was. Best to leave him alone and let him manage.

She set off to find Sintara among the dragons. Her bedroll bounced on her back as she walked. After three steps, she un-slung it and carried it clutched to her chest. The rasp on her arm was scabbed over and healing fast, but the long scratch down the top half of her spine didn't seem to be healing at all. Elsewhere, her scales had mostly protected her from Mercor's teeth, but there they had given way. Sylve had first noticed it when she in-sisted that Thymara take off her shirt so that she could bandage her arm. "What is this?" the girl had asked her.

"What is what?" Thymara had asked her, shivering still.

"This," Sylve said and touched a spot between her shoulder blades. The touch hurt, as if she had prodded an abscess. "It's like you cut it and it closed. When did this happen?"

"I don't know."

"I'm going to let it drain," Sylve said, and before Thymara could forbid it, the girl had flicked away the edge of a scab. She'd felt warm liquid trickle down her back and turned to see Sylve's expression of distaste as she dabbed at it. But the scaled girl had spoken no word of disgust as she prodded it and then poured clean water over it and bandaged it. It should have begun to heal. But the cut festered and was swollen and sore and some-times oozing in the morning. She had nothing to treat it with, and no desire to expose her lizard body to anyone's scrutiny. It would heal, she told herself stubbornly. She always healed. It was just taking longer this time. And hurting more.

The hunters had not fared well today. She smelled no meat,

only river fish cooking on the fire. Once, she had enjoyed fish and regarded it as a rare treat. Now, even as hungry as she felt, she decided her dry meat would be enough.

The dragons were disappointed, too. Several of the big males were roaming the mud spit in a disgruntled way. Ranculos waded in the shallows, as if he might be able to discover more food there. On plentiful nights, the dragons often gathered around the fire with their keepers. They all enjoyed the warmth. But tonight the beasts were hungry and more scattered.

It would have been hard to find Sintara in the dark if Thymara had used only her eyes. But all she had to do was grope along the unwelcome connection she felt to the queen dragon. Sintara was at the downriver spike of the sandbar, staring back the way they had come.

And she wasn't alone. As Thymara approached, she could hear Alise's voice raised in gentle reproach. "You sent her right into that, deliberately, with no preparation. Of course it was upsetting to her. I wouldn't want to stumble onto such a scene without warning. She has a sensitive nature, Sintara. I think you should have more care for her feelings."

"She can ill afford to be 'sensitive,'" the dragon replied scathingly.

Thymara halted, straining to hear what else they might say about her. She was becoming quite an accomplished eavesdropper, she thought sourly.

"She is already tough and strong." Alise boldly contradicted the dragon. "Coarsening her spirit will not make her a better person. Only a harsher one. I think it would be a shame for that to happen to her."

"It would be more of a shame for her to continue as she is—meek, bound by rules that she did not make, always holding in her words. Among dragons and Elderlings, we knew that every female is a queen, free to make her own choices and follow her own wishes. This is something Thymara must learn if she is to go on serving me."

"Serving you!" Alise spluttered. "Is that how you see it? That she is your servant?"

She had come a long way, Thymara thought, from those days when her every word to Sintara was framed as a flowery compliment. Now it seemed to her that Alise spoke to the dragon almost woman to woman. She wondered if she had changed that much. Or perhaps it was Sintara, confident enough of them to no longer bother exerting her glamour. Thymara grinned to hear Alise defend her, but an instant later, the woman paid the price.

"Of course she serves me. Or at least she has the potential to do so, if she rises to have the spirit of a queen. Of what use to me is a servant who grovels to other humans? How can she demand the best for me if she is always deferring to them? At one time, Alise, I thought that you, too, might serve me in such a way. But of late, you disappoint me even more severely than Thymara. And I do not see you trying to change. Perhaps you are too old and incapable of it."

Hurt could be expressed as silence. Thymara suddenly knew that, for she heard Alise's pain and it drove her out of the darkness. Dropping all pretense that she had not overheard their conversation, she sprang to the older woman's defense. "I do not know why either one of us would wish to serve such an arrogant, ungrateful creature as you!" she exclaimed as she stepped between them.

"Ah. Good evening, little sneak. Did you enjoy your time lurking in darkness, listening to us?" Aggression puffed out the dragon's chest, and she seemed almost luminous in her anger. A silvery blue glow surrounded her, setting off the growing rows of fringe on her neck. The dragon's light struck coppery ripples from the gown Alise wore. It was a breathtakingly beautiful sight, the gleaming copper woman with shining red hair against the silver and blue of the dragon. They were like a scene out of an old tale or a tapestry, and if Thymara had not been so angry with the dragon, her beauty would have captured her. Sintara sensed her wonder and began to preen herself, lifting her wings and shaking them out so that their glow was unmistakable. They were opalescent and larger than Thymara recalled them.

"I grow stronger and more beautiful each day," the dragon

echoed her thought effortlessly. "Those who have said I will never fly will one day eat their words. Only Tintaglia can rival me for beauty and power, and a day will come when that will not be so. I am not ashamed to say so of myself. I know what I am. So why should I tolerate the company of a timid little prey-beast, who bleats and squeaks her pity for herself, who will not even challenge the male who presents himself."

"Challenge the male . . ." Alise's icy voice melted and dribbled away in confusion.

"Of course." The dragon derided her lack of comprehension. "He has presented himself. He is strong enough and in good health. He follows you, sniffing after your scent. He flatters you and acknowledges your cleverness. You cannot hide from me that you are aware of his desire for you and that you find him attractive. But before you can take him, you should present to him a challenge. For you, there can be no mating flight, no battle in the air as he struggles to mount you and you evade him and test his skills in flight. But there are other ways of old that Elderling males once proved themselves. Set him a challenge."

"I am not an Elderling," Alise declared. Silently Thymara remarked that she did not challenge any of Sintara's other comments. So who was the suitor that Sintara deemed worthy of Alise? Sedric, she knew abruptly. The beautiful Bingtown man who had seemed to be at Alise's beck and call. Was Alise the reason he had come ashore tonight? Did he hope for a tryst with her? A voyeuristic thrill coursed through Thymara at that thought, shocking her. What was the matter with her? Sternly she refused to imagine them locked and rocking belly to belly as Jerd and Greft had been.

"And I am a married woman." Alise's second assertion seemed, not a statement of fact, but an admission of doom.

"Why do you bind yourself to a mate you do not desire?" the dragon asked. Her confusion seemed genuine. "Why do you obey a rule that only frustrates you? What do you gain from it?"

"I keep my word," Alise replied heavily. "And my honor. We entered into a bargain, Hest and I. In good faith we spoke promises to keep to each other and have no other. I wish I had not. Truly, I had no idea what I was giving up. For scrolls and a comfortable home and good food on the table, I bargained away myself. It was a stupid bargain, but one we have both kept in good faith. So, when all this is done, I will leave Leftrin and my dragons and my days of being alive. I will go home and do my best to conceive an heir for my husband. It is what I promised to do. And if you think me a squeaking and bleating prey-beast in the clutches of a predator, well, perhaps I am. But perhaps it takes a different kind of strength to keep my word when every bone in my body cries out for me to break it."

Sintara snorted disdainfully. "You do not believe he has kept his promises."

"I have no proof that he has broken them."

"No. You are the only proof that he has broken something. You are broken." The dragon's pronouncement was delivered heartlessly.

"Perhaps. But I have kept my word and my honor intact." Alise's voice had grown more and more ragged as she spoke. As she affirmed her honor, that she would keep her word, she bowed her face into her hands. For a time, she choked in silence. Then thick, painful gasps of mourning escaped her. Thymara stepped forward and hesitantly patted Alise's shoulder. She had never attempted to console anyone before. "I understand," she said in a quiet voice. "You are choosing the only honorable path. But it is hard for you. And even harder when people think you are a fool for keeping your word."

Alise lifted a tearstained face. Impulsively, Thymara put her arms around her. "Thank you," the older woman said brokenly. "For not thinking me stupid."

THE RAIN WAS coming down again, harder this time. Leftrin pulled his knitted cap down over his ears and squinted through the darkness and the downpour. He'd had a long day, and all he really wanted to do was settle down at his galley table with some hot tea, a bowl of chowder, and a redheaded woman who smiled at his jokes, and said "please" and "thank you" to his crew's efforts at courtesy. *Little enough,* he thought, *for a man to ask out of life.* As he'd clambered down to the shore and stalked off across the muddy flat, Tarman's painted gaze had followed him sympathetically. The ship knew his errand, and knew how much he disliked it.

It was just like that bastard Jess to demand he meet him out here in the rain and dark. They'd been exchanging silence and glares for several days now. Leftrin had been successfully avoiding conversation with the man by refusing to be alone with him. But tonight, just as he'd been getting ready to settle in by the warm galley stove, he'd found a note in the bottom of his coffee mug.

He'd done his best to slip away unobtrusively from his gathered crew. No one seemed to mark his departure. He moved quietly through the dark, veering away from the keepers and their bonfire. A burst of wind carried their laughter and the smell of cooking fish toward him as it whipped the flames higher. He'd no wish for anyone to see him ashore tonight.

Wind and the spattering rain and the dark all cloaked him as he approached the silver dragon. That, he took it, was the cryptic location for his meeting with Jess. "Meet me by silver or the secret is out." That was all the note had said, but it was a threat he could not ignore. The dragon had his front feet braced on something and was tearing chunks of meat loose from it. He knew a wild moment of hope that it was eating Jess. Another two steps and he could see that it had been something with four legs. The hunter had brought the dragon a bribe to keep him occupied while they talked. And it had worked. He watched the silver tear a leg loose from the carcass. The silver's condition had improved since he had first seen the creature, but he was still smaller and less healthy than the other dragons. His tail had healed, but he seemed to acquire parasites much more often than the other dragons. The dragon became aware of Leftrin and shifted to watch him as he chewed on the hoofed leg.

"Evening, Captain," Jess greeted him as he walked around the dragon's shoulder. "Fine night for a stroll."

"I'm here. What do you want?"

"Not so much. Just a little cooperation, that's all. I saw an opportunity this afternoon and thought we should take it."

"An opportunity?"

"That's right." Jess patted the dragon on its shoulder. The silver rumbled a growl at the hunter, but his focus was still on the meat. "He growls, but he's used to me. I've been slipping him an extra ration of meat every chance I got. He doesn't mind me at all now." As he spoke, he opened his coat, displaying a hatchet, two long knives, and one short-bladed one, all neatly sheathed in pockets concealed inside his vest. He tipped his head slightly toward the silver. "Shall we begin?"

"You're insane," Leftrin said quietly.

"Not at all." The man smiled. "Once he finishes eating that deer, he's going to want a very long nap. From the start, I planned for this possibility and came prepared. I cut that deer's belly open and put a large quantity of valerian and poppy in before I offered it to the silver. Enough to drop a dragon, I think. We'll find out soon enough." He pulled his coat closed against the wind and rain and stood grinning at Leftrin.

"I'm not doing this. We won't get away with it, and I'm just not doing it."

"Of course we'll get away with it. I've thought it all through. Dragon falls asleep, and we make sure it's forever. We spend a quiet hour or two claiming the most marketable parts. We take them back on board the *Tarman* and head downriver. Tonight."

"And the keepers and the other dragons?"

"In this wind and rain? They'll notice nothing until we're gone, and then they'll discover that we've disabled their boats. I doubt that anyone will ever hear of them again."

"And what do we tell the folks in Trehaug?"

"We don't even stop there. Downriver, fleet as an arrow, and then up the coast to Chalced. You'll live like a king there, with your lady. I've seen how you look at her. This way, at least, you end up with her."

"What do you mean?"

"I mean that the other way, the path I take if you refuse, you lose everything. I tell the dragons and the keepers that you used a dragon cocoon to give your precious Tarman a bigger supply of wizardwood. Your crew is in on it, obviously. They know how little they actually work to push that barge along. I don't think the dragons will think well of you, knowing that you've already butchered one of their kind for your own ends. I believe they're annoyed by such things. And your pretty red-haired lady may see you as not quite so honorable as she thought. False, even. Treacherous, if I do my work well.

"So, you see, you can help me harvest one mindless, unclaimed, stunted dragon and take your lady, crew, and yourself off to an indolent and indulgent life in Chalced. Or you can be stubborn and I'll unravel you and destroy everything you have or ever hope to have." He smiled, squinting into the rain as he added, "After they turn on you, I wouldn't be surprised if I ended up with both your ship and your lady. I've put in quite a few evenings cultivating trust and friendship among the keepers, while you wasted time courting your giddy little woman. And I suspect I'll have an ally in that Bingtown dandy. Or are you going to continue to pretend that all of you are innocent of any schemes?"

The dragon bent his head and picked up the animal's rib cage in his mouth. His jaws closed on it, crushing it. He began a slow mastication, crushing and folding the rest of the animal in on itself. Leftrin stepped toward the silver, intending to intervene. The dragon blasted a snarl at him past the meat in his mouth. The stench of his breath made Leftrin blanch and step back as much as the threat.

"Oh, he doesn't trust you," Jess snidely commiserated. "I don't think he'll let you rescue him. Stupid damn lizard. Looks like we're committed, Cap. Once he goes down, it's time to butcher. I'll just go take care of those boats right now."

The man's cockiness would have been enough to provoke Leftrin at any time without the threat to his dreams. As he passed Leftrin in the driving rain, Leftrin turned and launched himself at him. He'd beat him senseless and feed him to the dragon. *Poor Jess. Must have somehow provoked the dumb beast. Can scarcely blame a dragon for being a dragon, Alise.*

But Jess spun to meet him, teeth white in a merry snarl and a shining blade in his hand.

SINTARA WATCHED THE two human females in consternation. Now, what did this mean, this clutching and sharing of tears? It wasn't hunting, nor fighting, nor mating, nor any sensible activity that she could name. She wanted them to stop. "Did either of you bring me food?" she demanded.

Thymara stepped away from Alise and wiped her sleeve across her wet face. "I didn't have a chance to hunt today. I think the hunters got some fish."

"I already ate what Carson said was 'my share.' It was pitiful."

"I suppose I could go and—"

"Quiet!" Sintara barked at her. There was something, a distant noise like the roaring of a huge wind. She sensed distress and anger from the silver dragon. As always, his thoughts were poorly formed, but something was alarming him.

"What is it?" she roared at him and to the other dragons in general. The sound was growing louder now; even the humans could hear it. She saw Thymara turn her head and shout. Alise clutched at her and her head swiveled back and forth, seeking the source of the noise. The roar was coming closer, but she felt no increase in the wind or driving rain. The sound grew louder, with a grinding base to it mixed with sudden cracks and snaps.

"It's the river! It's a flood!" Mercor's bellow slammed into her mind, and with his warning, ancient memories leaped into Sintara's awareness.

"Fly! Get above the water!" she trumpeted, for in that moment she forgot what she was, half a dragon, bound to the earth. The darkness could not completely mask the danger. She stared upriver and saw white lace on a gray cliff face and tumbling tree trunks in the cliff's liquid face.

"Run for the trees!" Thymara shouted, but by then only the dragon could hear her small voice through the thundering water. She saw the two women, hands clutched together, turn and begin to run.

"Too late!" she bellowed at them. She stretched out her head, seized Alise by the shoulder and snatched her off her feet. The woman screamed. The dragon paid no attention as she craned her neck and set her down between her wings. "Hold tight!" she warned her.

Thymara was fleeing. Sintara thundered after her.

Then the wave hit them.

It was not just water. The force of it rolled boulders and carried sand. Old driftwood was tangled with trees newly torn from the earth. Sintara was bowled off her feet and pushed along. A log thudded against her ribs, knocking her sideways. The churning mass of water carried her inexorably downriver. For a moment, she was plunged completely underwater. She struck out, swimming vigorously for what she hoped was the surface and the bank. All was chaos, water, and darkness. Dragons, humans, boats, logs, and boulders mixed and mingled in the floodwater. Her head broke free of the water, but the world no longer made sense. Sintara spun in the current, paddling desperately. She could not find the shore. All around her, the water streamed white under the night sky. She caught a glimpse of Tarman's lights and saw an empty boat seized by the leafy branches of a floating tree. The immense driftwood log that had been the heart of the keeper's bonfire floated past her, streaming smoke and crowned still with a branch of glowing embers.

"Thymara!" she heard Alise shout, and only then became aware that the woman still clung to her wings. "Save her! Look, Sintara, see her! There! There!"

She didn't see the keeper girl, and then she did. The girl was trying to struggle free of a mass of floating brush. It had entangled her clothing. Soon it would engulf her and she would be pulled under as it sank. "Stupid humans!" Sintara bellowed. She struck out for her, only to be hit broadside by Ranculos as the water shoved him past her. When she recovered and looked at the floating mass of brush, the girl was gone. Too late.

"Thymara! Thymara!" Alise was shrieking, but her voice was full of hopelessness.

"Which way is the shore?" the dragon bellowed at her.

"I don't know!" the woman shrieked back. Then, "Over there! That way. Swim that way." Alise's shaking hand pointed in the direction they were already going. Encouraged, the dragon struck out more strongly. She could not climb the trees for safety, but she could wedge herself between them and wait out the worst of this flooding.

"There! Right there!" Alise shrieked again. But she was not pointing to the shore, but to a small, white, upturned face in the water. Thymara's hands reached out and up to her.

"Please!" she screamed.

Sintara bent her head and dragged her keeper from the river's grasp. "Mine!" she trumpeted defiantly around Thymara's dangling body. "Mine!"

Day the 17th of the Prayer Moon

Year the 6th of the Independent Alliance of Traders

From Erek, Keeper of the Birds, Bingtown

To Detozi, Keeper of the Birds, Trehaug

A message from Trader Korum Finbok of the Bingtown Traders, sent at the behest of and in support of a query by Traders Meldar and Kincarron, seeking more information about the departure of Alise Kincarron Finbok and Sedric Meldar on the liveship *Tarman*.

Detozi,

A small note. The families of Sedric Meldar and Alise Finbok are absolutely frantic, with both declaring that neither of them would voluntarily depart on an expedition that might take months before they return. Alise Finbok's husband is on an extended trading voyage, but her father-in-law has been persuaded to put his considerable fortune to work in an effort to gain more information. If you know of anyone capable of traveling swiftly up the river and taking a message bird or two with them, they might earn a substantial reward from this.

Erek

CHAPTER FIVE

WHITE FLOOD

Leftrin's hands locked around Jess's throat. The hunter was raining body blows on the captain's midsection. Leftrin thought he had cracked ribs from the beating and he tasted blood from his smashed lips, but he kept his grip. It was a matter of time. If he could throttle him long enough, the punishing punches would stop. Already they were losing strength and when both Jess's hands rose to clutch at Leftrin's wrist, he knew it was over except for that final stretch of endurance. The hunter clawed at his wrists, but Leftrin's hands were toughened, not just by scales but by too-frequent immersions in river water. His scar tissue resisted Jess's nails. He could not see Jess's face, but he knew his eyes would be bulging by now. He squeezed harder, imagining the man's tongue starting to protrude from his mouth.

Around the combatants, the wind swirled and the black rain battered down. The silver dragon had either abandoned the carcass or been unaffected by the drugs. He galloped in a clumsy circle around them, trumpeting in distress. Leftrin could not worry that the dragon's noise might bring the keepers down on them. If they came, he could show them Jess's knives, say he'd only been protecting the dragon. *Grip,* he told his weary hands and shaking arms. *Grip!* The pain was sickening. There was a roaring in his ears, and he feared he would pass out before he could finish the job. He squeezed, and still the hunter struggled, flinging his head forward in a futile effort to butt Leftrin in the face.

A wall of water, stone, and timber suddenly appeared behind Jess. Leftrin's mind froze that agonizing moment into a decade. He saw, clearly, the debris that showed in the white water. He knew that the wave would be acid and heavy with silt. This was a flood that had come a long, long way, collecting driftwood and tearing trees free from the banks as it came. He caught one glimpse of a huge elk carcass coming toward them, tumbling like a toy tossed in the air.

"Tarman!" he shouted, and let Jess's throat go. He spun to run for his ship, to save his beloved boat if he could.

But in that instant, time resumed. The water smashed him down as it devoured the sandbar. He saw nothing, knew nothing except the struggle of an animal that is suddenly thrust into a foreign element. There was no air, no light, no up, no down. Cold and force drove his breath from his body. *Good-bye,* he thought stupidly. *Good-bye, Alise. At least I didn't have to see you go back to another man.* A drowning death might be better than that other, slower torment.

Something bumped him. His hands and arms locked on to it and he rose with it, bursting into blackness. He gasped in both air and the water that streamed from his hair and skin, choked, went under again with the tumbling log, and then popped up again. The crest of the wave had passed them, but the river still flowed strong and possibly twice as deep as it had been. The speed of the current swept him down the river in a dangerous stew of trees, struggling animals and carcasses, and driftwood. He did not try to get on top of the log he clutched. Instead he resigned himself to regular duckings and held tight to it, hoping the current would hold him near the center of the river. He could hear the crashes and snapping as debris struck trees on the river's banks and tore them loose or smashed them down. He had one glimpse of a dragon, swimming frantically. Then his log turned, ducking him again, and when he came up, the dragon was gone.

As the river settled, he moved down the trunk toward the root end. There the wood was thicker, and the roots offered him more grips. He ventured to climb a bit higher out of the water and scanned the surface of the water. As the water calmed, the debris was spreading out, borne along on the still swollen river. The starlight and moonlight shone on the white water. He saw floating carcasses as black shapes. In the distance, he saw a large silhouette of a paddling dragon. He shouted, but he doubted that his voice reached it. The sounds of the rushing water, of trees groaning and giving way, of flotsam crashing together drowned his human voice.

Then he saw something that lifted his heart. Light sparkled, dimmed, and then grew steady to become a perfect circle of yellow lamplight. It could only be Tarman; someone had just rekindled a lamp on board him. The light gave sudden shape and meaning to what had been blackness against blackness. Tarman was distant, down current of Leftrin, but he knew his ship's low black profile. He drew his breath deep into his abused lungs, wincing at his aching ribs. He didn't waste his breath cursing Jess; with any sort of luck, the man was a corpse by now. Instead, he pursed his lips and pushed out a long, steady whistle. Another breath. Again, he whistled, the pitch a notch higher than before. Another breath.

Even before he pushed the sound out, he knew Tarman had heard him. The circle of light shifted as the ship wheeled toward him. The light vanished. For a time, he just clung to his log, breathing steadily and waiting. Then the lantern on Tarman's bow was kindled. He drew breath, whistled again, and watched the light almost immediately grow larger. Paddling with all his might, Tarman was coming for him. The barge's

thick sturdy legs and webbed feet would propel him against the
current. Swarge would man the tiller and the crew would break
out the sweeps, but Tarman would not wait for that pantomime
of help. The liveship was coming for his captain. He whistled
again, and low to the water, he saw the pale blue gleam of two
large eyes. Rescue was coming. All he had to do now was wait
for his ship to save him.

PERHAPS SINTARA ATTEMPTED to set her down beside Alise.
But the effort failed, and Thymara fell on top of the Bingtown
woman. Alise's arms closed around her in an engulfing embrace
that both kept her from sliding back into the water and sent a
spike of agony down her back as her clutching hands pressed
against Thymara's injury.

Thymara tried not to struggle against the grip that was saving her. An instant later, they were both starting to slide down
the dragon's sleekly scaled front shoulder. "Hold on!" Alise
screamed by her ear, and Thymara reached out for anything that
might offer purchase. Her scrabbling claws caught at the edges
of Sintara's scales; she was sure the dragon would have protested
angrily if she hadn't been struggling for her own life.

Alise's grip on Thymara had gone from saving the girl from
falling to clutching at her to stay on the dragon. Thymara risked
letting go with one hand and lunged for a better grip. She hooked
her hand over the joint where Sintara's wings were anchored to
her back. "Hold on to me!" she gasped to Alise, and used all her
strength to drag them back on top of the dragon.

Once they were on top, she managed to loosen Alise's grip on
her enough that she could slide forward. She seated herself just
in front of Sintara's wings, pushing her heels back and gripping
the dragon with her knees. It was not at all a secure perch, but
it was better than where she had been. Behind her, she felt Alise
settling into place. The Bingtown woman took a tight grip on
Thymara's belt, and suddenly there was a moment in which to
take stock of their situation.

"What happened?" she shouted back to Alise.

"I don't know!" Seated as close as she was, her words still barely reached Thymara's ear. The river roared around them. "A huge wave came down the river. Captain Leftrin told me that sometimes, after a quake, the river ran white for a time. But he never mentioned anything like this."

Wind snapped Thymara's wet black braids. All around them was a fury of sound. Her eyes could make no sense of what the faint moonlight showed her. The river was white as milk. As she clung to the struggling dragon, she shared the creature's panic and fury. And felt, too, her growing weariness. The water was filled with floating wreckage. Tree limbs and trunks, mats of uprooted bushes, and carcasses of drowned creatures bobbed and swirled in the river. When she stared toward the bank, it looked as if the flow of water now extended far under the forest eaves. As she watched, an immense tree swayed and began an impossibly slow fall. She cried out in terror, but there was nothing Sintara could do to avoid it. The tree was coming down, like a tower falling. It leaned, groaned, leaned again, and suddenly the river swept them past it and away from that danger.

"Dragon!" Alise shouted suddenly, and she stupidly let go of Thymara's belt with one hand to point downriver of them. "Another dragon. I think it is Veras!"

It was. Thymara recognized her by the crest that the dark green female had recently begun to grow. She was still swimming, but it seemed to Thymara that she was lower in the water, as if her weariness was pulling her under. Veras was Jerd's dragon. Thymara wondered where her keeper was, and then, like a second wave breaking over her, she realized she was not the only keeper swept away by the flood. The others had been gathered around the bonfire. All of them would have been inundated. And what had become of their boats and gear, of the *Tarman,* of all the other dragons? How could she have been thinking only of herself? Everyone, everything that made up her current life had been inundated and swept away. Her eyes swept the river in desperate search, but the light was too dim and there were too many objects floating and bobbing in the roiling water.

Beneath her, she felt Sintara's ribs swell as the dragon took a breath. Then a trumpeting cry burst from her. In the distance, Veras turned her head. A tiny sound like a bird's squawk reached her straining ears. Then another came, a deeper longer note, drawing her eyes to a massive swimming shape that had to be Ranculos. He bellowed again, and the sense of the sound reached her mind as well. "Mercor says swim for the bank. The trees will give us something to brace against. Hold in place until the water goes down. Swim for the bank!"

Sintara's ribs swelled with air again. With greater energy she trumpeted out the message, passing it on to any who might hear her. "Swim for the bank! Swim for the trees!"

Thymara heard it echoed by another dragon in the distance. And perhaps a second time. After that, at irregular intervals, she heard a dragon trumpet. It seemed to come from the direction of the shore. "Go toward the sound," she urged Sintara.

Following that advice was not an easy task. The current gripped them firmly, and the floating debris created obstacle after obstacle as Sintara battled toward the shore. Once they were caught in an eddy and spun around and around, until Thymara had no sense of direction left.

ALISE HELD TIGHT to Thymara's belt and gritted her teeth against the pain of her fresh scalds. Where her copper gown touched her, her skin was protected, but her cheeks and forehead and eyelids burned from the acid water. She turned her face up to the rain and felt its coolness as a blessing. She gritted her teeth, her lips pulling back in a sardonic smile. She could die here and she was worrying about a little pain. Ridiculous. She laughed aloud.

Thymara turned to stare at her. "Are you all right?"

For a moment, the sight of her eyes glowing pale blue in the night unsettled Alise. But then she nodded grimly. "I'm as all right as I can be. I've counted eight dragons so far; or at least I think I have. I may have counted some twice."

"I haven't seen any of the other keepers. Or the *Tarman*. Have you?"

"No." Alise bit the word off short. She wouldn't, couldn't worry now. The *Tarman* was a big boat; it had to be all right. Leftrin would come to find her and save her. He had to. He was her only hope now. For a moment she marveled that she could put so much faith in a mere man. Then she shook the thought from her mind. He was all she had that she could count on. She would not doubt him now.

All around them, the water seethed and roared. The sound pressed on her ears. The fury of the first wave had passed, but the water that followed it swelled the river and powered the current. Alise gripped with her knees as if she were riding a horse and held tight to Thymara's belt and prayed. All her muscles ached from being clenched so long. Sweet Sa, how long could sheer terror last? Beneath her, the dragon struggled, and seemed to swim less powerfully than she had. She wondered how much time had passed. The dragon must be getting exhausted. If Sintara gave up, then all of them would die. She knew she could not survive in the deluge without her. She leaned closer to the dragon's head.

"It's not far now, my beauty, my queen. See, there is the line of trees. You can make it. Don't try to swim straight to it. Let the current carry you but ease toward the shore, my gem, my priceless beauty."

She felt something from the dragon, some warming of strength, as if her mere human words encouraged her in a way that defied the physical challenges.

Thymara sensed it, too. "Great queen, you have to survive. The memories of all your ancestors depend on you to carry them forward through time. Swim! Or all they have been will be forever lost, and all the world will be less for that. You must survive. You must!"

The shore came closer so slowly. Despite their encouragement, Sintara's strength was flagging. Then the sound of trumpeting reached them. Along the shore, wedged against the trees, were dragons. They called to her, and Alise felt a thrill shoot through her when she heard thin human voices raised as well.

"It's Sintara! It's Thymara's blue queen! Swim, queen, swim! Don't give up!"

"Sweet Sa, there is someone on her back! Who is it? Who did she save?"

"Swim, dragon! Swim! You'll make it!"

Thymara suddenly lifted her voice. "Sylve? Is that you? Alise and I are here, Sintara saved us!"

Sylve's high voice reached them. "Don't try to climb up on the mat. You'll get tangled up. Push through it until you get to the trees at the edge. Then we'll get some big logs under you so you can rest, Sintara. Don't get tangled up! It's like a net; it will trap you and drag you down."

IN A MATTER of minutes, they were grateful for that advice. All manner of debris had fetched up against the shore. At the river's side, it was loose and floating, but the closer Sintara got to the trees, the more packed and tangled it became. Thymara clung to her dragon and felt that this final part of her struggle lasted at least a day. The safety of the trees loomed overhead, and never had she longed more to feel bark under her claws and hold fast to one of the immense giants and know she was safe. A dimness that was not quite light but indicated that morning was beginning somewhere had begun to permeate the sky and reach down toward the chaos on the water. Had they battled the water all night? Thymara could see the hulking shapes of dragons under the trees now. They were braced against the flow of the water, front paws wrapped around trees as they floated exhaustedly. At intervals, the dragons trumpeted; she wondered who they were calling. There were keepers there, too, perched in the lower branches of the trees. She could not tell how many or who, but her heart lifted with hope that all would be well. Only a few hours ago, she thought that she and Alise and Sintara might be the only survivors. Now she wondered if perhaps they had all escaped unscathed.

Sintara chested her way through the floating mat of debris.
It was hard for the dragon to accept the advice not to try and
clamber on top of it. Thymara could feel her weariness, her
need just to stop struggling and rest. Her heart leaped with joy
when she saw first Sylve and then Tats venturing out across
the packed branches and logs toward them. "Be careful!" she
shouted at them. "If you fall and go under, we'll never find you
under this mat."

"I know!" Tats was the one to reply. "But we have to pull
some of it out of the way so Sintara can reach the trees. We've
been able to help some of the dragons get at least a floating log
under their chests to help hold them up.

"That would be welcome," Sintara immediately replied, and
by that admission, Thymara knew she was far more tired than
she had thought.

"We have to get off her," she told Alise in a low voice. "The
mat looks thick enough to support us, if we go carefully."

Alise was already moving the sash from her gown. It was
longer than Thymara had expected, for the Bingtown woman
had looped it twice around her waist. "Tie this to your wrist,"
she suggested. "And I'll do the same. If one of us slips, the other
can save her."

Thymara clambered down first, half sliding down the dragon's slick shoulder. She was grateful for the sash on her wrist as
Alise pulled her up short of the mat and let her select her landing
spot. There was a nearby log with a branch sticking out. Thymara made the successful hop to it, and though it dipped and
rocked under her weight, it did not roll and dump her in. She
suspected that it had many submerged branches that were now
so tangled with other debris that it could not easily shift.

"It's good! Come down," she called back to Alise. She glanced
over to see that Tats had nearly reached the log and stepped onto
it. "Stay back!" she warned him. "Let me get Alise down and
onto this before you add any more weight to it." He halted
where he was, clearly displeased and anxious, but listening to
her. As Alise ventured down, clinging to Sintara's wing as she
came, she heard Sylve's voice on the other side of Sintara.

"We have to go slowly, or you'll dump me in the river. I'll come toward you on this log. As my weight pushes it down, you'll try to put a front leg over it. Then, as I back up, you'll try to edge sideways along it. So far, we've been able to help three dragons get some flotation this way. Are you ready to try?"

"Very ready," the dragon replied. She sounded almost grateful and very unlike her usual self. Thymara almost smiled. Perhaps after this, she might see her keepers in a different light.

She gasped aloud as Tats caught her by the arm. "I've got you," he said comfortingly. "Come this way."

"Let go! You're throwing me off balance." At the hurt look that crossed his face, she added more placatingly, "We have to make room for Alise on the log. Move back, Tats." As he obeyed her, she said in a quieter voice, "I'm so glad to see you alive that I don't know what to say to you."

"Besides 'let go!'?" he asked with bitter humor.

"I'm not angry with you anymore," she told him, a bit surprised to find it was true. "To your left, Alise!" she called as the woman, still clinging to Sintara's wing, groped for a place to set her foot. "A little more, a little more . . . there. You're right over it. Ease your weight down."

The Bingtown woman obeyed her, letting out a small squeak as the log initially sank under her weight. She lowered her other foot and stood, arms outstretched like a bird trying to dry its wings after a storm. No sooner was her weight off the dragon than Sintara made a lunge to try to get her front leg over the log that Sylve was weighing down. The dragon's abrupt movement sent the whole debris pack to rocking. Alise cried out but swayed with the motion, keeping her balance. Thymara, bereft of pride, crouched and then sat on the log. "Lower your weight!" she suggested to Alise. "We can crawl along the logs until we reach a place where things are a bit more stable."

"I can balance," the Bingtown woman replied, and although her voice shook a bit, she kept her upright stance.

"As you wish," Thymara replied. "I'm crawling." She suspected that her many years' experience in the treetops had taught her not to take risks unless she had to. She scuttled along the log to its widest end, where its snaggled roots reared up out of the river. There she stood, catching hold of the roots. Tats had preceded her. He now gave her a sideways glance and offered, "I'll show you the way I came out here. Parts of this mat are thicker than others."

"Thank you," she replied and waited for Alise to catch up with her, gathering up the slackened sash as she came. She glanced back at Sintara, feeling a bit guilty that she was letting Sylve do the work of caring for her dragon. The small girl moved confidently, instructing the dragon in what she wished her to do. Thymara sighed with relief. She could handle it.

"Sylve managed to recapture one of the boats," Tats said over his shoulder. "She's the one who pulled me out of the water."

"I remember when I thought she was too young and childish for an expedition like this," Thymara observed, and she was surprised when Tats laughed aloud.

"Adversity brings out the best in us, I suppose." They'd reached the first of the large trees. Thymara paused by it, resting her hand on it. It felt so good. It shivered in the passing current, but even so, it felt more solid than anything she had touched in hours. She longed to sink her claws in the bark and climb, but she was still tethered to Alise.

"There's one with some lower branches just over there," Tats told her.

"A good choice," she agreed. Under the trees, the debris was packed more tightly. It still bobbed under her feet with every step she took, but it was easy to dance across it to the tree that Tats had indicated. As she became more confident of simple survival, a hundred other concerns tried to crowd to the forefront of her mind. She held her questions until they reached the tree Tats had indicated. Thymara climbed a short way up it, sank in claws, and then assisted Alise as Tats gave her a boost to start her up the trunk. The Bingtown woman did not climb well, but between the two of them, they managed to get her up the trunk and onto a stout, almost horizontal branch. It was wide enough for her to lie down on, but she sat cross-legged in the exact middle and crossed her arms.

"Are you cold?" Thymara asked her.

"No. This robe keeps me surprisingly warm. But my face and hands hurt from the river water."

"I think my scales kept me from the worst of it," Thymara said and then wondered that she had said it aloud.

The Bingtown woman nodded. "Then I envy you that. This Elderling robe seemed to protect me from the water. I don't understand how. I got wet, but I dried very quickly. And where the gown touches me, I don't feel any irritation from the water."

Tats was the one to shrug. "Lots of Elderling stuff does things you wouldn't think it could. Wind chimes that play tunes when the wind blows. Metal that lights up when you touch it. Jewels that smell like perfume and never lose their scent. It's magical, that's all."

Thymara nodded and then asked, "How many of us are here?"

"Most of us," he said. "Everyone has scratches or bruises. Kase got a nasty gash on his leg, but the water seemed to burn it closed. So I suppose there's a mercy to that as we don't have anything to use for bandaging. Ranculos got hit in the ribs with something. When he snorts, blood comes out of his nose, but he insists he'll be fine if we leave him alone. Harrikin has asked that we do that. He says Ranculos doesn't want any of us fussing over him. Boxter got hit in the face with something; his eyes are blackened, and he can barely see out of them. Tinder hurt his wing, and at first Nortel thought it was broken. But the swelling went down and now he can move it, so we're thinking it's just a bad sprain. Lots of injuries for everyone. But at least they're here."

Thymara just looked at him. "What else?" Alise demanded

He took a breath. "Alum's missing. And Warken. Alum's dragon keeps trumpeting for him, so we wonder if he is still alive somewhere. We've tried talking to Arbuc, but no one can make sense of him. It's like trying to talk to a scared little child. He just keeps trumpeting and repeating that he wants Alum to come and take him out of the water. Warken's red is silent; Baliper won't speak to any of us. Veras, Jerd's dragon, is also missing. Jerd hasn't stopped weeping since she got here. She says she can't 'feel' her dragon, so she thinks she drowned."

"We saw Veras! She was alive and swimming strongly, but the current was carrying her downriver."

"Well, I still think that's good news. You should tell her."

Something in his voice alerted Thymara that worse news was to come. She held her breath, waiting for it, but Alise asked immediately, "What about Tarman and Captain Leftrin?"

"Some of us saw the ship, right after the wave first hit. The water went over the top of him, but we saw him bob up again, with white water streaming out of his scuppers. So he was upright and afloat the last time we saw him, but that's all we know. We haven't seen anyone from the boat's crews or any of the hunters, so we hope they were aboard and rode it out on Tarman."

"If they did, they'll come to find us. Captain Leftrin will come for us." She spoke with such heartfelt confidence that Thymara almost felt sorry for her. If he didn't come, she thought, Alise would be hard put to accept that she must rescue herself.

She looked flatly at Tats. "And what else?" she demanded.

"The silver dragon isn't here. And neither is Relpda, the little copper queen."

Thymara sighed. "I wondered if they would survive. Neither was very smart, and the copper was always sickly. Perhaps it was a mercy that they went so quickly." She looked at Tats, wondering if he would agree with her. But he didn't seem to hear her words. "Who else?" she asked flatly.

A small stillness followed her question, as if the world paused to prepare itself to grieve. "Heeby. And Rapskal. They aren't here, and no one saw anything of either of them after the wave hit."

"But I left him with you!" she protested, as if somehow that meant it were Tats's fault. She saw him wince and knew he felt the same.

"I know. One moment we were standing there arguing. The next, the water slapped us down. I never saw him again."

Thymara crouched down on the tree branch and waited for pain and tears to come. They didn't. Instead a strange numbness flowed up from her belly. She had killed him. She had killed him by getting so angry at him that she'd stopped caring about him. "I was so angry at him," she confessed to Tats. "What he told me ruined my idea of him, and I thought I'd just have to stop knowing him, stop letting him be near me. And now he's gone."

"Ruined your idea of him?" Tats asked cautiously.

"I just never thought he'd do a thing like that. I'd thought he was better than that," she said awkwardly.

Too late she saw that Tats accepted that judgment upon himself as well. "Maybe none of us are quite what the others think we are," he observed shortly and stood. He walked back toward the trunk, and she could not think of any words to call him back.

Alise called after him, "No one can know that he and Heeby are dead. He might have made it to the *Tarman*. Maybe Captain Leftrin will bring him back to us."

Tats glanced back at them. His voice was flat as he said, "I'm going to tell Jerd that you saw Veras. It might give her a little comfort. Greft has been trying to encourage her, but she hasn't been listening to him."

"That's a good idea," Alise agreed. "Tell her that when we saw her dragon, she was afloat and swimming strongly."

Thymara let him go. Let him go to comfort Jerd. It didn't matter to her. She had let go of him when she had let go of Rapskal. She hadn't really known either of them. It was much better to keep her heart to herself. She wondered if she were being stupid. Did she have to hold on to her hurt and anger? Could she just let it go and forgive him and have him back as her friend? For a moment, it seemed as if it were purely her decision; she could make what he had done an important matter or she could let it go as just something that had happened. Holding on to it was hurting both of them. Before she had known what he had done with Jerd, he'd been her friend. All that had changed was that now she knew.

"But I can't unknow it," she whispered to herself. "And knowing that he could do something like that does show me that he's a different person from what I believed."

"Are you all right?" Alise asked her. "Did you say something?"

"No, just talking to myself." Thymara lifted her hands and covered her eyes. She was safe and her clothing was starting to dry out. She was hungry, but the hunger was beyond her tiredness and hurt. She could wait to deal with it. "I think I'm going to find a place to sleep for a bit."

"Oh." Alise sounded disappointed. "I was hoping we'd go and talk with the others. Find out what they saw and what happened to them."

"You go ahead. I don't mind being alone."

"But—" Alise began, and Thymara suddenly saw her problem. She'd probably never climbed a tree before, let alone clambered around through a network of trees. Alise needed her help but didn't want to ask. Thymara suddenly longed for simple sleep and time alone. Her head was starting to pound, and she wished there were a private place where she could go to weep until she could sleep. Rapskal wandered through her thoughts with his insouciant grin and good humor. Gone. Gone from her twice now, in less than one night. Gone, most likely, forever.

Her chin quivered suddenly, and she might have given way right in front of Alise had Sylve not saved her. The girl came clambering up the trunk like a squirrel, with Harrikin close behind her. He climbed like a lizard, belly to the trunk, as Thymara did. Once they had gained the branch, he folded up his long lean body and perched with his back to the trunk. Sylve dusted her hands on her stained breeches and informed them, "We've got Sintara afloat and resting. Harrikin helped me and we got a couple of logs under her chest. We've jammed the logs against trees and the current should hold them there, but we roped them with vines just in case. She's not comfortable, but she's not going to drown. And the water has already begun to drop. We can tell from the water mark on the trees that it's going down."

"Thank you." The words seemed inadequate, but she didn't have anything better to offer her.

"It was nothing," she replied. "Harrikin and I are actually getting good at it. I never expected to learn how to float a dragon." She smiled, glanced at Thymara with red-rimmed eyes, and then away.

"Mercor and Ranculos?" Thymara asked. She would not mention Rapskal's name. Sharing the pain didn't help it.

"Mercor is weary but otherwise fine. I've asked him if he ever recalled anything like this happening before. Once, he said, one of his ancestors was foolish enough to fly around a mountain that he knew was about to explode. It was a tall one, covered with glaciers and snow, and he wanted to see what would happen when the fire met the ice. When it did erupt, the ice and snow melted instantly and flowed down the mountain, taking stone and muck with it in a thick soup. He said it flowed swift and far, almost out of sight. He wonders if that is what happened, somewhere far away from us, and the wave of it only reached us now."

Thymara was silent, trying to imagine such a thing. She shook her head. What Sylve was suggesting was on a scale far beyond anything she could imagine. A whole mountain melting and flowing away, clear out of sight? Was such a thing possible?

"And your dragon, Ranculos?" she asked Harrikin.

"Ranculos was clipped by a log in the first tumble of the wave. He's bruised badly, but at least his skin isn't broken so the water isn't eating into him." Sylve answered for him. Harrikin nodded slowly to her words. He'd become very still, and in repose he reminded Thymara even more of a lizard, right down to his jeweled unblinking eyes.

"You found a boat and rescued Tats?"

"It was random luck. I'd left my dish in the boat. The fish was nearly cooked, and I went back to get it. I climbed in and was sorting through my stuff when the wave hit. I held tight to the boat and eventually it came out on top of the water and upright. All I had to do was bail. But it snatched all my gear out. I don't have a thing except what I'm wearing."

Slowly it came to Thymara that the same was true for her. She had not thought her spirits could sink lower, but they did.

"Does anyone have anything left?" she asked, thinking desolately of her hunting gear, her blanket, even her dry pair of socks. All gone.

"We recovered three boats, but I don't think anything was in any of them. Not even oars. We'll have to make something that works. Greft has his fire pouch still, but it's of small use right now. Where would we set a fire? I dread tonight when the mosquitoes come. We're going to be miserable until the water goes down. And even then, well, my friends, we've hard times to face."

Alise spoke. "Captain Leftrin will come and find us. And once he does, and the water goes down, we'll go on."

"Go on?" Harrikin spoke softly, slowly, as if he could not believe his ears.

The Bingtown woman looked around at her small circle of startled listeners and gave a tiny laugh. "Don't you know your history? It's what Traders do. We go on. Besides"—and she shrugged—"there's nothing else we can do."

Day the 19th of the Prayer Moon

Year the 6th of the Independent Alliance of Traders
From Detozi, Keeper of the Birds, Trehaug
To Erek, Keeper of the Birds, Bingtown

Enclosed, a report from the Cassarick Rain Wild
Traders' Council as sent to the Trehaug Rain Wild
Traders' Council, concerning the earthquake, black rain,
and white flood, and the likely demise of the members
of the Kelsingra expedition, the crew of the *Tarman*, and
all dragons.

Erek,

*We have never seen such a flash flood as we have just endured.
Lives were lost in both excavation sites, the new docks that were
just built at Cassarick are gone, and a score of trees that fronted
the river were torn loose. It is only good fortune that so few
houses were lost. Damage to the bridges and to the Trader Hall
here is substantial. I doubt we will ever hear what has become of
the dragons and their keepers. I only received your bird message
about visiting the Rain Wilds a day ago. I hope you were not on
the river. If you are well, please, send me a bird to say so as soon
as you receive this.*

Detozi

CHAPTER SIX

PARTNERS

ater splashed against his face, startling him
awake from his nightmare. He coughed and spat. "Stop it!" he
choked and tried to put a threat in his voice. "Get out of my
room. I'm getting up. I won't be late."

Despite his plea, water slopped against his face again. His
stupid sister was going to get it now!

He opened his eyes to a new nightmare. He dangled face-
down from the jaws of a dragon. The dragon was swimming in
a white river. The sky had the uncertain light of dawn. Sedric's
head was barely above the water. He could feel the dragon's teeth
pressed lightly against the skin of his back and chest. His arms
and legs were outside the dragon's mouth, dragging through the
water. The water pushed against the swimming dragon, shoving
them steadily downstream. And the dragon was tired. She swam
with a dogged one-two, one-two stroke of her front legs. He
turned his head and saw that only the dragon's front shoulders

and head were still above water. The copper was sinking. And when her strength gave out and she went down, Sedric would go with her.

"What happened?" he asked, his voice a croak.

Big water. She gurgled her response, but the words formed in his mind. She pressed an image at him, a crashing wave of white filled with rocks and logs and dead animals. Even now, the moving face of the river was littered with flotsam. She swam downstream beside a tangled mat of creepers and small bits of driftwood. A dead animal's hoofed feet were partially visible in it. The river caught the tangle and spun it, and it dispersed.

"What happened to everyone else?" The dragon gave him no response. He was so close to the water's surface that he had no perspective. Nothing but water everywhere. Could that be so? He turned his head slowly from side to side. No *Tarman*. No boat. No keepers, no other dragons. Just himself, the copper dragon, the wide white river, and the forest in the distance.

He tried to recall what had come before. He'd left the boat. He'd spoken to Thymara. He'd gone looking for the dragon. He'd intended to resolve his situation. Somehow. And there his recall of events ended. He shifted in the dragon's mouth. That woke points of pain where the dragon's teeth pressed against him. His dangling legs were cold and nearly numb. The skin of his face stung. He tried to move his arms and found he could, but even that small shift made the dragon's head wobble. She caught herself and swam on, but now he was barely out of the water. The river threatened to start sloshing into her gullet.

He looked to see how far away the shore was, but could not find any shore. To one side of them, he saw a line of trees sticking out of the water. When he turned his eyes the other way, he saw only more river. When had it become so wide? He blinked, trying to make his eyes focus. Day was growing stronger around them, and light bounced off the white surface of the river. There was no shore under the trees; the river was in a flood stage.

And the dragon was swimming downriver with the current.

"Copper," he said, trying to get her attention. She paddled doggedly onward.

He searched his mind and came up with her name. "Relpda. Swim toward the shore. Not down the river. Swim toward the trees. Over there." He started to lift an arm to point, but moving hurt and when he shifted, the dragon turned her head, nearly putting his face in the water. She kept paddling steadily downstream.

"Curse you, listen to me! Turn toward the shore! It's our only hope. Carry me over there, by the trees, and then you can do what you wish. I don't want to die in this river."

If she even noticed he was speaking to her, he could not tell. One-two, one-two. He rocked with the dogged rhythm of her paddling.

He wondered if he could swim to the trees on his own. He'd never been a strong swimmer, but the fear of drowning might lend him a bit of strength. He flexed his legs experimentally, earning himself another dunk in the river and the knowledge that he was chilled to the bone. If the dragon didn't carry him to shore, he wasn't going to get there. And the way she was swimming now made him doubt that even she could make it. But she was his only chance, if he could get her to listen to him.

He thought of Alise and Sintara. He lifted a hand to touch Relpda's jaw, flesh to scale. His hands were tender, the skin deeply wrinkled from immersion in the river. They were red, too, and he suspected that if he warmed them up, they'd burn. He couldn't think about that now.

"Beauteous one," he began, feeling foolish. Almost immediately, he felt a warm spark of attention in his mind. "Lovely copper queen, gleaming like a freshly minted coin. You of the swirling eyes and glistening scales, please hear me."

Hear you.

"Yes, hear me. Turn your head. Do you see the trees there, sticking up from the water? Lovely one, if you carried me there, we could both rest. I could groom you and perhaps find you some food. I know you are hungry. I feel it." That, he realized, was disconcertingly true. And if he let his mind wander there, he felt her increasing weariness, too. Back away from that! "Let us go there so you can take the rest you so richly deserve, and I can have the pleasure of cleaning your face of mud."

He was not very good at it. Other than telling her she was pretty, he had no idea of what compliments would please a dragon. After he had spoken, he waited for a response from her. She turned her head, looked at the trees and kept paddling. They were not headed straight for the shore, but at least now, at some point, they'd connect with it.

"You are so wise, lovely copper one. So pretty and beautiful and shining and copper. Swim toward the trees, clever, pretty dragon."

He sensed again that warm touch and felt oddly moved by it. The aches in his body seemed to lessen as well. It didn't seem to matter that his words were simple and ungraceful. He fed her praise, and she responded by turning more sharply toward the river's edge and swimming more strongly. For an instant, he felt what that extra effort cost her. He felt almost shamed that he asked it of her. "But if I do not, neither of us will survive," he muttered, and felt a shadow of agreement from her.

As they got closer to the trees, his heart sank. The river had expanded its flow; there was no shore under the eaves of the forest, not even a muddy one. There was only the impenetrable line of trees, their trunks like the bars of a cage that would hold Relpda out in the river. In the shadow of the canopy, the pale water was a quiet lake without shores that spread off into the darkness.

Only one section of shore offered him hope. In an alcove of the surrounding trees, limbs and logs and branches had been packed together by a back current. All sorts of broken tree limbs and bits of driftwood and even substantial timbers had piled up there in a floating logjam. It didn't look promising. But once he was there, he could climb out of the water and perhaps dry off before nightfall.

That was as much as he could offer himself. No hot food and comforting drink, no dry, clean change of clothing, not even a rude pallet on which to lie down; nothing awaited him there but the bare edge of survival.

And even less for the dragon, he suspected. Whereas the wedged logs and matted driftwood might offer him a place to stand, she had no such hope. She swam with all her energy now, but it would avail her nothing. No hope for her and very little for him.

Not save me?

"We'll try. I don't know how, but we'll try."

For an extended moment, he felt her absence from his mind. He became aware of how his skin stung, how her teeth dug into him. His aching muscles shrieked at him, and cold both numbed and burned him. Then she came back, bringing her warmth and pushing his misery aside.

Can save you, she announced.

Affection he could feel enfolded him. *Why?* he wondered. Why did she care about him?

Less lonely. You make sense of world. Talk to me. Her warmth wrapped him.

Sedric drew breath. All his life, he'd been aware that people loved him. His parents loved him. Hest had loved him, he thought. Alise did. He'd known of love and accepted that it existed for him. But never before had he actually felt love as a physical sensation that emanated from another creature and warmed and comforted him. It was incredible. A slow thought came to him.

Can you feel it when I care about you?

Sometimes. Her reply was guarded. *I know it's not real, sometimes. But kind words, pretty words, feel good even if not real. Like remembering food when hungry.*

Sudden shame flooded him. He took a slow breath and opened his gratitude to her. He let his thanks flow out of him, that she forgave him for taking her blood, that she had saved him, that she would continue to struggle on his behalf when he could not offer her definite hope of sanctuary.

As if he had poured oil on a fire, her warmth and regard for him grew. He actually felt his body physically warm, and suddenly her dogged one-two, one-two paddling grew stronger. Together they just might survive. Both of them.

For the first time in many years, he closed his eyes and breathed a heartfelt prayer to Sa.

"TAKE YOUR FOOD and get up there. Keep looking," Leftrin told Davvie. "I want you up on top of the deckhouse, scanning in all directions. Look on the water, look for anyone clinging to debris, look at the trees and up in the trees. Keep looking. And keep blowing that horn. Three long blasts and then stop and listen. Then three long blasts again."

"Yessir," Davvie said faintly.

"You can do it," Carson said behind him. He gave the exhausted boy a pat on the shoulder that was half a push. The boy snatched up two rounds of ship's bread and his mug of tea and left the deckhouse.

"He's a good lad. I know he's tired," Leftrin said. It was half apology for treating the boy so gruffly and half thanks for being able to use him.

"He wants to find them as much as anyone else here. He'll keep going as long as he can." Carson hesitated, then plunged on with, "What about Tarman? Can he help us with the search?"

He meant well, Leftrin reminded himself. Nonetheless. He was an old friend, not part of the crew. Some things weren't spoken of outside that family, not even to old friends. "We're using the barge in every possible way, Carson, short of having it sprout wings and fly over the river. What can you expect of a ship?"

"Of course." Carson bobbed a nod that he understood and would ask no more. His deference bothered Leftrin almost as much as his question had. He knew he was short-tempered; grief tore at his heart even as he clutched at hope and kept desperately searching. *Alise. Alise, my darling. Why did we hold back, if only to lose each other this way?*

It wasn't just the woman, though Sa knew that overwhelmed him and ruined his brain for cold logic. All the youngsters, every one of them was missing. Every dragon, gone. And Sedric. If he found Alise but had to tell her he had lost Sedric, what would she think of him? And all the dragons gone, and her dreams gone with them. He knew how she felt about the dragons and the keepers. He had failed her, utterly failed her. There could be no good end to this search. None at all.

"Leftrin!"

He startled at his name and saw by Carson's face that he'd been trying to talk to him. "Sorry. Too long with no sleep," he said gruffly.

The hunter nodded sympathetically and rubbed at his own bloodshot eyes. "I know. We're all tired. We're damn lucky that tired is all we are. You're a bit beat up, and Eider may have a few cracked ribs, but by and large, we came through it intact. And we all know that we'll rest later. For right now, this is what I propose. My boat stayed with the *Tarman;* luckily I've the habit of bringing it aboard and lashing it down each night. I propose I take the spare ship's horn and set out on my own. I'll shoot down the river a ways, fast as I can, and then go right along the shore and search under the trees. You follow, but taking your time and searching carefully. Every so often, I'll blow three long blasts, just like Davvie, to let you know where I am and that I'm still searching. If either of us finds anything, we'll use three short blasts to call the other."

Leftrin listened grimly. He knew what Carson was implying. Bodies. He'd be looking for bodies, and for survivors in such poor condition that they could not signal their rescuers. It made sense. Tarman had been proceeding very slowly, first moving up the river to approximately where the wave had first struck them and then back down again, searching both the river's face and the shoreline. Carson's little boat could catch the current and shoot swiftly down to where they had begun to search and move downriver from there, searching the shallows.

"Do you need anyone with you?"

Carson shook his head. "I'd rather leave Davvie safe here with you. And I'll go alone. If I find anyone, the boat's small, and I'll want to bring them on board right away."

"Three short blasts will mean we've found something. Even if it's only a body?"

Carson thought, then shook his head. "Neither of us can do anything for a body. No sense one of us summoning the other and taking a chance on missing a survivor. I'll want some oil and one of the big cookpots. If we don't meet up before nightfall, I'll pull in, make a fire in the pot, and overnight there. The fire will keep me warm and serve as a beacon to anyone who might see it. And if I find someone near nightfall, I can use the horn and the firepot to guide you to us."

Leftrin nodded. "Take a good supply of rations and water. If you find anyone, they may be in bad shape. You'll need them."

"I know."

"Good luck, then."

"Sa's blessing on you."

Such words coming from the hunter made Leftrin feel even grimmer. "Sa's blessing," he replied and watched the man turn and go. "Please, please, find her," he whispered, and then he went back up on deck to put his own eyes on the river.

As he joined his crew on the deck, he felt their sympathy for him. Swarge, Bellin, Hennesey, and hulking Eider were silent and looked aside from him, as if ashamed they could not give him what he wanted. Skelly came to his side and took his hand. He glanced down at her, seeing his niece for a moment instead of his deckhand when she met his gaze. She gave his rough hand a small squeeze; her pinched mouth and a quick nod of her head let him know that she shared his concern. With no more than that, she left him and went back to her watching post. *They are a good crew,* he thought with a tight throat. Without a quibble, they had followed him on this jaunt up the river into unknown territory. Part of it was because that was the type of river folk they were: curious, adventurous, and confident of their skills. But a good part of it was that they would go where he and Tarman went. He commanded their lives. Sometimes that knowledge humbled him.

He wondered why he had bothered being evasive with Carson. The man was no fool. The crew's charade would not have fooled him for long. He knew the boat was sentient, and if he'd had any doubts, Tarman's rescue of Leftrin last night would have dispersed them. When he'd shouted, the barge had come straight to him, and despite the current, had held himself steady in the river until his captain was safe aboard him again.

Wrapped in a blanket but still dripping, shivering, he'd gone into the galley. "Is Alise all right?" he'd demanded, and the faces of his crew had told him all.

He hadn't slept since then. And he wouldn't sleep until he found her.

THE TANGLE OF floating debris was both too thick and not solid enough.

Relpda had carried Sedric to it. Once she had got close to it, she had pushed her way into it like a spoon pushing through thick soup. Driftwood and matted brambles, leafy branches and long, dead logs, freshly torn trees and wads of grasses had given way to her shoving and then closed up behind her. Chesting against the mess, she had either judged it solid or close enough, for she had dropped him. He'd fallen from her jaws athwart a couple of floating logs and started to slip between them. His stiff limbs had screamed as he frantically moved them, thrashing and crawling until he was on the larger and thicker of the logs. There he had clung, and he felt how it bobbed in the current. Worse, he felt how it shifted and threatened to break away from the tangled mess along the shoreline as the frantic dragon pawed and bumped at it as she attempted to clamber on top of it.

"It won't hold you, Relpda. Stop. Stop tearing it apart. You can't get on top of this; it's just floating bits of wood and reeds." He moved away from her to a part of the raft that her struggles were not affecting so violently. He could feel her rising panic coupled with her weariness and despair. She was tired, and he knew guiltily that if she had abandoned him, her reserves of strength would have been much greater. He wondered again why she had saved him at obvious cost to herself.

Then he wondered why he was doing nothing to save her.

There was a quick and guilty answer to that. Once she had drowned, she'd be out of his head forever. He'd know his thoughts were completely his own again. When he went back to Bingtown, he could live just as he always had and—

He thrust his selfishness aside. He was never going back to Bingtown. He was on a raft of debris over an acidic river. He inspected his stinging arms; the exposed skin looked like cured meat. No telling what the rest of him looked like and he was too cowardly to look. A shudder of chill ran over him. He hugged himself and tried to consider the incomprehensible situation he found himself in. Everything he had depended on in this savage place was gone. No ship, no crewmen, no hunters. No supplies of any kind. Alise was probably already dead, her body floating in the river somewhere. Sorrow smote him; he tried to push it aside. He had to clear his mind, or he'd join her.

What was he going to do? He had no tools, no fire, no shelter, no food, and no knowledge of how to get any of that for himself. He looked at the copper. He'd told her the truth. He had no idea of how he could save her. If the dragon died, the river would wash her away, and then he would die, too. Probably slowly. And alone. With no way to move up or down the river.

Right now, the dragon represented his only chance at getting out of here. She was his only ally. She'd risked her life for him. And asked so little of him in return.

Relpda gave a short trumpet, and he looked back at her. She'd pushed her way deeper into the floating wreckage. She'd hooked one of her forelegs over the end of a substantial log and was struggling to lift her other front leg over, but she was at the narrow end of the long, dead tree. As she put her weight on it, the log bobbed under. The log was threatening to slip out from under her and shoot up into the air. And the danger was great that she would sink beneath the floating debris.

"Relpda, wait. You need to center yourself on the log. Wait. I'm coming." He stared at her situation, trying to think how to remedy it. Sinking dragon, floating wood. He wondered if his weight on the high end of the log would be enough to hold it down while she put the other leg over.

She didn't listen to him, of course. She kept giving small hoots of effort while trying to hook her other front leg over the log. Her struggles were tearing at the matted debris. Pieces of it were breaking free from the outer edge and whirling back out into the river's current.

He tried again, focused himself at her. "Beauteous one, you must allow me to help you. Be still for a moment. Be still. Let me weight the log down for you. I'm coming now, lovely creature, queen of queens. I am here to serve you. You must not tear the packed wood apart. It might carry you away from me, down the river. Be as still as you can while I think of what to do."

He felt a touch of warmth and then a tiny message. *Serve me?* He felt her relaxing her struggles. It was pitiful, how quickly she put her belief in him. His wet clothes clung and chafed his red skin as he awkwardly moved from log to wedged driftwood to log. None of it was stable, and often he had but a moment to find his next step as his perch sank under him. But he reached the tangled roots of her log and seized hold of them. The log was long enough and he was far enough away from her that he thought his small weight might lever her greater one. He started to climb up on the root mass, to see if her end would rise. Then he realized his error. He needed to lower her end of the log to get it under her, not raise it. He suddenly wished he had more experience with this sort of thing. He'd never been a man who worked with his hands and back, and he'd taken pride in that. His mind and his manners had earned him his keep. But if he didn't learn, right now, how to help, then his dragon was going to die.

"Relpda, my glorious copper queen. Be very still. I am going to try to lift my end and shove the log under your chest. When it comes up, it may lift you a bit."

His scheme worked poorly. Whenever he tried to lift the floating end of the log, whatever he was standing on sank. Once he nearly lost his balance and fell under the floating tangle. He succeeded in moving the log slightly more under her chest, but when he gave up the task, her position was only marginally better than it had been. When she stopped kicking, she sank, but her back and head remained above the water. She fixed her eyes on him. He looked into them. Spinning pools, dark blue against copper. The colors in them were liquid. It reminded him of the shifting colors of her blood in the glass vial. Guilt stabbed him. How had he ever done such a monstrous thing?

Tired, she mooed at him. The sound beat against his ears, and the sensation of her exhaustion flooded his mind, weakening his knees. He braced himself against it, and he tried to send warmth and encouragement back to her.

"I know, my queen, my lovely one. But you must not give up. I'm doing my best, and I will help you." His weary mind weighed and discarded options. Push smaller pieces of wood under her. No. They'd simply dislodge. Or he'd fall in.

She shifted her front feet, seeking a better purchase. The end of the log lifted, splashed down again, and she nearly lost it. More debris broke from the edge of the mat and floated away in the river's hungry current. "Don't struggle, lovely one. The log you are on might break free of the others. Stay as still as you can while I think."

The wave of warmth that flowed through him stilled his worrying. For a moment, he was flushed with pleasure, and he felt a stirring of emotion, like infatuation. As·quickly as it had come, it faded. He clenched his hands. What had Alise called it? The dragon glamour. It felt good. Intoxicating and alive. Nearly, he reached after it and willed himself into it. Then she thrashed again, and once more he nearly fell into the water. No. He had to keep his distance and his own mind if he was to help her. A darker reason to stay separate came to him. If he let her join her thoughts too deeply with his thoughts and then she drowned— He shuddered to think of sharing that experience.

He looked at the dragon, at the sky to estimate his time, and around at the trees. The trees, he decided, would represent their best chance. It would be hard work, but if he could rearrange the debris so that the current braced the heavier logs tight to the trees, and then get her to move herself there, she might find a sturdier position. He looked at her, waited until she was looking at him, and then tried to push his mental image into her mind. "Lovely queen, I will move wood and make a safer place for you. Until I am finished, do not struggle. Hang there and trust me. Can you do that?"

Slipping.

"I'll hurry. Don't give up."

"I'll be damned," someone exclaimed in amused astonishment.

Sedric spun, his heart leaping with joy at the sound of a human voice. He slipped, caught his balance, and then squinted into the dimness under the trees.

"Up here." The man's voice was a hoarse croak.

He moved his eyes up and saw a man clambering down a tree trunk. His hands gripped the ridges of bark, and he stuck the toes of his boots in the cracks as he came quickly down. It wasn't until he turned to face him that Sedric recognized him. It was the hunter, the older one. Jess. That was his name. They'd never spoken much. Jess plainly had no use for him, and he'd never explained his one visit to Sedric's chamber. The man looked terrible, bruised and battered in the face, but he was alive and human and company.

And, Sedric quickly realized, he was someone who knew how to get food and water, someone who could help him survive. Sa had answered his prayers after all.

"How did you get here?" he greeted him. "I thought I was the only one left alive." He began immediately to make his way toward the man.

"By water," Jess said and laughed sourly. His voice was harsh and raspy. "And I shared your cheery thought about survival. Looks like that little quake we had a few days ago saved a second surprise for us."

"Does something like this happen often?" Sedric asked, already feeling his anger rise that no one had warned him.

Slipping. Distress was plain in the dragon's rumbled call and in the thought she pushed at him.

"A change in the water, yes. A flood like this, no. This is a new one for me, but not entirely ill fortune for either of us."

"What do you mean?"

Jess grinned. "Just that fate seems to have not only saved us, but thrown us together with everything we need for a most profitable partnership. For one thing, when I finally kicked my way to the surface, I found a boat caught in the same current that I was. Not my boat, unfortunately, but one that belonged to someone sensible enough to stow his gear tightly." He coughed harshly and then tried to clear his throat. It didn't help his rough voice. "It has a couple of blankets, some fishing gear, even a fire-making kit and a pot. Greft's, probably, but I'll wager that he'll never have need of it again. That wave hit so hard and so suddenly that it's hard to believe any of us survived. It almost makes me believe in fate. Maybe the gods threw us together to see how smart we were. Because if you're a clever fellow, we have everything we need for a very comfortable new life."

As Jess had croaked out his words, he'd dismounted from the tree's trunk and stepped onto a log. It bobbed beneath him as it took his weight. For a large man, he was graceful enough as he trod swiftly along its length. In the crook of one arm, he carried several round red fruit. Sedric wasn't familiar with what they were, but at the sight of them, both his hunger and thirst roared.

"Do you have water?" he asked the man, advancing cautiously across the packed debris toward him. Jess ignored him. It looked as if he reached the end of the large log and then clambered down into the water. Then Sedric realized that the boat was moored out of sight behind the big driftwood snag. Jess disappeared for a moment and when he stood up, he no longer held the fruit. Obviously he had stowed it in the boat he was standing in. A curl of uneasiness moved in Sedric's belly. The situation seemed plain to him. The hunter had climbed the tree, eaten fruit, and what he had brought down was his surplus that he intended to save. For himself. He must see how serious Sedric's situation was. Yet he stood there, in his boat, in his dried clothes, with his food, and made no offer of aid to him.

Jess leaned his elbows on the log that floated between him and Sedric and looked over at him. Sedric halted where he was, trying to make sense of the situation. When Sedric just returned his gaze, Jess cocked his head and wheezed, "I notice you aren't saying what you'll bring to our new partnership."

Sedric goggled at him. They were alone on a raft of ever-shifting flotsam in the middle of the forest, weeks from anywhere, and the man was trying to wring money out of him? It made no sense. Behind him, he heard the dragon thrash, felt a wave of anxiety from her, and then felt her calm as she realized the log was still partially under her. *Hungry.* His own thoughts about food had stimulated hers. Or perhaps it was her hunger he was feeling. He didn't know. He couldn't completely sort himself out from her anymore. *Afraid.* The thought came to him without a sound from her. *Careful.* Did she sense something he didn't?

He tried to focus his thoughts on the man's ridiculous statement. "What do you want from me? Look at me, man. I don't have anything to offer you. Not here. I suppose if somehow we got back to Bingtown . . ." He let the words trail off. It wouldn't be constructive to let him know that if they got back to Bingtown, he'd still have nothing. He tried to imagine facing Hest and admitting that he'd somehow lost Alise and with her Hest's hope of creating an heir who would assure his inheritance. He dared not think what his own family would think of him, let alone what Alise's might say. He'd been sent as her protector. What sort of a protector survived when his ward did not? If he went back to Bingtown alone, he'd have no career and no support from his family. He had nothing to offer this pirate.

"Nothing here, hey? Looks to me like you've got plenty here. Do I have to spell it out for you? Or are you still thinking that perhaps you can keep it all for yourself?"

The hunter stooped out of sight again and then brought up a gear bag from the boat. "Because from where I'm standing, man, if you decide to be greedy, I think you just die." He opened the gear bag, dug through it, and smiled, immensely pleased. "I'm sure this was Greft's boat now. Look at this. Knife and whetstone, all bundled nicely together. Could be a bigger tool, but it will still get the job done." As he spoke, he took out both items and began to lay the knife against the stone in slow, leisurely licks, as if they both had all the time in the world.

Sedric stood very still. What was the man asking of him? Was the gleaming blade a threat? What did he mean, "you've got plenty"? Was he making a sexual proposition? He'd shown nothing but disdain for Sedric before this. But Jess would not be the first man he'd encountered who publicly despised him and privately desired him. He took a breath. He was hungry and thirsty and the dragon's nagging anxiety scraped at his nerves and begged his attention. What was he willing to give Jess to ensure his survival? What would he give him to get him to help with Relpda?

Anything he wanted.

The thought chilled him, but he accepted it. "Just say what you want," he said brusquely, the words tumbling out more abruptly than he intended.

Jess stopped whetting the knife and stared at him. Sedric drew himself up tall and crossed his arms on his chest. He met his gaze levelly. Jess cocked his head at him, and then brayed out a coarse laugh. "Not that. No. Not interested one bit in that. Are you stupid or stubborn?"

He waited for Sedric to respond. When he didn't, Jess shook his head, his smile growing colder. He reached into his shirt, drew out a pouch, and opened it. As he tugged at the strings, he said, "Leftrin was stupid to think I was a fool. I know what happened. He saw a chance for money, and he thought that if he brought in his own people, he could make his deal direct and keep more of the split for himself. Well, I don't work that way. No one cuts out Jess Torkef." From the pouch, he took something the size of his palm. It was scarlet and ruby. He held it up between his thumb and forefinger and turned it to catch the light. It flashed in the sunlight. "Look familiar?" he asked Sedric mockingly and then laughed as first disbelief and then fury flushed Sedric's face.

It was the scarlet dragon scale that Rapskal had given Alise. Alise had entrusted it to Sedric, asking him to make a detailed drawing of it. Then she'd forgotten he had it, and he'd added it to his trove. "That's mine," he said flatly. "You stole it out of my room."

Jess smiled. "It's an interesting question. Is it possible to steal from a thief?" He turned the scale again, flashing it in the sun. "I've had it for days. If you missed it, you covered your anxiety well. I suspect you didn't even know it was gone. You're not quite as good at hiding things as you think you are. Most of what I found was disgusting trash, but not this bit. So I took it. Just for safekeeping, of course, to be sure I'd have something to show for this wild goose chase. Looks like it was a good thing I did. Everything else you had is probably at the bottom now."

Sedric had still not said a word. The hunter took his time putting the red dragon's scale back in the pouch, closing it, and slipping it back inside his shirt. "So," he said. "Looks like we each know what the other is about. And it's time to consider a new alliance. Leftrin was supposed to be a part of my deal with Sinad Arich. He was supposed to smooth the way and make it easy. But he didn't. Doesn't matter. He's gone now. And it's down to us. So you have two choices. You can step up and take his place in the deal, and we'll share. Or don't."

"Leftrin had a deal with you?" Sedric's mind was scrambling to put all the pieces together. What sort of a deal? To rob his passengers?

Tired, the dragon pleaded in the back of his mind. *Not safe.*

Hush. Let me think. Her heavy head was drooping on her weary neck. He appraised her and knew that if he didn't act, soon her muzzle would be touching the water. Take care of the most pressing issue first. Then puzzle out the rest. To Jess, he said, "Set all this aside for a moment. Can you help me with the dragon? She's tired and she's going to sink and drown if I can't help her float and rest somehow."

A slow smile spread across the hunter's face. "Now we're coming to terms, boy. Of course I'll *help* you with the dragon." He lifted the knife and turned it, making the blade flash in the sunlight.

"I don't understand you," Sedric said in a shaking voice. But abruptly he did.

The hunter jerked a thumb toward the copper. "I'm talking about the dragon. There's plenty there, for both of us. You help

me kill it, and butcher it fast before the river claims the carcass.
Then we load as much as we can in the boat, and we head back
for Trehaug. I know people there, people willing to make a
quick profit and not be curious about the source. I can go in
during the dark of night and get everything we need for us to
make a very comfortable trip down the river on a boat with a
crew who won't ask us any questions. Think about it. Everyone
else is dead. Everyone will assume you are dead, which means
you don't have to share with anyone. There will be no pursuit
and no questions. Just two very wealthy newcomers living a life
of ease in Chalced."

It was instinctive. He blocked the thought from the dragon's
mind as he would shield the eyes of a child from violence. He
tried to. He wasn't completely successful. He felt her anxiety
rise as she sensed his agitation without comprehending the reason for it. She looked at the hunter, recognized him. *Food?* she
queried hopefully.

"No food. Not yet," he spoke aloud to her without thinking.

The hunter barked out a hoarse laugh. "And that's what
you're bringing to the table, my little friend. You can hear her
thoughts. And you talk back to the damn things. I can hear
them a bit, but I try not to. Easier to be professional about these
things if you keep a distance, I think. Though it explains how
you got close enough to get as much as you did the first time.
Impressed me, I'll tell you. I'd been trying to figure out how
to do it for days. And here some little Bingtown fop just goes
ashore and takes what he wants."

"I don't know what you're talking about," Sedric lied. It was
a reflex. The hunter hadn't mentioned the blood. Did he know
about the blood? Did any of it matter anymore? The whole conversation was insane. He needed food and water and rest. He
needed to know if the man was going to help him or not. He
tried to sound as if he were not desperate. "Look, help me with
the dragon and give me some of that fruit you have. Anything.
I need to eat and rest. Then we can talk about what happens
next."

Jess cocked his head at him and said coldly, "No point to

feeding you if you don't intend to help me. And lying to me seems to be your way of saying you intend to keep it all to yourself. Though how you plan to make it work, I can't see. Shall I make it easier for you? I was awake that night. I saw you come aboard all bloodied. Been in a fight was my first thought, though I hadn't heard a peep of a row, and sound carries over water. But then, as you went up the ladder, I got a glimpse of what you were carrying. Glittery red, just like I'd been told. Dragon blood. And I was, as I've told you, very impressed. So I followed and in a bit I saw you come out of your cabin and throw your duds overboard. And that made it sure for me. Somehow you'd gotten blood out of a dragon and not been eaten or even caught. You were pretty savvy about hiding it, too. I went through your room more than once before I found your hoard. So. Let's just admit we're scoundrels and be honest scoundrels with each other . . . or as honest as scoundrels can be. We both shipped aboard the *Tarman* for the same reason. And I only shipped because I was promised that Captain Leftrin was going to grease things a bit for me, but I suspect his craze for that woman soured him on our kind of profit. Maybe he was hoping to keep everything for himself, woman, dragon parts to sell in Chalced, everything. Maybe you were the one who offered him a better deal. But the agreement was that he was supposed to help me, and in return, he was going to be well paid for his trouble. Very well paid."

His voice faded for a moment as he stooped down in the boat. When he came up again, he had a coil of line in his hand. He scowled at it and set it out beside the knife.

"Instead that son of a dog tried to kill me last night." He lifted his hand and felt about his throat gingerly. He growled and shook his head and went back to setting out his tools. "Double twist of fate, I suppose. That wave that hit kept him from strangling me, and I'm hoping it made an end of him. Love-blind idiot is what he is. Well, with a bit of luck, he's dead. And you've got your luck—you're alive." He held up a small hatchet, frowned at it, and then with a thunk seated it in the log beside the line.

"Bad tool for the job, but you use what you have. A bit like our captain. Leftrin got greedy and lost it all. If he'd lived up to his end of the deal, he could have had the kind of money we're going to have. Then the ugly old goat could have had any woman he wanted. Well, his loss is our gain. We'll have it all. Wealth, power, and any sort of woman we want, once we get back to Chalced." He leered at Sedric nastily, baring his little brown teeth, and added, "Or whatever you fancy."

He inspected his tools and they met his satisfaction. He set them out in a careful row. "So, you'll help me. Or you can be stubborn and try to keep it all for yourself. Try that, and I'll take just what I want. Won't be as easy without someone to handle the animal for me, keep it calm and lure it to the blade. But I can get more than enough to live the rest of my days as a very rich man." He thumbed the edge of the knife, nodded to himself, and looked directly at Sedric. "Well. Time for a decision. Shall we get on with it?"

Sedric swallowed. Reality seemed to re-form around him. Leftrin had been part of this man's plan to acquire and sell dragon parts? Then he'd probably just been using Alise all that time. Alise had been duped. And he'd been blind to the machinations going on all around him. He should have guessed. He should have known that he wouldn't be the only one to see the chance for profit. He'd known all along there had to be some bizarre motive behind the captain's apparent infatuation. So now what? Did he take the hunter's offer? Could he coax and calm the dragon until Jess got close enough for a kill?

The man had set it all out quite plainly. If he helped him, Jess would help him get to Chalced and sell what they had. He didn't need to go back to Bingtown at all. From Chalced, he could send Hest a message to come and join him. With the kind of money they'd have, there'd be no need for any more pretenses. They could go anywhere they wanted and live exactly as they pleased. He could have everything he'd dreamed of. He'd paid dearly already. Would it be so wrong to take some small measure of happiness for himself?

Jess was watching him closely. His raspy voice became persuasive, the threat gone from it. "Animal's going to die anyway. Look at it. It wasn't a prime specimen to start with, and now it's going to drown. So you might as well be kind and make the end a quick one and have something to show for your trouble." Jess hung the knife from his belt and gripped the fish spear firmly. He slung the coil of line from his free hand. "Tell her not to struggle, that I'm going to help her," he instructed Sedric in a low voice. "All I need you to do right now is keep her calm. Say I'm putting the rope on her to help her stay afloat. It's not as long as it could be; I'll need to get her to move closer to the trees so I can tie it off. Afterward, we'll have to work fast, before the carcass sinks. We'll go for the stuff that will keep and bring the most money. Teeth, claws, scales. It's going to be messy, rough work and you won't like it. But a little of this now will mean a lot of money later."

The copper was watching them anxiously. Suspiciously? How much could she really understand? Sedric chided his conscience. The hunter had said she was going to die anyway. Would it be better if she died slowly and her body sank to the bottom of the river for fish to eat? What good would that do anyone? After all he had gone through, didn't he deserve something for himself, some small bit of happiness? Didn't he deserve to finally stop living in deceit?

He kept his eyes on the dragon as Jess edged toward her. She looked back at him. Her eyes swirled as always, but darkness seemed mixed with their blue and gold now. He could feel her questioning him but not sense the fullness of her question. Did that mean she was dying? Was Jess telling the truth when he said it would be a mercy?

She hung at a slant from the log, one front leg hooked over it. Here at the edge of the river under the trees, the current was not as strong. Beyond her, deeper in the forest, standing water carried shimmers of light into the perpetual gloom. He noted in passing from the high water mark on the tree trunks that the water was starting to recede. But it was not happening quickly, and he doubted it would be soon enough to save her. As he watched, she gave a few feeble kicks of her hind legs, trying to push herself a little higher on the log. She was wearying of hold-ing her head so unnaturally high. She was hungry and thirsty and chilled. Dragons were creatures made for fierce sun and baking sand. The cool water sapped her energy and slowed her heart. He was not imagining it. Her eyes were spinning more slowly. She had never been strong or healthy. He looked at her and the welling of sorrow he felt ambushed him. He blinked his eyes and saw her through the opacity of tears.

You are leaving me?

Her childish interpretation of his reaction to their pending separation tore at his heart. He tried to take a breath, only to have it snag on something sharp inside him. *Little copper queen. I wish you could have flown.*

I have wings! The weary dragon cocked her head at him. Very slowly, she lifted her wings and opened them partially. They caught the light like hammered metal. They were larger than he would have supposed them, and more delicate. The spiderweb framework stood out against the leathery membrane and feathery scales. The afternoon light shone through them as if they were panes of stained glass.

"They are beautiful." He spoke the words aloud, sorrowfully, and felt her bask in the compliment.

"Beautiful is right. And the leather from them will last hundreds of years, according to the tales. But they're too big for us to harvest. They'd rot before we got down the river." Jess was edging toward her on a fallen tree. Branches covered in leaves were both impediments and handholds for him as he sidled along it. He halted where he was and laughed aloud at Sedric's scowl. "Don't glare at me. You know it's true. Keep her calm. All the debris has been loosened by her struggling, so the pack isn't as sturdy here. I don't want her to knock me into the water and have it close up over my head." He grunted as he worked his way cautiously along the floating tree.

He paused a man's length away from her. He was watching the dragon, not Sedric. He knew Sedric had no choice but to help him. "When I get closer, tell her to extend her head toward me. I'll get a rope around her neck and then I'll try to lead her in close to one of the big trees. As long as she's afloat and doesn't fight me, I should be able to get her where I want her."

He knew he couldn't save her. She was going to die. If Jess succeeded, at least her death would be quick. And it would serve a purpose. At least one of them could go on to live a decent life. The hunter would make it quick. He'd said so.

Danger? Relpda was watching Jess make his final approach. What was she sensing from him?

The hunter had nearly reached her. He balanced at the thick end of the fallen tree, just short of the upthrust of muddy roots that ended it. He was shaking out the rope and eyeing the dragon as he did so. Sedric marked that he still gripped the fish spear in one hand as he worked. His darting glance went from the dragon to Sedric and back again as he studied her neck and measured out line. "Keep her calm, now," he reminded Sedric. "There's not a lot of line here. Once I get the rope around her neck, I'm going to have to snub her up pretty close to the tree. But that will keep her head above the water afterward."

It wasn't something he was doing. He was here, but he couldn't stop it from happening. If he tried to intervene, Jess was capable of killing him as well. And what good would that do the dragon? It was her inevitable end. He watched it, feeling that he owed her that much, to witness her end. *I'm sorry,* he thought at her, and received only confusion in response.

"Okay, I'm ready." Jess was holding out a large loop of line. He had the fish spear trapped under his arm as he held the noose to one side of his body. "Tell her to reach her head out toward me. Slowly. Tell her I'm going to help her."

Sedric took a deep breath. His throat kept closing up. Give in to the inevitable, he counseled himself. "Relpda," Sedric said softly. "Listen to me, now. Listen carefully."

Day the 19th of the Prayer Moon

Year the 6th of the Independent Alliance of Traders

From Erek, Keeper of the Birds, Bingtown
To Detozi, Keeper of the Birds, Trehaug

Enclosed, a message from Trader Wycof to the First
Mate Jos Peerson of the liveship *Ophelia*, soon to dock at
Trehaug, informing him of the birth of twin daughters
to his wife on this day.

Detozi,

*An illness in my family has forced me to postpone all thoughts of
leaving Bingtown at this time. My father is seriously ill. I fear
that my hopes of visiting the Rain Wilds and finally meeting
you must be put off for the time being. I am disappointed.*

*Have you yourself ever considered a visit to Bingtown? I am
sure your nephew would be very pleased by such a visit.*

Erek

CHAPTER SEVEN

RESCUE

ight had been every bit as miserable as Thymara had feared it would be. The keepers had banded together to build a sort of platform, layering drift logs in alternating angles on top of one another. Leafy branches were torn down to provide cushioning over the bumpy logs. The resulting "raft" had not been sturdy, but there had been room for them to huddle together and commiserate while the mosquitoes and gnats feasted on them. There was no flat place to sleep, so Thymara had balanced her body on one of the wider logs. She had considered taking to the trees for the night but had finally decided to stay closer to the dragons and the other keepers. Every time she started to doze off, Alum's dragon would trumpet mournfully and she'd rouse. Too many times that night, tears had followed. The small sounds she heard from the others on the raft told her that she was not alone in her fears. Toward morning, not even the sorrow and sounds, let alone the buzzing, bites, and branch nubs could keep Thymara alert any longer. She had dozed down past the nightmares and grief to a deep sleep and had awakened chill and stiff and damp with morning dew.

The flooding was subsiding slowly. The high waterline on the nearby tree trunks was now shoulder-high on her. Next to her, Alise slept deeply, curled in a ball. Tats was just beyond her, breathing huskily. Jerd, she noted, slept tucked into the curve of Greft's body. For a moment, she envied them the warmth they shared and then dismissed the thought. That wasn't for her. Boxter and Nortel were perched on the edge of the platform, staring out at the flooded forest and talking softly. The dragons were hunched on their log perches. They looked uncomfortable and precarious, but they were sleeping heavily. The chill of the water and the deep shade of the trees had plunged them into deep lethargy. They probably wouldn't stir until midmorning, or later.

Thymara nudged Sylve and whispered, "I'm going to see if I can find us some food," and then picked her way through her sleeping comrades. Log by log, she clambered over the pack of floating debris to the closest major tree trunk. It had no branches within reach, but her claws served her well as she scaled it. It was strange how good it felt to be back in the trees again. Safer. She might still be hungry, thirsty, and insect bitten, but the trees had always befriended and sheltered her.

She had not gone far when the forest rewarded her for her efforts. She found a trumpet vine and drank the nectary water from the blossoms with only a small twinge of guilt. She had no way to carry the meager mouthful that each flower offered her. She'd drink now, renew her own strength, and hope she'd find something she could transport back to her friends. There was not really enough liquid to quench her thirst, but at least her tongue no longer felt like leather. When she had emptied every flower, she climbed on.

The exertion required a different use of her arms and shoulders than she had become accustomed to, and soon the injury on her back began to leak fluid again. It did not hurt as much as it had, though she could feel the skin pull every time she reached for a new handhold. The tickle of liquid down her spine was distracting and annoying, but there was nothing she could do about it. Twice she saw birds that would have been easy prey for her if she'd had a bow, and once she hastily dropped down to a lower limb and changed trees when she came across a large constrictor snake who lifted his head and eyed her with interest. At that moment, she decided that her decision to sleep on the raft instead of in the trees had been a good one.

She was looking for a good horizontal branch to allow her to cross to another tree when she encountered Nortel. He was sitting on the branch that was her chosen path, and from the way he greeted her, she suspected he'd seen her and watched her progress down the trunk.

"Find anything to eat?" he asked her.

"Not yet. I got some water from a trumpet vine, but I haven't found any fruit or nuts yet."

He nodded slowly, then asked her, "Are you alone?"

She shrugged and wondered why his question made her uncomfortable. "Yes. Everyone else was asleep."

"I wasn't."

"Well, you were talking to Boxter. And I like to hunt and forage alone. I always have." She took another step toward him, but he made no sign of moving to allow her to pass him on the branch. It was wide enough that he could easily have moved to one side. Instead, he remained perched where he was, looking up at her. She didn't know Nortel well; she'd never realized his eyes were green. He was not as scaled as most of the other boys, and what he did have, around his eyes, was very fine. When he blinked, his lashes caught the light and sparked silver at her.

After a long moment, he said, "I'm sorry about Rapskal. I know you two were close."

She looked away from him. She was trying not to think of Rapskal and Heeby and whether they had died quickly or struggled for a long time in the water. "I'll miss him," she said. Her voice went thick and tight on the words. "But today is today, and I need to see what food I can find. May I get past you, please?"

"Oh. Of course." Instead of just sliding to one side, he stood up. He was taller than she was. He turned sideways on the branch and motioned that she should edge past him. She hesitated. Was there a challenge in how he stood there or was she imagining it?

She decided she was being silly. She edged past him, sliding her feet and facing him as she did so. She was halfway past him when he shifted slightly. She dug her toenails into the bark of the branch and hissed in alarm. He immediately caught her by the arms and held her facing him. His grip on her arms was firm, and she was closer to him than she wanted to be. "I wouldn't let you fall," he promised her, his face solemn. His green eyes bored down into hers.

"I wasn't about to fall. Let go."

He didn't. They were frozen in a tableau, looking at each other. A struggle would almost certainly mean that one or both of them would fall. The smile on his face was warm, the look in his eyes inviting.

"I'm getting angry. Let go now."

The warmth faded from his eyes, and he granted her request. But he slid his hand down her arm before he lifted it away. She hopped past him, resisting the urge to give him a slight shove as she did so.

"I didn't mean to make you angry," he said. "It's just . . . well, Rapskal is gone. And I know you're alone now. So am I."

"I've always been alone," she told him furiously and then strode off along the branch. She wasn't fleeing, she reminded herself, only leaving him behind. When she reached the next trunk, she went up it more quickly than a lizard and refused to look back to see if he was watching her climb. Instead, she concentrated on climbing higher, heading for the upper reaches of the canopy where more sunlight increased the chances of finding fruit.

Fortune favored her. She found a bread leaf vine parasitizing a handprint tree. The fat yellow leaves didn't offer much flavor, but they were filling and crisp with moisture as well. For a time, she perched and ate her fill, then tore several trailing strings of leaves from it. She wound the vines into a loose wreath and put them around her neck hanging down her back.

She started back down and on the way saw a sour pear tree only a few trunks away. She crossed to it. The fruit was past its prime and slightly wrinkly, but she doubted her friends would be fussy. With no other way to carry it, she filled the front of her shirt and then went more slowly, trying to avoid crushing the food she carried. When she reached the tree by the river's edge and climbed down to the flotsam raft, she was surprised to find that many of the keepers were still sleeping. Tats was awake; he and Greft were trying to kindle a small fire at the root end of one of the big snags. A thin tendril of smoke wound up into the morning air. As she approached, she saw Sylve and Harrikin crouched at the edge of the packed driftwood. She watched as Sylve reached out with a long stick and then dragged something closer. It wasn't until she was near that she realized they were pulling dead fish from the river. Harrikin was cleaning them, sticking a claw in each belly, slitting it open, and scooping out the guts before adding it to the row of fish beside him.

"Where are the dragons?" she called anxiously to them.

Sylve turned to her and gave her a weary smile. "There you are! I thought I'd dreamed you telling me you were going hunting, but then you were gone when I woke all the way. The acid run killed a lot of fish and other creatures. The dragons have moved upriver. They've discovered an eddy full of carrion and are eating their fill. I'm glad there's something for them. They're tired from treading water and so much swimming, but at least they won't be hungry after this. Even Mercor was beginning to be bad-tempered, and I was afraid a couple of the bigger males were going to fight this morning."

"Did Sintara go with them?"

"They all went, each more jealous than the next, to be sure of getting a fair share. What did you bring?"

"Bread leaf and sour pear. My shirt is full of sour pear. I couldn't think of any other way to carry them."

Sylve laughed. "We'll be glad to have them, no matter how you got them here. Greft and Tats are trying to get enough of a fire going that we can cook the fish. If it doesn't work, I suppose raw will have to do."

"Better than nothing, certainly."

Harrikin had been quiet through their conversation. He was never much of a talker. The first time she had seen him, he had reminded her of a lizard. He was long and slender, and much older than Sylve, but she seemed very comfortable with him. Thymara had not realized that he, too, had claws, until she watched him using them. He looked up from his task, caught her eyes on his hands, and nodded an acknowledgment to her.

A little silence fell over the group. Unanswered questions were answered by it. No one spoke of Rapskal, and in the distance, she heard Alum's dragon give a long, anxious cry. Arbuc still called for his missing keeper. Warken's red dragon, Baliper, held his mourning silence. The remaining keepers were still marooned on a raft of floating debris. Nothing had changed. Thymara wondered in passing what would become of them if their dragons abandoned them here. Would they? Did the dragons need them any longer? What if they decided to travel on without them?

She looked up to see Tats coming toward them and wondered if she looked as bad as he did. His skin was scalded red from the river water, and his hair stuck up in tufts. The water had attacked his clothing as well, mottling the already-worn shirt and trousers. He looked haggard, but he still managed to put on a smile for her. "What are you wearing?" he asked her.

"Our breakfast. Bread leaf and sour pear. Looks like you have a fire going for the fish."

He glanced back to the little blaze that Greft tended. Jerd had come from somewhere to join him. She leaned against him quietly as he broke dry bits of root from the end of the snag and fed it to the small fire he'd kindled in the main nest of roots. "It wasn't easy to get it going. And the fear is that if we succeed too well, it may spread to the rest of the debris pack and send us fleeing again. We don't have much security here, but at least we're still afloat."

"And the water is going down. But if we must, we would take to the trees. Here. Hold your shirt out."

Tats lifted the front of his shirt to form a sling, and Thymara reached down her own shirt front to extract the sour pears she had carried inside her shirt against her belly. The wrinkled fruit were no relation to true pears, but she had heard that the flavor was similar. When she had emptied her shirt into his, she followed him back to Greft's fire. She feared there would be awkwardness when she got there, comments or mockery, but Jerd only turned away from her while Greft said simply, "Thanks. Any chance of more?"

"These are past the season, but I could probably find more on the tree. And where one bread leaf vine grows, there are usually others."

"That's good to know. Until we know more of our situation, we're going to have to manage whatever food we can acquire carefully."

"Well, there's plenty of dead fish floating in the river. The current is pushing the floaters up against the debris pack." This was from Sylve. She and Harrikin carried a line of fish suspended by a stick shoved through their gills.

"They won't be good much more than a day or so," Harrikin observed quietly. "The acid in the water is already softening them. We probably shouldn't try to eat the skin, only the meat."

Thymara removed her garland of bread leaf vine and began to strip the leaves from them methodically. Tats had already divvied the fruit into piles. Now he began to deal the leaves out as well. With the fish, each keeper would have an adequate breakfast. There was no sense worrying about dinner just yet.

Greft seemed to have the same thought. "We should hold some food back for later," he suggested.

"Or we can give each keeper a share and tell them, 'that's it for the day, ration yourself,'" Tats countered.

"Not everyone will have the self-discipline to be wise about it," Greft spoke the words, but it didn't sound like an argument. Thymara suspected they were continuing an earlier discussion.

"I don't think any one of us has the authority to ration the food," Tats said.

"Not even if we've provided it?" Greft pushed.

"Thymara!"

She turned her head to Alise's voice. The Bingtown woman teetered awkwardly along one of the logs. Thymara winced to look at her. Her face was pebbled with blisters and her red hair was a tangled mat that dangled halfway down her back. Always before, Alise had been so clean and well groomed. "Where did you go?" she demanded when she was still most of a log away.

"Out to look for food."

"By yourself? Isn't that dangerous?"

"Not usually. I almost always hunt or gather alone."

"But what about wild animals?" Alise sounded genuinely concerned for her.

"Up where I travel, I'm one of the larger creatures. As long as I watch out for the big snakes, tree cats, and little poisonous things, I'm pretty safe." She thought briefly of Nortel. No. She didn't intend to mention that incident at all.

"There are other dangers besides wild animals," Greft observed darkly.

Thymara glanced at him in annoyance. "I've been moving through the trees all my life, Greft, and usually much higher in the canopy than I went today. I'm not going to fall."

"He's not worried about you falling," Tats said in a quiet voice.

"Then someone should say plainly what he *is* worried about," Thymara observed sourly. They seemed to be talking about her and deliberately making the words go past her without meaning.

Greft glanced at Alise and away. "Perhaps later," he said, and Thymara saw Alise bridle. His words and look had pointed her out as an outsider, someone not to be brought into keeper affairs. Whatever it was that was chafing him, Thymara already wanted to defy whatever older, male wisdom he intended to inflict on her. From the look on Jerd's face, he had annoyed her as well. She shot Thymara a look that was full of venom, but Thymara could not master the coldness to be angry at her. Grief for her missing dragon had ravaged Jerd. Her tears had left scarlet tracks down her face. Impulsively, she addressed her directly.

"I'm sorry about Veras. I hope she manages to rejoin us. There are already so few female dragons."

"Exactly," Greft said, as if that proved some point for him.

But Jerd looked at her, weighed her comment, and decided Thymara was sincere. "I can't feel her. Not clearly. But it doesn't feel like she's gone, either. I'm afraid that she's injured somewhere. Or just disoriented and unable to find her way back to us."

"It will be all right, Jerd," Greft said soothingly. "Don't distress yourself. It's the last thing you need right now."

This time both Thymara and Jerd shot him furious looks.

"I'm only thinking of you," he said defensively.

"Well, I'm thinking and speaking about my dragon," Jerd replied.

"Perhaps we'd best get the fish cooking before the fire burns too low," Sylve suggested, and the alacrity with which the fish were taken up and fixed on wooden skewers over the fire attested to how uncomfortable the near quarrel was making everyone.

"Have you asked the other dragons if they can feel her?" Sylve asked Jerd as they began to ferry the cooked fish and other foods from the fire to the main raft. Boxter had found shelf mushrooms and onion-moss to share, welcome additions to an otherwise bland meal.

Jerd shook her head mutely.

"Well, my dear, you should!" Alise smiled at her. "Sintara and Mercor would be the best ones to approach with this. I'll ask Sintara for you, shall I?"

The words were said so innocently, with such a hopeful helpfulness. Thymara bit down on her anger. "Do you really think so?"

"Of course. Why wouldn't she?"

"Well, because she is Sintara," Thymara replied, and Sylve laughed.

"I know what you mean. Just when I think I understand Mercor and that he will do any simple favor I ask of him, he asserts he is a dragon and not my plaything. But I think he might help with this."

Jerd struggled for a moment and then asked quietly, "Would you ask him, then? I didn't think to ask the other dragons. It just seemed to me that I should know if she is alive or dead. I should be able to feel it, without help."

"Are you that close to Veras?" Thymara asked and tried not to let envy creep into her voice.

"I thought I was," Jerd said quietly. "I thought I was."

ALISE LOOKED AROUND the circle of dragon keepers. In her hands, she held two broad, thick leaves topped with a piece of partially cooked fish. A mushroom and a tangle of shaggy greenery topped the fish. She balanced a fruit that Thymara had called a "sour pear" on her leg. They'd given her the same share that any other keeper had received. She'd slept alongside them and now ate with them, but she knew that, despite her efforts, she was not one of them. Thymara did not make as much of their differences as the others did, but the girl still deferred to her in a way that kept her at a distance. She felt that Greft resented her, but if she'd had to say why, the only reason she would come up with was that she was not of the Rain Wilds. It made her feel desperately alone.

And being so useless did not make it any easier.

She envied how quickly the others seemed to have adapted and then reacted to their situation. They shifted their lives and responded to recover from the disaster so quickly that she felt both old and inflexible in comparison. And they spoke so little of their losses. Jerd wept, but she did not endlessly rant. The calm the keepers showed seemed almost unnatural. She wondered if it was the response of people who had grown up with near disaster at every turn. Quakes were not a rarity to them, any more than they were to the people of Bingtown. But all knew that in the Rain Wilds, quakes were more dangerous. So many of the Rain Wilders worked underground, salvaging Elderling artifacts as they unearthed the buried halls and chambers of the ancient cities. Cave-ins and collapses were sometimes triggered by quakes; had the keepers been inured to loss from an early age?

She wished they had been less reticent. She wanted to howl at the moon, to shake and rant, to weep hopelessly and fall apart. She longed to talk about the *Tarman* and Captain Leftrin, to ask if they thought the ship had survived, to ask if they expected the captain to come searching. As if talking about rescue could make it a reality! It would have been strangely comforting to discuss it all, over and over. Yet in the face of all these youngsters simply dealing with this disaster, how could she?

She picked the steaming fish apart with her fingers and ate it with bites of the mushroom and strands of the onion-moss. It did, indeed, have the flavor of onions. When she finished, she ate the "plate" it had been served on. The bread leaf was untrue to its name; there was nothing of "bread" about it. It was thick and starchy and crisp, but to her palate, unmistakably vegetable. When she finished it, she was still hungry. The sour pear at least helped her with her thirst. Despite its wrinkled skin, the fruit was juicy. She ate it right down to its core and only wished there was more.

Yet with every bite, her thoughts were elsewhere. Was Leftrin all right? Had the *Tarman* weathered the wave? Poor Sedric would be frantic with worry about her. Were they looking for them right now? She wanted to believe that, wanted to believe it so desperately that she realized she hadn't been exerting herself to better their situation. Captain Leftrin and the *Tarman* would come to rescue them. Ever since Sintara had plucked her out of the water, she'd believed that.

"When the water goes down, do you think there will be solid land here?" she asked Thymara.

Thymara swallowed her food and considered the question. "The water is going down, but we won't know about land until it goes all the way down. Even if there is land, it will be mud for some time. Floods come up quickly in the Rain Wilds, and go away slowly, because the earth is already saturated with water. We won't be able to walk on it, if that is what you are thinking. Not for any great distance."

"So. What are we going to do?"

"For now? For now, those of us who can forage or hunt will.

The others will do what they can to make things more comfortable here. And when the water goes down, well, then we'll see what else is to be done."

"Will the dragons want to continue our journey?"

"I don't think they'll want to stay here," Tats said. Alise realized he was not the only one listening in on their conversation. Most of the keepers within earshot were focused on his words. "There's nothing for them here. They'll want to move on, if they can. With us or without us."

"Can they survive without us?" The question came from Boxter.

"Not easily, not well. But they've mostly led the way, and mostly found the resting places each night. They've learned to hunt a bit. They're stronger and tougher now than when we started. It wouldn't be easy, but none of this journey has been easy for them. I don't say they'd choose to go on without us."

Tats paused. Alise waited, but Thymara was the one to continue his thought. "But if we cannot go on with them, if we have no way to accompany them, then they'll really have no choice. Food will run short here for them. They'll have to leave us."

"Couldn't they carry us?" Alise asked. "Sintara rescued Thymara and me and carried both of us to safety. It wasn't easy for her to swim with us. But if they were wading through the shallows as they usually do . . ."

"No, they wouldn't," Greft decided.

"It would compromise their dignity too much," Thymara said quietly. "Sintara saved us. But to her, that is different from acting as a beast of burden and carrying us along."

"Mercor might carry me," Sylve injected. "But he has a different nature from the others. He is kinder to me than most of the dragons are to their keepers. Sometimes I feel like he is the eldest of them, even though I know he came out of his case on the same day."

"Perhaps because he remembers more," Alise dared to suggest. "He seems very wise to me."

"Perhaps," Sylve agreed and for the first time shared a shy smile.

"If the dragons go on without us, what becomes of us?" Nortel asked suddenly. He had moved closer to Thymara. He seemed focused on the discussion, but his proximity still made her uncomfortable.

"We survive as best we can," Tats said. "Right here. Or in whatever place we can find."

"It would not be so different from how Trehaug was founded," Greft pointed out. "The original population of the Rain Wilds were forcibly marooned here by the ships that were supposed to help them find a good spot to start a colony. Of course, there were more of them, but still, it's similar."

"Wouldn't you try to return to Trehaug?" Alise asked. "You have three boats." To her, it seemed the obvious course of action, if the dragons abandoned them. It would be an arduous trek, either slogging through mud and swamp or traveling through the trees, but at least safety beckoned at the end.

"I wouldn't," Greft said quietly. "Not even if we had enough boats to carry us all and paddles to steer them."

"Nor I," Jerd echoed him. After a moment, with a small catch in her throat, she added, "I couldn't."

Alise watched as Greft took her hand. Jerd turned her head away from him and looked out across the water. Alise noticed unwillingly that some of the keepers openly spied on the two while others looked away. Plainly they were a couple, and it was equally plain that this bothered some of the keepers. Thymara watched them, her eyes hooded and her thoughts private.

"That's a decision that's a long ways from now," Tats declared. "I'm more concerned about what we're going to do today and tonight."

"I'm going foraging," Thymara said quietly. "It's what I'm good at."

"I'll go with you, to help carry," Tats declared. Across the circle, several of the young men glanced at him and then away. Nortel looked down, glowering. Boxter looked thoughtful. Greft opened his mouth as if to say something and then closed it again. Then he said, "A good plan," but Alise was certain that was not what he had originally planned to say.

"Is there any way that we can have a fire tonight?" Sylve asked. "The smoke might keep off some of the insects, and the fire might be a beacon if anyone is trying to find us."

"I could help with that," Alise declared instantly. "We could construct a little raft, like the sleeping raft, only smaller, and put the fire on that, so there'd be no chance of it spreading to where we're sleeping. We could tether it with some of these creepers." She leaned over and picked up one of the bread leaf vines, now stripped of food. "We'd need more, of course."

"We'll bring back more vines," Tats volunteered.

"Harrikin and I can dive for mud. If we can find a way to bring it up, we'll plaster mud on the fire platform, and it will last longer," Lecter said.

"But the water's so acid!" Alise objected, thinking of their eyes. Both of the youths were so scaled she didn't think their skin would take much harm.

"It's not so bad." Lecter shrugged his spiny shoulders. "Acid level is going down all the time. Sometimes it's like that after a quake. Big gush of acid water, then back to almost normal."

Almost normal was still enough to scald Alise's skin, but she nodded. "Build a platform, plaster it with mud, gather the driest wood we can find, and braid a good tether so it doesn't get away from us. That's a lot to get done before nightfall."

"It's not like we have an alternative," Boxter observed.

"Thymara. Do you want help with your gathering?" Nortel threw the question out almost as a challenge.

"If I need any, I have Tats," the girl replied.

"I can climb better than him," Nortel asserted.

"You only think so," Tats responded instantly. "I can give her any help she needs."

Thymara glanced from Tats to Nortel and her face darkened. For a moment, her scales seemed to stand out more vividly. Then she said flatly, "The truth is, I don't think I'll need help from either of you. But Tats can come with me if he wishes. I'm leaving now, while the light is good."

She stood as she spoke, flowing effortlessly to her feet, and strode off toward the forest without looking back. To Alise, she

seemed almost to dance across the floating logs between her and
the closest tree trunks. Once she reached one, she went up as
quickly as a lizard. Tats followed her, and it seemed to Alise that
he struggled hard to match her speed as his human hands found
grips on the rough bark of the tree.

As Nortel rose, Greft spoke. "Nortel, we could use you here,
to help put the fire raft together."

Nortel froze. He said flatly, "I intend to go foraging for food."

"See that food is all you forage for. We are a small group,
Nortel. We cannot quarrel among ourselves."

"Tell that to Tats," he said and then walked away. He chose
a different tree trunk for his ascent, but Alise suddenly feared
for Thymara and wished she could go after them. Something
had changed in the group, and she wasn't sure what it was. She
glanced at Greft, but he did not meet her eyes. Instead he said,
"Today is clear and tonight probably will be as well. But there
is no telling what weather tomorrow may bring. We're uncomfortable enough without being wet. Let's see if we can make a
shelter."

Alise felt as if she had been plunged into the intimate affairs of
an extended family she didn't know well. There were currents
here she hadn't suspected, and she abruptly wondered what her
status was as an intruder. Thymara was the only one she felt she
knew at all. She glanced at Sylve; the girl had at least smiled at
her. As if she felt the older woman's eyes, Sylve turned to her and
said quietly, "Let's go build our fire platform."

"TELL HER TO extend her head toward me!" Jess barked at him.
He was perched at the end of the log, holding his makeshift
noose open. "I can't get this around her neck if she doesn't reach
her head toward me."

The log Sedric was standing on shifted slightly under him,
and he felt a moment of vertigo. He looked up at the noose
and tried to make a firm decision. Abruptly, he gave his head
a shake, snapping himself out of that peculiar drifting state the
dragon could put him in. Just end it. She'd be dead, he'd have

his mind to himself and a fortune in his pocket. He could have Hest. If he still wanted him after all this.

That last thought shocked him. Of course he wanted Hest. He'd always wanted Hest, hadn't he? Wasn't Hest and the love he felt for him what all this was about? He cleared his throat. The love he'd felt . . .

"Relpda."

She swung her swirling gaze to him.

Jess shook the noose out larger. Sedric could see his intent now. Noose her, snub the line off, and kill her. It wasn't going to be pretty or easy. Before she died, she would know he had betrayed her. He'd feel the pain of that, her anger and reproach, right alongside the pain of her death. She'd saved his life. And his thanks to her was that he was going to profit from her death.

The price was too high. Hest wasn't worth it.

The shock of that realization jolted him; no time to dwell on it.

He reached toward the dragon, mind and heart. *Relpda, get away from Jess. Don't let him get near you. He wants to kill you!* He dared not speak aloud to her.

Kill? Alarm. And confusion. She hadn't understood. The exhausted dragon clung to the log and stared up at her executioner. Her eyes spun faster suddenly, but she made no move to get away. It was too much for her, he'd tried to put too much information in the thoughts he sent her. Keep it simple. And have some courage!

"Relpda, get away! Flee! Don't let him near you. Danger. Danger from him!"

Danger? Hunter bring food. Run away? Too tired.

He'd tipped his hand to the hunter, and it still wasn't going to be enough to save her. Jess's teeth showed in a snarl as he turned toward Sedric. "You damn little fop! I was going to make it quick for her. Well, you've spoiled that and now you'll both pay."

The hunter was quick. He dropped the noose and shifted his grip to the fish spear. It was a small weapon; it couldn't possibly hurt her. Please, Sa! "Relpda, get away! Go now!"

Sedric was already in motion, but he knew he'd never get there in time. He grabbed a stick floating in the water and flung it at Jess. Not even close. The hunter laughed aloud, then drew back the spear and plunged it into the dragon.

A blast of pain shot through Sedric. It stabbed him in the top of his shoulder, and his left arm suddenly went numb. He stumbled and went down, one of his legs slipping between the floating pieces of wood. His frantic snatch at a log kept him from going under completely. He bit his tongue, and strangely the one pain drove the other way. The log bucked, but he got a leg over it and struggled up from the water, looking around wildly. Everything was happening too fast.

Relpda trumpeted shrilly. The fish spear stuck out of her, and brilliant scarlet blood was sheeting over her scaled shoulder. Her wings were half open and she flapped them, splashing feebly as she struggled to keep her sliding grip on the log. The hunter was in the water. One of her flailing wings must have hit him and knocked him in. Good. But he had already caught hold of a log and was starting to drag himself up. In another moment he'd be on the raft with them. Sedric knew he couldn't fight him. The man was too big, too strong, too experienced. *Weapon, weapon!* The hatchet! The hatchet by the boat.

Sedric danced across the wildly rocking wood in a frantic race for the boat. If he had not been terrified, he would have crossed the debris raft on his hands and knees. But faced with imminent death, he leaped and dashed like a scalded cat, traversing logs that bobbed and tried to roll, leaping wildly from one to the next. Jess seemed instantly to divine Sedric's intention. He hauled himself up, cursing and spitting, and hurled himself in furious leaps across the packed driftwood. Twice the hunter went down between logs and hauled himself up again, and still he managed to stand suddenly between Sedric and the small boat, a knife held blade out and low in his dripping right hand. Water streamed from his hair and down the sides of his scaled face as he promised Sedric, "I'm going to cut you and string your guts across this driftwood pack and leave you to die here."

I'm sorry. Please don't kill me. I just want to live. I couldn't let you kill her. His mind flipped through a hundred things to say and discarded them all as useless.

Flee! Flee! the copper trumpeted at him. It seemed an excellent idea and perfectly aligned with Sedric's own impulse, but he dared not turn his back on the man. If he was going to die, it wasn't going to be with a knife in his back. He heard an immense splash as Relpda lost her precarious perch on the log and went under. *Cold, wet, dark, no air.* For that instant, Sedric froze.

Jess dived at him, knife leading the way, and it was the man's spring forward on the floating log that propelled Sedric's sudden sideways lurch. The knife, hand, and man went past him, not meeting the expected resistance. It was the impulse of a moment to put his hand on Jess's back and shove as the hunter plunged past him. The hunter stepped off the log, onto the floating mat of driftwood. For a moment the tangled morass of weeds and wood held him up and then he dropped down through it with a furious shout. He flung his arms wide and splayed them out on the floating branches, twigs, and moss clumps. Somehow he stayed above water, cursing at Sedric, unable to clamber out.

In two steps, Sedric was in the boat. He'd thought it would feel solid under him. Instead, as he jumped into it, it lurched and bucked. He fell, knees down, onto the thwarts, catching his ribs painfully. Safe. Safe in the boat. Where was the hatchet? And where was Relpda? "Dragon, where are you?" he shouted. He stood up on his knees, looking all around. To his horror, he could not feel her. And Jess had vanished, too. Was he drowning under the mat? It was hard to feel sorry for him.

Suddenly, like a vengeful water spirit, Jess shot up and out of the water right next to the small boat. He caught hold of the side. As he dragged himself up, the boat heeled over and Sedric cried out in terror that he'd be spilled into the stinging water again. Instead, the big wet man levered himself into the boat. Sedric immediately tried to abandon the small ship, but Jess tackled him around the legs. He fell hard, slamming his ribs and belly against the edge of the boat and the driftwood log it was tied to. The hunter grabbed him by the back of his shirt and his hair, jerked him back into the boat, and hit him, hard, in the face.

Other than some boyish scuffles, Sedric had never been in a real fight. Sometimes Hest was rough with him, when he was in a mood to take their engagement in a harsher direction and enforce his dominance. In their early days together, Sedric had been aroused by such rough play. But in the last year or so, Hest had seemed to reserve it for times when Sedric had displeased him in some other arena. There had been a few times when the thrill of feeling Hest's aggression had changed into the dread that his lover would do real damage to him in the throes of his tigerish play. Worse, Hest seemed to relish waking that fear in Sedric. Once, Hest had throttled him nearly unconscious yet had not paused in his own pursuit of pleasure. It was only when he had rolled away from him that Sedric had been able to shift to where he could get a clear breath. With black spots dancing before his eyes, he'd gasped out, "Why?"

"To see what it would be like, of course. Stop whining. You're not hurt; you've just had your feelings ruffled."

Hest had risen and left him there. And Sedric had accepted Hest's judgment that he wasn't truly hurt. The recollection flashed through his mind and with it, the resolution he'd buried shortly afterward. *Never again. Fight back.*

But Jess's attack was beyond anything Hest had ever done to him. To be struck so hard in the face shocked him as much as stunned him. He hung in the hunter's grip, trying to find the strength to lift his hands, let alone make fists of them. Then the man laughed aloud, and the sound filled Sedric with a panicky strength. He shot his fist forward as hard as he could into the center of the Jess's body, just below his breastbone. Jess let out a sudden whuff of air and sat down hard in the boat.

For half a breath Sedric was on top of the hunter, raining blows on him, but he was dazed and could not put any strength behind them. Jess lunged up and wrapped his arms around Sedric. Then, as effortlessly as if Sedric were a child, he rolled with him, trapping him beneath his weight. Then the hunter's heavy hands settled around his throat. Sedric's own hands rose to catch at the man's thick wrists. They were wet and cold and slickly scaled; he could not get a grip on them. The man forced him down and back across the seat in the middle of the boat, pushing him into the rancid bilgewater as the seat bit into his back. He kicked wildly, but his feet connected with nothing. He clawed at the man's face, but the hunter's skin seemed impervious to pain or penetration.

Sedric gave up trying to attack Jess or even to defend himself. All he wanted to do was escape. His flailing hands groped for the side of the boat. One hand gripped it, and he tried to pull himself out from under and away from Jess. But the man's hands were locked on his throat and his weight pressed him down.

Sedric had never felt so powerless.

Not since the last time Hest had held him down and laughingly told him, "I'll decide how it's going to be. You'll like it. You always do."

But he didn't. Not always. And suddenly all the anger he'd ever felt at Hest for not caring if he enjoyed it or not, for laughing at him when he dominated him, rushed through him just as his desperately groping hand found the handle of the hatchet.

It was stuck firmly in the hard dry log that floated beside the boat, but his was the strength of desperate anger. He jerked at it spasmodically. Luck, not intent, decreed that as it suddenly bucked loose, the heavy blunt end of it connected with the back of Jess's skull.

It startled the hunter more than stunned him. His grip slacked and through a red mist, Sedric saw Jess roll his head to one side as if to look for an unsuspected attacker. *Fight him. Fight him.* The dragon's furious thoughts fed him strength. He swung the hatchet again, awkwardly, but with deliberate force and direction. It connected, this time with the hunter's jaw, knocking it sideways with a loud crack. Jess shrieked. Sedric dragged a deep breath, then half of a second one into his lungs. Jess was making noises, but Sedric's ears were ringing and Jess's diction was ruined by the hatchet hitting him yet again. And suddenly Sedric heard himself croaking out, "I'll kill you! I'll kill you."

I'll kill for you. That thought bounced back to him, a reptilian echo.

A last flailing strike hit the hunter between the eyes, and that did stun him. Sedric dropped the heavy hatchet into the bottom of the boat. He pushed hard at Jess and the man flopped off him with a groan, half over the low side of the boat. He was only unconscious for a moment. "You bas—!" he croaked. He drew back his arm, and all Sedric could see was a meaty fist headed toward him.

Then an immense splash rocked the boat. Relpda's head and shoulders shot up out of the matted debris to tower momentarily over the boat. *Hunter food!* she announced and bent her head. Sedric had never really seen the inside of a dragon's maw before. She opened her jaws impossibly wide, and he could see inside, see the immense swallowing muscles at the sides of her throat, and the row of sharp teeth that curved inward. Her mouth came down over the hunter's head and shoulders like a poacher popping a sack over a rabbit. He had one brief glimpse of Jess's eyes so wide that the whites showed all around them. Then Relpda closed her jaws.

There was a sound, a sound between a shearing of bone and a crushing of meat. Relpda's head rose, and she pointed her muzzle at the sky. Her head jerked twice as she swallowed.

Jess's bloody hips and legs fell into the boat beside Sedric. He kicked at them in reflexive horror and the pelvis flopped over the side, followed by the legs. Relpda gave a squeal of protest and dived after them. The wave of her passage rocked the boat wildly. Blood and water mingled in the bottom of the boat, sloshing back and forth around the dropped hatchet.

Sedric leaned over the side of the boat, staring after them. "That didn't happen," he slurred. He lifted the back of his hand to his mouth and then took it away. Bloody. He turned his head and looked at the hatchet in the boat's bilgewater. Blood streamed from it in tiny threads and mingled with the water. There was hair on it, too. Jess's hair. "I killed him," he said aloud. The words came strangely to his ears.

Delicious.

THE AFTERNOON PASSED without incident. Thymara and Tats didn't talk much. She didn't have much to say, and keeping up with her left Tats short of wind. She made sure of that.

The way her feelings about him vacillated bothered her more than her actual emotions. When she was around the others, it was easier to pretend that nothing had changed between them. Did that mean that perhaps nothing really *had* changed? Was she angry at him or not? And if she was, what was the reason? Sometimes, she could see that she had no real basis for her anger. There had been no mutual understanding between them. He had not broken any promise to her. Surely he was free to do as he pleased, just as she was. She could be dispassionate about it. He'd mated with Jerd. That was their business, not hers. And now that Jerd was with Greft, it had even less to do with her.

But then her hurt would break through, and she'd feel indignant and slighted all over again. The least he could have done was let her know sooner. If Rapskal had known of it, how private could it have been? Why had he let her be ignorant of it so long? It made her feel so stupid, so naive. *My pride,* she thought. *It's my pride that's broken, not my heart. I'm not in love with him. I don't want an exclusive claim on him. I don't want him to claim me. We are just friends, friends who have known each other for a long time. And he kept a secret from me and made me feel stupid.* Just her pride. That was all.

It might be true, but it wasn't what it felt like.

Spurred by emotion, she climbed higher and more swiftly through the trees than she usually would, making Tats struggle to keep up with her. She found food and by the time he caught up with her, she had gathered most of it. Tats had fashioned his shirt into a crude carry-sack. As soon as he arrived, she packed whatever she had found into it and moved on. Other than discussing what food she had found and what they might next look for, there had been little conversation. She could see that Tats was aware she wasn't really talking to him, but he seemed content to leave the situation alone.

They returned to the floating morass that was their current sanctuary just as it became too dark to see under the trees. On the river, there was still some light from a distant sunset. The others had been successful, both in raising a small shelter on their raft, and in creating another platform for their floating fire. The yellow light it cast was cheering. As Alise had suggested, it was tethered to their sleeping raft in such a way that it could be quickly shoved away if the fire began to spread. For now, the welcome light and warmth it gave off cheered everyone. Boxter and Kase were tending it, stripping branches of leaves and tossing them on the fire to create a haze of smoke to drive insects away. Thymara was not certain that she preferred eye-watering smoke to stinging insects, but she was too weary to argue with them about it.

The dragons had returned for the night. It was somewhat comforting to see their hulking silhouettes braced against the trees that barred them from entering the flooded forest. They were becoming more adept at capturing their own timbers and hooking their rib cages over them to float. She wondered if they had come back because they missed the humans, or only because they knew their keepers would help shore them up and keep them afloat for the night. Sylve and Harrikin seemed to have devised a technique for trapping several logs under a dragon's chest. The dragons were not thrilled with their night's lodgings, but it was better than treading water. The acid-killed fish had proven both a boon and a liability to the dragons. They had eaten to satiation, but their bulging bellies were uncomfortable, and more so when braced against a log.

"And they're tired of being in the water. Really tired. Some are complaining that their claws are getting soft," Sylve said as she sat next to Thymara when they ate that night. To her surprise there had been meat to cook as well as the fruit and vegetation that she and Tats had foraged. A disoriented riverpig, half drowned and stupid with weariness, had climbed right out on their raft. Lecter had clubbed it. It had not been a large animal, but it had been fat, and it tasted delicious to Thymara.

Greft walked behind them on his way to sitting down and commented, "There's no use their complaining about soft claws. No one can do anything about it."

Thymara rolled her eyes at Sylve, and the girl bent her head over her plate to hide a smile. "I'm sure the dragons will take that thought to heart," Thymara muttered to her, and they both laughed softly. She glanced up just in time to see Greft giving her a dark look. She returned his gaze with a flat stare and then went on with her eating. She didn't respect him, and she refused to quail before him.

The sleeping shelter was small, and the floor was very uneven despite a layer of leafy branches. The positive side of that was that everyone was a bit warmer when packed so closely together, but it also meant that no one could shift positions without disturbing two others. It had been decided that they would keep a watch on the fire outside, adding wood to feed it and adding leaves for smoke. "Flames to signal anyone who might be trying to find us. Smoke to keep the insects away," Greft had needlessly informed them all.

The task was trickier than Thymara had thought it would be. There was a layer of matted leaves and mud between the fire and the mass of floating wood that made its platform. When it was Thymara's turn to keep the watch, Sylve came to wake her and showed her how to feed the fire without letting it burn down deep into the lower part of its raft. Sylve left her sitting on the edge of the main raft with a plentiful supply of leafy branches and a stack of broken dry wood for the fire.

Thymara sighed as she settled into her task. Her back hurt, in a way that was different from her aching muscles. She'd pushed herself as well as Tats today; she had only herself to blame for her weariness. But she was very tired of the injury along her spine and the dull ache she endured at all hours.

Night had passed into its quietest hours. The evening birds had stopped their calls and swooping insect hunts and settled for the night. Even the buzzing, stinging insects seemed less prevalent. She watched the reflection of the firelight on the water. Occasionally, a curious fish would make a slow shadowy pass beneath the mirroring water, but for the most part, all was still and calm. The river lapped placidly against the logs as if it had not tried to kill all of them only a day and a half ago. The dragons looked like strange ships as they dozed, heads bent and half their bodies hanging under the water. She tried simply to enjoy the night without thinking, but her thoughts ranged from Rapskal to the silver dragon and back to Alum and Warken. Three of the keepers were missing and probably dead, and three dragons, all female. That was a blow. Veras had still not appeared; Mercor had told Sylve that he had not felt her die but that she should not take that as an assurance that Veras was still alive. It was maddening news to Jerd, and she had seemed more weepy rather than less after hearing it.

"I need to talk to you."

Thymara startled and then felt angry she had done so. Greft had ghosted up behind her; she hadn't even felt the raft rock as he approached her. It hadn't been an accident that she'd been unaware of him; he'd wanted to surprise her. She glanced up at him, keeping her face expressionless, and asked, "Do you?"

"Yes. For the good of us all, I need some answers from you. We all do." He hunkered down beside her, closer than she wanted him to be. "I'll put it simply. Is it to be Tats?"

"Is what to be Tats?" The question irritated her and she let him hear it in her voice. If he wanted to be mysterious and officious, then she could be obtuse.

His scaled face, always a study in flat planes, hardened. His lips were so narrow, it was hard to tell if he clenched his jaw or not. She suspected so. He crouched down beside her and spoke in a low growl. "Look. No one understood why you chose Rapskal, but I told them all that it didn't matter. You'd made your choice and we had to respect that. A few wanted to challenge him. I forbade it. You should appreciate that. I respected your first choice and kept the peace for you.

"But Rapskal is gone now. And for all our sakes, the sooner the matter is settled, the better it is for all of us. So choose and make it clear."

"I don't know what you're trying to say. But I think I prefer not to know. This is my watch and I'm doing my task. Go away." She spoke flatly, torn between anger and fear. Greft seemed somehow inevitable tonight, a force she must deal with, and a force she seemed unlikely to defeat. His words were either mysterious, or made a horrible sense. She didn't want to know which.

But he wouldn't spare her ignorance. "Don't pretend," he said harshly. "You aren't good at it. You heard me warn Nortel earlier today. If you've chosen Tats, well, then, you've chosen him. Make that choice plain to the others and there won't be any problems. I'll see to that. Tats isn't what I would have picked for you, but even in a time and place of new rules, I respect some of our oldest traditions. I was largely raised by my mother, and she kept the old rules, the rules from when the Rain Wilds were first settled. Back then the Traders agreed that a woman could stand on an equal footing with her husband and make her own choices. That I am alive today is due to my mother's choice. She kept me, and she demanded that others respect her right to do so. And so I see the wisdom of letting women have a say in their lives, and I'm willing to respect it. And to demand that others respect it also."

"And who made you the king?" she demanded. She was afraid now. Had she been blind to this, as well? Did the others accept him as leader, and beyond leader, as someone to set the rules and dictate their lives to them?

"I put myself in charge when it became plain to me that no one else was equal to the task. Someone has to make the decisions, Thymara. We can't all blithely go our own ways, letting things fall out as they may. Not if we hope to survive." He annoyed her by picking up wood and putting it on her fire. It caught almost immediately. She retaliated by poking it off the fire into the river, where it hissed and then bobbed next to the fire raft. He got her message.

"Fine. You can defy me. Well, you can try. But life and fate are what you can't defy. Fate has given us a bad balance here. Even with three males out of the picture, the ratio of keepers is still badly skewed. Do you want men to fight over you? Do you want to see our fellows injure one another, create lifelong vendettas with one another, so that you can feel valuable?" He turned his head and looked at her, his eyes dark and unreadable in the night. "Or are you waiting to be raped? Does that sort of thing excite you?"

"I don't want that! That's despicable!"

"Then you need to choose who you will accept as a partner. Now. Before all the males start competing for you. We are a small company. We can't afford to have boys hurting one another over you. Nor can we allow anyone to force you. Where that would lead, I can imagine only too well. Choose a mate and have it be over."

"Jerd didn't choose. She mated where she wanted." She flung it at him as the only weapon she could find. "Or didn't you know that?"

"I know that all too well!" he snarled back. "Why do you think I had to step in and take charge of her? She was being foolish, setting the men against one another. A black eye here, a bruised face there. It was starting to escalate. So I took her and made her mine, to keep the others from quarreling. She wasn't my first choice, if you want to hear me say that. I don't think she's as intelligent as you are. Nor as competent to survive. I let you know of my interest from the very beginning, but you preferred Rapskal the no-wit to me. I forced myself to accept that decision, even though I thought it was a poor one. Well, he's gone now. And I'm with Jerd, for better or worse, at least until the child is born. Because that is the only way I could force the others to stop striving to win her regard. I can't very well claim you as well. So before the rivalry and competition for your attention become violent, you'd best make a choice and stick to it."

Thymara's head whirled. A child? Jerd was pregnant? Was there a worse time and place to be pregnant? What had she been thinking? And before she drew another breath, she wondered angrily what any of the males had been thinking. Had any of them considered that they might be fathering a child? Or, like Rapskal and Tats, had it simply been a thing she was allowing them to do, and because they could, they did? Anger washed through Thymara.

"Who is the father of Jerd's child?"

"It doesn't matter really, does it? I'll claim it, and that will be that."

"I think you go about claiming too many things already. You may have appointed yourself king or leader, Greft, but I have not. I'll tell you bluntly, I don't accept your authority over me. And I am certainly not going to 'choose' one of the 'males' simply to stop the others from quarreling. If they are stupid enough to fight one another over something that is not theirs to claim, then let them."

She nearly stood up and walked away. But her watch was not over, and the fire was her responsibility. She looked at him flatly. "Go away. Leave me alone."

He shook his head. "You may wish it to be that simple, but it isn't. Wake up, Thymara. If you don't choose a protector and if I don't enforce your choice of one, who is going to protect you? We are alone out here, now more than ever. There are four females and seven males. Jerd is with me. Sylve has chosen Harrikin. If you think—"

"*Four* females? I can't believe what I'm hearing. Are you including Alise in your crazy plans?"

"She's here and she's female, so she's included. That choice isn't mine; it's simply the reality of what is. I'll let her adjust for a time before I speak with her about it. The reality is this, Thymara. We are all marooned here together. Just as the original Rain Wild settlers did, we will have to learn to make our homes here. This is where our children will be born and grow up. We, right now, this little huddle of sleeping people, are the seeds from which a new settlement will grow."

"You're insane."

"I am not. The difference between us is that you are very young, and you think that 'the rules' mean something when there is no law and punishment to back them up. They don't. If you don't choose someone and make that choice plain, then someone will choose you. Or several someones. And you'll either end up going to whoever battles his way to the right to claim you or being used by several men. I'd sooner not see the outcome of that."

"I choose no one."

He stood slowly, shaking his head. "I don't think that's an option for you, Thymara." He turned away from her and then turned back. He spoke disdainfully. "Perhaps Tats *is* the best match for you. You can probably make him wait and lead him about by the nose until it suits your fancy to come to his bed. But he isn't what I would choose for you and I'll tell you why, plainly. He's too tall; if he gives you a child, it will be too large for you to birth easily. I know you've said you won't listen to my advice, but I suggest that you look at Nortel. He is one of us in ways that Tats can never be, and he's more compatible in size. You don't have to be with him forever. It's possible that eventually you'll take a different mate, or possibly several in your lifetime."

He took a step away, then halted and looked back at her again. For a moment, his gaze seemed almost sympathetic. "Don't think this is something I'm imposing on you. I simply happen to see people and situations for what they are. While the rest of you were singing songs and telling stories about the fire, I was talking with Jess. There was a man with book education and ideas. I'm sorry he's gone. He opened my eyes to a lot of things, including how the greater world works. I know you think that I'm overbearing, Thymara. The truth is, I want us all to survive. I can't force you to do this. I can only point out to you that, right now, you have the opportunity to make a choice. Wait too long, even a few days more, and that choice may be taken from you. Once men have fought over you and one has claimed you, it will be too late for anyone to assert you have the right to choose your own mate. Then you'll have to live with what you have."

"You are monstrous!" she cried in a low voice.

"Life *is* monstrous," he replied imperturbably. "I was trying to make it less so for you. To make you aware that you should choose while you still can."

He moved quietly and gracefully across the shifting logs. She watched him reenter the shelter. All peace had gone out of her night. Did Jerd know the sorts of things he said about her? He'd preferred her. That thought sent a shiver down her spine, and not of the pleasant kind. She recalled now that she had initially found him attractive. It had been flattering to have an older man pay attention to her. But even then, she recalled, he had been talking of "changing the rules." Somehow his claim of honoring the Rain Wild traditions that women could determine their own futures rang false to her.

"I won't be pushed," she said aloud to the night. "If they fight one another, that's their problem, not mine. If any one of them thinks that somehow they can claim me that way, he's going to find out he's wrong."

She had not been aware of Sintara on the edge of her thoughts until the dragon responded sleepily, *Now you are thinking like a queen. There may be hope for you yet.*

✦ ✧ ✧

Day the 21st of the Prayer Moon

Year the 6th of the Independent Alliance of Traders
From Detozi, Keeper of the Birds, Trehaug
To Erek, Keeper of the Birds, Bingtown

Enclosed, from the Rain Wild Traders' Council at
Cassarick and from the Rain Wild Traders' Council
at Trehaug, a list of those confirmed dead from the
calamitous quake, flood, and collapses in the excavation
cities, said scroll to be posted in the Traders' Concourse
at Bingtown and to become part of the Traders' Records
there.

Erek,

*This is a substantial list. When you receive it, please take time to
sit down with my nephew Reyall and tell him gently that there
have been losses in our family. Two of his cousins were working
in the excavation at the time of the flood. No trace of either has
been found. These lads were his playmates as he was growing
up. This news may be hard for him, and the family wishes that
you may give him time to make a visit home and mourn with us.
I know it is hard to spare your apprentice, but if you can comply
with this request, you will have my everlasting gratitude.*

Detozi

✦ ✧ ✧

CHAPTER EIGHT

HORNS

The dragons woke her. Alise had heard nothing before their trumpeting calls jerked her from her slumbers. All around her in the crowded shelter, keepers were rolling to their knees. The raft shifted, and a wave of vertigo washed over her. She clenched her teeth. She missed her nights on the *Tarman,* when the barge was beached and the world was still beneath her. And she missed Leftrin, more than she dared think about.

The dragons trumpeted again, not in unison, but in a ragged response to a sound she hadn't heard. She heard Sintara's clear clarion call, and Mercor's bull bellow. Fente's note was a drawn-out shriek, while Nortel's lavender dragon made a sound like a bow thrumming. "What is it?" she asked, but only heard her question echoed in half a dozen voices. A jam of bodies trying to exit the shelter plunged her back into dimness and tipped the crude raft. She waited where she was, looking up at the blue sky through the crude roof woven of leafy branches and wondering if some new disaster was about to befall them all.

By the time she could join the others outside, all the dragons were roused. Among their excited trumpeting, in a small gap of quiet, she heard both the winding of a long horn call and the cry of another dragon. "Veras! It's Veras!" Jerd shrieked. She went scuttling over the packed logs, heading for the unstable edge of the floating debris pack, and Greft went scrambling after her. He caught her by the shoulders and held her back from falling in as Veras approached. In her wake, periodically blowing three short blasts on a horn, was one of the hunters from the *Tarman*. Alise's heart leaped and then sank at the sight of him. It was Carson, Leftrin's friend. But he was not Leftrin, and the barge was nowhere in sight.

A hail of questions peppered them both as they drew nearer. Carson didn't even attempt to reply. He abandoned blowing his horn and applied his efforts to his paddle to swiftly approach the shore. By the time he could toss a line to one of the awaiting keepers, Veras had already thrust her way into the packed debris and was allowing a weeping Jerd to stroke her face. Alise crowded forward with the keepers to hear what tidings he might bring.

"Are you all here and safe?" was his first question, and when Greft shook his head, the hunter's face fell into lines of disappointment.

"The *Tarman* and Captain Leftrin are just around the last bend. They should be showing any minute now. As soon as he's here, he'll take you on board and get a hot meal into you. Not much we can do for the dragons just yet, but the river's been dropping fast since dawn. I hope that by this evening, there will be some shallows where they can at least stand and take some rest."

Lecter had caught the rope and secured the small boat to their raft as Carson spoke. Now the hunter clambered nimbly from the boat to the raft and looked around at the gathered people, grinning. As he scanned the waiting faces, hope slowly died. "Who's missing?" he asked.

"Who's on board the *Tarman*?" Greft countered.

Carson looked annoyed with him but answered, "Captain Leftrin and the full crew came through just fine. Big Eider banged up his ribs some, but nothing's broken so far as we can tell. My boy Davvie's on board, too. We lost our other hunter, unless Jess is here with you. And what about Sedric? Is he here?"

"Sedric!" Alise gasped his name. Sedric was missing? She'd always thought he was safe on board the *Tarman*. He'd been there, in his cabin, when she left. How could he be missing, unless the barge had taken a terrible beating in the wave? Had his shelter been torn free, had he been drowned in his bed? The devastating news that Sedric was definitely missing collided with her joy that Leftrin was fine and would soon appear to rescue her. It was as if neither emotion would allow her to fully experience the other, and so she was trapped between them, feeling disloyal and numb. She worked her way around the clustered keepers and through them until she stepped out in front of Carson. At the sight of her, a sudden smile lit his face.

"Alise! You are here! Well, that will take away the captain's greatest fear." A light of cautious hope spread over his face. "And Sedric? Is he with you?"

She shook her head as Carson sidestepped Greft and came straight to her. She found her voice and tongue, though she could scarcely draw breath to push out the words. "I thought he was on the *Tarman*." A devastating guilt dizzied her. She'd made him come with her. And now he was missing. Dead. Sedric was no swimmer, no tree climber. He was dead. Unthinkable. Impossible. *Don't think on it, don't allow it to be real.* She cleared her throat, and her tongue babbled on without her. "Now that Veras has returned, we are missing only the copper dragon, the silver one, and Heeby. Of keepers, we've seen nothing of Rapskal, Alum, or Warken. Are any of them with you?"

A silence fell, and when Carson slowly shook his head, low groans and sighs met his denial of their hopes. "They're gone, then," Alise said aloud, and she hated the finality of her words. It was like pronouncing them dead.

"I intend to keep looking." Carson's words jolted her back to awareness of the world around her. The keepers were milling around and talking, absorbing this latest piece of news. Veras had rejoined the other dragons; Jerd, Sylve, and Harrikin were working together to show her how to use the logs to float so she could rest.

"I found her wedged between some trees," Carson told her. His gaze had followed hers. "She'd climbed up there when she was too weary to swim anymore. That probably saved her life. But as the water went down, she found herself wedged. She'd probably have gotten herself out after she starved a bit more, but I'm glad it didn't come to that."

Alise met his eyes. "You're trying to tell me that the others may be in similar situations somewhere. Stuck, but alive."

"That's what I'm going to keep believing. Excuse me." He turned away from her, lifted the horn to his lips, and blew three short but deafening blasts. This time, in the distance, she heard an answering horn. He turned back to her with a smile and raised his voice so that all on the raft could hear him. "And that will be the *Tarman*. We'll ferry all of you out to the barge as soon as we can. The floats for the dragons are a good idea. We may be able to make them a bit more sturdy with line from the *Tarman*. If the river continues to fall, they probably won't need them much longer.

"Jess is still missing, and I'm going to continue searching rather than hunting. So I suggest that gathering any food you can find would be an excellent idea. You're going to have to do more toward feeding yourselves for a few days, until we can resume hunting again."

Greft had come to stand just behind Carson's shoulder. He looked irritated, Alise thought, and wondered what could annoy him about being rescued. When he spoke, his words sounded like a rebuke.

"If you've finished chatting with Carson, I've some important information to share with him, if he'd give me his attention. The wave that struck us deposited most of us in the trees along here. I gathered those I could find, and the dragons called to one another until they found one another. We've been able to pro-

vide for ourselves here. I'll organize some of the keepers to collect more food for tonight. Most of it will be fruit or vegetable.
Luckily, I kept my wits about me, and we caught three of our
boats. No paddles remained; they were tossed about and almost
all our gear was lost. It will make it hard for us to help bring in
meat or fish for the dragons."

Carson nodded slowly. "Damn shame. We can carve some
paddles, but that will take time. And the missing gear will be
largely impossible to replace. We can try to make some fish
spears, too, even if they're not much more than sharpened sticks.
But at least you're all alive."

Greft's eyes narrowed. Alise realized that was not the response he had expected from the hunter. "Saving lives seemed
a bit more important to me than saving gear," he said tartly. "I
did the best I could at the time."

He'd expected the hunter to praise him, she realized. To give
him the credit for saving the keepers. "And of course you were
very helpful to Thymara and me when Sintara brought us here,"
Alise interjected, hoping to soothe his ruffled feathers. He flicked
a glance at her that was like a slap. It suddenly reminded her of
Hest and how annoyed he would get, even in a social situation,
if she spoke during what he deemed "a man's conversation." Her
sympathy for him evaporated. Almost vindictively she added,
"Thymara has been doing most of our providing. I'll speak to
her now about going out."

She turned and walked away from them, surprised by the
strength of the anger washing through her. *He isn't Hest,* she reminded herself fiercely and, in doing so, realized the true source
of her anger. In a short time, the man she had come to love
would be here beside her again.

And her husband still stood between them.

THREE SHORT BLASTS of the horn!

The first time he heard it echoing back to him, he hadn't
dared to hope. Sounds traveled strangely across the wet lands of

the Rain Wilds. Leftrin had not seen Carson for some hours. He had vanished around one of the gentle bends in the immense river. Then Tarman had been delayed when Davvie had spotted exactly what Leftrin had most feared to see: a body tangled in the driftwood and debris along the side of the river.

It had been Warken, and he had not drowned but been smashed against the flotsam in the river. Carefully they had taken up the body of the young keeper, wrapped him in a fold of canvas, and laid him on the deck of the barge. Every time he passed the body, it seemed an ill omen of things to come. How many more draped bodies would weight Tarman's deck before this day was out?

So he had been cautious when he first heard the three short blasts clearly. He had Davvie signal back and then had asked Tarman to make haste. Even as the barge picked up speed, he reminded himself that the three short blasts could signify anything; Carson could have discovered more bodies just as easily as survivors. But as the boat rounded the bend and came in sight of the tiny camp and its smoldering signal fire, his heart had leaped. He had squinted at the small figures in the shade of the great trees and tried to make out who might be there.

Sooner than he had a right, he saw her. There was no mistaking the sun glinting off that head of glorious red hair. He'd given a roar of delight and felt an answering surge of speed from his ship. "Easy, Tarman! We'll be there soon enough!" Swarge had bellowed, and the ship had reluctantly slowed. Not even a liveship was immune to every danger the river offered. Now was not the time to discover a submerged rock or a waterlogged snag.

It was hard to remain on board and wait patiently for Carson to begin the slow process of ferrying the keepers back to the barge. He dared not let Tarman go nosing in among the debris. The push and wake of the bigger ship could easily disrupt the fragile unity of the mat and send the keepers plunging into the cold river water. No. No matter how he longed to somehow fling himself across the distance that separated them, he stood firmly on the deck of his ship and waited. He muttered imprecations when he saw that Carson's first passengers were Greft and Jerd and Sylve.

Despite his disappointment, he was still able to welcome them warmly aboard. All three looked a bit worse for wear, but the girls both hugged him and thanked him for finding them. He sent them off to the galley for hot fish soup to warm them up. "Get some food in your bellies and you'll be your old selves. But I have to warn you, go easy on the fresh water! Share a bucket and a rag for now. Until we get rain or the river goes down so we can make a sand well, we're going to have to conserve. Off you go now!"

And the girls had gone, obedient and grateful, while Leftrin watched Carson heading back to the floating mat for more passengers.

"Captain." Greft's officious voice was an unwelcome distraction.

"What is it?" he said, and upon hearing the impatience in his own voice, he added, "You must be as weary and hungry as the others. Why don't you get yourself some soup?"

"Soon enough," Greft replied brusquely. "First, we have to lay our plans for what will happen next. Three keepers and three dragons are still missing. We have to discuss plans for either continuing or abandoning the search."

Leftrin shot a look at the younger man. "I'll make it easy for you and tell you my plans, son. First, I'm sorry to tell you that only two keepers are still missing. We found young Warken dead in the river only a few hours ago. And second, we'll continue our search for at least another day and perhaps two. Once we have the rest of the keepers aboard, Carson will set out to see if he can find anyone else. We'll either hold here with the dragons, or leave a few keepers here with the dragons and follow Carson more slowly. That just may depend on what the river does. The water is going down fast. I think whatever broke loose upriver has just about passed us by now."

"Captain, in my opinion, there isn't much point in our delaying our journey. You'd only be wasting time and precious fresh water. What you've told me about Warken saddens me, but it confirms what I've feared since we first pulled ourselves out of the water. I think the others are dead. And I feel that . . ."

"Go feel whatever you're feeling in the galley, lad. On the *Tarman,* the only opinion that counts is the captain's, and oh, looky, that's me. Go on with you, now. Eat something. Sleep. You'll more clearly remember who I am and who you are, and that you're standing on the deck of *my* ship."

His words were considerably gentler than how he would have addressed a deckhand who so far forgot himself as to speak to his captain like that. Besides, he could see Alise stepping into Carson's tippy little boat and he wanted to watch her come aboard without distractions.

He saw the youngster's jaw snap shut and marked the baleful look in his eye. Well, he'd get over it. And if he didn't, he'd just get smacked down a bit more firmly the next time. Leftrin didn't watch him leave. His eyes were locked on the boat, which Carson was paddling crosscurrent toward them.

Abandoning all pretense, he left the top of the deckhouse and descended quickly to the deck. He stood by the railing and waited for her, grinning stupidly. When the small boat was alongside and she looked up at him with her eyes so gray in her poor water-scalded face, his heart ached for her. "Oh, Alise!" No other words came to him. Her red hair was a tangled tumble down her back. She still wore the copper gown he had sheathed her in. Thank Sa for Elderling artifacts. He leaned over the railing, and as soon as he could, he put his hands lightly on her wrists as she climbed up the ladder.

And when he helped her over the railing and onto the deck, he didn't let her go. He folded her in his arms and held her gently against him, mindful of how sore her skin must be but also knowing, "I'm never, ever going to let you get that far away from me again, Alise. Sa be praised that you're here and safe. I'm not letting you go again. I don't care what anyone says."

"Captain Leftrin," she said softly. She leaned her brow against the side of his jaw. Was it an accident? Did he imagine the quick brush of her lips against his throat? A shiver, a flush of heat, ran over him and he stood perfectly still, as if a rare bird had deigned to alight on his shoulder. She pulled herself slightly back from him and looked up into his eyes. "It's so good to be safe with you," she said. "I knew you'd come for us. I knew it."

Could she ever have said a more touching thing to him? He was so pleased by her words that he felt both foolish and extremely manly at the same time. He grinned fiercely and held her closer for a moment. Then, before she could request to be released, he set her free. Never did he want her to feel trapped by him.

Her next words brought him firmly back to earth. "Do we know what befell Sedric? Was he lost overboard during the wave?"

"I am so sorry, Alise. I don't know. I thought he was in his cabin. I'd gone ashore to . . . check on things. I was there when the first wave hit." He had to think fast now. No one knew he'd gone to meet Jess. No one connected him to the hunter at all. In his heart, he knew he'd killed the man. He'd given him a bad enough beating that he could not possibly have survived his time in the water. He'd killed him, and he couldn't regret doing it. That didn't mean he wanted to let anyone else know that he'd done it. It was his secret, and he'd take it to the grave with him. "It was sheer luck that the *Tarman* found me in the dark and took me aboard." Another lie. Didn't he owe her better than this? He plowed ahead with his tale. "Sedric might have been on deck and got washed overboard when the water hit. Or he might have been ashore. All I know is that when I went looking for him, he wasn't here. And neither were you."

"And it's my fault, for dragging him into this." She spoke the words quietly but firmly, as if it were a fault she had to confess.

"I don't see how that's true," he offered her.

"I do."

The depth of guilt in her voice unnerved him. "Now, Alise, I don't think there's any future in following that thought. We've been looking for him, and we're going to continue looking for him. We're not giving up. As soon as we've settled what we're

doing with the dragons, we'll make our plans to continue the
search. We found you, didn't we? We'll find Sedric, too."

"Captain?" It was Davvie.

"What is it, lad?"

"Everyone coming on board is really thirsty and hungry.
How much food and water do I let them have?"

The ugly reality of that question reminded him that he was
a captain as well as a man. He gave Alise a final apologetic look
and turned aside from her, saying, "I have to deal with the survivors right now. But we're going to keep looking for Sedric. I
promise."

SHE NOTICED HE didn't promise to find Sedric. He couldn't. Her
relief at being found, her joy at seeing Leftrin and knowing he
was safe, had passed in a matter of heartbeats. Any joy, any relief
seemed selfish to her just now as she wondered where Sedric was
and what sort of condition he was in. Dead? Dying as he clung
to a log somewhere? Alive and helpless somewhere on the river?
He wouldn't know how to take care of himself, not in this sort
of situation. For an instant, she saw him beside her, dapper and
clever, smiling and kind. Her friend. Her friend whom she had
dragged away from all he enjoyed and held dear, and brought to
this savage place. And it had destroyed him.

She made her way to her cabin and was grateful to close the
door behind her. Soon enough, she'd have to deal with everyone again. For now, she needed a few moments to find herself.
Habit made her strip off her clothing. The long Elderling gown
still looked perfectly intact. She gave it an experimental shake.
A fine shower of dust fell from it; no mud clung to it, no snag
or tear showed in the fabric. She dragged it over her hands and
it flowed like a molten fall of copper. Such a marvel! A gift far
too rich for a married woman to accept from a man not her
husband. The thought ambushed her, and she thrust it ruthlessly
aside.

The gown had swiftly dried once she was out of the river and had kept her warm during those rough nights. And somehow, where it had touched her body, the scalding from the river was far less. Suddenly self-conscious, she raised her hands to her face and then touched her wild hair. Her skin felt rough and dry, her hair like a bundle of straw. In the dimness, she looked at her hands. The skin was reddened, her nails snagged and rough. She felt a double shame, not just that she looked so awful but that she could care about how she looked at such a time.

Feeling shallow, she nonetheless found scented lotion for her hands and soothed her face with it. She dressed in some of her now well-worn clothing and then spent time working at the snarls and tangles in her hair. Then a fresh wave of despair struck her. She had successfully lost herself in the tiny routine of tidying up her self. Now that it was finished, her loss and guilt roared back. For a brief moment, she tempted herself with going to the galley for a hot cup of tea and a piece of ship's bread. Hot tea would taste so good after her days without it.

Sedric had no tea.

It was a sudden silly thought, but it brought tears to her eyes. A trembling ran through her and then was still. "I don't want to think about it," she admitted aloud. When she had been stranded, she'd made herself believe that he was safe on board the ship with Leftrin, even though she had no reason to suppose that Leftrin or the *Tarman* were intact. She'd hidden her fear from herself. And now that she had to face it, she was still burying it, still hiding behind chapped hands and rough hair and cups of tea. Time to face it.

She left her room and walked quickly to Sedric's cabin. The keepers were mostly aboard now; she could hear the buzz of talk from the galley. She passed Davvie, the ship's boy, staring disconsolately out over the water. She stepped around him and went on, leaving him to his thoughts. Skelly was talking to Lecter, both their faces etched with sorrow. His eyes lingered on the girl's face. She heard Skelly ask him something about Alum. Lecter shook his head, the spikes along his jaw quivering. She slipped past them quietly.

She tapped on Sedric's door and, half a heartbeat later, cursed herself for stupidity. She opened the door and went in, closing it behind her.

Had absence sharpened her awareness? Everything in the room seemed wrong. It smelled of unwashed clothing and sweat. The blankets were rucked about like an animal's nest, the floor littered with discarded garments. Untidiness was very unlike Sedric, let alone this sliding into grubbiness. Her guilt hit her with a double sharpness. Sedric had been suffering from dark spirits for days, ever since he had poisoned himself with bad food. How could she have left him alone so much, even if he had been unpleasant and cold to her? How could she have visited this room for even a few minutes and not admitted how he was declining? She should have tidied things for him here, kept it as clean and bright as she could. The signs of his despondency were obvious in every part of the room. For one shocking moment, she wondered if he had deliberately done away with himself.

Knowing it was ridiculous, a mercy performed too late, she gathered his unwashed garments and carefully folded them, setting some aside to launder. She shook out his bedding and remade his pallet. A promise to herself—a foolish promise—that he would return and be relieved to find a tidy room waiting for him. She took up the bundle he had been using for a pillow and shook it to fluff it.

As she did so, something fell to the floor. She stooped in the darkness and groped until her fingers found a fine chain. She lifted it and held it to the light. A locket swung from it. It gleamed gold and flashed even in the dim light. She had never seen Sedric wear it, and the moment it had tumbled from its hiding place in his pillow, she knew it was something private. She smiled even as her heart ached. She'd never suspected that he had a sweetheart, let alone that she'd gifted him with a locket. With a sudden wrench, she understood his reluctance to be stolen away from Bingtown, and his agony over being gone so long. Why hadn't he told her? He could have confided in her, and then she would have understood his driving need to return. His melancholy of the last week suddenly shone in a

different light. He was heartsick. With her free hand, she caught
the locket as it swung.

She had not intended to open it. She was not the sort of woman
who pried and spied. But as her hand closed on the locket, the
catch sprung and it opened in her hand. With an exclamation
of dismay, she saw that a lock of gleaming black hair was now
escaping from its golden prison. She opened the locket the rest
of the way to tuck it back in, and then stopped. Gazing up at
her from the locket's confines were features that she recognized.
Whoever had painted the miniature had known him well, to
catch his face at just that moment before he burst into laughter.
His green eyes were narrowed, his finely chiseled lips pulled
tight enough to partially bare his white teeth. The painting was
the work of a skilled artist. She looked down at Hest smiling up
at her. What did it mean? What could it mean?

She sank down slowly to sit on Sedric's bed. With trembling fingers, she poked the curl of black hair, tied with a single
golden thread, back into the locket. It took her three tries before
it would stay snapped shut. And when it was closed, the mystery
only enlarged. For engraved on the outside of the golden clam-
shell was a single word. "Always," she whispered to herself.

She sat for a long time as the afternoon sunlight outside the
small window slowly died. There could be but one explanation.
Hest had had the locket made and entrusted it to Sedric to give
to her. Why had he done such a thing?

Always. What did that word mean to her, coming from Hest?
Had he feared to lose her? Did he actually care for her, in some
thwarted bizarre way that he could not confess to her face? Was
that what this locket was supposed to tell her? Or had it been
intended as a threat, that "Always" he would keep a hold on her?
No matter where she went, no matter how far, or how long she
stayed away, Hest held her leash. Always. Always. She looked
at the locket in the palm of her hand. Carefully, she lifted the
chain and puddled it in a golden coil around the closed locket.
She shut her fist around it, thrust her hand inside Sedric's pillow and dropped it. Carefully, she set the pillow down on his
pallet.

Her eyes roved around the small place where she had kenneled Sedric. Dim and small and crowded. Untidy. Completely unlike his personal chambers at their home in Bingtown. He loved high ceilings and tall windows open to the breeze. His desk and shelves were always a model of organization. Hest's servants knew to stock his room daily with fresh flowers, that he loved fragrant applewood burning in his small fireplace and hot tea served on an enameled tray. Scented candles in the evening and mulled wine. And from all that, she had snatched him away and condemned him to this. "Sedric, I will make it up to you. I promise. Just be alive. Just be where we can find you. My friend, I've treated you badly, but I swear it was not with intent. I swear."

She stood on her tiptoes to open the small windows to the evening breeze. As soon as they had water for washing, she'd see that his clothes were laundered and hung fresh in his wardrobe. It was all she could do. She refused to consider the futility of promises made to a dead man. He had to be alive and he had to be found. That was all there was to it.

"THAT'S SIMPLY NOT POSSIBLE." Thymara spoke firmly.

"We are not asking you," Sintara rejoined. "It's his right."

"We do not eat our dead," Tats said stiffly.

Evening had fallen, and much to the relief of everyone the river had finally subsided to an almost normal level. The dragons were still belly-deep in water, but now they had river bottom to stand on, even if it was thick with a fresh coat of silt and muck. The crew had moved the barge to an anchoring spot that was close to the dragons without threatening the barge with getting stranded. Every keeper had had a hot meal, even if it had been a small one.

Plans for the next day had been set. The keepers, dragons, and the barge would remain where they were for the next two days while Carson traveled a full day down the river and back up again, looking for survivors or bodies. Davvie had wanted to go with him and been refused. "I can't load the boat up with passengers here, lad. I need room to ferry back anyone I find."

Kase had offered to accompany him in one of the other boats, but with the makeshift paddles they had, Carson had said he would only slow him down. "Use the time while I'm gone to see what you can do about carving out some decent paddles. Davvie and I have some extra spear- and arrowheads. Jess had a good stock of hunting equipment in his chest on board, but don't raid that just yet. I've still got hopes that we'll find him alive. He's a pretty savvy riverman. It would take more than a big wave to do him in, I'll wager."

Everything had been decided, and some of the keepers were already settling for the night when the dragons had waded out to surround the barge and Baliper had made his outrageous demand.

Now Mercor spoke. "You are free to eat or not eat whatever you desire. As are we. We do devour our dead. It is Baliper's right to feed on the body of his keeper. Warken should be given to him before his meat rots any more." The dragon turned his head to look at his own keeper. "Are my words not clear? What is the delay?"

"Mercor, mirror of both the sun and the moon, what you ask is against our custom." Sylve seemed calm, but her voice trembled a bit. Thymara suspected that she did not often defy her dragon.

The great dragon spun his eyes at her. "I am not asking. To reach Warken's body, Baliper may have to damage your boat. This, we think, would distress all of you. So, to aid you, we suggest you put his body over the side."

"It's what we'd have to do soon in any case," Captain Leftrin pointed out in a low voice. "We've nowhere to bury him. So, the river will have him in any case, and moments after he's in the river, the dragons will have him. It's what they do, my friends."

If he was seeking to console them, Thymara thought, he was doing it in an odd way. There was not a one of them who could look at Warken's draped form and not imagine herself or himself lying there.

Sintara picked up the image from Thymara's mind and agilely turned it against her. "If you died tomorrow, which would you wish? To rot in the river, eaten by fishes? Or be devoured by me, and your memories live on in me?"

"I'd be dead and thus I wouldn't care either way," Thymara replied brusquely. She felt the dragon was using her against the rest of the keepers and was not entirely comfortable with that.

"Exactly my point," Sintara purred. "Warken is dead. He no longer cares about anything. Baliper does. Give him to Baliper."

Harrikin suddenly spoke up. "I wouldn't want to just sink down in the muck of the river bottom. I'd give myself to Ranculos. I want everyone here to know that now. If something does befall me, give my body to my dragon."

"Same for me," Kase said, and predictably Boxter echoed him with a, "Same."

"And I," Sylve chimed. "I am Mercor's, in life or death."

"Of course," Jerd conceded, and Greft added, "For me, also."

The assents rounded the circle of gathered keepers. When it came back to her, Thymara bit her lip and held her silence. Sintara reared up out of the water, standing briefly on her hind legs to look down on her. "What?" she demanded of the girl.

Thymara looked up at her. "I belong to myself," she said quietly. "To get, you must give, Sintara."

"I saved you from the river!" The dragon's outraged trumpeting split the darkening sky.

"And I have served you from the day I met you," Thymara replied. "But I do not feel that our bond is complete. So I will hold my thoughts until such time as a decision must be made. And then I will leave it up to my fellow keepers."

"Insolent human! Do you think that you—"

"Another time." Mercor cut into their quarrel. "Render to Baliper what is his."

"Warken wouldn't have had a problem with it," Lecter said decidedly. He straightened from where he'd been leaning on the railing. "I'll do it."

"I'll help," Tats said quietly.

"Keepers' decision," Leftrin announced, as if they had waited for his permission. "Swarge will show you how to use a plank to slide his body over the side. If you want words said, I'll say them."

"There should be words," Lecter said. "Warken's mother would want that."

And so it went, and Thymara watched it unfold and wondered at the strange little community they had become. *I am and am not a part of this,* she thought as she listened to Leftrin say his simple words and then watched Warken's body slip over the railing on a plank. She wanted to turn her head away from what would happen next but somehow she could not. She needed to see it, she told herself. Needed to see how the keepers and their dragons had become so intertwined that such an outrageous and macabre request could be seen as reasonable and even inevitable.

Baliper was waiting. The body slid out from under its draping and as it entered the river, the dragon ducked his head and seized it. He lifted Warken, his head and feet dangling out either side of his mouth, and carried him off. The other dragons, she noted, did not follow him, but turned away and half swam, half waded back to the shallows at the edge of the river. Baliper disappeared upriver into the darkness with his keeper's body. So it was not a simple devouring of meat that humans would otherwise discard. It meant something, not just to Warken's dragon, but to all of them. It was important enough to them that when Baliper's demand had been initially refused, they had massed and made it plain that they would not let him be denied.

The other keepers reminded her of the dragons. They dispersed quietly from their places along the railings. No one wept, but it did not mean no one wished to. Seeing Warken dead, really dead, had brought home the reality of Rapskal's absence. He was gone, and the chances were that if she saw him again he would be like Warken, battered and bloated and still.

The keepers congregated in small groups. Jerd was with Greft, of course. Sylve was with Harrikin and Lecter. Boxter and Kase, the cousins, moved as one as they always did. Nortel trailed after them. And she stood apart from all of them, as she so often seemed to do. The only one who had refused her dragon. The only one who never seemed to know what rules the group had discarded and which ones they kept. Her back ached abominably, she was river scalded and insect bitten, and the loneliness that filled her up from the inside threatened to crack her body. She missed Alise's company, but now that they were back on the barge and she had her captain's attention, she probably wouldn't want to spend time with Thymara.

And she missed Rapskal, with a keenness that shocked her.

"Are you all right?"

She turned, startled to discover Tats standing at her side. "I suppose I am. That was a hard, strange thing, wasn't it?"

"In some ways, it was the simplest solution. And Lecter had spent a lot of time with Warken; they partnered in the boats most days. So I'm willing to believe that he knew what Warken would have wanted."

"I'm sure he did," Thymara replied quietly.

They stood for a time, staring over the river. The dragons had dispersed. Thymara could still feel, like a fire radiating cold, Sintara's anger with her. She didn't care. Her skin hurt all over, the injury between her shoulders burned, and she didn't belong anywhere.

"I can't even go home."

Tats didn't ask what she meant. "None of us can. None of us was ever really at home in Trehaug. This, here, on this barge tonight, this is as close to home as any of us have. Alise and Captain Leftrin and his crew included."

"But I don't fit in, even here."

"You could if you chose to, Thymara. You're the one keeping a distance." He moved his hand, not putting it over hers, but setting it on the railing beside hers so that his hand touched hers.

Her first impulse was to move her hand away. By an effort, she didn't. She wondered both why she had wanted to move it away, and why she hadn't. She didn't have an answer to either question, so she asked Tats a question of her own. "Do you know what Greft said to me about you?"

The corner of his mouth quirked. "No. But I'm sure it wasn't flattering. And I hope you recalled that you know me far better than Greft can ever hope to."

So at least it hadn't been a male conspiracy to get the lone uncommitted female to make a choice. That made her opinion of her fellow keepers rise slightly. She kept her voice level and noncommittal as if she were speaking about how pleasant the night was. "He came out when I was on watch last night and asked if I'd chosen you. He explained that if I had, I'd best declare it clearly, or let him know at least so that he could enforce my choice with the others. He said, otherwise, there might be a lot of competition. That some of the other keepers might even challenge you or start fights with you."

"Greft is a pompous ass who thinks he can speak for everyone," Tats said after a profound silence. Just as she was ready to dismiss her experience with Greft as an aberration, he added, "But I'd like it if you said to everyone that you had chosen me. He's right about that; it would make things simpler."

"What 'things' would it make simpler?"

He gave her a sideways glance. They both knew he was treading on shaky ground now. "Well. One thing is that it would give me an answer. One that I'd like to have. And another is—"

"You've never even asked me a question," she broke in. She spoke hastily and was appalled to realize that she'd just pushed them deeper into the quagmire.

She wanted to run away, to get away from this stupidity that stupid Greft had triggered with his stupid lecture. Tats seemed to know that. He put his calloused hand over hers. She could feel the softness of his palm against the scaled back of her hand. The warmth from that touch flooded through her, and for a moment her breath caught. Her mind flashed to Jerd and Greft, entwined and moving together. No. She forbade the thought and reminded herself that her hand under his was probably cold, slick with scales, like a fish. He did not look down at the hand he had captured. He took a breath and puffed it out. "It's not a question. Not a specific question. It's, well, I'd like to have what Greft and Jerd have."

So would she.

No! Of course she didn't. She denied the thought.

"What Jerd and Greft have? You mean mating?" She didn't completely succeed in keeping accusation out of her voice.

"No. Well, yes. But they also have a certainty of each other. That's what I want." He looked away from her and spoke more gently as if she were fragile. "I know Rapskal has not been gone that long, but—"

"How can anyone seriously think that Rapskal and I were anything more than friends?" she burst out indignantly. She jerked her hand out from under his and used it to push back the hair from her face.

He looked surprised. "You were always with him, all the time. Ever since we left Cassarick. Always sharing a boat, always sleeping together . . ."

"He always lay down to sleep next to me. And no one else ever offered to share a boat with me. I liked him, when he wasn't making me cross or annoying me or saying strange things." Suddenly her diatribe against him seemed disloyal. She halted her words and admitted in a whisper, "I liked him a lot. But I never imagined I was in love with him, and I don't think he ever thought of me that way. In fact, I'm certain of it. He was just my peculiar friend who always looked on the bright side of things and who was always in a good temper. He always sought me out. I didn't have to work to be his friend."

"He was that," Tats agreed quietly. For a moment, that mourning silence held, and during it she felt closer to Tats than she had for a long time. Thymara broke the silence at last. "What was the other reason?"

"What?"

"You started to say and I interrupted you. What was the other reason you thought it would be best if I declared that I was— that I was with you." She tried to find a better euphemism, couldn't, and gave up on it. She looked at him directly and waited.

"It would settle things. Put an end to speculation. There is, um, some bad feelings. From the others. Nortel has made a few comments—"

"Such as?" she asked him roughly.

He became blunt. "That I'm not one of you, and that you belong with someone of your own kind, someone who can really
understand you."

"That sounds like Greft stirring the pot again."

"Probably. He says lots of things like that. Late at night, around
the fire. Usually after the girls have gone to sleep. He talks about
how things are going to be, when we reach Kelsingra. According
to Greft, we'll build our own city there. Well, it won't be a city
at first, of course. But we'll settle there and make homes. Eventually others will come to join us there, but we keepers will be the
founders. We'll make the rules.

"And when he talks like that, he unfolds things so logically
that it does start to seem like it must be the way he says it's going to be. And usually, it comes out like he says it will. When
we found out that Jerd was, well, going to have a baby, he said
someone would have to be responsible, even if she didn't know
whose it was. And he said he'd set the example, and he did. And
then, later, he said that Sylve was too young to have to make
decisions for herself. He picked out Harrikin for her, because
he was older and would have more self-control. He told him to
start out by being her protector. And he did, and it worked out
that Sylve chose him."

"Sylve said that?" She was shocked.

"Well, not directly. But it's obvious to all of us. And Greft
said that even though no one could figure out why you'd chosen Rapskal, that was how it was and no one was to interfere. It
made me angry at first. I didn't think you'd 'chosen' him. But
I was, well, I was with Jerd when he said it. So I couldn't very
well say . . ." He let his words trickle away, took a breath, and
tried again. "And everyone respected what he said. No one tried
to come between you two. But Rapskal is gone now. I hope
he'll turn up, but if he doesn't, I wanted you to know that I was,
well, waiting and hoping."

She decided to put an end to all of it, immediately. "Tats. I
like you. A lot. We've been friends for a long time. And I'm sure
that if anyone can understand me, it's you. But I'm not 'choosing' you or anyone else. Not now, and maybe not ever."

"But . . . not ever? Why?"

Her annoyance blossomed. "Because. That's why. Because it's up to me, not Greft, not you, not anyone else. I won't be told I have to 'choose' as if there is some time limit and after that, it will not be my choice anymore. I want you and Greft and everyone else to know that perhaps *not* choosing one of you is a possible choice for me."

"Thymara!" he protested.

"No," she said flatly, forbidding whatever it was he was going to say. "No. And that's the end of it. You can tell Greft that, or he can come and talk to me and I'll tell him."

"Thymara, that's not—"

Whatever he was going to say was interrupted by a distant sound. At first, Thymara thought it was a horn. She'd heard that Carson was going to look for other survivors, but wasn't sure if he'd left already or was going to go in the morning. Then she heard the sound again and realized it was not a horn but a dragon calling.

From the mucky shallows, first Mercor and then Fente replied. Kalo chimed in with his bull's roar, and Sestican echoed him.

"Who is it?" Tats demanded of the darkness.

Thymara's heart leaped in sudden hope. She strained her ears, listening to the distant dragon's response. Then she shook her head in disappointment. "Not Heeby. Heeby is shriller than that."

Arbuc suddenly trumpeted, a clear and long call. Silver-green, he moved out of the shallows and into the current. The moonlight touched him, and he seemed to gleam with joy. He swam steadily down the current, toward the unseen dragon. When he lifted his voice again, his thoughts rode loud on it. "Alum! Alum, I come for you!"

Tats and Thymara leaned on the railing, craning and trying to force their eyes to see farther into the blackness. The other keepers were joining them, and she heard Captain Leftrin's bellow, "Who is it? Has anyone sighted it yet?"

"It's the silver!" someone on the stern yelled suddenly. "It's the little silver dragon! And Alum is with him! They're both alive."

"Silver! You're alive!" There was no mistaking the joy in

Sylve's shout of greeting to the dragon. He turned his head toward her and, for a moment, looked almost intelligent.

"I'm so glad!" Tats exclaimed, and Thymara nodded silently. She watched the homecoming, sick with envy. Alum tried to embrace his dragon, but Arbuc had grown too large. He transferred from the little silver's back to Arbuc's broad one and then leaned forward against his dragon as if by pressing his heart against him, he might become one with him.

What was wrong with her? Why didn't she have that sort of a bond with Sintara? Or with anyone? She glanced at Tats surreptitiously. He leaned far out on the railing, grinning. Why didn't she announce she'd chosen him? Why couldn't she be like Jerd and charge into things? Jerd had obviously sampled a number of males. Now Greft had proclaimed she was his, and she didn't seem displeased with that. Would it be so hard? To just take what was offered, without making a commitment?

The silver, obviously pleased with himself, lashed river water to a froth with his tail and then, spreading his wings, "flew" in a series of splashes to join the other dragons in the shallows. The other keepers crowded the aft railings, laughing and shouting and pointing. She began to drift in that direction.

Without warning, Tats took her hand again. He tugged at her until she turned back to face him. "Don't be so sad. Rapskal and Heeby might still be alive. We won't give up hope just yet."

She looked up at him. He wasn't that much taller than she was, but the expedition had changed him. He'd muscled out, his shoulders and chest built up by the paddling in a way that was very different from the muscles of a tree-climbing gatherer. She rather liked it. Her eyes moved over his face. The small tattoo of a horse, legacy of the slavery of his infancy, was only an unevenness against his windburned skin in the fading light. The spiderweb was nearly gone. This close to him, she could smell him, and that, too, was not unpleasant. Her eyes met his and she realized how dark they were. His smell suddenly changed, and she realized she was sucking on her own lower lip as she studied his face. She saw him take a breath and dare himself.

She acted before he could take the decision from her. She leaned in, turning her head slightly and putting her mouth on his. Was this how it was done? She had never kissed anyone on the mouth. Awkwardness and worry assaulted her. Tats's arms suddenly moved up and around her, pulling her body against his. His lips moved on hers. *He knows how to do this,* she thought, and knew an instant of fury at where he'd learned it. Well, she wasn't Jerd and whether she kissed the right way or not, he'd soon discover that she did things her own way. She shook her head slowly, moving her lips back and forth against his. *Scale on softness,* she thought, and briefly lost herself in that sensation. His hands wandered up her back and their touch on the tender area between her shoulder blades made her twitch with pain.

"What is that?" he demanded.

Embarrassment flooded her. "It's nothing. I got cut in the river. It's sore."

"Oh. Sorry. It feels really swollen."

"It's sensitive."

"I'll be careful."

He bent his head to kiss her again. She let him. Then, from somewhere else on the boat, she heard someone's voice raised in a question. Someone replied. They weren't alone here. Not really.

She pulled her mouth from his and bowed her head. He folded her in close to him and kissed the top of her head greedily. She felt his warm breath, and it sent a shiver down through her. He laughed softly at that. "Is this my answer?" he asked her, his voice deeper than she'd ever heard it.

"To what question?" she asked, sincerely puzzled.

"Are you choosing me?"

Almost, she wanted to lie to him. She didn't. "I'm choosing to be free, Tats. To not have to choose, not now, not ever if I don't want to."

"Then, then what does this mean?" He hadn't released her, but there was a stiffness to his embrace that hadn't been there before.

"It means that I wanted to kiss you."

"And that's all?" He leaned back from her, and she looked up at his face.

"For now," she admitted. "That's all."

She was meeting his gaze now. A trick of the light moved stars in his dark eyes. He nodded at her slowly.

"That's enough. For now."

✧ ✧ ✧

Day the 22nd of the Prayer Moon

Year the 6th of the Independent Alliance of Traders

From Detozi, Keeper of the Birds, Trehaug

To Erek, Keeper of the Birds, Bingtown

In a sealed message cylinder, specific to his family and sealed with wax imprinted with his seal, a confidential message from Trader Sworkin to Trader Kellerby.

Erek,

I am both saddened by the news that your father has been ill and relieved to know that you were not on our river when the world went mad. I wish to assure you of our family's hospitality should you have the opportunity to come for a visit with us. If the other bird keepers could take charge of your flock and responsibilities for a time, perhaps you could accompany Reyall when he returns home to visit, if indeed that visit is possible. I would greatly enjoy finally meeting you after all these years of exchanged notes.

Detozi

✧ ✧ ✧

CHAPTER NINE

DISCOVERIES

S*edric.*

"No. Go away. Let me sleep."

Sedric.

"I just want to sleep."

Sedric.

"What?" He projected all his annoyance into the word. It hurt. He lifted his hand to his jaw, then gingerly explored the whole side of his face. It hurt. Of all the bruises that Jess had given him, this one hurt the worst. One of his eyes still wouldn't open all the way.

"I'm hungry." Her actual voice was a rumbling, gargling sort of sound. The meaning of it rode into his mind as a thought. No time to worry about his own pain. She pushed his own physical state aside with concerns about her own. She was hungry.

"Well, I don't have any more hunters to feed you."

????

"Never mind. I'm getting up. I'll see what I can do for you."

He was still trying to forget yesterday's events and their bloody culmination.

The second time Relpda had surfaced, Jess's lower half had been in her jaws. She'd treated Sedric to one more shocking glimpse of the sheared torso, then merrily tossed the remains into the air, caught them so that they aligned with her throat, and with a couple of jerking motions, swallowed the hunter's hips and legs.

He'd turned his head away, retching hopelessly. When he heard a splash and felt the raft rock, he'd guessed it was safe to look back. She'd vanished under the water again. He'd taken a shuddering breath and curled forward over his belly. That left him looking at the pool of mingled blood and river water in the bottom of the boat. He'd scrabbled out of it and perched on the log beside it, trying to think what he must do next.

The hunter was dead. He and the dragon had killed Jess. If they hadn't, Jess would certainly have done his best to kill both of them. Yet it all seemed so monstrous, so hugely outside his experience that he could scarcely grasp it. He'd never expected to kill a man; he'd never expected even to fight or hurt another man. Why would he? If he had remained in his correct place, in Bingtown, working as Hest's assistant, nothing like this would have ever befallen him.

If he'd remained with Hest, nothing like this would have ever happened to him.

Suddenly that had been a thought that could cut both ways.

The dragon had surfaced noisily. *Better,* she'd told him. *Not so hungry.*

"I'm happy for you."

The words had been an empty courtesy, but in return she'd given him a flood of warmth. The surge of affection he felt from her had temporarily pushed all pain from his body. She'd followed it with a request. *Need help. To get on the wood again.*

"I'm coming." And he'd actually managed to help her to a safer perch, one where she could rest.

Sometime before nightfall, he'd recovered enough that he'd

eaten the fruit that Jess had harvested. His lips were broken and his face hurt where Jess had struck him, but he ignored the pain to eat. The fruit was both food and drink for him, and he was shocked at how much better he felt for it. That done, he'd inventoried the supplies in the boat. The best discovery had been a wool blanket, even if it was wet and smelly. He'd spread it out to let it dry as much as it would before dark.

He'd forced himself to proceed logically, even to gathering up the piece of line and the fishing spear that Jess had dropped when he'd decided that killing Sedric was more important than killing the dragon. Relpda had watched him from her precarious perch on the logs. When he'd picked up the spear, she'd shuddered and he'd felt her dislike for the weapon.

"I might be able to get food for us with this," he suggested doubtfully.

Yes. Maybe. But hurt. See?

And so he'd had to examine her injury. It was still leaking blood, but her dip beneath the water seemed to have partially cauterized it. "You need to keep that as dry as you can," he'd counseled her. "No more diving."

Sedric angry?

Her query had actually sounded anxious. Her tone made him stop to consider her question. "No," he answered honestly. "Not angry. We do what we have to do. We had to kill him or he would have killed us. You ate him because, well, it's what dragons do. You were hungry. I'm not angry."

Sedric kill. Sedric protect. Sedric feed Relpda.

"I suppose I did," he said after a time of horrified reflection. "I suppose I did."

Sedric my keeper. You will change.

"I'm changing already," he admitted.

Yes. Change.

He wasn't sure he enjoyed contemplating that.

That night the damp blanket had provided him with some shelter from the incessantly humming insects, but it could not keep at bay his stinging thoughts. What was he going to do? He had a boat that he didn't know how to manage, a slightly injured dragon, and a small array of tools that he didn't know how to use. He didn't know if any of the others had survived, nor if he should look for them upriver or downriver. No matter which direction he went in, he was fairly certain the dragon would follow him.

Follow, she'd assured him. *Follow Sedric. Relpda and Sedric together.*

Just as he'd accepted that thought, she'd rattled him in a new direction. *Easier to think, easier to talk with you here.* And in case he hadn't taken her meaning, she'd sent him a flush of warmth through the connection they shared.

It had been a long time before he'd been able to sleep, and now that he was awake again, none of his problems seemed simpler. The dragon obviously expected him to feed her. He rubbed his swollen eyes cautiously and tossed his smelly blanket aside. Slowly he sat up and then clambered awkwardly out of the boat. He was too stiff to move comfortably, and he was quite literally sick of every object moving in reaction to every move he made. He was hungry and thirsty, the whole side of his face was swollen, his clothes stuck to his itching, stinging skin, his hair was plastered to his scalp. Abruptly, he stopped enumerating his misery to himself. No point to that except to make himself more miserable.

Fix.

Again that warm flush suffused him. This time, as it faded, everything hurt less.

"Are you healing me?" he asked in wonder.

No. Making you not think about pain so much.

Like a drug, he thought. Not as reassuring as thinking he was healing, but less pain was good, too. So what should he do?

Find food for me.

Her thoughts were clearer and more cogent. Less separate from his own, he feared. He pushed that thought away as something he couldn't worry about right now. Right now he had to find a way to feed the dragon, if only to lessen the hunger pangs she was sharing with him. But how?

There was no quick and satisfying answer to that. The day

was mild, the river calmer and the water less white. He had the tools of a hunter, if not the skills. He had a boat. And he had a dragon.

All he needed to do was decide what to do with those things.

The closest he came to a decision was walking away from the boat and taking a piss into the river. When he was finished, he spoke. "So, Relpda, what shall we do now?"

Get food.

"Excellent idea. Except I don't know how."

Go hunt. He felt the mental nudge she gave him. It wasn't comfortable.

He thought of arguing with her and then decided there was no point to it. She was right. They were both hungry, and the only solution was that one of them find food. And she certainly wasn't going to do it. He recalled that he had seen Jess coming from the trees with fruit. If the hunter had found fruit up there, then chances were that some remained. Up there. Somewhere.

Meat. Fish, she insisted. She shifted uncomfortably on the log that supported her. One end of it abruptly broke free of the tangled debris and dipped lower into the water. *Slipping!* She trumpeted her fear as her thought slammed his mind. Frantically, she reached out and seized a second log with her front claws. Her grip held and she pulled the log closer, managing to hitch herself up partially onto both of them.

"Good girl! Clever dragon!" he praised her.

And in return, he received that wave of warmth that eased his hurts. But with it came a message. *And tired. So tired. Cold, too.*

"I know, Relpda. I know." They weren't just comforting words. He did know exactly how tired she was, and how her weariness dragged at her. Her front legs ached from hanging on. All her claws felt odd, soft and sore. Her back legs and tail were weary from thrashing. Abruptly she opened her wings and beat them, trying to lift herself higher on the logs. They were stronger than he had thought they were. He felt the wind they stirred and saw her chest rise almost out of the water. For all that, it didn't help her at all. It just disrupted the tangle of wood and debris in the eddy. As Sedric watched, a clump of tangled weeds broke free and floated off down the river. Not good.

"Relpda. Relpda. Listen to me. We have to get more logs under your chest and give you a place to rest. Once you are safe, then I can hunt for food for you."

Rest. A world of longing was in the single word.

SHE'D SLEPT LATE, yet when she emerged onto the deck, she saw that some of the keepers were sleeping still. Alise wondered if weariness or sorrow weighted them. Two who were not sleeping were Thymara and Jerd. The two girls were on the bow of the *Tarman,* their legs dangling as they sat on the railing and talked. Alise was mildly surprised to see them together. She had not thought they were friendly with each other, and after what Thymara had told her about Jerd, she doubted they ever would be. She wondered what they were talking about, and if they would welcome her if she joined them. She'd had female friends in Bingtown, but she'd never cherished those friendships as much as some women did. There was a reserve in her that perhaps other women thought cold; she'd never been able to confide in her friends the most intimate details of her marriage, though many had insisted on sharing such with her.

Yet she thought that now she would welcome another woman's thoughts. Since her discovery of the locket yesterday, her mind and emotions had been in turmoil. Why would Hest have such a gift made, why entrust it to Sedric, and why hadn't Sedric passed it on to her? These were questions she could not share with Leftrin; if there was guilt to bear in these matters, it belonged to her alone. It was a question only Sedric could answer, and Sedric was gone. She reined her mind away from that sorrow. Not yet. She would not mourn him yet. There was still hope.

She wandered the boat, looking for Bellin. When she finally found her, she was in the deckhouse, sitting on Skelly's bunk. Bellin's face was serious, and she held both of Skelly's hands. Tears had tracked down the girl's face recently. Bellin's eyes flickered to Alise's face, and a very slight change in her facial expression told Alise to go away silently without alerting Skelly to her presence. Alise gave a small nod and ghosted away, back to pacing a circuit of the deck.

Thymara had rolled her trousers up to her knees. As she swung her legs, her scales glittered silver in the sunlight. She sat hunched over, but Jerd sat straight and tall, almost pushing her stomach out. Alise envied them: they had so much freedom. No one fretted that they were showing too much leg, or even that they might fall in. Everyone on the vessel assumed they knew what they were about and left them to it. They reminded her of Althea Trell and how competently she had moved about the deck of the *Paragon*. Althea, she reminded herself, was of Bingtown Trader stock, just as she was. So she could not really blame where she came from for the limitations on her. No, she realized slowly. She was the one who had accepted those limitations and brought them with her. She was the one who lived by the restrictive rules.

She thought of Leftrin with frustration and longing. She sensed in him tenderness and passion, two things she had never received from Hest. Leftrin woke like feelings in her. Why couldn't she just go to him and give herself to him as she longed to? The man obviously wanted to bed her, and she wanted him.

There was a wild part of her that insisted they were too far up this strange river, and that she did not need to worry about what might happen to her after she returned to Bingtown. That part believed that she might never return at all. And whether she died on this mad adventure or lived it out to the end, shouldn't she live all of it, have all of it, instead of holding back from it? Coldly she realized that Sedric was not here to look at her with doleful accusing eyes. Her conscience was gone; she could do as she pleased.

"It's a lovelier day with you on the deck, my dear."

She felt a warm rush of pleasure at hearing his voice and turned to find Leftrin bearing down on her. He carried two cups of tea. As she took the heavy, stained mug from his calloused and scaled hand, she thought of how she might have flinched away from him only a month ago. She would have wondered if the mug were clean and tsked over the stale tea. Now she knew that the mug had been given only a tiny swirl of water to clean it, or perhaps been wiped out with a rag. Knew and didn't care. As for the tea, well . . . She toasted him with her mug. "Best tea to be had for miles around!"

"It is that," he agreed. "And the best company to be had in the entire world, I'm thinking."

She laughed softly and looked down at her hands. Her freckles were dark against her water-scalded skin. She didn't want to think about her face and hair. She had glanced at them in the small dim mirror in her cabin after she had brushed and pinned up her hair and given it up as hopeless. "How can you give me such outrageous compliments and not sound foolish doing it?"

"Maybe you're the right audience for such words. And maybe I don't care if I sound foolish, for I know it's the truth."

"Oh, Leftrin." She turned to look out over the river, resting her teacup on the ship's railing. "What are we going to do?" She hadn't known she was going to ask him that. The question came out of her as naturally as the steam that rose off her tea.

He purposely misunderstood her. "Well, Carson left before dawn. We're going to hold in place here for a day. The dragons can rest a bit and gorge some more. A little bit upriver, they found an eddy full of acid-killed fish. So we'll let them eat and rest while Carson continues the search. He'll go another full day down the river. If he finds survivors, he'll guide them back to us. If he finds nothing, he'll give it up and come on back to us. He took the horn with him, and the sound carries quite a ways. I heard him blow three long blasts, not that long ago."

"I didn't hear it."

"Well, it was faint, and I'm accustomed to listening for such things." Something in his tone rang oddly to her. She sensed a secret but was willing, for now, to let it go.

"Do you think he'll find anyone else?"

"It's impossible to predict a thing like that. But we found almost all our survivors in one place. So, it seems to me that what that river picked up in one place, it kept mostly together and dumped in another place."

He stopped talking, but she pieced his logic together. "So you think that if anyone survived to be found, they would have been with us."

He nodded reluctantly. "Most likely. But we found that dragon off by herself."

"And Warken's body."

"And the body," he agreed. "That says to me that most everything that was in our area when the wave hit was carried by the wash to this area."

She was silent for a time. "Heeby and Rapskal? The copper dragon?"

"Probably dead and on the bottom. Or buried under debris. Dead dragons that size wouldn't be hard to spot."

"And Sedric?"

His silence was longer than hers had been. Finally he said, "Speaking bluntly, Alise, the keepers survived because they're tough. Their skin can stand up to these waters. They all know how to climb a tree if they can get to one. They're made for this life. Sedric wasn't. There was no muscle to that man to begin with, and his long days of lying abed, sick or not, would only have weakened him more. I try to imagine him swimming in that wave, and I can't. I fear he's gone. It's not your fault. I don't think it's my fault, either. I think it's just what happened."

Did he mention fault only because he secretly knew it was her fault? "I brought him into this, Leftrin. He wasn't your idea of tough, I know. But in his own way, he was strong, capable, and very competent. He was Hest's right hand. I'll never know why he decided to send him with me." Her words stuttered to a halt. Unless Hest had believed that she deserved the kind of watching over her that Sedric had tried to provide.

"I wasn't saying he wasn't a good man, only that I doubted he was a good swimmer," Leftrin said gently. "And we don't have to give up hope. We've got a strong man looking for him. I think Carson wants to find him as badly as you do."

"I'm grateful to him. I don't know how to thank him for being so determined."

Leftrin gave a small cough. "Well, I think he's hoping that Sedric will do the thanking. Them being the same kind of men and all."

"The same kind of men? I can't think of two men more unlike."

Leftrin shot her an odd look and then shrugged. "Like enough in the ways that matter to them, I'm thinking. But let's let that go. It's enough to say that Carson won't give up easily."

"So why did you do it, then? If you didn't think you were, well, in love with him?"

Jerd lifted one shoulder. "I guess that I'd decided I was going to live my own life just as soon as I left Trehaug. It was like keeping a promise to myself. And"—she smiled wryly—"he was the first. It was flattering, I guess, that someone as soft-skinned as him would, well, want me. I don't have to explain that to you. After a lifetime of being told that no one should touch you, that no one would or could touch you because you were born too much of a monster? Then a soft-skinned boy with a gentle manner doesn't seem to think it matters . . . that just made me feel free. So I decided to be free."

"So." Thymara swallowed and tried to think how to phrase her next question. She was the one who had sought Jerd out. And she'd been surprised that the other girl hadn't rebuffed her attempts at conversation. Neither of them had brought up Thymara's spying on her and Greft. With a bit of luck, neither of them would. Perhaps Jerd was as uncomfortable about that as she was. She considered her question one last time. Did she really want to know?

"So, then, he came to you. Not you to him."

Jerd glanced across at her and made a disparaging face. "I

followed him into the woods. Is that what you're asking? Or are you asking who touched whom first? Because I'm not sure I remember . . ." She sat up straighter, put her hand on her slight belly, and asked, "Why do you care, anyway?"

Thymara was suddenly sure that Jerd did remember, perfectly well. And she saw that she had just handed the other girl a little knife that she could use to dig at her anytime she wanted. "I don't know," she lied. "I just wondered."

"If you want him, you can have him," Jerd offered magnanimously. "I mean, I've got Greft, you know. And it isn't like I wanted Tats permanently. I wouldn't take him away from you."

So she thought she could. Could she? "And you didn't want Rapskal permanently?" Thymara countered. "Nor any of them?"

If she'd thought to pierce the other girl, she'd missed. Jerd gave a laugh. "No, not Rapskal! Though he was sweet, so boyish, and so handsome. But once with him was enough for me! He laughed in such a silly way; very annoying. Oh! I'm sorry he's gone, though. I know you were close, and I'm sure you didn't find his silly ways annoying at all. It must be very hard for you to lose him."

The bitch. Thymara willed her throat not to close, her eyes not to tear, and failed. It wasn't that she'd been in love with him. He was just too strange. But he'd been Rapskal and her friend; his absence left a hole in her life.

"It is hard. Too hard." Without apology or explanation, Thymara swung her legs to the other side of the railing and hopped down. As she did, she felt a brief vibration of sympathy from Tarman. As she walked away, she let her hand trail along the railing, assuring him of her mutual regard for him. She saw Hennesey, the mate, give her an odd look and immediately lifted her hand from the railing. He gave her a slow, unsmiling nod as she passed. She'd crossed a line just then and she knew it. She wasn't part of Tarman's crew and had no right to communicate with the ship that way. Even if he had started it.

That thought brought an unwelcome comparison to what

Jerd had said about Tats. She forced herself to think about it. Did it matter if Tats had initiated things with Jerd? Wasn't it something that was over and done with?

"Now, JUST STAY like that. Rest and don't move. I'll try to find more food for you."

"Very well."

Sedric looked again at the dragon on her bed of logs and marveled at all of it, at the logs they had moved together, at how he had visualized it and created it, and how he had managed to get her up and out of the water. In the process of finding logs he could move and shifting them toward her, he had discovered several large dead fish floating in the water, and one carcass that might have been a monkey. Touching the soft dead things had been disgusting. *Not fresh,* she had complained, but she'd eaten them. Then, despite the sting of the water, he'd scrubbed most of the stink from them off his hands.

"We work well together." She spoke in his ears and in his mind.

"We do," he agreed, and he tried not to wonder too much if that were a good thing.

It had taken the morning and half the afternoon to achieve this. He'd seen that if he could force several of the larger logs up against the trees, he might be able to secure them there and make a dragon-size raft. He'd begun with one log that was already butted firmly against several thick trees. The eddying current held it there. He'd moved the brush, small branches, and other debris that was packed between it and another log. It had been wet heavy work, and his soaked clothing still chafed against his river-scalded skin. Long before he had finished, his hands were stiff and sore, his back ached, and he felt almost dizzy from the effort. Relpda had been impatient as he worked, mooing her distress and fear. Slowly her anxiety had crept into irritation and anger.

Help me! Slipping. Help. Not do wood. Help ME!

"I'm trying to. I'm building something for you, something you can get onto."

Anger made her thrash both tail and wings, nearly knocking him into the water. "Help now! Build later!"

"Relpda, I have to build first, then help."

NO! Her wild trumpeting split the sky, and the force of her thought staggered him.

"Don't do that," he warned her. "If I fall in the river and drown, you'll be alone. No one to help you."

Fall in, I eat you! Then no build trees. She sent him the thought silently but with no less force.

"Relpda!" For a moment, he was both outraged and terrified that she would threaten him. Then the cold current of fear that underlay her words snaked through his heart. She didn't understand. She thought he was ignoring her. "Relpda, look: if I can push enough of the big trees together here and make them stay, then—"

Help Relpda NOW!

She pushed him again with her thought, and he almost blacked out. He responded in anger. "Look at what I'm trying to do!" And he shoved back hard against her stubborn little lizard brain, sending her the image of a thick raft of logs and branches, with Relpda curled safely upon it.

She snorted furiously and hit the water with her wings, splashing him. Then, *Oh,* she exclaimed. *Now I see. It all makes sense. I'll help you.*

Her sudden fluency astounded him. "What?"

I'll help you push the logs into place. And clear the brush that blocks them from fitting snugly together.

She was in his mind, using his vision, his thoughts, his words. He shuddered at the sudden intimacy, and she shivered her hide in response. He tried to pull back from her and couldn't. On his second effort, she reluctantly parted her thoughts from his.

Relpda help?

"Yes. Relpda help," he'd replied when he felt he could form words of his own again.

And she had. Despite her weariness and the soreness of her clawed feet, she swam about, pushing debris out of the way and shoving logs where he indicated. When their first effort came to pieces, she'd given one shrill trumpet of protest and despair. And then, when he called her back to their task, she'd come. She'd listened to him as he directed her to sink logs and push them under their row of timbers. When he told her she'd have to tread water while he roped their latest effort with their pitifully short piece of line, she'd done it. And then, cautiously, she'd clambered up onto her uneven bed of logs. And rested. Her body began to warm. He hadn't realized how much her exhaustion had been affecting him until she suddenly relaxed. He nearly fainted with her relief.

Sleep now.

"Yes. You sleep. It's what you need most right now."

He himself needed food. And water. How pathetic to long, not for wine or well-prepared food, but a simple drink of water. And now he was right back to where he had been hours ago, except that most of his daylight was gone. Soon darkness would fall, and he'd be back to huddling under a smelly blanket in a small boat. He glanced at the sky and decided that he had to at least try to find where Jess had found the fruit.

Meat. She'd been following his thoughts sleepily, and the idea of fruit didn't please her. *Find meat.* She let the sharpness of her hunger touch him. He was appalled. He'd just fed her!

Not enough.

"Maybe I'll find some meat." Then, trying to accept the desperation of their situation, he forced himself to say, "I'll try."

He walked back to the boat and looked at the selection of animal-killing tools that remained to him. The hatchet still lay in the bloody bilgewater. His gorge rose as he picked it out and set it on the seat to dry. Jess's blood, diluted with slimy water, was on his hands now. He knelt and thrust his hand down through the matted debris and into the river water to sluice it off. To his surprise, it did not sting as he had expected it to. Was he becoming accustomed to it? A glance around at the river showed him that not only was it far less acid than it had been, but that the level was much lower. The high water mark on the tree trunks was well over his head now.

He worked his way over to the cage of tree trunks that edged the river, stepping from log to log. Sometimes they bobbed deeper than he expected, and one spun under his foot, nearly dumping him into the river. But at last he stood at the edge of the forest, looking up at the trees. He knew he'd seen Jess descend one of those trunks, but they all suddenly looked much smoother than they had before. When was the last time he'd climbed a tree? He couldn't have been more than ten years old, and it had been a friendly apple tree, its branches laden with sweet fruit. The memory of those apples made him swallow hard against his hunger. Well, no help for it. Up he must go.

The horn's long low call startled him. He spun to face it as Relpda lifted her head and trumpeted out a response to it. The sound seemed to come from all around him. He stared around wildly, even looking up into the trees. Relpda was gazing upstream and as he watched her, she lifted her chin again and trumpeted.

By hops and tiptoeing runs, he ventured to the very edge of the packed debris and peered upriver. The light on the water dazzled him and for a time he could see nothing. Then, as if salvation were appearing in response to his most heartfelt dream, he made out the outline of a small boat and a man at the oars. And it was coming toward them. He lifted both his arms and waved them over his head. "Hey! Over here, over here!" he shouted, and in response, the man in the boat lifted a hand and waved at him.

Slowly, so slowly, the boat and its occupant grew larger. Sedric's eyes ran with tears, and not all of them were from the effort of keeping his light-dazzled gaze on the water. Carson recognized him before he knew the hunter. "SEDRIC!" he cried, sending his deep-chested shout of joy across the water to him. Then the hunter redoubled his efforts with the oars. It still seemed an eternity before Sedric could kneel and catch the line that Carson tossed to him. He drew the boat in close to the logs and then didn't know what else to do. He was grinning foolishly, trembling with relief.

"Thank Sa you're alive! And the dragon, too? That's a double miracle, then. And she's up and out of the water! How did you do it? Look at you! The river worked you over, didn't it? Here, let me take that and I'll make her fast. What do you need first? Water? Food? I thought I'd find you half dead if I found you at all!"

He stood shaking as Carson did all the talking for both of them. In moments the boat was secured to the edge of the debris island, and without his asking, Carson was offering him a waterskin. He drank greedily, paused to mutter, "Sa be praised and thank you," before drinking again. Carson watched him, his grin white in his beard. He looked weary and yet so triumphant that he shone.

As Sedric returned the waterskin to him, the hunter pushed a flat ship's biscuit into his hands. Sedric suddenly felt giddy with the smell of food. Perhaps he swayed on his feet, for Carson caught his elbow. "Sit down. Sit down and eat slow. You're going to be all right now. You've had a bad time, but everything's come right now. For you, too!" he assured Relpda as the dragon trumpeted her protest that Sedric was eating and she wasn't. Sedric was grateful but suddenly so hungry he could scarcely focus on Carson's words or Relpda's complaints. He broke off a piece of the hard bread and chewed it slowly. His jaw hurt, and he couldn't chew on the bruised side. Swallowing food made the pain worth it. He broke off another bite and ate it slowly.

Carson left him and went over to speak with the dragon. When he came back, he was shaking his head in admiration. "That's a nice bit of work there; it will probably fall apart if she moves around at all, but having a place to haul out is better than any of the other dragons have had."

The words slowly penetrated Sedric's mind, and he remembered that there were more things in the world to consider than just food and water. He spoke with his broken mouth full. "Who survived?"

"Well, more survived than went missing. Took us a day or two, but we've gathered up most everyone. Now that I've found you and the copper, we're only missing Rapskal, his dragon, and Jess. We found poor Warken dead, and Ranculos is badly bruised, but other than some injuries, everyone else is fine. How about you? You look more battered than anyone else."

He touched his face self-consciously. "A bit."

Carson gave a low laugh. "From here, it looks like more than 'a bit' to me. So. It's only you and the dragon here. No one else?"

"Only us," he replied guardedly. How would Carson feel if he knew that he and Relpda had killed the other hunter? He had frequently seen the two men together on the boat, and they often partnered each other in their hunting tasks. Now was no time to risk offending his savior. If he said nothing about Jess, no one would ever know.

Unless Relpda said something.

A tremor of fear went through him. The dragon reacted to it. *Danger? Eat hunter?*

"No, Relpda, no. No danger. The hunter will find food for you, but not right now." He mended her words as best he could and then said to Carson quietly, "She's been a bit more confused since the big wave."

"Well. I think we all have. But she has a point. She has to be ravenous. She was never fat to begin with, and it looks like the last couple of days have winnowed her down. Relpda? I know that dragons prefer fresh meat, but I saw an elk carcass floating not far from here. Shall I show you where?"

"Bring to Relpda. Relpda tired."

"Carson tired, too," the hunter muttered, but it was a good-natured complaint. "I'll go put a line on the stinking thing and pull it down here. You want me to leave the water with you?"

"Don't go!" The words were out of his mouth reflexively. Rescue had only just arrived.

Carson grinned and put a gentle hand on his shoulder. "Don't worry. I'll be back. I've gone to all this trouble to find you. I'm not about to abandon you here." Carson's gaze met Sedric's, and the words seemed to come from the hunter's heart. Sedric didn't know what to say.

"Thank you," he managed at last. He looked away from the man's earnest gaze. "I must seem a coward to you. Or an incompetent idiot."

"Neither one, I assure you. I won't be long. I'm leaving the water with you. It's all we've got right now, so go as easy on it as you can."

"It's all we've got? Why did you let me drink so much?" Sedric was horrified.

"Because you needed it. Now, let me go get Relpda some nice rotten elk, and then I'll be back. Maybe I'll still have enough light to go up the trees and look for more food for us."

"Jess—" Sedric halted his words. He'd nearly told him that Jess had found fruit nearby. Stupid, stupid, stupid. Don't mention the other hunter.

"What?"

"Just be careful."

"Oh, I'm always that. I'll be back soon enough."

THE WATER HAD gone down. There was still plenty of dead fish to eat. It wasn't fresh, but it was filling. She wasn't dead. At least, not yet.

Sintara shifted her weight. Her feet were sore from the constant immersion. The water was less acid than it had been, but her claws still felt soft, as if they were decaying. And she had never had less hope for herself.

She, Sintara, a dragon who should have ruled the sea, the sky, and the land, had been picked up and tumbled head over heels like a rabbit struck by a hawk. She'd floundered and gasped. She'd clung to a log like a drowning rat. "No dragons have ever endured what we have," she said. "None has ever sunk so low."

"There is nothing 'low' about survival," Mercor contradicted her. As always, his voice was calm, almost placid. "Think of it as experience hard won, Sintara. When you die and are eaten, or when your young hatch from the egg, they will carry forward your memories of this time. No hardship endured is a loss. Someone will learn from it. Someone profits from it."

"Someone is tired of your philosophizing," scarlet Ranculos grumbled. He coughed, and Sintara smelled blood. She moved closer to him. Among the dragons, his injury was the most serious. Something had struck his ribs as he tumbled in the flood. She could sense the pain he felt with every breath. For the most part, their scaled bodies had protected them. Sestican had a bruised wing that ached when he tried to open it. Veras complained of a burned throat from swallowing acid water. The lesser bruises that they all had scarcely seemed worth mentioning. They were dragons. They would heal.

The river had retreated as the day wore on. There was something of a shore now. Bushes festooned with streamers of dead vines stuck up in a long bar of silty mud. It was a relief to be able to stand, to have her belly out of water, but walking about in the thick sucking mud was almost as wearying as swimming.

"So what would you have me say, Ranculos? That after we have come this far, through so much adversity, we should now lie down and die?" Mercor came slogging over to them. To stand so close to one another was not a normal behavior for dragons, Sintara recognized. But they were not normal dragons. Their years huddled together in the limited space near Cassarick had changed them. In times like these, times when they were weary and uncertain, they tended to gather. It would have been comforting to lie down and sleep next to Ranculos. But she would not. The mud was too deep. She would stand and doze tonight and dream of deserts and hot dry sand.

"No. Not here, at least," Ranculos replied wearily.

Big blue Sestican slogged his way over to them. Mud streaked his azure hide. "Then it's agreed. Tomorrow we move on."

"Nothing is agreed," Mercor replied mildly. The gold dragon opened his wings and shook them lightly. Water and mud pattered down. His peacock-eyes markings were streaked with grime. She had not seen him so dirty since they had left Cassarick.

"Strange," Sestican commented sourly. "It sounded to me that we had decided not to lie down and die here. So the alternative would be, I think, to keep moving on, toward Kelsingra."

"Kelsingra," said Fente. She made the name sound like a curse. The little green dragon fluffed out the fronds of her immature mane. If she'd been properly grown, it would have appeared threatening. As it was, she reminded Sintara of a green-and-gold blossom on a skinny stem.

"I, for one, see no reason to wait for the keepers. We don't need them." Kalo wandered over. He limbered his wings as he came, spreading their blue-black expanse and shaking them to rid them of mud. They were larger than Mercor's. Was he attempting to remind them all that he was the largest and most powerful male?

"You're splattering mud all over me. Stop it." Sintara lifted the frills along her neck, confident that her own display was at least as intimidating as his.

"You're so covered with mud now, I don't know how you'd tell," Kalo complained, but he folded his wings all the same.

Sintara was in no mood to let him make peace so easily. "And you may not need your keeper, but I've a use for mine. Tomorrow I will have them both groom me. I might have to stand in mud, but there's no reason I must wear it."

"Mine is negligent. Lazy. Full of himself. Angry at everyone." Kalo's eyes spun with anger and unhappiness.

"Does he still think that perhaps butchering a dragon and selling him like meat would solve his problems?" Sestican baited him happily.

Kalo rose to it. No matter how often he complained of what a poor keeper Greft was, he would not tolerate comments critical of him. Even after Greft had made his obscene suggestion, Kalo had snapped at any of the others who dared complain about him. So now he opened his jaws wide and hissed loudly at Sestican.

He seemed as surprised as any of them when a bluish mist of venom issued from his mouth, to hang briefly in the air. Sintara lidded her eyes and turned her face away. "What are you about?" Fente demanded angrily. The little green splattered mud up on all of them as she scampered out of reach of the cloud. Sestican immediately stretched his own jaws wide and gathered breath.

"Stop!" Mercor commanded. "Stop it, both of you!"

He had no more right to issue orders than any other dragon. *Nonetheless, that never prevented him from doing it,* thought Sintara.

And almost always, the others obeyed him. There was something in his bearing that commanded their respect, even their
loyalty. Now he waded closer to Kalo. The big blue-black
dragon stood his ground, even half lifting his wings as if
he would challenge Mercor. But the golden dragon had no
intention of seeking battle. Instead, he stared intently at the
other big male, his black eyes whirling as if they gathered up
the darkness around them.

"Now do that again," Mercor challenged him, but not as
male to male. Rather he stared at Kalo as if he could not believe
what he had witnessed. He was not alone. The other dragons,
sensing something about the urgency in Mercor's voice, were
drawing nearer.

"But downwind of us!" Sestican interjected.

"And put some heart in it," Mercor added.

Kalo folded his wings. He did it slowly, and slowly was how
he turned away from the gathering dragons, to face downwind
of them. If he was attempting to make it appear he was not
obeying Mercor, he failed, thought Sintara. But she kept the
thought to herself, for she too wished to see if he could, indeed,
spit venom. All of them should have been capable of it since they
emerged from their cases, but none had achieved reliability or
potency with that most basic weapon in a dragon's arsenal. Had
Kalo? She watched his ribs swell as he took in air. This time, she
saw him work the poison glands in his throat. The muscles in
his powerful neck rippled. He threw back his head and snapped
it forward, jaws opening wide. He roared and a visible mist of
bluish toxin rode with the sound. It drifted in a cloud over the
water. She was not the only dragon to rumble in amazement.
She watched the toxin disperse and heard the very soft hiss when
acid met acid as it settled on the water.

Before anyone else could react, Fente propelled herself out
into the open river. She shook herself all over, opened her wings
wide, and threw back her head. When she launched her toxin
with a trumpet like a woman screaming, the cloud was smaller
but more dense. Again and again, she shrieked it forth, until on

her fourth try there was no visible sign of poison. Nonetheless, she turned to all of them and proclaimed, "Make no mistake. You may all be larger than I am, but I am just as deadly as any of you are. Respect me!"

"It would be wiser to save your toxins for hunting rather than making a show of them," Mercor rebuked her mildly. "You have no way of knowing how long it will take you to recover them. If you saw game right now, it would escape you."

The small green dragon spun to face them. Now the layered fronds of her immature mane stood out stiffly around her neck. She shivered them, a move more serpent than dragon. "Don't preach to me about wisdom, golden one. Nor hunting. I do not need your advice. Now that I have my poison again, I am not sure that I even need your company."

"Or your keeper?" Ranculos asked in mild curiosity.

"That remains to be seen," she snapped. "Tats grooms me, and it pleases me to hear him praise me. I may keep him. But having a keeper does not mean I must stay in company with you or those other raggle-taggle keepers. Nor do I need to be near keepers so disrespectful they speak of butchering a dragon as if he were a cow." She beat her wings, stirring air and spattering water. "I have my poison and soon I will be able to fly. Then I will need nothing of anyone save myself."

"So Heeby spoke of flying, too," Sestican said quietly.

"Heeby. That's not even her true name. She couldn't even summon her true name. Heeby. That's a name for a dog or a rather stupid horse. Not a dragon."

"Speak no ill," Mercor advised her. "Her end might be the same one we all meet."

"She didn't end because she never began," Fente retorted. "Half a dragon is no dragon at all."

Privately, Sintara agreed with her. The dimmer dragons still distressed her in a way she could not explain. To be around a creature with the shape of a dragon but to have no sense of that creature thinking the thoughts of a dragon was unsettling. One night she had overheard some of the keepers telling "ghost" stories to one another and wondered if that were not the same sensation. Something was there, but not there. A familiar shape with no substance to it.

And that was exactly what she saw now as the silver dragon with no name laboriously paddled out into the river. His tail had long healed, but he still held it stiffly as if the skin were too tight. His body had muscled from travel, and since his keepers had wormed him, he had put on healthier flesh. But his legs were still stumpy and short. The wings he now spread were almost normal, however. All the dragons watched in silence as he lifted them carefully, flapped them several times in imitation of Fente, and then drew back his head. When he snapped it forward, jaws wide, Sintara saw that his teeth were twice the size of Fente's and double rowed. And the cloud of toxin that came forth with his guttural roar was thick and nearly purple. The droplets were large and they fell, hissing, onto the river's surface. Sintara turned her face away from the acrid scent of strong venom.

"This half a dragon," the silver said, "can make you no dragon at all." He turned to glare at them, making sure they understood the threat. "Name? I *TAKE* a name. Spit my name. My name what I do. Fente, say my name."

The small green dragon spun away from him. She tried to remove herself in a dignified way, but dragons were not designed for swimming. She looked hasty and awkward as she scuttled out of his range. Spit laughed, and when Fente turned her head to hiss at him, he released a small cloud of floating toxins at her. The river wind wafted it away before it could do her any harm. Even so, Mercor reacted to it.

"Spit, save your venom. One of our hunters is gone, and our keepers have lost several of their boats and almost all their weapons. They are not going to be able to hunt as productively as they once did. All of us must strive harder to make our own kills. Save your venom for that."

"Maybe I eat Fente," Spit suggested poisonously. But then he turned and paddled back to the shallower water. He waded out onto the muddy shore and with a fine disregard for the filth, flung himself down to sleep. Sintara suddenly envied him. It would be so good to lie down. She could sleep. When she woke, Thymara and Alise could clean her. She was already dirty, so a bit more mud wouldn't make any difference. And it was time they both showed some gratitude for her saving them.

Her mind made up, she slogged to what she judged the highest point on the mudbank and eased herself down to sleep. The mud accepted her shape, coldly at first, but as she lay still, almost as a bed of thick grasses would, it warmed her. She lowered her head to her front legs to keep her nose out of the mud and closed her eyes. It was so good to lie down.

Around her, she could hear the other dragons following her example. Ranculos found his old spot beside her, favoring his left side as he lay down. Sestican settled on the other side.

The dragons slept.

$\diamond \diamond \diamond$

Day the 24th of the Prayer Moon

Year the 6th of the Independent Alliance of Traders

From Erek, Keeper of the Birds, Bingtown

To Detozi, Keeper of the Birds, Trehaug

In this case, a message from Hest Finbok, delivered by pigeon from Jamaillia to be sent on, by the swiftest means possible, to the barge *Tarman* and its passengers Sedric Meldar and Alise Finbok, directing them to return to Bingtown at the earliest possible moment. Traders in Cassarick and Trehaug to be informed by a general posting in both Trader Concourses that no debts incurred by these two will be honored by the Finbok family after the 30th day of the Prayer Moon.

Detozi!

Someone sounds very unhappy! I confess I am becoming intrigued. Has she run off with his secretary? But why decamp to the Rain Wilds? The gossip here is that both of them seemed well content with their lives, so all are astounded and scandalized at the prospect.

Erek

$\diamond \diamond \diamond$

CHAPTER TEN

CONFESSIONS

Relpda tore into the carcass with no complaints about how it stank. Sedric wished he could share her equanimity about it. She stood now always at the edge of his mind and thoughts. The stench of the meat and its rank flavor were like ghost memories in his mouth. He pushed them away, trying not to let it taint the fruit that Carson had gathered.

The hunter had come back as he had promised. Relpda had still been reluctant to reenter the water, so the two men had maneuvered the floating carcass within reach of her raft. It was streaked with mud and had been sampled by scavengers. Relpda didn't care. Since they had delivered it to her, her only thought had been to fill her belly.

The smooth-barked trees that had defied Sedric had yielded to Carson. For such a large man, he was very spry. He appeared to have no more difficulty ascending than a spider had in running up a wall. Sedric had tried to follow him, but his river-scalded hands were too tender for climbing. He'd given up when he was just over twice his height up the tree. Even backing down had been tricky. When he launched backward from the trunk, he'd landed badly. Now his ankle was tender.

Carson had returned from his climb just as darkness was falling. He cradled a sling of fruit, some like the stuff that Jess had brought, and two other kinds, one yellow and sweet, and the other the size of his fist, hard and green. So many plants and trees grew in the Rain Wilds, and he knew so little about any of it. He picked up one of the green fruits and turned it in his hands until Carson took it from him without a word and tapped it on the log between them as if it were a hard-boiled egg. The thick green shell peeled away from a pulpy white skin. "Eat it all," Carson advised him. "They don't taste like much, but there's a lot of moisture in them."

Carson had talked himself out. Sedric had heard the full tale of the wave hitting the ship, and how they had ridden it out, recovered the captain, and then discovered most of the missing keepers. Sedric has been shocked to discover that Alise had not been safely on board the vessel, and relieved she was safe. He'd let the hunter talk himself all the way to silence. Now he watched Sedric. He watched him closely, not with a direct stare, but from the corner of his eye and through his lashes. He shared the fruit out evenly between them, with no mention that Sedric hadn't done a thing to earn his. Even after he fed the dragon, Sedric kept waiting for Carson to bring up a scheme to kill the creature and make a profit on it. If the other hunter and the captain were in on that plot, it only made sense that Carson would be, too. And if Jess had shared his knowledge of Sedric's specimens with Carson, that would explain him and Davvie being so attentive and visiting Sedric's room so often. They'd both know that he had brought dragon blood on board the *Tarman*. Find that trove, and they'd be wealthy men.

When the fruit was gone, Carson had fetched a heavy iron pot from his boat, poured in a small amount of oil, and set fire to it. He cut bits of wood and resinous branch tips from the drier hunks of driftwood and fed the fire in the pot. It gave off smoky light and welcome heat and kept some of the insects at bay. The two men sat, watching the night deepen over the river. Stars began to show in the strip of sky overhead.

Carson cleared his throat. "I thought you couldn't talk to the dragons. Couldn't understand what they said at all."

Sedric didn't have a planned answer to that. He ventured close to the truth. "That changed when I began to be around them more. And after she rescued me, after she carried me here, well, we began to understand each other better." There. True enough and an easy explanation to remember. The best sort of lie. He stared off across the flat surface of the river.

"You don't talk much, do you?" Carson observed.

"Not much to say," Sedric replied guardedly. Then his manners caught up with him. "Except thank you." He forced himself to turn and meet Carson's sincere eyes. "Thanks for searching for us. I had no idea what I was going to do next. I couldn't get up a tree to find fruit, and I've never been a hunter or a fisherman." More formally he added, "I am in your debt." Among Traders, those words were more than a nicety. They acknowledged a genuine obligation.

"Oh, you looked like you were managing well enough," Carson replied generously. "But usually a man in your situation would be full of his tale, how the wave hit you and what you did . . ." He let his words trail away hopefully.

Sedric looked off into the darkness. Tell as much of the truth as he could. That would be safe. "I don't remember the wave hitting. I'd gone ashore to— to stretch my legs. When I came around, Relpda had hold of me and was keeping my head above water. Of course, she was swimming downriver with me, and I had quite a time persuading her that we needed to head for what used to be the shore. I was afraid she'd be exhausted before we got here. But we made it."

"Yes. We did." The dragon spoke around a mouthful of meat. She was pleased with herself. Pleased to hear Sedric tell of how she had saved him.

"I'm not surprised you don't recall everything. Looks like you took a hard knock to the head."

Sedric lifted a hand to his swollen face. "That I did," he said quietly. And he tried to let the conversation die. It was almost pleasant to be still in the night next to the flickering fire in the pot. He was still hungry and he ached all over, but at least he didn't have to wonder how he was going to survive the next day. Carson would take care of him, would get him back to the *Tarman.* His smelly little cabin beckoned him now, a haven from open water and starvation. There would be clean clothing there, and hot water and a razor. Cooked food in the galley. Simple things that he suddenly valued. *That wasn't very admirable,* he thought. Earlier in the day, he'd been able to take care of himself and a dragon. Yesterday, he'd been capable of killing to stay alive. But now he was ready to abandon all pretense of being competent in this world and let someone else do all the worrying and the thinking.

No wonder Hest had been able to discard him so easily.

Planning to smuggle dragon parts to Chalced was the closest he'd had to a personal plan of action in years. And look how well that had turned out! Almost as well as his previous suggestion that Hest marry Alise. Such happiness that had brought to all three of them. When had he let go of his own life? When had he become a bit of driftwood caught in Hest's current, tossed and turned and shaped by him and then, eventually, washed up here with the other debris? Idly he watched Carson add a piece of twisted white wood to the pot. Yes. That was him. Fuel for another man's flames.

Carson sighed suddenly. He seemed disappointed but game to forge ahead. "Well. Here's our plan for tomorrow, then. I'd like to get up as early as we can see and head back upriver to the *Tarman.* Captain Leftrin and I agreed that I wouldn't go more than a day's paddle downriver, but I'll admit that I covered a lot more distance than I thought I would. I may have to paddle hard to get back to him before sunset tomorrow. Think your dragon will be ready to travel by then?"

His dragon. Was she his dragon now?

Just thinking that question turned her awareness toward him.

Yes. You are my keeper. And I'll be ready to journey tomorrow. On to Kelsingra!

"On to Kelsingra," he affirmed quietly. "We'll be ready to travel."

Carson grinned. The smile and the firelight transformed the man's face. He was not, Sedric suddenly realized, that much older than he was. "Kelsingra," Carson agreed. "The end of the rainbow."

"You don't believe we'll get there?"

The hunter shrugged his shoulders. "Who cares? It will make a better tale if we do. But I've gone on longer expeditions than this with far humbler goals. This one called to me for a lot of reasons. Get Davvie out and about and away from danger. But I think I'm along for the same reason Leftrin is. A man wants to do something that leaves a mark. If we find that city, or even if we just find the place that it used to be, we'll have set the Rain Wilds and Bingtown on their ear. How often does a fellow get a chance to do something like that? At the very least, we've expanded the map. Every night, Swarge sits down and does his sketches and entries, and Captain Leftrin adds his notes. Jess was keeping a log of his own. I've put in a bit or two about the game we caught and what sorts of trees and riverside we found. All that information will go into the records and be stored at the Rain Wild Traders' Concourse. Years from now, when someone wants to anchor up for the night, they'll be doing it on the basis of what we've told them. Our names will be remembered. *The* Tarman *Expedition to Kelsingra*. Something like that. That's something, you know. That's something to be part of."

Sedric had been staring at the firepot as Carson spoke. Now he glanced at him surreptitiously. For the first time he saw the animation in his face. His deep-set brown eyes shone, and his lips, nestled in his beard, curved in a smile of purest satisfaction. Sedric had never heard anyone so pleased over such an intangible thing. He'd seen Hest in a paroxysm of joy over closing a rich deal, and he'd witnessed his father drunkenly celebrating a partnership in a trading trip. Always it had been about the wealth, the money, and the power and status that went with it. That had been the measure of the man, the status of the Trader in Bingtown. And it was how a man was measured in every town in Chalced and in Jamaillia and every other civilized place he'd ever visited. So he watched Carson and waited for the quirk of the lips or the bitter laugh that would expose his mockery of himself.

It didn't come. And although he'd said he'd come along for the same reason as Leftrin, he hadn't mentioned the taking of dragon parts and the riches to be made from them.

"It sounds like the stuff of dreams," he said, mostly to fill in the gap in the conversation, but wondering if it might provoke the man to confide the larger plan to him. Before he went back to the *Tarman,* he needed to know how ruthless Captain Leftrin was. Was Alise in physical danger from the man?

"I suppose. Every man has a dream. But I'm not telling you anything. You and Alise, documenting the dragons and ferreting out what they can recall of the Elderlings. It's the same thing, exploring territory where no one has gone, at least not in a long time."

"There will be money to be made from this," Sedric ventured.

Carson did laugh then. "Maybe. I rather doubt it. If it comes about, it will likely be after I'm in my grave. Oh, some of the keepers see it that way." Carson smiled as he shook his head. "Greft's full of himself; he's going to be the founder of a new Rain Wild settlement, the keepers will claim the wealth of Kelsingra as their own, and the dragons will help them defend their claim. The ships and workers will come up the river, there will be trade, and he'll be a rich man."

"Greft says that?" Sedric was shocked. He respected Greft's intelligence, but the young man had always seemed to be too full of hostility to have grandiose plans for himself.

"Not to me, of course. But he whispers it to the other keepers, as if such talk would stay in one place. I suspect a lot of his notions came from Jess. Jess is fond of claiming to be both worldly wise and well educated. By which I think he means that he once read a book. He has filled that boy's head with all sorts of nonsense." Carson leaned over and snapped a snag off a piece of the floating pack. The way he broke it spoke of extreme annoyance.

When he spoke again, he sounded calmer. "Oh, it may happen that Kelsingra is found and we establish a settlement there, but not the way he visualizes it. For one thing, he hasn't got enough people, and too few of them are female. He's barely got the population to start a village, let alone a city. And Rain Wilders, as I'm sure you know, don't breed easily. The babies who manage to be born sometimes live less than a year. And a Rain Wilder is an old man at forty." Carson scratched his scaly cheek above his beard. "So, even if a big discovery does persuade a boatload of new settlers to come, the new will likely outnumber the old, and they'll have their say about how things are done. And while Greft and the other keepers may discover riches, well, you can't eat Elderling artifacts. Don't we all know that! As long as the Elderling treasures remained in the Rain Wilds, it did no one any good. We had to ship them out to where people could come to bargain for them. That's why Bingtown is the big trading town and Trehaug isn't; if we didn't trade, we'd starve. And if we do find Kelsingra, and there is treasure there, the Traders driving the deals for those things will know that better than anyone. Men experienced at squeezing every bit of fat out of a deal will come. King Greft would have to sit at their bargaining table and play by their rules. Still. By the time Davvie's a full man, there might be a future for him in Kelsingra."

He cleared his throat and poked another dry stick into his firepot. Sedric was silent, picturing Greft or any of the keepers at a trading table with Hest. He'd eat them alive and pick his teeth with their bones.

A fat silver fish leaped suddenly out of the water after a low buzzing insect. It fell back into its world with a splash, and Carson laughed aloud. "Listen to me, spinning dreams and tales as if I were a minstrel. If anything of Kelsingra remains, and if we find it . . ."

"What if we find nothing?"

"Well. I've wondered that, too. At what point will Captain Leftrin give up and say that we're going back to Trehaug? To be honest, I don't see him doing that. For one thing, the keepers and the dragons can't go back. There's nothing there for them. He has to keep going until he finds somewhere that those creatures can live. And that would be nearly as big a discovery as Kelsingra." Carson scratched his beard thoughtfully. "For another, as long as Leftrin pushes on, he has Alise at his side. The minute he turns that barge around, he's just counting down the days until he loses her." He lifted an eyebrow at Sedric and added, "Pardon me if I'm talking out of turn, but that's how I see it.

"I overheard him and Swarge talking about it one night. Leftrin listens to his crew, more than most captains, and that's why so many of them have been with him so long. He wanted to know if Swarge and Bellin were discontented and wanted to turn back. Swarge said, 'It's all one to us, Cap. No homes in the trees waiting for any of us. And this river has to come from somewhere. We follow it far enough, we're bound to come to something.' And Leftrin laughed and said, 'What if what we come to is a bad end?' and Swarge said, 'A bad end is just a new beginning. We've been there before.' So. I think they'll keep going, until they find Kelsingra or the *Tarman* can't crawl any farther."

He poked the firepot again and seemed to take genuine pleasure in the drakes-tail of sparks he freed. "And I'll go with them. After all, I've got nothing and nobody calling me back to Trehaug. Or anywhere."

His statement seemed to be a question in disguise. Sedric considered it. He shrugged and answered it. "I've got no choice, do I? There's a life waiting for me back in Bingtown. One I'm rather good at, even if I can't survive on my own out here. But I've no way to get back to it. So I'm doomed to return to the *Tarman* with you and endure whatever comes next. I'm trapped."

And he was and he knew it. Even so, he regretted how mean and small his words seemed following Carson's more generous view of the world.

Carson's face shifted. The corners of his mouth dropped, and his eyes became solemn. He dropped the stick he'd been stirring the fire with into the pot and leaned back a bit. With both his big hands, he pushed his wild hair back from his face. When he spoke, his voice was tight. "You don't have to go back, Sedric. Not if you hate it that much. I've got the boat and the basic tools of my trade. I could take you downriver. It wouldn't be an easy trip, but I'd get you back to Trehaug. And from there, you could go home."

"What about the others?" Sedric asked reluctantly, trying to keep his rising excitement out of his voice. And then, as the complication came to him, "And what about the dragon?"

Yes. What about me? Her voice was a sleepy gurgle.

"Oh. That's right. The dragon." Carson smiled ruefully. "Strange, how a small detail like a very large dragon can slip my mind for a time. I suppose I'm still thinking of you as Alise's assistant rather than as a keeper." He was quiet for a time, and the bubble of excitement that Sedric had felt at the prospect of an early return to Bingtown began to subside.

Carson shrugged. "We could make sure she got back to the other dragons. After that, she'd have to manage on her own. We'd have to go upriver first anyway. I couldn't just vanish; Leftrin would think I was dead, and Davvie would be crazy with fear and sorrow. I wouldn't do something like that to a friend, let alone a boy who depends on me. And I'd want to ask Leftrin to let me out of my contract to hunt. A bad time for me to be asking that, with Jess missing. And you'd want to say good-bye to Alise, I'm sure . . ." His voice dwindled away. "I guess neither of us is as free as I was thinking we were," he said softly. "Too bad."

"Too bad," Sedric agreed sickly. He was silent for a time, and then he observed, "Just a few minutes ago, you were talking about how wonderful it was to be part of something big like this expedition. Mapping the river, looking for an ancient city. Why would you offer to walk away from that just to take me to Trehaug?"

Carson grinned. He met his eyes frankly. "I like you, Sedric. I *really* like you. Haven't you figured that out yet?"

The man's frankness astounded him. He stared at the hunter, at his scaled skin above his bearded cheeks, his wild hair, and his scruffy clothing. Could he have been more unlike Hest?

A moment too late, he realized he should have given some response to that honest offering. Carson had already looked away from him. He gave a tiny shrug. "I know you've got someone waiting for you to come back. I think he was an idiot to let you go in the first place. And of course, I don't forget the differences between us. I know what I am, and I got my place in the world. And most of the time, I'm pretty satisfied with my life."

Sedric found his voice. "I wish I could say the same," he offered, then knew it had come out wrong. "I mean, I wish I could say I'd found satisfaction in my life. I haven't." There had been moments of it, he thought. Time spent with Hest in some of the more exotic cities they'd visited, times of excellent wine and rare foods and the prospect of a long, merry evening in a finely appointed inn. Had that been satisfaction with his life, he suddenly wondered, or simply hedonistic satiation? Uncomfortably he sensed that Carson was right. The differences between them were extreme. He suddenly felt shamed but also a bit angry. So he liked things to be nice; so he enjoyed the fine things life could offer. That didn't make him shallow. There was more to him than just enjoying what Hest's money could buy him. Carson's voice called him back to reality. His voice sounded resigned.

"It's getting late. We should get some sleep. You can have the blanket."

"There's another blanket in the other boat," he said.

"Other boat?" Carson asked him.

He'd relaxed too much. The truth had slipped out. Then he wondered how long he would have lied? Would he have kept his silence tomorrow, let them abandon supplies and gear that were even more precious now than when they had left Trehaug?

"It's tied up on the other side of that big snag over there." He tossed his head toward it, and then sat, guilty and silent, as Carson gracefully rose and crossed the mat of rocking logs and debris to look down on it. He stared at the firepot. He heard the big man thud gently down into the bottom of the boat. In a moment, his voice came through the dimness. "This is Greft's boat and his gear. One thing about him, he's good at taking care of what's his. If I were you, I'd be careful with his stuff. He's going to want it all back, and in good condition."

A few moments later, Carson returned. The blanket was slung over his shoulder. He tossed it to Sedric, not hard but not softly either. Sedric caught it. It was still damp in places. He'd intended to spread it out to dry in the sun and forgotten.

"So," Carson said, sitting down on the log again. "That's Greft's boat. And you didn't tie the knots that are securing it. What's the whole story? And why didn't you tell it?" There was a chill in his voice, a cold spark of anger.

Sedric was suddenly too tired to dissemble. Too tired to be anything but honest. "I did tell you what happened to me. I saw this pack of logs here, and Relpda brought me here. Then I found out that Jess was already here. He'd been swept away, too, but he'd found a boat. And he'd got here before I did."

"Jess is here?"

A simple question. If he answered it truthfully, how would Carson react? He looked at him wordlessly. No lie came to him and he didn't dare tell the truth. He fingered the massive bruise on the side of his face as he tried to decide where to begin. Carson's deep eyes were fixed on his. A furrow had begun to show between his brows, and his mouth was suspicious. *Talk. Say something.*

"He wanted to kill Relpda. Cut her up into parts, take the parts to Chalced and sell them."

For a long moment, Carson was silent. Then he nodded slowly. "That sounds like something Jess was capable of doing. Sounds like what he was trying to get Greft to persuade the keepers to do. So what happened?"

"We fought. I hit him with the hatchet."

"And I ate him." There was satisfaction in Relpda's quiet rumble.

The copper distracted Carson completely from what Sedric had said. His head swiveled to face her. "You ate him? You ate Jess?" He was incredulous.

"It's what dragons do," she replied defensively. Sedric's own words, coming out of her mouth.

Sedric found himself justifying it. "Jess wanted me to help him trick her into keeping still while he killed her. I wouldn't. So he stabbed her with a spear and then came after me. Carson, he was going to kill her and cut her up and sell her. And he didn't care if he had to kill me first to do it."

The hunter's head swiveled back to regard Sedric skeptically. His eyes wandered over Sedric, his bruised face and battered condition, assigning new meaning to what he saw. Sedric felt his muscles tighten as he faced that gaze, fearing that soon it would turn to judgment and condemnation. Instead, he saw disbelief slowly become admiring amazement.

"Jess was one of the nastiest fellows I'd ever had to work alongside. He had a reputation for being a dirty fighter, the kind who didn't stop even after the other fellow was willing to give in. And you stood up to him for your dragon?" He glanced over at Relpda. Nothing remained of the elk carcass. She'd eaten it all.

"I had to," Sedric said quietly.

"And you won?"

Sedric just looked at him. "I'm not sure I'd describe it as winning."

The comment surprised a guffaw out of Carson. Then Relpda intruded.

"And I ate him. Sedric fed him to me." She seemed to savor the memory.

"That isn't exactly what happened," Sedric hastily interposed. "I never intended for that to happen. Though I'll admit that at the time, what I mostly felt was relief. Because I wasn't sure if anything else would have stopped him."

"And Jess is what happened to your face, then?"

Sedric lifted a hand to his jaw. His cheekbone was still tender, and the swollen inside of his cheek kept snagging on his teeth. But he felt almost strangely proud of his injury now. "Yes, it was Jess. I'd never been hit in the face like that before."

Carson gave a brief snort of laughter. "Wish I could say that!

I've caught plenty of fists with my face. Though I'm truly sorry
to see it happen to yours."

Almost timidly, the hunter put out a large hand. The touch of
his rough fingers on Sedric's face was gentle. Sedric was shocked
that such a slight brush against his cheek could send such a rush
of feeling through him. The fingers pressed gently around his
eyes socket and then the line of his cheekbones. He sat very still,
wondering if there would be more, wondering how he would
react if there was. But Carson dropped his hand and turned his
face away, saying hoarsely, "Nothing's broken, I don't think.
You should heal." A moment later, he fed another stick to the
firepot. "We should get some sleep soon if we're going to get
up early."

"Jess said Leftrin was in on it." Sedric blurted the statement
out, letting it be its own question.

"In on what?"

"Killing dragons and selling off the parts. Teeth, blood, scales.
He said that whoever had sent him had said that Leftrin would
be willing to help him."

Carson's dark gaze grew troubled. "And did he?"

"No. That was part of Jess's complaint. He seemed to feel
Leftrin had cheated him."

Carson's expression lightened somewhat. "That seems likely
to me. I've known Leftrin a long time. And over the years,
once or twice, he's been involved in a few things that I found,
well, questionable. But slaughtering dragons and selling off their
bodies? No. To Chalced? Never. There are a number of reasons
why I couldn't imagine him getting involved with something
like that. Tarman being the big one." His brow wrinkled as he
stared into his fire. "Still, it would be interesting to know why
Jess thought he would."

He shook his head, then stood up slowly, rolling his shoulders
as he did so. He was surprisingly graceful for his size, catching
his balance easily as he stepped down into his small boat. His
own blanket was neatly stowed, folded, and shoved high under
the seat out of the damp. Sedric still clutched the damp and

wrinkled blanket Carson had tossed at him. He looked at Carson's boat, at every item in a precise location, and he suddenly felt childish and ashamed. Over in the other boat, a hatchet was probably rusting from its immersion in the bloody bilgewater. Carson had arrived and had seen to every need that he and the dragon had, without a single wasted movement. Sedric hadn't even remembered to spread his blanket out to dry.

He wondered how Carson saw him. Incompetent? Self-indulgent? Rich and spoiled? *I'm not truly any of those things,* he thought. *I'm just out of my place right now. If we were back in Bingtown, and he came to where I was helping Hest prepare to negotiate a trade, he'd see what I truly am.* Carson would be the incompetent and useless one there. Then even that thought seemed self-indulgent and spoiled, a child's wish to show off for someone he desired to impress. What did it matter what Carson thought of him? When had he begun to care what an ignorant Rain Wild hunter thought of him?

He shook out the smelly blanket and slung it around his shoulders. Within its shelter, he sat hugging himself. And thinking.

NIGHT WAS FULL dark around Tarman. Captain Leftrin walked his decks. The night sky was a black strip sprinkled with glittering stars. To one side of the barge, the river stretched out to an invisible distant shore. On the other side the forest loomed, making the barge small. At the foot of the forest, on a narrow muddy bank, the dragons slept. On the roof of the deckhouse, laid out in neat rows as if they were corpses, the keepers slept. And Leftrin was awake.

Swarge was supposed to be on watch, but he'd sent him off to his bed. The entire crew was asleep. The river was down, Tarman was safely snugged on mud for the night, and his crew deserved a rest. It would be the first full night of sleep any of them had had since the wave hit. They all needed the rest. Everyone needed to sleep.

Even Alise. That was why she had sought her room early. She was exhausted still. He began another slow circuit of the decks.

He didn't need to walk laps around his ship. All was safe and calm now. He could have gone off to his own bunk and slept and left Tarman to watch for himself. No one would fault him for that.

He passed Alise's door. No light shone from under it. Doubtless she was asleep. If she had wanted his company, she would have lingered at the galley table. She hadn't. She'd vanished immediately after dinner. He'd hoped that she would stay. He faced that fading hope frankly. It would have been the first and only night that they'd been together on board his ship without Sedric's presence as a reminder of who and what she was. He had hoped to steal this one night from her Bingtown life and possess it as something of their own.

But she'd excused herself from the table and vanished into her own room.

What did that mean?

Probably that she was a lot smarter than he was. Which, he told himself, he'd known all along. What intelligent man would want to share harness with a woman stupider than himself? His Alise was smart, and he knew it. Not just educated but intelligent.

But he wished she hadn't chosen to be smart on this particular night.

And what sort of a man was he, that he felt Sedric's absence as a sort of relief rather than a loss? The man had been Alise's friend since childhood. He knew that. He might find him an annoying spoiled twit of a fellow, but Alise cared about him. She was probably wondering if he was dead or in dire circumstances tonight. And here he was, brutishly thinking only that the watchman was gone.

He finished his circuit of his ship and stood for a time on Tarman's blunt-nosed bow. He leaned on the railing and looked at the "shore." Somewhere there the dragons slept in the mud, but he couldn't see them. The forest was pitch before his eyes. He spoke to his ship.

"Well, tomorrow's another day, Tarman. One way or another, Carson will return. And then what? Onward?"

Of course.

"You seem so sure of it."

I remember it.

"So you've told me. But not the way it is now."

No. That's true.

"But you think we ought to keep going?"

The others have no choice. And I think it's the least we can do for them.

Leftrin said nothing. He glided his hands lightly along the bow railing, thinking. Tarman was an old ship, older than any of the other liveships. He was one of the first to have been put together from wizardwood, as it was known then. He hadn't been designed to be a trading ship of any kind, only a simple wooden barge, given a thick layer of the only sort of wood that seemed impervious to the Rain Wild River's acid rages. In a tradition much older than Bingtown or even Jamaillia, Leftrin's ancestor had painted eyes on his ship not only to give it a wise expression but as a superstition that the barge would literally "watch out" for itself on the dangerous waterway. At the time, the only known properties of wizardwood were that it was hard and heavy and could withstand acid. No one had known then that after lifetimes of human presence on board, a liveship could attain its own awareness. That would not be discovered until the first sailing ships with figureheads were carved from the stuff.

But that didn't mean that Tarman hadn't become aware. It didn't mean that his captains hadn't known and felt his presence.

The sailors of Leftrin's lineage had known there was something peculiar about their ship, especially those who grew up on his deck, who slept and played aboard him. They developed an affinity for both the barge and the river, an instinctive knack for navigating and for avoiding the ever-shifting sandbars and hidden snags of the forest waterway. They dreamed strange dreams that they seldom shared except with other members of the family. The dreams were not just dreams of the river and sliding silently through it. They had dreams of flying and sometimes dreams of swimming in a deep and blue-shadowed world.

Tarman had become aware, just as all liveships eventually did.

But he had no mouth to speak with, no carved hands or human face. He was silent, but his eyes were old and knowing.

Perhaps Leftrin should have left him that way. Things had been good between them. Why had he desired to try to make them better?

The wizardwood log had been both a windfall and a complication in his life.

He'd made his plans so carefully. He'd reduced his crew to a handful of men whom he absolutely trusted. He'd found men who had worked wizardwood, men with sterling reputations for honesty and carpentry skill. He'd scrimped and saved and bartered for the tools he needed to have. And when all was ready, he'd transported them to where he had found and secured the log of wizardwood.

And he had done it knowing that it was neither log nor wood.

He'd run Tarman aground, and then with lines and pulleys he'd winched the barge up into an isolated inlet along the river's shore. He'd lost most of a summer's work to that project. The wizardwood log had to be cut into rough planks and blocks on site and then fastened to Tarman. The barge had to be lifted up on blocks to allow the workmen access to the bottom; the soft ground along the river meant that every day, the blocking had to be reinforced and releveled.

But when all was finished Tarman had what the barge had conveyed to Leftrin it most desired. Four stout legs with webbed feet and a long tail had been added to the hull. Tarman could now go almost anywhere he and his captain wished to go.

It had taken several weeks for Tarman to get complete motion in all his limbs. Leftrin had been terrified for him the first time the blocks were jerked out from under the hull. But Tarman had caught himself, with difficulty, and slowly dragged himself back into the river. The ship's eyes had gleamed with satisfaction as he propelled himself about in the shallows. He was equally content to swim in the river or crawl along in the shallows. His crew became more a sham than a workforce. They preserved the illusion that Tarman was a barge like any other.

Every scrip and scrap of leftover "wood" had been stowed in-

side Tarman as dunnage. Not so much as a sliver of the stuff had
he sold; that would have been breaking faith with his ship. He
respected the dragon stuff Tarman was made from. As the weeks
and months passed, he had sensed the ship integrating his new
material and memories. Tarman's placid nature had changed; he
had become more assertive and adventurous, sometimes even
edging into mischievousness. Leftrin had enjoyed the changes
in his ship just as much as if he'd been watching a child grow
to manhood. Tarman's eyes had become more expressive, his
connection to his captain more eloquent, and his efficiency as a
barge a wonder. If any of the other Traders suspected Leftrin's secret, none asked about it. Almost every Trader had his own store
of undisclosed magic or technology. Not prying too deeply into
the affairs of others was an essential part of being a Trader. Leftrin had had no problems, and his profits had steadily grown.

All had been well until one of the carvers had flapped his
mouth to that Chalcedean trader, and the hunter had come on
board to threaten them, his own kind. Leftrin gritted his teeth
so hard that it made a noise. Beneath him, he felt Tarman dig his
feet into the mud in anger. *Betrayal! Betrayal is not to be tolerated.
The traitor must be punished.*

Leftrin immediately loosened his grip on the railing and
calmed his own emotions. The captain of a liveship always had
to keep a rein on his darker thoughts. His emotions could infect
his ship in dangerous ways. The strength and clarity of Tarman's
response startled him. He seldom conveyed his thoughts so directly. He had not realized the ship felt so strongly about the
hunter. So now he calmly pointed out that the river had done
their task for them. Jess was gone, most likely drowned.

At that thought, he sensed a wave of grim satisfaction from
the ship, tinged with a bloody amusement. Did the ship know
more of Jess's fate than he had shared? Leftrin wondered uneasily. And then he hastily turned his thoughts away from that. The
liveship had a right to his own secrets. If he had seen Jess struggling in the water and deliberately turned away from him, that
was the ship's business, not Leftrin's.

Don't be troubled about that. I didn't need to do anything so crude.

He ignored the amusement in the ship's tone. "Well, I'm glad of that, Tarman. I'm glad of that. If I'd had to face that, well. Just glad it was a decision that didn't come my way." He sensed the ship's calm assent. "And tomorrow we can expect Carson to rejoin us."

Yes. You should expect that.

Sometimes the ship just knew things. The ship had heard Carson's horn when he'd first found the survivors and told Leftrin. The captain had learned better than to ask him how he sensed things or to ask for details. Only once had Tarman been in a mood to tell him anything, and then he had only said, *Sometimes the river shares its secrets with me. Sometimes, but not always.* For tonight, Leftrin simply accepted that tomorrow the hunter would rejoin them, and he asked no more. Instead he suggested, "Think we'll head upriver tomorrow, then? Or anchor another night here?"

Probably another night here. The dragons can use a bit more rest, and there is still dead fish for them to feed on. If they are going to take rest, they may as well have it while there is food. Even if it is rank food.

"Will they sicken on it?"

Dragons are not such a feeble race as humans. Carrion displeases the palate and eating too much of it can bring on a bellyache. But dragons can eat what they must, and when dead fish is all that is to be had, then they will eat it. And go on.

"As shall we, then," Leftrin affirmed.

As was agreed, the barge reminded him.

"As was agreed," the captain concurred. For he had not been quite honest with Alise in that small matter. The fact was that even before he had docked in Cassarick, he had known that he and Tarman would be escorting the dragons up the river. It was why he had been able to load so swiftly and depart. The fact that it dovetailed so completely with Alise's plans had seemed like fate to him, as if he were predestined to enjoy her company. It had been a wonder and a pleasure to see her shine at that meeting.

She's not asleep. She's in the sneaking whiner's chamber.

"I think I might just go check on that. See if she's having trouble sleeping."

Think you might have the cure for such wakefulness? the ship asked him in amusement.

"Perhaps some quiet talk with a friend," Leftrin returned with what dignity he could muster.

Didn't know you'd already introduced her to your "friend." You go along. I'll keep watch here.

"Watch your words!" Leftrin rebuked his ship, but felt only Tarman's amusement in response. "You're chatty tonight." He made the comment not just to divert the ship's attention but because he had seldom experienced such clarity of thought from Tarman. It was much more common for him to have an unusual dream, or to sense emotions through his connection to the ship. Direct conversation with Tarman was highly unusual and he wondered at it.

Sometimes, the ship agreed. *Sometimes, when the river is right and the dragons are close by, it all seems easier and clearer.* There was a time of stillness and then Tarman added, *Sometimes you are more willing to hear me. When our thoughts align. When we agree on what we want. We both know what you want right now.*

He lifted his hands from the railing and went in search of Alise. Despite his attempt at rebuking the barge, a small smile crept across his face. Tarman knew him far too well.

He stood for a time on the dark deck outside Sedric's door. Tarman was right. A very faint glow was visible at the crack at the bottom of the door. He tapped lightly and waited. For a time, all was silence. Then he heard the scuff of feet on the deck and the door opened a crack. Alise peered out, limned against a faint candle glow.

"Oh!" She sounded surprised.

"I saw the light coming out from under the door. Thought I'd best check on who was in here."

"It's only me." She sounded disheartened.

"I see that. May I come in?"

"I'm . . . I'm in my nightrobe. I came here from my cabin when I couldn't sleep."

He could see that also. Her nightrobe was long and white and rather plain, the simple lines of it interrupted only by the complex curves of the woman inside it. Her red hair had been brushed and plaited into two long braids. It took years away from her face. Her little bare feet peeped out the bottom of the robe. If she'd had any idea of how desirable it made her look, she'd never have dared open the door to anyone!

But her eyes and the end of her nose were reddened from crying. And it was that more than anything else that made him step into the room, close the door firmly behind him, and take her into his arms. She stiffened slightly but did not resist him, even when he pulled her close and kissed the top of her hair. How could she smell like flowers still? He closed his eyes as he embraced her and heaved a heavy sigh. "You mustn't cry," he told her. "We haven't given up hope yet. You mustn't cry and you mustn't torment yourself like this. It doesn't do a bit of good for anyone."

He refused to think anymore. He stooped and kissed her left eye. She gasped.

When he kissed her other eye, her arms rose and linked tight around his neck. He put his mouth on hers, and her lips opened so softly and easily to his that his heart shook. She was trembling, pressed hard against him. He held the kiss, feeling and tasting the warmth of her mouth. He straightened up and still she clung to him, not letting him break the kiss. He lifted her easily and she hooked her knees over his hips with no pretense of keeping her legs together.

"Alise," he gasped, warning her.

"Don't talk!" she responded fiercely. "No talking at all!"

So he didn't.

Two shuffling steps crossed the small room. He tried not to crush her as he lowered her to the bed, but she would not let go of him and he all but fell on top of her. He was between her legs, nothing but the canvas of his trousers and the bunched fabric of her nightdress between them. He pressed himself against her, warning her, wanting her. Instead of heeding the warning, she surged up against him. He kissed her again, finding her breasts free within her nightdress. He hefted the weight of them while he kissed her, found her ripe nipples and gently teased them.

She made a small sound in her throat and pressed herself into his hands.

Emboldened, he slid a hand down her belly and lifted his body slightly from hers to touch her with his fingers. She gasped, and gave the unmistakable shudder of a woman in climax. He was astonished and almost insufferably pleased at her responsiveness. He hadn't even entered her!

But if he thought his brushing touch had satisfied her, he was wrong. When she opened her eyes to look at him, her gaze was wild and hungry. "Don't stop," she warned him.

"Alise, are you cert—"

He didn't even complete the sentence. She stopped his mouth with hers, and her groping hand found him and made her desire plain.

ALISE OPENED HER other hand. The locket with Hest inside it fell, to the bedding, to the floor. It could have fallen into the river itself. She didn't care.

Day the 25th of the Prayer Moon

Year the 6th of the Independent Alliance of Traders

From Erek, Keeper of the Birds, Bingtown
To Detozi, Keeper of the Birds, Trehaug

Enclosed, part one of a missive from the Bingtown
Traders' Council to the Rain Wild Traders' Councils at
Trehaug and Cassarick, being the public accounting of
the Bingtown Traders' expenses and income for the year,
for purposes of shared taxation. Three copies of each
accounting to be sent by bird, and one by ship.

Detozi,

*I am sure all are anxiously awaiting to hear how our taxes will
rise yet again this year! With Bingtown still, in some places,
rebuilding public works and the Market damaged by the
Chalcedeans, and both Cassarick and Trehaug needing funds
for the shoring up of the excavations, I wonder if taxes will
ever go down to what they were five years ago. My father is on
the mend at last, but his recent illness has renewed my parents'
anxiety about my lack of a wife and children. Silly me, to think
that might be MY business!*

Erek

Chapter Eleven

REVELATIONS

ome time short of dawn, she'd wakened him. "We should go back to our own beds," she whispered.

He gave a long sigh of resignation. "In a minute," he lied. He stroked her hair, twined a lock of it around his finger. It tugged gently, pleasantly against her scalp.

"I had a dream," she heard herself say.

"Did you? So did I. It was nice."

Alise smiled into the darkness. "I dreamed of Kelsingra. It was a strange dream, Leftrin. I think I was a dragon in my dream. Because I saw the city, well, as if it were small and I were looking down on it. I've never even imagined seeing a city that way. All the rooftops and spires, the roads set out like veins in a leaf, and the river was the biggest silver road of all. The river was so wide, but the city was still on both sides of it. You know, in my dream, the city looked as if it had been planned to be seen from above. Like a strange form of art . . ."

She let her voice drift away. In the bed beside her, Leftrin shifted. When he moved, she became more aware of him, of where his body touched hers and how he smelled. She spoke reluctantly. "I think we should both go back to our rooms."

The candle had long since guttered out. Sedric's small room was black. Leftrin sat up slowly. Cold air touched her where his body had pressed against hers in the narrow bed. She smiled to herself. She'd slept next to a naked man. Actually slept with his arms around her, her cheek against the hair of his chest, her legs tangled with his.

She'd never experienced that before.

In the blackness, she heard him find his trousers and shirt. The canvas trousers made an interesting sound as he drew them up his legs. She heard him shoulder into his shirt. He stooped to find his shoes and picked them up. "I'll walk you to your door," he whispered, but, "No. Go along. I'll be fine," she told him.

He didn't ask her why she wanted him to leave. For that, she was grateful. She heard the door open and close, and then she moved. Her nightgown was on the floor. It was cold and damp in places, but she pulled it on over her head. One of her braids, she noted, had come out of its plait. She shook out the other one. By touch, she smoothed the rucked blankets on Sedric's bed. She found his "pillow" and put it back in place. She felt around on the bedclothes and on the floor, but did not find the locket. She told herself again that she didn't care. It was a worthless artifact of a life no longer connected to her. She slipped from the room, closing the door behind her.

It was only a short flit to her own room. She closed the door behind her and found her bed. The blankets seemed cold and unused as she crawled under them. Her groin ached, her face and breasts were rasped from his beard, and his smell was all over her. She wondered at what she'd done, defiantly decided she didn't care, but still could not close her eyes. She cared about what she had done. She cared about it more than any decision she'd ever made in her life. She stared up into the darkness, not repenting it but reenacting every moment in her mind. His hands had touched her so, and he'd made those small sounds of enjoyment, and his beard had brushed her breasts when he had kissed them.

It had all been so new to her. She wondered if she had been wanton or only womanly. Had they behaved like animals toward each other, or was this how people who loved each other touched and tasted and devoured each other? She felt as if she'd experienced it all for the first time.

Perhaps she had.

She closed her eyes. Thoughts of Sedric's fate, of Hest in Bingtown, of her proper friends and her mother's pride, and of her eventual return to that life threatened her.

"No." She spoke aloud. "Not tonight."

She closed her eyes and slept.

HE STOOD BAREFOOT on his deck, looking out over the shore. His shoes were in his hand. "Tarman, what are you about?" he asked his ship quietly.

The response that came was enigmatic. He didn't hear it. He felt it as much through his bare soles on the deck as he did in his heart. The ship was keeping his own counsel.

He tried again. "Tarman, I know that dream. I thought it was mine. Something you wanted me to see."

This time there was a shiver of assent in the air. A shiver, and then silence.

"Ship?" he queried.

But nothing responded. And after a time, carrying his shoes, the captain of the *Tarman* sought his berth.

CARSON HAD ROPED the small boats together. That was humiliating, as if he were riding a horse that someone led, but Sedric appreciated how sensible it was. So instead of protesting it, he had devoted his efforts to seeing that the line between the two stayed slack. He was willing to admit that he was incompetent at keeping a small boat out of the main current and moving upstream in a river. He was not willing to admit that he didn't have the strength to row his own boat and must be towed back to the barge.

There was a price to pay for that pride, and he was paying it now. Every stroke of the oars had become an effort. His hands had blistered, the blisters had popped and run, and now he gripped raw flesh to bare wood. Carson turned his head and shouted back to him. "Not much farther to go now! Everyone will be glad to see you and the dragon and the boat! Losing it was a significant loss."

Probably more significant than losing a Bingtown fop, Sedric thought savagely. He knew that Carson didn't intend to insult him, only point out that they would be triply welcomed. Knowing that didn't help. In the last day and night, he had seen himself in a different light, and he found it very unflattering. Useless to remind himself that in Bingtown business circles, he was a competent clever fellow. He was known in all the better taverns to have a lovely clear tenor for drinking songs, and the wine shops saved their best vintages for him. No one could fault his taste in silk. Given charge of Hest's itinerary, every voyage under his control went flawlessly.

And none of that mattered here. Once he would not have cared about Carson's regard at all. He would have been content to wait out each boring day on the barge until he could return to Bingtown and his proper life. Now he found himself hungry to show that he could distinguish himself in places other than the bargaining table. Or the bedroom. The thought loomed again, and this time he faced it. Had Hest truly valued him as a business partner? Or had he kept him at his side solely because he was amusing and pliable in the bedroom?

Off to the side of the boats, the copper dragon lumbered through the shallows. The river was almost down to its former level. She seemed cheery to be moving upriver again. Soon she would rejoin the other dragons, and their endless journey would continue. She slogged along, sometimes holding her tail up out of the river's flow and sometimes letting it trail behind her. She kept a touch on his mind, rather like a small child gripping a handful of her mother's skirts. He was aware of her without having her intrude too much into his mind. Right now, she had sun on her back, mud under her feet, and she was just starting to feel hungry. Soon they'd have to help her find food, or she'd become fractious. But for now, she had everything she desired from life and was content with it. She was such an immediate creature that she almost charmed him until he realized how amoral she was.

Rather like Hest.

That thought ambushed him, breaking the pattern of his rowing. He stared straight ahead, trying to decide if he had just discovered something or was only indulging his anger at Hest yet again. Then the rope between the two small boats went tight, jolting him back on the seat and causing Carson to look back at him. The hunter allowed the river to push him back alongside Sedric's boat. "You're tired? If you're tired, we can pull over to the trees for a time." The brown eyes were full of sympathy. He knew that Sedric was unaccustomed to physical labor. That morning, he'd offered to let Sedric just sit in his boat while Carson did all the rowing and towed the other boat behind them.

He longed to do just that. Just admit that he was a weakling and not fit to survive out here. "No, I was just scratching my nose. Sorry!"

"Well, let me know if you need a rest." Carson simply stated the possibility. Sedric looked for mockery behind the words and found none. The hunter pulled on his oars again, drawing his boat ahead.

Sedric leaned into his rowing again. Carson had turned his gaze back to the river. He watched the man's back and tried to copy the way he moved his oars. His broad shoulders and muscular arms moved steadily with the seeming ease of an animal breathing. As he rowed, his head made small movements, watching the water, the passing trees, the dragon, the water. He was like the dragon, Sedric realized. He had his mind on what he was doing, and did it well, and that was enough for him. Sedric knew a moment of pure envy. Would that his own life was that simple.

Could it be?

Of course not.

His own life was a mess. He was out here, far from where he could be successful at anything. He'd taken blood from a dragon, and worse, he'd tasted it, and now he knew the lowness of what he'd done, and what he'd contemplated doing. How could he ever have imagined that they were simply animals, like a pig or a sheep, to be slaughtered as a man pleased? He thought of the bargain he'd struck with that merchant Begasti and shuddered. As soon he would traffic in a child's heart or the fingers of a woman!

And here was where that ill-founded plan had brought him. He was far from home, and getting farther away every day. His plan for becoming án incredibly wealthy man and spiriting himself and Hest away from Bingtown seemed more unlikely and reprehensible every moment.

He tried to bring that fantasy back to life. He imagined himself and Hest in a beautifully appointed room, regarding each other over a table laden with a perfectly prepared meal. In his dream, there had always been tall doors open to a fragrant garden illuminated by the setting sun. In his dream, an astounded Hest was always demanding to know how he had acquired all this for them, while Sedric leaned back in a chair, a glass of wine in his hand, and silently smiled.

He imagined it all in detail, the laden sideboard, the wine in his glass, the silk shirt, and the birds calling as they flitted from bush to tree in the evening garden. He could recall every bit of his dream, but he could not make it move, could no longer hear Hest's intrigued and eager questions, could no longer make his own face smile as he would have smiled and shaken his head, refusing all answers. It had become unruly, a dream turned to nightmare in which he knew that Hest would have had too much to drink, and that he had refused the fish as overcooked and leeringly commented on the serving boy who came to clear the dishes. The real Hest would have asked him if he'd whored himself out on the streets to get this money. The real Hest would disdain whatever Sedric presented, would have

criticized the wine, found the house too ostentatious to be taste-
ful, would have complained that the food was too rich.

The Hest of his dreams had been replaced by the man Hest
had steadily become over the last two years, the mocking, sour
Hest, the impossible-to-please Hest, the domineering Hest who
had banished him here for daring to disagree with him. The
Hest who had begun to bludgeon him, more and more often,
with reminders that the money they spent was Hest's, that Hest
fed him, clothed him, and gave him a place to sleep at night.
What had Sedric thought? That by becoming the source of the
wealth and taking control of it, he could make Hest go back to
the man he had thought he was?

Or had he wanted to become Hest, to be the man in charge?

His oars dug deeply into the water. His back and neck and
shoulders and arms all ached. His hands burned. But not even
that pain could drown out the truth. From the beginning, from
their very first time together, Hest had enjoyed dominating
him. Always, he had sent for Sedric, and Sedric had come to
him. The man had never been tender, never kind or consider-
ate. He'd laughed at the bruises he'd left on Sedric, and Sedric
had bowed his head and smiled ruefully, accepting such treat-
ment as his due. Hest had never really gone too far, of course.
Except for that one time, when he had been drunk, and Sedric
had enraged him by trying to help him up the stairs of the inn.
That one time, he'd been truly violent and drawn blood when
he struck him. He'd fallen down the stairs. But only that one
time—and the time when, in vengeance because Sedric had not
agreed with him that a merchant had deliberately cheated him
but suggested it was only an error, Hest had left the inn in a
carriage without him, forcing Sedric to run through the most
dangerous part of a rough Chalcedean town in order to board
the ship minutes before it sailed. Hest had never apologized for
that, only mocked him to the merriment of several of the fellows traveling with them.

One of them, he now recalled, would be with Hest now.
Cope. Redding Cope, with his plump little mouth and stubby-
fingered hands, always hanging on Hest's every word, always

eager to win a smile from him with his sly mockery of Sedric. Well, Cope would have Hest to himself now. Savagely he wished the man small joy of it. Perhaps he might find the prize he had won was not what he had thought it to be.

THYMARA HAD LEFT the barge early in the morning, after begging the use of one of the small boats from Captain Leftrin, who had seemed in an uncommonly generous mood that morning. He had ordered Davvie to row her ashore in the remaining ship's boat, telling her to hallo from the trees when she wanted a ride back to the vessel. She'd taken a couple of carry-sacks and promised she'd try to find fresh fruit or vegetables for them all.

She hadn't told Tats she was going. She hadn't told anyone. Still, she hadn't been that surprised when he came to help them put the small boat over the side. And when he'd clambered down the ladder and sat down behind her, that hadn't surprised her either.

She had the amount of time it took Davvie to row them ashore to consider how to react to Tats's presence. Davvie's friendly chatter kept him busy until then. Evidently he'd just become friends with Lecter and was full of questions about him. Tats answered as well he might. Lecter had always been a bit aloof; none of them knew him well. Thymara was happy for him; she didn't know Davvie well, either, but had noticed how alone he seemed to be. She understood Leftrin's decision to keep a distance between his ship's crew and the keepers, but she had pitied Davvie as the only youngster on the ship. She hoped for his sake that Leftrin would loosen his rules a bit and allow his friendship with Lecter to continue.

Davvie nudged the small boat up onto the bank of the river as close as he could get to a tree's outthrust roots. She and Tats disembarked onto the knees of the trees. From there, Thymara sprang for the trunk and was able to sink her claws in and scrabble up. Tats bid Davvie farewell and then followed her more laboriously. Once they reached the branches, they both traveled more easily. Neither one of them said much for a time, other than, "Watch out, it's slippery here," or "Stinging ants. Move quickly."

She led and he followed, moving in parallel to the river's edge, moving upstream as she traveled higher into the branches.

"Where are we going?" he asked her at last.

"Looking for fruit vines. The kind with air roots. They like the light along the riverbank."

"Good. I don't feel like having to climb all the way up to the canopy today."

"I don't either. We'd waste most of our time just going up and coming down again. I want to gather as much food as we can today."

"Good idea. It's going to be harder to feed everybody now. Most all our fishing gear is gone. Along with most of our other supplies. Our blankets are gone. We lost a lot of knives."

"It's going to be harder," she agreed. "But the dragons have got better at feeding themselves. I think we'll be all right."

He was quiet for a time, following her along a horizontal stretch of branch. Then he asked, "If you could go back to Trehaug, would you want to?"

"What?"

"Last night you said you couldn't go home. I wondered if that was what you really wanted to do." He followed her silently for a time, then added, "Because if it was, I'd find a way to take you there."

She stopped, turned, and met his eyes. He seemed so earnest, and she suddenly felt so old. "Tats. If that was what I really wanted to do, I'd find a way to do it. I signed up to be part of this expedition. If I left it now . . . well. It all would have been for nothing, wouldn't it? I'd just be Thymara, slinking back home, to live in my father's house and abide by my mother's rules."

He furrowed his brow. ' "Just Thymara.' I don't think that's such a bad thing to be. What do you want to be?"

That stumped her. "I don't know. But I know that I want to be something more than just my father's daughter. I want to prove myself somehow. That what I told my da when he

asked why I wanted to go on this expedition. And it's still true."
They'd come to the next trunk and Thymara started up it, digging her claws into the bark. The same claws that had condemned her to a half life in Trehaug might be her salvation out
here, she thought.

Tats came behind her, more slowly. When Thymara reached
a likely branch, she paused and waited for him. When he caught
up with her, his face was misted with sweat. "I thought only
boys felt things like that."

"Like what?"

"That we had to prove ourselves, so people would know we
were men now, not boys any longer."

"Why wouldn't a girl feel that?" Her eyes had caught a glint
of yellow. She pointed toward it, and he nodded. At the end of
this branch, out over the river, a parasitic vine garlanded the
tree. The weight of hanging yellow fruit sagged both vine and
branches. It swayed and she saw the flicker of wings. Birds were
feeding there, a sure sign the fruit was ripe. "I'm going out
there," she told him. "I don't know if the branches will take
your weight."

"I'll find out," he replied.

"Your choice. But don't follow me too closely."

"I'll be careful. And I'll stick to my own branch."

And he was. She ventured out onto the branch, and he transferred to one beside it. She crouched, digging her claws in as she
ventured toward the vine. The farther she went, the more the
branch sagged.

"It's a long drop to the river, and shallow down there," Tats
reminded her.

"Like I don't know," she muttered. She glanced over at him.
He was belly down on his branch, inching out doggedly. She
could tell he was afraid. And she knew that he wouldn't go back
until she did.

Proving himself.

"Why wouldn't a girl want to prove herself?"

"Well." He gave a grunt and inched himself along. She had to
admire his nerve. He was heavier than she was, and his branch

was already beginning to droop with his weight. "A girl doesn't have to prove herself. No one expects it of her. She just has to, you know, be a girl."

"Get married, have babies," she said.

"Well. Something like that. Not right away, the having babies part. But, well, I guess no one expects a girl to, well—"

"Do anything," she supplied for him. She was as far out as she dared to go, but the fruit was barely within her reach. She reached out and took a cautious grip on a leaf of the vine. She pulled it slowly toward her, careful not to pull the leaf off. When it was near enough, she hooked the vine itself with her free hand. Carefully she scooted back on the branch, pulling the vine with her as she went. Most of the parasitic vines had very tough and sturdy stemwork. She'd be able to pull it in from here and pluck as much fruit as she wanted.

Tats saw that, and she credited his intelligence that he stopped risking himself immediately and backed along the branch. He sighed slightly, watching her. "You know what I mean."

"I do. It didn't used to be like that, with the early Traders. Women were among the toughest of the new settlers. They had to be, not only to live themselves but to raise their children."

"So maybe having babies was how a girl proved herself, back then," he pointed out, an edge of triumph in his voice.

"Maybe," she conceded. "To some degree. But this was before any of the tree cities were built or Trehaug unearthed or any of it. It was just survival days at first, figuring out how to get drinkable water, how to build a house that would stay dry, how to make a boat that the river wouldn't eat . . ."

"It all seems pretty obvious now." He was working a smaller branch back and forth.

"It usually is, after someone else thinks of it."

He grinned at her. He'd broken the branch free. Now he stripped it of most of its leaves and then used it to reach out and hook a different vine. Slowly and carefully, he pulled the vine toward him until he could catch hold of it. She twisted her mouth and then grinned back at him, conceding his cleverness. She opened her pouch and began to methodically strip fruit from the vine into it. "Anyway. Back then, women had to be able to do a lot of different things. Think of different ways to do things."

"And the men didn't?" he asked innocently.

She'd come to a bird-pecked fruit. She tugged it off, shied it at him, and went on picking. "Of course they did. But that doesn't change my point."

"Which is?" He'd opened his own pack and was loading it now.

What was her point? "That at one time, Trader women proved themselves just as men did. By surviving." Her hands had slowed. She looked out through the leaves, over the river, into the distance. The far shore of the river was a misty line in the distance. She hadn't realized how much it had widened until now. She tried to put her unruly thoughts in order. Tats was asking her the very same questions she'd been asking herself. She needed to formulate the answer for herself as much as she did for him.

"When I was born," she said, careful not to look at him. "I was deemed unworthy to live. My father saved me from being exposed, but that only proved something about him. It didn't say anything about me. All the time I was growing up, I could look around and see people who didn't think I'd deserved to live." Including her mother. She wouldn't mention that to him. It sounded self-pitying, even to herself. And it had nothing to do with what she was saying. Did it? "I worked alongside my father. I gathered just like he did. I did all the work that was expected of me. But it still wasn't enough to prove that I deserved to live. It was just what was expected of me. What would have been expected of any Rain Wild daughter." She did look at him then. "Proving I could be ordinary, despite how I looked, wasn't enough for any of them."

His hands, tanned brown, worked like separate little animals, stripping the fruit and loading it into his pack. She'd always liked his hands. "Why wasn't it enough for you?" he asked her.

There was the rub. She wasn't sure. "It just wasn't," she said gruffly. "I wanted to make them admit that I was as good as any of them and better than some."

"And then what would happen?"

She was quiet for a time, thinking. She stopped her gathering to eat one of the yellow fruit. Her father had had a name for them, but she couldn't remember it. They didn't commonly grow near Trehaug. These were fat and sweet. They'd have fetched a good price at the market. She got down to a fuzzy seed and scraped the last of the pulp off with her teeth before she tossed it away. "It would probably make them hate me more than they already did," she admitted. She nodded to herself and smiled, saying, "But at least then they'd have a good reason for it."

Tats's backpack was full. He pulled the drawstring tight. She'd never seen that pack before; probably ship's gear. He picked another fruit, took a bite of it, and then asked, "So, for you, it wasn't about proving yourself and then being able to break their rules? Get married, have babies."

She thought about it. "No. Not really. Just making them admit that I deserved to live might have been enough for me." She turned her head and added, "I don't think I really focused on the 'get married, have babies' part of it. The rules about us were just the rules about us."

"Not for Greft," he said, shaking his head. He'd finished the fruit. He put the whole seed in his mouth, chewed on it for a moment, and then spat it out.

"Greft and his new rules," she muttered to herself.

"You never wanted to live without the rules they put on you? Just do what you wanted to do?"

"The rules are different for me than for him," she said slowly.

"How?"

"Well, he's male. Women like me . . . just about as often as we give birth to children who can't or shouldn't survive, we don't survive ourselves. The rules about not having husbands or having children, my father said they were there to protect me as much as anything else." She shrugged one shoulder. "Greft changes the rules, it's no risk for him, is it? He's not the one who's going to go into labor out here with no midwife. He's not the one who'll have to deal with a baby who can't survive. I don't think he's ever wondered what he's going to do with that baby if Jerd dies and the baby lives."

"How can you think of such things?" Tats was aghast.

"How can you *not* think of them?" she retorted. She let go of the vine and settled her carry-sack on her shoulder. She stared out through the leaves at the distant shore. After a time, in a quieter voice she said, "It's all very well for Greft to talk about new rules. It infuriates me when he says that I 'must make my choice soon' as if my only choice is choosing which male. To him, it probably seems so simple. There's no authority out here to tell him that he can't do a thing, so he does it. And he never thinks about the reason that rule came to be. To him, it's just a bar that keeps him from doing what he wants."

She turned her head to look at him. "Can you see that for me, it's just another rule that he's talking about putting on me? His rule is that I have to choose a mate. 'For the good of all the keepers,' to keep boys from fighting over me. How is that better than the old rule?"

When he didn't answer, she glanced back out over the river. "You know, I just now realized something. Jerd and Greft, they think that breaking the rules is the same as proving themselves. To me, breaking an old rule doesn't mean anything except that they broke a rule. I don't think Jerd is braver or stronger or more capable because she did it. In fact, right now, with a baby growing in her belly, she's more vulnerable. More dependent on the rest of us, regardless of how hard that makes it. So. What does that prove about Jerd? Or the boys who slept with her?"

In unfolding her thought, she'd forgotten to whom she was speaking. The stunned look on Tats's face stopped her words. She wanted to apologize, to say she hadn't meant it. But her tongue couldn't find the lie. After a few moments of his silence, she said quietly, "My bag is full. Let's take what we have back to the barge."

He bobbed his head in a brusque nod of agreement, not looking at her. Had she shamed him? Made him angry? Suddenly it all just made her tired, and she didn't want to understand him or have him understand her. It was all too much trouble. It was so much easier being alone. She stood and led the way back.

She was only about three trees away from where they had left the boat when she saw Nortel coming up a trunk toward them. She halted where she was, moving back on the branch to make room for him. He came up fast and when he reached the branch he halted there, looking from her to Tats and back again, breathing hard with the effort of his climb. "Where have you been?" he demanded. Thymara bridled at the unexpected question.

"Picking fruit," Tats replied before she could say anything.

"How can you think that's fair?" he asked Tats. "You heard what Greft said. We all agreed. She gets to make her decision and *then* we all abide by it."

"I didn't—" Tats began, but Thymara raised a sudden hand, halting his words. She looked from one to the other. "*What Greft said,*" she repeated, making the words a demand for clarification.

Nortel let his gaze settle on Thymara. "He said we all had to play fair, and not take advantage of your situation." He shifted his eyes back to Tats. "But that's what you're doing, isn't it? Taking advantage of being old friends, of her mourning Rapskal. You're using every excuse to be around her all the time. Not letting anyone else even get the chance to talk to her."

"I went with her to pick fruit. We've lost a lot of hunting equipment. We need to gather what food we can, while we can." Tats spoke in a flat voice. His words were reasonable, but the sparks in his eyes were not. They were, she suddenly knew, a challenge. She saw how Nortel swelled his chest, and she saw a pale lavender light kindle behind the green of his eyes. He reminded her, she thought, of his dragon and suddenly recognized what she was seeing; here was a male, come to challenge all comers for the right to be her mate. A strange thrill went through her. Her heart leaped and raced, and she felt her skin flush.

"Stop it," she growled low, to herself as much as to the males.

She did not have to turn to know that Tats was responding to Nortel's challenge. "I don't care what stupid things Greft says. He can't set rules about who talks to me or when. Nor can he insist that I make some 'decision' that exists only in his mind. I have no intention of choosing anyone. Not now, perhaps not ever."

Nortel licked his narrow lips and then accused Tats, "You said something to her, didn't you? Something to set her against the idea."

"No, I didn't!"

"Nortel! Talk to me, not him!"

His eyes shifted between them. "That's exactly what I'd like to do. Leave, Tats. Thymara wants to talk with me."

"Make me."

"Stop it!" She hated that her voice rose to a shriek and broke on the words. She sounded hysterical and frightened, when in truth she was angry. "I don't want this," she said and tried to make her voice calm and reasonable. "This isn't going to convince me of anything."

It was as if she hadn't spoken. Nortel squared his shoulders and leaned slightly to one side to stare past her at Tats. "I *can* make you, if that's how you want it," he offered.

"Let's find out, then."

She was suddenly disgusted with both of them. "Fight if you want to," she declared. "It won't prove anything to me or anyone else. And it won't change anything." She tucked her carry-sack tight to her ribs, measured the distance to the next lower branch and leaped. It was not that far of a leap, and her claws were out and ready. Perhaps it was the bag that threw her balance off. In any case, she landed slightly off center on the branch, slipped, and, with an outraged cry, was suddenly falling.

She only fell perhaps a dozen feet before her outstretched hands caught another branch. With a practice born of years, she dug in claws, swung herself around, and was suddenly up and on it. Even so, she hunkered down, teeth gritted against the pain in her back. When she'd missed her grip and twisted, in her panic her back muscles had spasmed. The wound on her back felt as if it had torn. Her injury had not been comfortable, but at least it had been quiescent and perhaps beginning to heal. Now it felt not only torn but as if something were jammed in it. She reached back a cautious hand, but found that the motion hurt too badly for her to complete it. She couldn't even touch it to see if it was bleeding.

Above her, both boys were yelling her name, and then accusing each other of making her fall. Let them fight then. It meant nothing to her. Stupid, stupid, stupid. And stupider yet was that tears stung her eyes.

THEY'D HEARD THE horn long before they saw anything. The three short blasts proclaimed that Carson was returning and that he had found someone. Leftrin watched as the keepers gathered on the deck of his barge, straining their eyes downriver and talking to one another in low voices. Rapskal and Heeby? The copper dragon? Jess? Sedric?

Personally, he doubted it was Jess. He'd done his best to make certain that the hunter would never return before the wave struck. But if he had survived, what then? How much would he say, and to whom? When the copper dragon came in sight, trudging alongside the two boats, there were cries of relief and joy from the keepers. He squinted, surprised to see that there were two boats. He stared for some time at the figure paddling the second boat and then bellowed out, "It's Sedric! He's found Sedric! Alise! Alise! Carson's found Sedric! He's alive and it looks like he's unhurt."

He heard the patter of feet on his deck and a few moments later, she joined him on top of the deckhouse. "Where? Where is he?" she demanded breathlessly.

"There." He pointed. "Paddling the second boat."

"Sedric paddling a boat?" she said doubtfully, but a moment later she said, "Yes, that's him. I recognize the color of his shirt. I can't believe it! He's alive!"

"He is," Leftrin said. Unobtrusively, he took her hand. He

didn't want to ask her in words, but he had to know. Did Sedric's survival change things between them?

She squeezed his hand. Then she let go of it. His heart sank.

ALISE WATCHED THE two boats approach and tried to separate
her emotions. She rejoiced that her friend Sedric had survived.
She dreaded the return of her husband's witness. She was angry
at him that he had withheld Hest's token from her and amazed
to see him engaged in such a physical endeavor as paddling a
boat.

The dragons were trumpeting to the copper, and Relpda was
responding joyously. At such times, Alise heard their sounds
only as sounds. She felt that she understood the dragons only
when they intended that humans should hear and understand
them. She was not positive that was so, but she suspected that
there were some communications they kept to themselves. She
should make a note of that idea in her journal, she thought, and
instantly felt guilty. It had been days since she had updated her
journal or added any new observations about the dragons. She'd
been too busy surviving and discovering herself, she decided.
Of her time in the water and how the dragon had saved her, she
would write. But of last night? That would remain hers and hers
alone, forever.

She and Leftrin had not spoken of it. Today, when they had
met at the galley table, and later as she strolled the deck with
him, they had maintained their decorum. She had tried not to
blush, tried not to stare meaningfully into his eyes. Their si-
lences had spoken more than their words. She did not intend to
become a figure of speculation and gossip among the keepers,
and she suspected that Leftrin would just as soon keep his privacy from his crew intact. Now she wondered if she would ever
again have the opportunity to be alone with him, to speak of
what it had meant to her.

Sedric returning was like all her Bingtown past coming back
to envelope her. Once he stepped onto the deck again, she was
no longer simply Alise. She was Alise Finbok, wife to Hest

Finbok, who would some day be Trader Finbok and control the
Finbok vote on the Bingtown Traders' Council. By virtue of
their marriage, she owed him not just fidelity but the hope of
an heir, and beyond that, she owed him and his family and her
own family the decorum and propriety that was necessary for
everyone's social survival.

She didn't want Sedric to come back. She didn't want him to
be dead, but if by a wish she could have safely transported him
back to Bingtown, she would have done so in a breath.

Day the 26th of the Prayer Moon

Year the 6th of the Independent Alliance of Traders

From Erek, Keeper of the Birds, Bingtown

To Detozi, Keeper of the Birds, Trehaug

A message from Erek, Keeper of the Birds, Bingtown, to Detozi, Keeper of the Birds, Trehaug. In a sealed case, the travel arrangements for Apprentice Reyall to return home to his family to observe a period of mourning, at the expense of the bird keepers. A shipment of twenty-five swift pigeons and six kings has been entrusted to his care on the way. With our deepest sympathy and warmest regards.

CHAPTER TWELVE

THE LOCKET

I ate a man! I ate the hunter!" Relpda was triumphant. She blasted the news to all of them, trumpeting it out before she even reached them. She waded out of the shallows and onto the mucky beach to greet them. "He threatened my keeper! We fought him and we ate him!" Her next words unsettled the disrupted dragons even more. "My keeper has proven himself worthy. He drank my blood to speak to me, and now he is mine. I shall make him an Elderling, the first of a new kind."

"This has not been discussed!" Mercor objected.

"You gave him your blood?"

"How will you make him an Elderling?"

"What is she talking about?"

"SILENCE!" Ranculos blasted them with a roar. And when the other dragons fell into a stunned quiet, he rounded on the little copper female. "What have you done?" he demanded of her. "You, with less than half the proper wits of a dragon, you have given blood to a human? You have begun to change him? It is bad enough that so many have begun to change, simply from proximity to us. Do you not recall what was decided, ages ago? Have you forgotten the Abominations? Would you bring more of them into existence?"

"What are you talking about?" Sintara exploded. "Stop speaking in riddles! Is there a danger here for us? What has she done?"

"She's eaten a hunter, for one thing. A hunter who was supposed to help provide food for us!" Ranculos sounded outraged.

Spit snorted. "Feed myself now. Don't need hunter or keeper."

"No human has brought us food of any kind for several days now," Veras pointed out quietly.

"They haven't needed to. There has been plenty of dead fish for us," Sestican said.

As the long afternoon had approached evening, the dragons had returned to the vicinity of the barge. The river had continued to drop. Mud-laden bushes and clumps of grass were reappearing as the water continued to retreat. Tonight, at least, Sintara was looking forward to sleeping in a relatively dry spot. And tomorrow, they would resume their upriver journey. Life had almost seemed to be returning to normal before the copper reappeared.

"One of us should speak to her, not all of us, or we will get no sense at all out of her." Sintara left the other dragons to approach the copper. She regarded her closely. Relpda had changed. She moved her body with more certainty, and she communicated more clearly. Something had happened to her. She focused herself on the little copper dragon. "Relpda. Why did you eat the hunter? Was he dead already?" she asked the smaller female.

Relpda considered the question as she waded out of the water and up the mud beach toward the gathered dragons. "No. But he wanted to kill me. And so my keeper attacked him. And then, when I saw that my keeper was trying to kill him, I took him for meat. It was a good kill for me." The copper looked around. "There was fish?"

"The fish is eaten. Tomorrow we will have to move on." Sintara tried to bring her back to the topic. She noticed that the other dragons had quietened to listen. "What do you mean, your keeper drank blood? And who do you claim as your keeper?"

Relpda bent her head to rub her muzzle against her front leg. It put more mud on her face than it cleaned off. "Sedric," she said. "Sedric is my keeper now. He came to me and took my blood and drank it, to be closer to me. We think together now. All is clearer to me than it was. I shall make him my Elderling. That is my right to do."

"You will make an Elderling?" Sestican was confused.

"I am trying to get sense out of her! Be quiet!" Sintara hissed.

"We cannot change humans unless we are willing to be changed by them." Mercor spoke wearily, ignoring her request. His words stilled her. There was something there, something to be remembered.

"Cannot or should not?" Sestican demanded.

"I do not understand!" Fente lashed her tail.

"Then be quiet and listen!" Sintara opened her jaws on the smaller female, a threat that venom might follow. Fente slunk aside from her, then spun and hissed at her.

"Stop it!" Ranculos roared. "Both of you!"

Mercor looked around at them sadly. His eyes, black on black, whirled slowly. "So much has been lost. Even as we grow stronger and move closer to becoming true dragons, I am frightened every day by the holes in our memories. I know I should not assume that each of you remembers what I do, but I continue to make that mistake. It appears, Fente, that Relpda recalls that which some of the rest of you have forgotten. Elderlings can be created by dragons, deliberately. Sometimes, as is happening with our keepers, humans undergo changes simply by virtue of extensive contact with us. In the days when Elderlings and dragons shared cities and lives, Elderlings were shaped by the dragons who favored them, much as a human gardener might prune a tree. Deliberately and carefully, choosing well what they began with, a dragon created an Elderling. In the lifetimes that our kinds have been apart, many of the Rain Wilders have taken on some of the lesser aspects of Elderlings, with few of the benefits."

"How?" Sintara demanded. "With no dragons about, why should they change?"

"It served them right," Ranculos said in a low voice. "Those who killed dragons in their cases, those who handled and carved what should have become dragons, those who stole and used the artifacts and magics of the Elderlings, they are the ones who have suffered the consequences most deeply. It is fitting. They took what was not theirs to take. They meddled in the stuff of dragons. The changes came upon them, and upon their offspring. They suffered shorter lives and stillborn children. They deserved it."

"You speculate," Mercor cautioned him.

"I speculate with reason. It is no coincidence. In their heart of hearts, the humans know what is true. Look whom they chose to give us as our 'keepers.' They gave us the ones so deeply changed that they scarce can live among the other humans. They have scales and claws, it is hard for them to breed, and their life spans are shortened. That is what befalls humans who meddle in a magic that has not been freely given to them. They used the stuff of dragons, our blood and bones, and they changed. But with no dragons to guide the change, they became monstrous."

"And the Abominations," Mercor asked in his deep, rolling voice. "What of them? Are they, too, a punishment well deserved?"

"Perhaps," Ranculos replied recklessly. "For it is as you said. Dragons cannot change humans without risk that they will change us. It was long suspected that dragons who associated too much with Elderlings and humans would harm themselves or their offspring. An egg hatches and it is not what it should be . . ."

"Must we speak of obscenities? Is there no decency left among us?" Their words had wakened memories in Sintara, memories long dormant. Once, one of her ancestors had chosen a human and shaped an Elderling for herself. The physical changes in such a creature were less than half of it. Properly prepared, an Elderling gained a life span that, while not even close to that of a dragon, was sufficient to allow at least some wisdom and sophistication to accrue. It was amusing, even comforting, to have such an Elderling. It was pleasant to be flattered, to be "immortalized" in verse and paintings and poetry. Elderlings became companions for dragons in a way that other dragons could not be. With an Elderling, there was no competition, only the comfort of their admiration, the pleasures of grooming, and, yes, the stimulation of conversations.

But in every pleasure there is a danger, and some dragons spent too much time with their Elderlings and were, in turn, changed by them. It was not something that was lightly spoken of. No dragon wished to accuse another of such an obscenity, but it was undeniable. Dragons who spent too much time in the company of humans changed. The changes were not as obvious as what befell humans who spent too much time in the company of dragons, but the evidence was there, all the same. And in the next generation, when eggs hatched from, it was suspected, two such dragons, the offspring were not serpents but Abominations.

It was not a thing for dragons to admit to outsiders. It was not even a thing for dragons to discuss among themselves. Sintara turned aside from them all, affronted by the coarseness of the conversation. Mercor ignored her disdain as he spoke severely to Relpda.

"I think you have done a foolish thing, Relpda. I am not sure you are capable of guiding a human to an Elderling state. If you are careless, or unskilled, or even forgetful, the consequences for the human can be dire, even fatal. This is a human who had not even begun on a path of change. What entered your mind to make you choose him for such an honor?"

"He could not even hear us speak when first he walked among us," Sintara interjected. "He thought us beasts, like cows. He was very arrogant, and extremely ignorant. I cannot think of a human less deserving of such an honor."

Relpda lashed her tail warningly. "It was my decision. It is my right. He came to me, seeking the contact. When I felt his mind brush mine, I chose him. And now he is chosen by me. That is all any of you need to know. I do not recall that the decision to create an Elderling was ever a shared decision. It is not one now."

"In your anger, your words and thoughts come clear," Mercor observed mildly.

"I use his mind. It is nothing to you."

"It is something to you, something you may regret depending upon. What if he should decide he does not wish to be bound to you? What if he should decide to leave and return to his Bingtown?"

"He will not." Relpda spoke with finality.

Sintara, disturbed, moved away. It was not the first time she had been forced to confront the idea that her memories were incomplete. She tried to focus her mind on the floating fragments of recall the talk had stirred in her. One of her ancestors had willingly and consciously created an Elderling. Could she recall how it was done?

Only in fragments. Blood had been involved, she knew that. Had there been more, the giving of a physical token? A scale? There was something back there, an elusive memory that swam at the very edges of her recall.

"Sintara."

She had been thinking too deeply. She had not even noticed Mercor's quiet approach. She tried to appear unsurprised as she turned to him. "What is it?"

"Are you aware of the changes your keeper is going through?"

She stared at him for a moment and then asked distantly, "Which keeper?"

He was unruffled. "The one who is what the humans would say 'heavily touched by the Rain Wilds.' Thymara."

"I have not paid a great deal of attention to her changes, though she is more scaled than she was when we began our journey."

"So her other changes are not deliberate? They are not gifts from you?"

What other changes? "She is scarcely worthy of any gifts from me. She is both arrogant and disobedient. She fails to praise me or to be grateful for my attentions. Why would I choose her for a gift?"

"It is a question I am asking of any dragon whose keeper seems to be undergoing obvious changes. Although Relpda has announced her intention, I would not have been surprised if others had quietly chosen such a path."

"And have they?" She was suddenly curious.

"Only Relpda has offered a blood change to her keeper."

She considered his words for a time, then said, as if merely confirming a thought rather than asking a question, "Of course, there are other paths to creating an Elderling."

"Yes. They are more time-consuming and in most cases, less radical. They are no less dangerous if one is careless with the human."

"She was careless, not I. When she removed the rasp snake from me, some of my blood spattered on her face. Perhaps in her mouth or eyes."

Mercor was silent for a time. "She changes then, a blood change. If you do not guide it, it could be very dangerous for her."

She turned away from him again. "It seems strange to me that a dragon should care about what is dangerous for a human."

"It is strange," he admitted. "Yet it is as I told you all, and as Relpda's new abilities show. One cannot change a human without being changed by her. Or him."

He waited for a time, but when she neither looked at him nor made any response, he moved quietly away.

SIMPLE PLEASURES. SIMPLE human pleasures. Hot food and drink. Warm water to wash in. Soothing oil for his abused skin. Clean clothing. He hadn't even had to talk much. Carson had handled all the questions and told their story in a much abbreviated yet embellished form to an appreciative audience while Sedric had focused his entire attention on the platter of steaming stew and the mug of hot tea placed before him. Even the rock-hard ship's biscuit had, when soaked in stew gravy, seemed almost delicious.

Leftrin had been there, and Alise, looking guilty and remorseful. She had sat down at the table with him, saying little after her initial embrace at their reunion, but watching him intently as he ate. She had been the one to measure out water and put it to warm for him, even bringing the steaming bucket to the door of the room for him. When she had tapped, he had opened the door for her and let her bring it in.

"I'm sorry there's so little water to spare for bathing. When the river goes down more, we should be able to dig sand wells again. For now, it's so murky still that all we get is mud soup."

"It's fine, Alise. It's more than enough. All I want to do is sponge myself off and get some salve on my scalds. I'm glad to see that you're safe. But I'm so weary right now." His words skipped across the top of their relationship, refusing to engage her any more deeply than if he were speaking to Davvie. Not now. He needed to be apart from all of them for a time, but especially her.

She did not miss the distance he set between them. Her words were full of courtesy, but she still tried to reach him. "Of course, of course. I won't bother you just now. Make yourself comfortable first. But afterward . . . I know you are tired, Sedric, but I need to talk to you. Just a few words before you rest."

"If you must," he said in his weariest voice. "Later."

"As you wish, then. I am so glad you are alive and found again."

And then she was gone. He'd sat down on his bunk and let himself relax. Strange, how his little musty, fusty room could seem almost cozy after all he had recently experienced. Even the rumpled pallet looked inviting.

He'd let his filthy ragged clothing fall to the floor as he disrobed. He took his time washing himself. His skin was too tender to hurry. Even as he dreamed of a tub full of hot, sudsy water, he was grateful for this small mercy. The water had cooled and turned a nasty shade of brown by the time he was finished. He found a clean nightshirt and donned it. It was an incredible pleasure to have something soft next to his abused skin. Washing had shown him that the large bruise on his face was merely the most obvious of the injuries that Jess had dealt him. There were bruises on his back and on his legs that he scarcely remembered getting.

After he was as clean as he could get with such limited water, he smoothed scented oil on the worst of his scalds, frowning over how little he had left. Someone had laundered some of his clothing. He dressed himself, looked at his discarded clothing, and realized it was little more than rags now. With his foot, he pushed it toward the door.

That was when he heard the faint jingle of metal against the floor. He lifted his candle and peered closer, wondering what he could have dropped. There, on the floor, was his locket. Habit made him open it. And there, in the candle's dim light, Hest looked out at him.

He'd commissioned the tiny portrait from one of the best painters of miniatures in Bingtown. The man had to be good; Hest had sat for him only twice and was very ungracious about both appointments, acceding to the request only because Sedric had pleaded for it as a birthday gift. Hest had thought it overly sentimental, as well as dangerous. "I warn you, if anyone catches a glimpse of you wearing it, I shall deny all knowledge and leave you to their mockery."

"As I expect," Sedric had replied. Even then, he now saw, he had begun to accept that perhaps his feelings for Hest were deeper than any Hest had for him. Now he looked down into the supercilious smile and recognized the slight curl of his lip that the artist had caught so accurately. Not even for a portrait could Hest think of him with respect, let alone love.

"Did I make you up?" he asked the tiny picture. "Did you ever exist as the person I longed for you to be?" He snapped the locket shut, coiled the chain into his palm and closed his hand around it, then sat on the edge of his flat, hard bunk, his loosely clenched hands to his temples. He closed his eyes and commanded his memories. One kiss that Hest had initiated in gentleness rather than as demand. One openhanded touch that was pure affection and nothing else. One word of praise or affection, unhinged by sarcasm. He was certain there had been such moments, but he could not call one to the forefront of his mind.

Unbidden, the thought of Carson's hand brushing his injured face came to him. Strange, that the calloused hand of the hunter had been gentler than any touch he had ever received from the gentlemanly Hest.

He'd never met anyone like Carson. He hadn't asked him to conceal his role in Jess's death, yet when he had been recounting his rescue of Sedric, the hunter's name hadn't come into it. He hadn't mentioned the boat, letting all the others assume whatever they wished about it. Before they had left the debris raft, Carson had insisted on cleaning out the boat, scrubbing away the bloodstains and bailing out the stinking bilgewater. He'd cleaned the hatchet and restored it to its sheath. Not once during that operation had he mentioned that he was obscuring all traces of the murder.

Carson had simply done it and shielded him since then from the questions. He imagined that sooner or later, it would come out. Relpda was too proud of what she had done to keep quiet forever. But he was grateful it wasn't just now. His own secret was too tightly tied to Jess's death. He didn't want anyone picking at one thread to discover where it might lead. For although Carson doubted that Leftrin had been involved with Jess, Sedric was not too sure. It would explain so many things: why he had set out on such a ridiculous and unprofitable errand, why he had cozied up to Alise, and how Jess had become a member of the party so easily. Yes. He was certain there were secrets that Leftrin wasn't sharing with anyone. And he feared that if Leftrin thought those secrets were threatened, he might take action. The captain, he felt, was capable of anything. Discovering his secret had only confirmed the opinion Sedric had had of him since the beginning.

And what of his opinion of himself? What of his own dirty little secrets?

He lowered his hand and looked at the closed locket he still clutched in his hand.

Throw it overboard.

No. He couldn't quite bring himself to do that. Not yet. But he would not wear it, nor sleep with it under his pillow anymore. He'd set it aside, where he wouldn't see it by accident. He would put it with the other mementos that now shamed him.

He was on his knees, working the concealed catch on the wardrobe when he heard the knock on the door. "A moment!" he cried, flung himself back into bed, and then thought to ask, "Who is it?"

"It's Alise," she said, opening the door as she spoke. She carried a candle. Uninvited, she entered his room and shut the door behind her. She stood a moment, looking down at him, and then exclaimed, "My poor Sedric. I am so sorry about everything that has befallen you as a result of this journey. If I could take on your suffering as my own, I would."

"You don't look much better than I do," he replied, surprised into honesty.

He saw a flash of hurt in her eyes as her hand flew to her cheek. "Well, yes, I'm as scalded as you are, on my face and hands. The river water wasn't kind to either of us. If it hadn't been for Sintara, both Thymara and I would have drowned. But, well, here we are, both of us intact, and not all that much the worse for wear." She smiled apologetically.

"I had thought that you were safe aboard the boat," he said in wonder. "The wave caught you too, then."

"Indeed. Even Captain Leftrin was washed away in it. Luckily for him, his crew found him quickly. But Thymara and I only returned to the *Tarman* a day before you did."

"Alise, I'm so sorry. I must seem so thoughtless to you. I never even asked you about your experience. Tell me now." *And ask me no questions about what befell me.*

Her smile grew warmer. She sat down on the edge of his bed. "There's not much to tell. The wave hit us, Sintara fished us out of the water, and when we struggled to what had been the shore, we found many of the other keepers there. Not all, unfortunately. I'm sure you've heard that we lost Warken and young Rapskal and his dragon, Heeby. Still, it could have been so much worse. Other than some bruises and cuts, most of us emerged unscathed. Though you look as if you took quite a battering."

He touched the bruised side of his face and shrugged. "It's healing," he replied.

"I'm glad," she replied, letting the topic go so easily that he immediately knew she had something else on her mind. Her eyes were wandering around his small room, her glance lingering on the floor near his bed, as if she were looking for something. Anxiety uncoiled in him and slithered in his belly. She'd been in here in his absence; he knew that. She'd tidied the room. Had she found his hidden cache of dragon parts? No. That couldn't be it. If she even suspected him of doing such a dastardly thing, she'd have accused him immediately. There was something else. He waited. When her words came, they shocked him.

"Sedric, does Hest love me?"

She asked the outlandish question with the naiveté of a child. And like a child, there was both longing and dread in her voice. He tried to think what answer she wanted so he could give it to her. He settled for saying, "Surely I'm not the one to ask such a question. He married you, didn't he? Doesn't he give you nearly everything you ask for? Including this extended journey?"

"He gives me everything he must give me, everything that our bargain binds him to give me. I have his name and stature, money to spend as I wish, the opportunity to use all my free time poring over old scrolls. I have lovely clothing, an excellent chef, and a well-appointed home. When he wishes me to, I welcome his guests. I do everything that he expects me to do. I . . . I've cooperated with his efforts to get an heir from me . . ."

She'd had excellent control of her voice and face right up until then. But suddenly, on the final breathless words, her face crumpled, her nose turned red, and tears began to leak from her eyes. It was a transformation as sudden as it was shocking.

In a heartbeat, she went from composed and contained Alise to someone he didn't know. She hunched at the foot of his bed, her hands covering her face, weeping noisily and messily. And, he realized with rising alarm, uncontrollably. "Alise, Alise," he begged her, but her sobs only grew more spastic, shaking her entire body. He sat up, every muscle in his body aching, and put a cautious arm around her. She turned to him and huddled against him, her shoulders shaking with her grief.

"What is it?" he asked her, dreading whatever secret she was about to spill. "Alise, what is wrong? What brought this on?"

His question seemed to reach her. Perhaps it gave her permission to speak of whatever it was that distressed her so. She drew herself more upright and groped in her pocket for a kerchief. The one she drew out was stained and torn, more fit for a Jamaillian street urchin than a Trader's wife. Nonetheless, she dried her face with it, took a breath, and spoke. She watched her candle in its holder as she talked, never glancing at him.

"When Hest first courted me, I was skeptical of his intentions. He was such an eligible bachelor, such a prize, and there I was, a younger daughter, not pretty and with no prospects and scarcely any dowry. It actually made me angry that he would court me. I kept thinking it was some sort of wager or cruel jest. I even resented how he intruded into my life and work. But as our courtship went on, he was so charming that somehow I persuaded myself that not only was I infatuated with him but that he concealed a similar feeling for me." She gave a strangled laugh.

"Well, he concealed it very well, and continued to do so for all the years of our marriage. He has the cleverest way of twisting words, of delivering a compliment that leaves everyone at the table smiling for me while only I see all the barbs it carries. To everyone else, he shows such a fair face. He seems an attentive, even a doting, husband to our friends and families. Yet to me . . ." She turned suddenly to face him. "Is it me, Sedric? Do I expect too much? Are all men like him? My father was sometimes tender, sometimes merry, and always kind to my mother.

Was that only for show before us children? When they were alone, was he cold and boorish and cruel?"

There was such need in her question, such honest confusion that he felt carried back in time to when they had been much younger. She had sometimes asked him such questions then, in full confidence that he was older and wiser in the ways of the world. Without thinking, he took her hand, and then wondered at himself. How could his feelings about her weathervane so freely? It was mostly her fault that he was in the forsaken place on this dreary vessel, and now bonded to a simpleminded dragon. How could he feel sympathy for her?

Perhaps because it was mostly his doing that she was locked in a marriage that was equally forsaken and dreary, bonded to a man who regarded her with the sort of affection usually reserved for a dog with mange?

"Hest isn't like us," he said, and he wondered if he had ever said a truer thing. "I don't know if he loves anyone, in the way that we use the word. Certainly he values you. He knows that you are his hope for an heir." His supply of glib words suddenly dried up. "Oh, Alise," he said, sighing. He put his arm across her narrow shoulders. "No. He doesn't love you. Yours is a marriage of convenience. It was convenient to Hest to have a wife, to settle down and try for an heir. His parents had begun to insist that he behave as a respectable Trader's son should. With you, he could present those aspects without changing his ways too much. I am sorry, my friend. He doesn't love you. He never has."

He was braced for her to collapse into sobs. He was prepared to comfort her as well as he could. He did not expect her to suddenly sit up straight and square her shoulders. She sighed deeply, but no new tears welled. She sniffed a couple of times and then said flatly, "Well. That's that, then. It's what I expected. Probably what I deserve. I made a deal with him. I keep telling myself that. Maybe now that I've heard the truth from you as well, I can believe it all the way through my heart. And decide what I'm going to do about it."

That sounded dangerous. "Alise, my dear, there is little you can do about it, except to make the best of it. Go home. Live respectably. Continue your studies, and add to them what you've learned from this expedition. Have a child, or children. They will love you as you deserve."

"And loving them, I could condemn them to having a father like Hest?"

He could not find a response to that. He tried to imagine Hest as a father and could not. Children and sardonic wit would not blend. Elegance and wailing babies? A supercilious smile and a five-year-old offering a flower. He cringed at each thought. She was right, he slowly conceded. A child might be what Hest wanted and needed, for the sake of providing his line with an heir. But Hest as a father was the last thing that any child needed. Or deserved.

Alise wiped tears from her reddened cheeks. "Well. I have no solution to my dilemma. I promised to be his wife, to lie with him, to give him a child if I could. I gave my word. It was a bad bargain to be sure, but what am I to do? Just sail up the river and disappear forever?"

Her query sounded almost hopeful, as if he might accede to such a wild idea.

"You can't." He spoke the words bluntly. She couldn't know he was answering his own question as well. He wanted to run away almost as much as she did. But the Rain Wilds was no place for either of them. Difficult as things were at home, they didn't belong here. As often as he told himself that he could not go back, he knew even more clearly that he could not stay here.

She hung her head, looking at the floor, almost as if she had lost something there. When she brought her eyes up to meet his, a blush reddened her windburned cheeks to an even darker shade. "I came into your room while you were gone. When I thought you might be drowned and forever lost to me. I felt terrible at how I had neglected you. I imagined a hundred terrible things had befallen you—that you were dead, or lying injured somewhere, stranded and alone." Her eyes wandered over his face, lingering on his bruises. "So I tidied your room and took your clothing to wash, thinking that if you did return, you'd know how badly I'd felt. And in the course of doing that, of straightening your bedding and so on, I— what's that?"

He'd been dreading what she was obviously about to tell him. She'd found the secret compartment and the vials of scales and blood. But the look of shock on her face now startled him. She leaned closer to him, lifting a hand. He leaned away from it, but she touched the side of his face anyway. Her fingers slid down his cheek and trailed along his jawline. She'd never touched him in such a way, let alone looked at him with such horror.

"Sweet Sa have mercy," she said breathlessly. "Sedric. You've begun to scale."

"No!" He denied it fiercely. He jerked his face from her touch, replaced her hands with his own, and ran his fingers over his face. What did he feel? What was this? "No, it's only roughness, Alise. The river water scalded me, and then I was out in the wind and the sun. It's not scaling! I'm not a Rain Wilder, why would I grow scales? Don't be foolish, Alise! Don't be foolish!"

She just looked at him, her face locked between horror and pity. He rose abruptly from his bed, went to his wardrobe, and took out the little mirror he used for shaving. He hadn't shaved since his return to the ship—that was all she was seeing. He looked into the mirror intently, bringing his candle close as he felt along his jawline. His skin was rough there. Just rough. "I need to shave. That's all. Alise, you gave me a turn! What a wild notion. I'm tired now, but I'll shave in the morning and put a bit of lotion on my face. You'll see. Scaling. What an idea!"

She continued to stare at him. He met her eyes, daring her to disagree with him. She folded her lips in and bit them and then shook her head to herself.

"I'm very tired, Alise. I'm sure you understand." *Just leave. Please.* He wanted to look more closely at his face but not while she was here watching him.

"I know you must be tired. I'm sorry. Well. I've spoken about everything except the one thing that brings me here. And I don't know how to approach that except bluntly. Sedric. Before we left Bingtown, when we were planning this journey . . . did Hest ever entrust to you a token for me? A keepsake? Something that, perhaps, you were to give me during our journey?"

He stared at her, honestly baffled. A keepsake from Hest for her? What could she be thinking? Hest was not the type to give keepsakes to anyone, let alone someone who had so seriously and recently irritated him. He didn't say that. He merely shook his head, silently at first and then, as she narrowed her eyes and looked at him suspiciously, more vehemently. "No, Alise, he gave me nothing to pass on to you. I swear."

"Sedric." Her tone told him to stop pretending. "Perhaps he told you not to tell me of it or give it to me unless I, oh, I don't know, unless I lived up to some standard he expected or . . . I don't know. Sedric, speak bluntly to me. I know about the locket. I found it when I made up your bed. The locket with Hest's portrait in it. The locket that says *Always* on the back."

At her first mention of it, he felt his heart give a hitch and then beat wildly. He felt dizzy and black spots danced before his eyes. The locket. How could he have been so foolish as to leave it where anyone might see it? When first he'd had it made, he'd promised himself to wear it always, to remind him every moment of the person who had so changed his life. *Always*. He'd had it engraved on the case. The little gold case that he'd paid for himself. The birthday gift that he had given himself. What a stupid, thoughtless, wretchedly apt gesture that had been!

And now his silence had lasted too long. She stared at him, a sick and reluctant triumph in her eyes. "Sedric," she said.

"Oh. That locket." A lie, he needed a lie. Some sort of excuse, some reason he would have such a thing. "It's mine, actually. It's mine."

The words came out so easily. Then they hung, irrevocable and unmistakable, in the silent air of the room. All turned to stillness. He didn't look at Alise. If she continued to breathe, he couldn't hear it. He was breathing, wasn't he? Slow and shallow. Can one unmake a moment? He willed it not to be, tried to make it unhappen with his stillness.

But she spoke, nailing the reality to what he had just said with the most damning words of all. "Sedric, I don't understand."

"No," he replied lightly, glibly, as if the admission meant nothing at all to him. "Most people don't. And lately, I'll admit I scarcely understand it myself. Hest? Hest and *Always* on the same locket? What an unlikely combination." He laughed, but the sound fell in brittle pieces all around him. Moved by what, he could not say, he reached into the bundle he used for a pillow and pulled out the locket. "Here. You can have it, if you wish. A gift from me rather than Hest."

"So you . . . I don't understand, Sedric. You had it made? You had it made to give to me? But Hest must have known of it. He sat for the portrait, didn't he? It's so like him that he must have!"

Boldly he pressed the catch on the locket and opened it. Hest looked out at both of them, sardonically pleased at the mess he had made of their lives, at the friendship of years that was now crumbling away at his touch. He looked into Hest's eyes as he spoke. "Oh, yes, he sat for it. I commissioned Rolleigh to paint it. It was very expensive and Rolleigh was justifiably insulted by Hest's cavalier attitude toward the sittings and the finished portrait. He was supposed to come six times, in the evenings after dark, to a very private place for the sittings. He only came twice. And Rolleigh wanted to show him the miniature before it was put into the locket. Hest did not even come to see it and thank the painter for the likeness. That fell to me. And if Rolleigh was ungracious, well, I can scarcely blame him. Hest was unpleasant and condescending about the whole thing. And he told Rolleigh that if he knew what was good for him, he'd keep the matter of both the sitting and the portrait secret."

From time to time as he spoke, he glanced over at her. She sat there, freckled and unlovely, her wild red hair abandoned to its own inclinations. It had danced free of the pins she had put in it, to curl loosely around her windburned brow and cheeks. Her clothing was clean, but worn. Her blouse was just beginning to fray at the seam. She looked like what she had been when Hest married her; a member of Bingtown's genteel but down-at-the heel middle class. And in her eyes there was only confusion, with not even the slightest flicker of suspicion of what he was actually telling her.

"I don't understand why you paid to have him sit for a portrait, Sedric, let alone a miniature to put in a locket. If you wished to give—"

"Alise, can you be so unaware, even at your age? Let me speak plainly. I love your husband. I loved him for years, even before he thought to marry someone to put a respectable façade on his household. Now do you understand?"

She was beginning to. Pink had started to suffuse her face, and her eyes were widening in shock and horror. He didn't wait for her inevitable questions.

"Yes. He is my lover. When we travel by sea, when we are abroad, even after you are asleep at night in your own home, we share a bed. For me, there has never been anyone else. Only Hest. Forever, I thought, when I so foolishly had this damned locket created for myself. Here. Have it, if you wish, *Always* and all. I wish I could give you Hest along with it. But somehow I doubt that he was ever mine, to keep or to give away."

She stared at the locket as if he held a tiny coiled snake in his hand rather than a piece of jewelry. He tipped his hand and let it slither onto the bed between them. He was trembling slightly. Over the years, he'd imagined this moment of revelation in so many ways, but never like this, with them sitting side by side on a bed in a dim room, both frozen in agony. He had thought Hest would be present, that they might tell Alise together before he stole her husband out of her life. He had thought there would be shrieking, hurled threats and thrown objects, slaps and hysteria. But as she sat there, absorbing the betrayal and deception of years, reordering her perception of him and her life, she was silent. She swayed a tiny bit, like a tree in a high wind, and he feared for an instant that she would faint.

"You and Hest," she said awkwardly, at last. "You love each other. He holds you, kisses you, touches you. That's what this means?" She touched the coiled chain of the locket and then drew her finger back as if the cold metal had burned her. Her question had burned him.

He'd been so strangely calm up to now. He'd been able to tell her his life's largest secret, without any display of emotion. But now the tears seeped up, flooding his eyes, and his throat closed as if distant hands were choking him. "I've loved him. I don't think he loves me anymore. If he ever truly did." He bowed his face into his hands and the tears came. Had he thought he'd told Alise his most private secret? He'd been wrong. The deepest secret in his life was the one he had just uttered aloud for the first time, the deception he had hidden from himself.

He felt her stand. She would hit him now, she'd call him the names he had feared ever since he was a boy. He waited.

Instead, he felt one of her hands hesitantly touch his head and then smooth his hair, just as his mother had stroked him when he was a small boy. "I'm so sorry for you, Sedric. I'm angry and I'm hurt; I never thought you capable of such deception and betrayal of our friendship. But mostly I'm so sorry for both of us. Especially you. How could you love such a man? What a worthless waste of your heart. Look how it has destroyed both our lives. With Hest, there is no chance of happiness for either of us. But I don't think he'd care about that at all."

He couldn't say anything. He couldn't lift his face from his hands, could not even mutter an apology to her. He felt her cross the room. She took her candle with her, and when she left, the light diminished by half. The door shut firmly.

He sank into his bedding. There. It was done.

He'd just destroyed the last good thing in his life. His friendship with Alise was gone, shattered by what he and Hest had done to her. It shamed him now to think that he'd ever suggested such a marriage to Hest, even when he was in his cups. It shamed him more that he'd allowed Hest to follow through on it. What would it have taken to stop it? One call on Alise to inform her quietly of Hest's true intentions? Of course, that would have betrayed what he was to her. And possibly brought misery crashing down on him then and there. Hest would have cast him aside. No doubt of that. And found a way to discredit him completely.

Why was it only now that he could admit how ruthless the man could be? If he were back in Hest's presence for an hour, if Hest threw a casual arm across his shoulder, or made Sedric his evening's companion for food and theater and wine, would he forget and forgive him? When Hest focused on him, when Hest was in full howl as he rampaged through any city in search of entertainment and mischief, then he could make Sedric feel as if he owned the world. To be Hest's chosen companion for a night of raucous play was the most invigorating, heady rush of exhilaration that Sedric could imagine. Even now, in the depths of his despair, a sour smile came to his mouth as he recalled such evenings.

Arm in arm with Hest, surrounded by cohorts of well-dressed friends, they had stormed public houses and theaters from Chalced to Jamaillia. When Hest wished to, he could charm the most recalcitrant tavern owner into keeping his doors open and paying his minstrels for an extra hour. With that suave smile and a scattering of coin, he could procure the best tables, the finest seats in the playhouse, the best cuts of meat, and the finest wine. And people always smiled as they gave it to him. People who only knew his public face found him charming and gracious and witty. To be his companion at such a time, to be his chosen, preferred companion was to be toasted and honored right alongside Hest.

The smile slowly faded from his face, leaving only the bitterness. Never again. Never again would he be publicly lauded alongside Hest.

Never again would he be privately belittled and humiliated as the price of those hours.

That thought should have cheered him. Instead, he tried to imagine a life without Hest. He tried to imagine returning to Bingtown to find himself turned out of Hest's home, reviled by Alise. Would she tell others? Dread gaped wide to consume him, but then a cruel comfort came. She would not. She could not tell anyone without revealing how she had been deceived and that her marriage had been a lie from the start. If she told, she would lose everything: her library, her studies, her social standing. She'd have to return to her father's house, to live at the edge of poverty, a woman who would be either pitied or mocked by all who had known her.

The same fate would await him, if she told.

But even if she did not, he feared it would be little better. He was virtually certain now that Hest was preparing to cast him off. He suspected he would return to find himself replaced. He, too, would have to return in humility to his father's home and hope to be taken in and given work. The well-funded society of Hest's friends who had welcomed him would not snub him, not at first. But he would not be able to afford such company, and once they found that he had lost Hest's regard, few would wish to be seen as his friend. Hest's displeasure had frozen out more than one friend or acquaintance over the years that Sedric had known him. It had been but one more of the uglier facets of Hest's character that he had once been able to ignore. Now it would be the sole facet turned toward him.

No. There was nothing to go back to. Nothing at all.

His spirits sank and gloom closed in all around him. Even the room seemed to become darker. He closed his eyes and wondered how much courage it would take for him to end it. Once he had imagined he could throw himself into the water and drown, that once that decision had been undertaken, it would be irrevocable. Well, he knew better now. Once in the water he would struggle. Whether he willed it or not, he would shout for help.

And I would come to save you. Again.

As the thought entered his mind, a warm feeling suffused him. Comfort and contentment, without reason, rose up and permeated him as if he were an earthenware mug filling up with hot tea. He struggled briefly, trying to find his way back to his misery. And then, like a flame claiming a wick and sending forth life, he suddenly wondered why he was holding so tightly to that misery. He let go again. His dragon's affection filled him and warmed him and crowded out the pain that had been there.

There. You see? We're going to be all right. Both of us.

"MY OLD FRIEND, we need a private word or two."

Leftrin looked up from scowling at his mug of coffee. It was the second pot made with the same grindings today, and it was both weak and bitter. He thought about dumping it over the side and then reminded himself that it was marginally better than plain hot water. He turned to his old friend. "Finding a place for a private word is going to be the trick," he said. He and Carson both turned, putting their backs to the aft rail and looking over the decks of the *Tarman*. Keepers and crew mingled in conversation knots. Harrikin and Sylve and Skelly sat cross-legged on the roof of the deckhouse. Skelly was pointing up at the stars and telling them something about them. Boxter and Kase were belly down on the deck, arm wrestling. Alum and Nortel were keeping them honest while Jerd looked on grinning. Greft stood next to her, scowling. As Leftrin watched, the boy worked his mouth and then rubbed the sides of his jaw as if it pained him. The shape of his face was changing; it looked uncomfortable.

Past the keepers, he could see the silhouette of Swarge and Bellin, heads together, leaning on the railing, talking. As his eyes roved the decks, seeking a quiet spot, he found none.

"My stateroom, then," he said quietly, and Carson followed him. He lit a candle in the galley and then led the way to his small room.

"So, what is it, then?" Leftrin asked him as he shut the door behind them. He pushed the candle into its holder and then sat down on his bunk. Carson, his face grave, sat down on the chair by the chart table. He took a heavy breath.

"Jess is dead. Believe it or not, Sedric and the copper killed him. Sedric says he had to kill him because Jess was planning to kill his dragon and sell the body parts in Chalced."

"Sedric killed Jess?" Leftrin's disbelief was plain in his voice. He had been so sure that he had killed Jess. How that bastard had survived his beating and a drowning was nothing short of a miracle. And then to be killed by a Bingtown fop and a dim-witted dragon?

"He and the dragon both said so."

Leftrin scrambled for words. "Don't get me wrong, that man needed killing if anyone ever did. It just seems so unlikely that Sedric was up to the job, let alone he'd do it to defend a dragon . . ." He let his comment trail away. If Carson had killed the hunter and was, for whatever reason, putting the deed at Sedric's door, he wanted the man to know he could own up to it and Leftrin wouldn't think less of him.

"The deed was done before I got there. Nothing left of Jess but some blood in Greft's boat. Dragon ate him."

"Well, that's fitting," Leftrin said quietly. He tried not to smile. He wouldn't tell Carson that his earlier fight with the hunter had probably softened him up substantially for Sedric. It was over. He heaved a sigh that was part relief and part amazement. Sedric had finished the deed for him. He owed the man a debt of thanks.

"It's fitting because Jess was on board to harvest dragon parts. Right? And you knew about it. Maybe had an agreement about it?"

Silence filled up the room like cold water filling up a sinking vessel. He hadn't seen that coming. Carson was quiet, waiting. Leftrin cleared his throat and made his decision. Truth time. "Here's how it was, Carson, exactly. Someone had me over the fire and thought they could demand I do this. They said they'd be sending someone on this expedition who would be hunting dragon bits for the Duke of Chalced. I didn't agree to it; it was just done to me. At first, I wasn't even sure who their man was. I even thought it might be you, from one comment you made. Then, not too long ago, Jess made it clear to me that he was the one and he expected me to help him."

Carson was sitting quietly, listening as only he could. He nodded slowly and let Leftrin take his time and pick how he told his story.

"Just before the wave hit? I was on the beach, doing my best to throttle the life out of Jess. All this time, I've been thinking that I'd done the job, or maybe the wave had finished it. So I'm surprised it was Sedric. But I'll admit that I'm just glad it was done."

"So that's all there was to it? You don't have plans to butcher a dragon and sell the parts to Chalced?"

Leftrin shook his head. "I'm a lot of things, Carson, and a lot of them aren't nice. But I'd never betray the Rain Wilds that way."

"Or Alise?" Carson watched his face as he asked him.

"Or Alise," Leftrin agreed.

✦ ✦ ✦

Day the 29th of the Prayer Moon

Year the 6th of the Independent Alliance of Traders

From Erek, Keeper of the Birds, Bingtown
To Detozi, Keeper of the Birds, Trehaug

In a sealed case, covered in wax and marked with his signet, a message from a friend to Jess Torkef, to be left at the Frog and Oar tavern with Innkeeper Drost, until called for.

Detozi,

Please send a bird back to me with a note to let me know of Reyall's safe arrival. If you would, let us try it on one of the swift pigeons he is bringing with him. It would be particularly interesting to me if you sent me a duplicate note on a regular bird, releasing both at dawn of the same day. I wish to see if our efforts to breed for speed are yielding a measurable advantage to our birds. As for the kings, large and lovely as they are, I have had no success with them as messengers. They are too heavy-bodied to be fast, and many of them seem indifferent about returning to the home coop. They are, I fear, condemning themselves to be meat birds.

Erek

✦ ✦ ✦

CHAPTER THIRTEEN

CHOICES

I t was strange to move upriver again, as if nothing had happened. Thymara stood on the *Tarman*'s deck, the tool in her hand forgotten, and watched the jungly riverbank slowly slide by her. When she was in her own little boat, she'd never really had a chance to look down at the shore like this and see how the banks of the river changed as the hours of the day passed by. She missed being in her small boat but was almost glad it was gone. If it still existed, she'd have been paired with someone who wasn't Rapskal, and it hurt to imagine that.

Counting Carson's boat, they were reduced to five small boats, and only three had a full complement of gear. The *Tarman* had shipped extra oars for all the boats, she had discovered to her relief. Even so, the keepers had to rotate their days on the water. And when they were not in the small boats, they served on board the barge, doing whatever the captain asked them to do.

The expedition was now short on everything; knives, bows and arrows, spears, and fishing tackle had been lost, not to mention blankets, spare clothing, and the few personal items that each keeper had brought along. Greft had repeatedly congratulated himself on how well he had stowed his gear. It made Thymara want to hit him. It was sheer luck that his boat had wedged in the same tangle where the Bingtown man washed ashore. If it hadn't, he would have been as beggared as the rest of them. As it was, he now functioned as a hunter alongside Carson. Those two boats had departed at dawn, with Davvie helping Carson and Nortel riding along with Greft. She was just as glad; Nortel had come to her with a bruised face and muttered an apology for "treating her like trade goods" and then walked away. She wondered if the words were his or Tats's, and if Tats hoped to gain anything by forcing Nortel to apologize to her.

And there was her other painful subject. She didn't want to think about Rapskal's death, and she didn't want to waste time thinking about Greft's stupid plan for their lives.

"You won't finish it that way."

Tats's voice called her back from her pondering. She considered her clumsy attempt to shape a piece of wood into an oar. She knew next to nothing about woodworking, but even she could see that she was making a bad job of it.

"It's just busywork, anyway," she complained. "Even if I get this to where someone can use it, the river will eat it in a matter of days. Even our old oars were beginning to soften and fuzz at the edges, and they'd been treated against the acid water."

"Even so," Tats said. "When the ones we're using give out, the oars we're carving now will be our only spares. So we'd best have some." His effort did not look much better than hers, except that he was further along with it. "Any oar or paddle is better than none," he comforted himself as he looked at his handiwork. "Would you brace this for me while I try to use the drawknife on it?"

"Of course." She was happy to set her own tools down. Her hands were tired and sore. She braced the half-finished oar as Tats went to work with the drawknife. He handled the tool awkwardly, but still managed to shave a short curl of wood from the oar's handle before the tool bounced over a knot.

"I'm sorry about the other day," he said quietly.

They hadn't spoken about it since the incident. He hadn't tried to put his arms around her or kiss her since then; he probably knew the reception he'd get. His face wasn't as battered as Nortel's had been, but a black eye was still fading. "I know," she said shortly.

"I told Nortel he had to apologize to you."

"I know that as well. I suppose that means you won."

"Of course!" He seemed insulted that she had to ask.

He'd stepped right into her trap. "What you won, Tats, was a fight with Nortel. You didn't win me."

"I know that, too." From being apologetic, he was moving toward angry.

"Good," she said, biting the word off short. She picked up her chisel again, trying to decide where to set the blade to take another chunk out of the wood when Tats cleared his throat.

"Um. I know you're angry at me. Would you still hold the oar while I try to shape it?"

That wasn't really the question he was asking. She picked up the end of the oar and braced it again. "We're still friends," she said. "Even when I'm angry with you. But I don't belong to you."

"Very well." He placed the drawknife carefully and then drew it down the shaft of the oar. She watched how his brown hands gripped the handles of the tool, how the muscles in his forearms stood out. This time the curl of wood he shaved away was longer. "Let's turn it this way," he said and guided the oar through a half turn. As he set the drawknife to it again, he asked, "What would I have to do to win you, Thymara?"

It was a question she had never considered. As she thought about it, he said into her quiet, "Because I'm willing to do it. You know that."

She was startled. "How can you be willing to do something when you don't even know what I might ask?"

"Because I know you. Maybe better than you think I do.

Look, I've done some stupid things since we left Trehaug. I admit it. But—"

"Tats, wait. I don't want you to think that I'm going to give you a list of tasks you have to do. I won't. Because I wouldn't know what those things would be. We've been through a lot lately. You're asking me to make a big decision. I'm not playing a game when I say that I don't think I'm ready to make that decision. I'm not waiting for you to do something or give me something or even be something. I'm waiting for me. There's nothing you can do to change that. Nothing Greft can do."

"I'm not like Greft," he said, instantly insulted.

"And I'm not like Jerd," she replied. For a moment, they stared at each other. Thymara narrowed her eyes and firmed her chin. Twice Tats started to speak, and then paused. Finally he said, "Let's just make this oar, shall we?"

"Good thought," she replied.

EVENING WAS FALLING as Sedric emerged from his room. He'd spent the day alone and in darkness, for his last candle had burned down to nothing and he hadn't wanted to ask anyone for another one. He'd fasted as well. He'd half expected Davvie to come tapping on his door with a tray of food, but that hadn't happened. Then he'd recalled that Carson had told him he'd be keeping the boy clear of him. Just as well. *Just as well if everyone stayed clear of me,* he'd thought. Then he'd heard the self-pity in that statement and despised himself.

Hungry, thirsty, and bleak of spirit, he emerged onto the deck as the sun was going down. He found the barge nosed up in a creek bed, one of numerous tributaries that fed the Rain Wild River. Sometimes the water they offered was clear and almost free of acid. It seemed to be the case with this one, for most of the keepers and crew had gone ashore, leaving the ship almost deserted. When he paused at the railing to look, most of the boys were engaged in a water fight. The stream was shallow and wide, the water running swiftly over a sculpted sandy bed. The shirtless keeper boys were stooping to splash one another, laughing and shouting. The last light of the summer's end sun glinted on their scaled backs. Green, blue, and scarlet glints ran over them, and for one brief instant, he saw beauty in their transformations.

Beyond the youths, he saw Bellin kneeling by the stream as Skelly poured a stream of water over her soapy hair. Good. At least now there would be plenty of fresh water to replenish their supplies.

The dragons, too, were enjoying the water. Their gleaming hides showed that their young tenders had given them a good grooming. Relpda was among them, shiny as a copper coin. He wondered who had groomed her, and he felt guilty. He should take better care of Relpda. He didn't know how. He scarcely knew how to take care of himself, let alone anyone else.

The beach near the stream mouth was not large, but there was enough room for the dragons to be comfortable for the evening and for the keepers to have a bonfire. The fire was small now, but as he watched, two of the keepers approached with a branchy evergreen log and tossed it onto the flames. For a moment he thought they'd smothered the fire; then the darker smoke of burning needles rose, followed by a sudden leap of tongues of flame. The sweet smell of burning resin perfumed the evening air. The wave had left plenty of firewood scattered along the banks of the river. So. They would build a large fire for the night, and the keepers would be sleeping ashore.

He sniffed the air and realized that the smell of baking fish rode on the bonfire smoke. His stomach rolled over with an audible gurgle. He was suddenly horribly hungry and thirsty as well. He wondered where Alise and Leftrin were. They were the last people he wished to encounter right now, Alise because of what she knew about him and Leftrin because of what he knew about the man. It troubled him that he had not found a way to tell Alise yet. He didn't want to talk to her at all, let alone dash her dreams. But he would not betray her again. He would not stand by and watch her deceived.

He crossed the deck quietly, almost surreptitiously. At the door of the deckhouse he paused and listened. All was quiet within. Almost everyone had gone ashore, he imagined, to take advantage of the opportunity to bathe, to enjoy themselves at the bonfire, and to share hot fresh food. He opened the door and entered as silently as a scavenging rat. As he had hoped, a large pot of coffee was on the back of the small iron stove in the galley. The only light in the room came from the fire gleaming through the door crack of the stove. A covered pot was muttering; probably the eternal fish soup that was always kept simmering for the crew. He'd seen water and fish and vegetables added to the pot; he could not recall that he'd ever seen it emptied and washed. No matter. He felt as if he were still hungry from his days of isolation. Hungry enough to eat anything.

He did not know his way around the small galley. Moving carefully in the dimness, he found mugs hanging on hooks and plates stored vertically in a rack. He filled a mug with some dubious coffee, and finally found a stack of bowls on a shelf with a railing. He took one down, ladled soup into it, and got a round of ship's bread from the sack. He could not find spoons or forks. He sat down at the small galley table alone and took a sip of the coffee.

Weak and bitter but coffee all the same. He lifted the bowl of soup with both hands and sipped from the edge. The flavor was strongly fishy with overtones of garlic. He swallowed and felt warmth and strength funneling down his throat. It was good. Not delicious or even tasty but good. He suddenly understood the copper eating the rotted elk. On a basic level, when a man or a dragon was hungry enough, any food was good.

He was eating the soft chunks of fish and vegetable from the bottom of the bowl, scooping them up with his fingers, when the door of the deckhouse opened. He froze, hoping that whoever it was would walk past to the bunk room. Instead, she came into the galley.

Alise looked at him, hunched over his food, and without a word, opened a cupboard and reached into a bin. She took out a spoon and set it on the table for him.

Still silent, she poured herself a mug of the horrid coffee and stood, holding it in her hands. In the gloom, he was not sure if she was staring at him or not. Then she sighed, came to the table, and sat down opposite him. "I hated and despised you for several hours today," she said conversationally.

He nodded, accepting the judgment. He wondered if she could see his face in the dark.

"I'm over it now." Her voice was not gentle but resigned. "I don't hate you, Sedric. I don't even blame you."

He found his voice. "I wish I could say the same."

"I've grown so accustomed to your witty remarks over the years." Dead. That was how her voice sounded. Dead. "Somehow they are not as amusing as they once were."

"I mean it, Alise. I'm ashamed of myself."

"Only now."

"You sound as if you are still angry."

"Yes. I'm still angry. I don't hate you; I've decided that. But I'm angry in a way I've never been angry before. I think that if I hated you, I'd just hate you. But once I realized that only someone I loved could hurt me this badly, I realized I didn't hate you. And that is why I'm so angry."

"I'm sorry, Alise."

"I know. It doesn't really help, but I know you're sorry. Now."

"I've been sorry about it for a long time, actually. Almost from the beginning."

She flapped a hand at him, as if to shoo his excuses away. She sipped her coffee and seemed to debate something with herself. He waited. Finally, she spoke, in an almost normal voice. "I have to know this. Before I can go on with anything, before I can make any decisions, I have to know. Did you and Hest, did you make fun of me? Laugh at how gullible I was, how sheltered that I never even suspected? Did Hest's other friends know? Were there people I knew, people I thought were my friends, who knew how stupid I was? How deceived I was?"

He was silent. He thought of small dinner parties, held late in the evening, in the private upper rooms of inns in Bingtown. Brandy after dinner in Hest's den with some of their circle, and merriment that went on long after Alise had tapped on the door to wish them good night and retired to her bed.

"I have to know, Sedric." Her words called him back to the cramped and grubby galley. She was watching him, her face pale in the dimness. Waiting for the truth.

In her position, he would have felt the same way. The need to know how foolish he had appeared, how many people had known. "Yes," he said. The word cut his mouth. "But I didn't laugh, Alise. Sometimes I spoke out for you."

"And sometimes you didn't," she added ruthlessly. She sighed and set her mug down on the table. It was a small sound in the quiet room. She lifted her hands and hid her face in them. He feared she was crying. If she was, he knew he should comfort her, but he would have felt like a fraud doing it. He had been a party to creating this humiliation for her. How could he offer the comfort of a friend? He sat still, not speaking, waiting for her to make a sound.

But when she lowered her hands from her face, she only sighed heavily. She picked up her mug and took a sip of her coffee. "How many?" she asked conversationally. "How many people in Bingtown knew what a fool I was?"

"You weren't a fool, Alise."

"How many, Sedric?"

"I don't know."

"More than ten?" She was relentless.

"Yes."

"More than twenty?"

"I think so."

"More than thirty?"

"Possibly." He took a breath. "Probably."

She laughed bitterly. "So you were not very discreet in your indiscretion, were you? Was I the only one who didn't know?"

"Alise . . . you don't understand. Men like us, we have our own society, one that is mostly invisible to Bingtown society at large. We create our own world. We have to, because if we didn't, we wouldn't be allowed . . . You are not the only wife who has no idea of her husband's preferences. There are other wives in Bingtown who do know, and just accept it. My sister believes you are one of them, from something she once said to me. Some of those husbands are fathers, some of them do love their wives, in their own ways. It's just that . . . well . . ."

She had clenched her hands into fists. "Sophie knew?"

"Yes. Sophie knows. The way she spoke, she believes you knew and agreed to it. For a time I hoped you did. Then I mentioned it to Hest one day, and he laughed at me."

Her brows were knit as she puzzled over this. Then she asked abruptly, "How did Sophie know? Did you tell her?"

"I didn't have to. She's my sister. She just knew." He paused to think about that. "She always knew," he added quietly.

Alise drew a small breath, sighed it out. "I don't know which would be more humiliating, really. To have your sister think I was a deceived fool, or to think I was a party to your arrangement." She looked aside from him. "At least Hest didn't pretend he cared for me. Looking back, I suppose that he did offer me a strange sort of honesty. I knew he didn't want me, that he came to my bed only because he must, to make a child. I supposed he had another woman or women somewhere; I could never understand why he hadn't married someone he actually liked. But now I know. He couldn't."

He bowed his head to her cold reasoning.

"When I try to imagine you and him together, when I think of you embracing him, kissing his mouth, and him holding you tight . . . in the very house where we lived. Both of you coming down to breakfast with me after a night together, both of you planning . . ."

He was appalled. "Please don't, Alise. I don't want to talk about that."

"Was he tender to you, Sedric? Did he say he loved you, bring you small gifts? Remember what scents you liked, what sort of sweets?"

She wasn't going to let it go. Did he owe this to her? Did he have to endure this? He took a breath and admitted it. "No. That was how I was to him. He was never that way to me."

"Then how was he?" There was an edge of tears in her voice. "What did he do to make you love him?"

He stopped to think about it. It hurt. "He was Hest. You've

seen him. It was easy to fall in love with him. He's handsome and well dressed. Graceful on the dance floor. Charming. When he wants to, he can put his attention on you and make you the most important person in the world. He was strong. I felt . . . protected. Lifted up by him. I couldn't believe he wanted me, that he'd chosen me. He was so beautiful that just to have him notice me was all the gift I could imagine. I was dazzled. He did buy me gifts. Clothing. Pipes. A horse. I look back and I think now, those things were not really for me. They were things he gave me so that I would look how he wanted me to look. So I would not shame him with my shabby clothing or my poor taste in horseflesh. I was like . . . like cloth. Like something he had cut and sewn into a garment that suited him."

He had been staring at the table, at the almost-empty bowl, the cheap earthenware mug, the unused spoon. Now he lifted his eyes to look at her. In the dimness, her face could have been a paper mask with holes cut for the eyes. She was full of stillness, he thought. But no. All the stillness was on the surface. Beneath that quiet, she seethed.

"I'm not going back."

He stared at her, unable to make the connection between what he had said and what she had replied.

"I'm never going back to Bingtown," she clarified. "I'm never going back to where anyone knows me, knows how I was deceived, how I was shamed. That was something Hest did to me, using me that way. But I won't let him make that be who I am. I won't be cut and sewn into something that suits him."

"Alise—"

"He broke his vows to me. He voided our contract. I'm no longer bound to him, Sedric, and I've no reason to return to him. I'm staying here. On the *Tarman* with Leftrin. I know he'll have me. I don't care if he wants to marry me or not. I'm staying with him."

"You can't. You shouldn't." Now was not the time to be telling her this. He did not want to mix the two things together in her mind. But he couldn't let her get up from the table and walk away without knowing. He couldn't let her do something irrevocable, something that would allow yet another man to deceive her.

"Alise. You shouldn't trust him." His words stopped her. Her hand was on the door.

"I know that's what you think, Sedric." She didn't even turn to look back at him. "I know you think he is uneducated and socially beneath me, crude and unmannered. And you know something? He is those things. But he loves me, and I love him, and I've discovered that that matters more than all the things you think are important." She opened the door.

"Alise, he is deceiving you."

For a moment she stood in the doorway. Then she closed the door again, softly. He could not see her face, but he could imagine how the insecurity would flicker through her eyes. A man had made a fool of her before. A man she had trusted as a friend had deceived her for years. Could she trust her own judgment? Was it happening again?

"I don't enjoy telling you this."

"Yes, you do," she said harshly. "But say it anyway. How could he be deceiving me? How? Does he have a wife I don't know about? Immense debts somewhere? Is he a murderer, a liar, a thief? What?"

He ground his teeth, wondering how he could tell her without revealing his part in Jess's death. He wanted to keep that private. It was bad enough that both the dragon and Carson knew. He was surprised to realize that it was his dragon he was shielding as much as himself. He didn't want the other keepers to know that she had killed and eaten a human. Just tell her about Leftrin. He wouldn't say how he knew. "You must know that the Duke of Chalced is ill. He has made it plain that there will be rich rewards for anyone who brings him the dragon parts that he thinks will cure him. For that matter, any part of a dragon that ends up in any market will command a high price."

"Of course I know that. How could I study dragons and be unaware of all the traditions about the medicinal values of dragon scale or blood or liver or tooth? I don't doubt that some of that tradition is true. So?"

Out with it. "Leftrin is in league with people who intend to make the duke happy. He plans to gather or may already be collecting specimens from the dragons to sell in Chalced."

"He wouldn't." A hitch in her words as she thought. She was asking herself if it was possible. "He has no time, no opportunity!" she objected. "Running the ship takes up every bit of his time."

"He has been out around the dragons, helping get the rasp snakes off them, helping tar their injuries. He could do it, Alise. A scale or two here, some blood there. Waiting for the chance to plunder more from a dying or dead dragon. That would be the big payoff for this expedition. If a dragon dies or is injured, and he could collect parts from it, he could abandon the keepers and dragons and leave immediately for Chalced and rake in a rich reward."

"This is insanity! I won't, I can't believe it."

"It's true."

"How do you know?"

"I'm not at liberty to say."

"Oh." She put a world of disgust into that one word. "Innuendos and rumors. Well, Sedric, I'll put an end to it. I'll simply ask him."

"You shouldn't do that, Alise. I truly believe you don't know him, don't know what he is capable of doing. Jess, Jess the hunter, he told me things. There. Now you know. Jess told me that he was in partnership with Leftrin to get the dragon parts. He told me there was a plan to meet a Chalcedean ship at the mouth of the Rain Wild River as soon as they had what they needed. But they had a falling-out over it, and it came to fists."

"Why would Jess even talk to you, let alone confide such things in you?" He heard the small doubts piling up in her mind. Detail might convince her.

"Believe it or not, he thought I might help him get close to the dragons. Because of how I go among them with you. He knew you had given me that red scale to draw. He actually stole it from my cabin while I was sick. He said it alone was worth a small fortune. He thought that if we could get a scale from a dragon, perhaps we could get more things. Enough to make us all rich."

She stared at him through the gloom. He could hear her breathing. "Leftrin would not be a party to such a low scheme."

"He was. I fear he is. And I fear that if you bring it up to him, he may become violent. Or find a way to get rid of both of us. Alise, I'm telling you the truth. And you have to ask yourself, if you don't know this about him, what else do you not know?"

"I think I do know him. I think I know him better than you might suspect."

She flung those words at him and he knew. The depth of the lurch he felt surprised him. She'd slept with the man. Slept with that smelly, ignorant riverman. Alise, the sweet little girl he had known since her childhood, the respected Bingtown lady, had gone to the bed of that man. For a moment, he was wordless with dismay. Then he knew he had to do it. Deploy his final weapon against her blind infatuation.

"Alise, you think you know him. You thought you knew me, and Hest. But we deceived you for years and you never suspected us. I'm sorry for that, truly sorry. And that's why I'm trying to keep you from falling prey to that type of trickery again. Leftrin isn't worthy of you, Alise. You need to stay away from him."

In the dim light of the galley, he could see the motion of her shoulders as they rose and fell. She was fighting back sobs. She caught her breath. Her voice went shrill with the tightness of her throat. "Did I say I didn't hate you, Sedric? I think I was mistaken."

"Hate me, then," he replied. "I probably deserve it. I'll accept it as the price I pay, as what I owe you for how I deceived you for years. But don't waste yourself on that lout, Alise. You deserve better."

She made no reply to that, only shut the door firmly behind her as she left.

He sat a long time, alone in the dark. It was a reflex to lift the mug and finish off the last mouthful of cold, bitter coffee. He stood to leave and then looked back at the dishes on the table. He should tidy up after himself, stop being the spoiled Bingtown do-nothing he was accused of being. Tomorrow, maybe. Not tonight. His scene with Alise had exhausted him. The bleakness of his spirits weighed him down with a weariness that had nothing to do with sleepiness or tiredness. He just wished he could make everything stop, just for a while. He sighed and scratched his cheek. Tomorrow, there would be more wash water on board. He'd be able to heat some and shave. He'd never worn a beard before, never realized how itchy it could be. He scratched again, more vigorously.

Hair came off under his nails. When he shook his hand, the falling hairs glinted briefly in the moonlight from the window before falling. What was this? He'd never lost hair before! He scratched his head, pulled his hand free, and found a number of long strands dangling from his nails.

Stress and worry, he told himself. The effects of the acidic river water. That was all. He scratched more slowly along his jawline. His fingernail caught under something, lifted it. No. He moved his finger carefully, found the edge of the next scale. He caught the edge of it, lifted until it pulled painfully against his skin. Not a fleck of dirt, not dry skin. A scale growing on his face. A line of scales on his jaw. He felt dizzy and sick.

He walked his fingers up the nape of his neck, feeling the thin line of scales that followed his spine there. They were fine and flat now, like the scales on a trout. There were little scales growing on his scalp, loosening his hair as the scales replaced the hair. He felt his chapped lips with his fingertips. Not there yet. His breath came faster. But soon there would be, and the scales on his jaw and brows and on the nape of his neck would grow thick and curved and horny as a hoof.

You are unhappy?

He slammed his thoughts shut and ignored the floating sense of confusion that followed his exclusion of Relpda. His heart was thudding in his ears. Could this be real? It was an awful dream. He dared himself, then scratched his head violently with both hands. When he lowered them, strands of hair clotted his fingers. He shook them free and then hastily left the galley, letting the door bang shut behind him.

He started to head for his room, but halted halfway there. What was he going to do? Go inside his glorified packing crate, curl up on his pallet of rags, and whimper to himself? Hadn't he done enough of that lately? Hadn't he learned it did nothing?

The bow of the ship was nosed up on the stream's delta of sand. It overlooked the bonfire and the dragons and the keepers eating and talking together. He turned the other way, toward the stern and walked aft. Here he had a view of the glinting river as it flowed swiftly past the ship. Overhead, the moon was nearly full in a field of twinkling stars. He could look out and see no sign of humanity at all. The sounds of the keepers living their lives came from behind him to reach his ears. They were merry tonight. Plenty of fresh water and baked fish. All was well in their simple world. Not for him.

"I have nothing left," he said to the night. He counted off his losses to himself. No Hest. No home in Bingtown. No fortune. His friendship with Alise was in shreds. No face. If he returned to Bingtown, people would turn away from him in disgust, some because Hest had cast him off and some because his beauty was gone. Among his circle, to befriend someone whom Hest had cut off was rather dangerous. No respectability, no prospects. So what was there for him?

Nothing. Years of nothing ahead of him.

For three heartbeats, he considered Alise's solution. Stay in the Rain Wilds. Never go home. But she had someone who would take her in and care for her. He had no one, save a dragon. A dragon who was devoted to him. But how long would that last, if she discovered why he had first come to the Rain Wilds? He dared not think too much about it lest she discover his thoughts. He did not understand how she could not remember that he had come by darkness, to pluck scales from her and fill vials with her blood. Did she not recall it? How could she know that about him and still care for him?

Some day, she would realize it.

He thought of what that would mean. For the first time in his life, when Relpda touched minds with him, he had actually been able to feel the love that another creature had for him.

Daily her mind developed, her thoughts grew clearer and stronger. What would she feel for him when she realized that he had come to her, not as a friend but as a butcher?

And would she share that feeling with him, as she had shared her love? What would it actually be like to experience the hatred and loathing she would feel for him?

A shudder ran over him. He realized abruptly that he had not lost everything. He still had the love and regard of a simple creature. He could think of no way to avoid eventually losing that. He could not imagine enduring it. With sick certainty, he saw his only exit from his problems.

Don't think about what he was about to do. Don't let the dragon pick up on his thoughts and thwart him. Even warning himself brought her attention back to him. He wanted to say good-bye to her, to tell her it wasn't her fault. It wasn't. She'd done her best by him, saved him time after time. He felt a surprisingly sharp pang of sorrow at the thought of hurting her. He had an impulse to take off his boots and jacket. How silly was that? What difference could it make?

Sedric? Sedric?

Not right now, dear.

You are scared? Something hunts you, something comes to hurt you?

No. No, I'm fine. Everything is going to be all right.

No, you are frightened. Sad. Something is bad.

As gently as he could, he pushed her away from his thoughts. No time to waste. He could feel her clamoring outside his walls, raising an alarm with herself. Time to get it done before she could puzzle out what he was up to. He studied the water off the stern of the barge and chose a place where he could see the current running. He climbed up on the aft railing and judged the shining black water below him. Would it be deep enough and swift enough? It wouldn't take much. He'd never been a swimmer. Jump. Just jump and don't struggle. That was all. He deliberately exhaled, crouched, and sprang.

He hit hard, slamming on his side. His head slapped something that burst into light. He thought he'd breathed out, but a weight on top of him forced a gasp from his lungs. No water. Nothing made sense . . . "Can't . . . breathe . . ." he wheezed out.

The weight rolled off him. Sedric sucked in a breath, and for a dazed minute could not make sense of where he was or what had just happened. His eyes focused. He lay face-to-face with the hunter, Carson, on the *Tarman*'s deck.

"I knew you'd try something," Carson panted by his ear. "Saw it in your eyes when you left the galley earlier today. I told your dragon to let me know if she was worried. And she did." Carson dragged in a breath. "I had to run all the way up from the bonfire. You're lucky I got here in time."

Sedric's body was demanding air, and all he could do was wheeze. Funny. He wanted so badly to die, but when his body wanted air, it didn't care what his intentions were. All his thoughts stopped until he had air. When he'd had three full breaths, he asked bitterly, "Lucky?"

"Very well, then. I'm lucky. I caught you in time. I didn't have to get wet coming after you." Carson was smiling, very slightly. His dark eyes studied Sedric's face. "Why were you trying to drown yourself?"

"My life is over. I might as well be dead."

"How is that so?"

"You should have let me go. I want to die. I've lost everything."

"Everything?"

"Everything. Hest was finished with me. I see that now. That's why he sent me off with Alise. I confessed it all to her, admitted everything to her. She hates me now. Or she's very angry with me, she can't decide which. I haven't protected her. I betrayed her as a friend, and now she's making a terrible mistake, but she no longer trusts me, so my warnings are useless. If I go back to Bingtown, I'll be penniless and jobless. Hest will see that I'm despised by everyone in our circle. So I can't go back." Sedric's voice was getting ragged. He felt childish, recounting his woes to Carson in such a disorderly list. He bit his tongue before he could say a word about betraying the dragon. He still had a small chance of taking that secret to his grave. It didn't help that the big man just regarded him with those dark eyes and that half smile. He tried to sit up, to be away from him, but Carson's arm across him suddenly grew heavier, pinning him down.

"Stay there a moment. Catch your breath. There's something else bothering you. What is it?" That deep gaze bored into him, demanding confidence.

As if the simple question were a glamour he could not resist, he heard himself babbling his final secret. "The dragon's in my head. We're linked. I can't be free of her. She . . . she loves me. And that only makes me feel worse, because I don't really deserve it. She's a kind little creature . . ."

"Little?" Carson's was incredulous.

"Young, then. So young and in her own way, innocent. She's always aware of me, and especially so when I think of her." Tears had begun to spill from his eyes. He was ashamed of them. Hest had always mocked him when he wept. He turned his face away from Carson and looked up at the sky. He could already feel the dragon. Relpda offered her warmth. She tried to wrap it around him, to reassure him, but he cocooned himself in his own hard misery and held her off. He felt a hand on his jaw and flinched.

"Easy," Carson said. "No one's going to hurt you." Gently he turned Sedric's face back to his. "I don't think there's anything so terrible about someone loving you, even if she's a dragon. So what else pushed you to this? What is so terrible you can't live past it?"

Sedric swallowed. Carson hadn't lifted his hand from his face. He moved his forefinger carefully to swipe away a tear. When was the last time anyone had touched him with simple kindness?

"I've started to scale." The words came out tighter, higher pitched. He couldn't keep the panic out of his voice. "Along my jawline. And on the back of my neck."

"It doesn't usually happen to grown men. Let me see." Carson leaned up on an elbow and looked down at him intently. He walked his fingers along Sedric's jawline. "Mmm. You may be right. There's a little scaling there." He smiled a small smile. "Your beard is as soft as a puppy's fur. Let me check the back of your head." He slid his hand around the back of Sedric's skull, and let his fingers trace a line down the nape of his neck. "So you have," he said softly. "Scales."

He took a deep breath. "Better and better," he said gently. He sounded pleased and for some reason, Sedric felt very hurt by that. Why would Carson enjoy his misfortune? And then, with his hand cupped around the back of Sedric's neck, the hunter slowly lowered his mouth onto his and kissed him. Sedric went still with astonishment. Carson's lips were gentle but demanding. When he broke the kiss, Sedric discovered that Carson had gathered him into his arms, holding him with strength but not cruelty. Cradling him against him. Something in him broke. He lowered his face to the rough fabric of Carson's shirt and wept. Sobs rose out of him and broke him. He cried for all the things he'd thought he'd had but had never possessed. Wept for what he'd let Hest make him, how he'd deceived Alise, for what he'd thought of doing to Relpda. He cried because it was suddenly safe to do so. The hunter said nothing. He didn't move other than to pull him closer. As the last tears finally left him, Sedric felt the dragon's affection surround him.

I know you took my blood. Even then, you did not want to kill me. You drank my blood and gave me a link to your mind, to clear my thoughts. It will be all right, Sedric. I won't betray you. No one need ever know.

The simple acceptance and forgiveness washed through him like a flood. It tumbled him and drowned him as the wave of water had not. He could not and found that he did not wish to resist it. Mindless warmth flushed through him again, taking away all thought of his problems, washing away his despair and leaving comfort.

He felt his whole body relax.

And Carson put two fingers under his chin, lifted his face, and kissed him again.

After a time, the hunter pulled his mouth away and said hoarsely, "If you've changed your mind about killing yourself, I've thought of something else you could do tonight."

Sedric tried to find his own thoughts, to summon again everything that had filled him with despair. Carson must have seen it in his face.

"Don't," he suggested softly. "Just don't. Not now. Don't question it, don't hesitate." He pushed his body back from Sedric's and rose to his feet. Then he leaned over, offering Sedric a hand. He took it, felt the hunter's rough and calloused palm against his, and let Carson help him to his feet.

"Let me take you to your room," Carson offered quietly.

"Yes."

THYMARA WALKED AWAY from the bonfire into the night. It should have been a good evening. The night weather was mild, her stomach was full of fish and creek greens, she had been able to bathe and wash her hair and drink all she wanted this afternoon. She had scrubbed Sintara until the arrogant queen shone bluer than any summer sky. She hadn't praised her with words and had been annoyed when Sintara had turned to her and said, "You are right in your heart. No other dragon here can compare to me."

No thanks for her grooming had she offered. Thymara had seethed, but silently, and had soon left her. The rest of the afternoon, she helped Tats, Harrikin, and Sylve groom the keeperless dragons. That had been a challenge.

Baliper had been morose and uncooperative, still mourning Warken. Spit had presented the opposite problem. Newly cheeky and dangerously aggressive, the little silver had not wanted anyone to leave off grooming him as he basked in the attention of several keepers at once. Thymara had been relieved when Alise, her hair still damp from washing, had joined them and kept him occupied. Poor Relpda had submitted to grooming, but all the while, she had kept her eyes on the *Tarman,* palpably missing Sedric. Thymara had felt outrage on her behalf. "What sort of a man allows a dragon to save him and then ignores the poor creature?" she'd demanded of Alise. And then been jolted with surprise when Alise had defended him, saying, "I'm not surprised. He has problems of his own to deal with just now. It's best to leave him alone with them."

The copper had been more direct with her. "My keeper!" she'd hissed at Thymara, and though the exhalation had been venomless, Thymara had made no more disparaging remarks about Sedric.

When evening was full and they gathered by the bonfire to bask in its heat and eat together, she had seen that the others were healing from their losses. She was glad for them. All missed Jess's storytelling. When Davvie brought out his pipes and began to play, the music sounded thin and lonesome. Then, to the startlement of all, Bellin had come down from the *Tarman,* carrying her own pipes. Without fanfare, she had sat down beside Davvie and joined her music to his, wrapping his melody in an accompaniment that made it seem more than enough to fill the night. Stoic Swarge was more pink cheeked than his wife, visibly prideful over her talent. The music was beautiful.

But that was when Thymara had slipped away from the company. For when she had turned to Rapskal, looking forward to sharing her astonishment and pleasure, he simply wasn't there.

It seemed obscene and cruel that she had forgotten, even for a few moments, that he was dead and gone. It seemed a betrayal of their friendship, and suddenly the beauty of the music cut her too deeply and she had to go away from those who sat by the fire enjoying it. She'd stumbled off into the darkness until she came to the stream. There, she'd sat on a fallen tree and listened to the mutter of the water. Behind her, the light and warmth of the bonfire and the music seemed to come from a different world. She wondered if she belonged in it anymore.

The silence of the forest was no silence at all to her ears. The water moved, and insects ticked in bark and moss. Up above her, something small and clawed stalked through the branches; probably a little tree cat looking for lizards gone motionless with the evening chill. She listened intently and heard the final pounce and a thin squeak before the little predator gave a short purr of satisfaction and then made its purposeful exit. Probably taking its kill off to a safe place to enjoy it.

"What if I just stayed here?" she asked the night quietly. "Clean water. The firmest land I've ever seen; there is sand in the creek bottom, not muck. The hunting should be good. What do I need that I couldn't find here?"

"Company?" Tats suggested from the darkness. She turned and saw him as a silhouette against the orange firelight. "Or have you had enough of people? Mind if I join you?"

She moved over on the log instead of answering him. She wasn't sure what her answer would have been.

"By now, he would have had everyone up and jigging with him," Tats said to the night.

She nodded silently. Tats reached over and picked up her hand. She let him. He handled it in the darkness, sweeping his thumb across her palm, counting her fingers with his. He ran his nails lightly over her claws. "Remember when you thought these were a bad thing to have?" he asked conversationally.

She drew her hand back into her lap, suddenly self-conscious. "I'm not sure I ever really thought that. They've always been useful to me. I just knew I'd have to live with everyone else thinking they'd limit me."

"Yes, well, more than once on this expedition, I've wished I had claws like you." Matter-of-factly, he recaptured her hand and warmed it between both of his. It felt good; she hadn't known it ached until he gently rubbed it and soothed the ache away. Tension began to seep out of her body. He slid a little closer to her. "Give me your other hand," he told her, and she complied without thinking about it. He held her hands in both of his, rubbing them gently.

For a time, they were silent. The noises from the bonfire came to them, and one of the dragons hooted in alarm about something, but it wasn't Sintara, and she ignored it. When Tats put one of his arms across her shoulders and pulled her closer to lean on him, she allowed herself to do so. He rested his cheek on her hair. She wasn't surprised when he ducked his head in to kiss her. It was easy to allow him to do that, easy to let the spreading warmth of sensation drive all thoughts from her mind.

The second time his hand brushed her breast, she knew it wasn't an accident. Did she want to do this? Yes. She refused to think that it might lead to things she wasn't ready to allow him. She could always say no if it came to that. She didn't need to say it yet.

He kissed the side of her neck, her throat, and she leaned back, letting him. His mouth slid lower and suddenly a voice said, "Well, it appears a decision has been reached."

They leaped apart, Tats coming to his feet and whirling to face Greft. His hands were already cocked into fists. "You spying sneak!" he hissed.

Greft laughed. "Turnabout is fair play. Ask Thymara." He turned around, ignoring Tats's physical challenge. "I'll tell the others for you," he offered. "I think they've a right to know." He walked away.

"Nothing has been decided. Nothing!" Thymara shouted after him.

He laughed mockingly and continued on his way back to the fire. He favored one hip as he walked, and Thymara selfishly hoped that his Rain Wild changes were making him ache.

"That bastard," Tats said with feeling. Then he turned to her and cocked his head. "Nothing?" he asked her.

"It's . . . it's not a decision," she said. "We were just kissing."

In the darkness, with no touch joining them, he seemed very far away from her. "Just kissing?" he asked her. "Or just teasing?" He crossed his arms on his chest. She could barely see him in the dimness.

"I wasn't teasing," she said defensively. More quietly she added, "I wasn't thinking about what we were doing."

For a time, he was quiet. Her body still tingled from his touch. She thought of stepping closer to him, of letting him resume where he had left off. Perhaps he was thinking the same thing, for he suddenly said, "Thymara. Yes or no?"

She didn't have to think about it. She forced herself to speak quickly before she could change her mind. "No, Tats. It's still no."

He turned and walked back to the bonfire, leaving her alone in the darkness.

$\diamondsuit \quad \diamondsuit \quad \diamondsuit$

Day the 3rd of the Gold Moon

Year the 6th of the Independent Alliance of Traders

From Detozi, Keeper of the Birds, Trehaug

To Erek, Keeper of the Birds, Bingtown

Enclosed, the formal invitation for all Rain Wild Traders and Bingtown Traders to attend the upcoming Harvest Festival Ball in the Rain Wild Traders' Concourse at Trehaug. To be widely posted and to be duplicated and personally delivered to the Traders listed within.

Erek,

As you have requested, I released four birds at dawn of this day, at precisely the same moment, all bearing identical messages that Reyall had indeed arrived safely home. Two of them were from the batch of swift pigeons that arrived with Reyall two days ago, and two were standard messenger birds. I delayed their flight by two days to allow the swift birds time to recover from their voyage and to limber their wings in the fly pen. The moment the birds were released, all four took immediate flight. I will admit to a moment of jealousy as I watched them go, wishing that I, too, could so effortlessly undertake the journey to Bingtown. Please keep me informed of this experiment. I should like to know how many days it takes them to make the journey, and if the swift pigeons are appreciably faster than our standard messenger birds. I have set the kings aside in breeding cages, allowing only one bird of each mated pair to take flight at a time. So far, they seem well able to provide for themselves, and all have selected

nesting boxes. I will keep you apprised of this project as well. If it succeeds on a small scale, I could see that a family could found its fortune on such a meat production venture. I am glad to hear that your father's health has improved. You are not the only one pestered by family to take a mate and settle down. One would think my mother had a nesting box awaiting me, to hear her nag that I need to find a husband soon!

Detozi

CHAPTER FOURTEEN

DIVERGENCE

After two days of steady rain, the weather had suddenly changed. Bright blue skies overhead gave a false promise that summer might return. The fog and the clouds drew back, revealing changes in the countryside. The river had changed gradually, with the far bank slowly advancing back toward them. Perhaps, Leftrin thought, they had finally passed through the remains of the wide lake that the dragons had spoken of. But it was just as likely, he told Swarge, "That nothing is as they remember it. And anything that they tell us of how things used to be can be worse than useless to us. If we rely on it instead of our own river sense, and they're wrong, we could go nosing into all sorts of trouble."

Swarge had nodded gravely but said nothing, as was usual with him. Leftrin hadn't really expected any conversation from him, but he would have welcomed more than a nod. He felt he'd been left too much alone with his own thoughts lately.

Alise had been quiet for days, almost withdrawn. Oh, she smiled at him, and once or twice, she had taken his hand, so he did not think she was seriously regretting their interlude together. But she had shown no signs of attempting another rendezvous. The one night that he had tapped softly on the door of her darkened cabin, she had not answered him. After a time of anxious loitering, he had cursed himself for acting like a silly boy. She had shown him that when she wanted him, she'd make it plain. He'd not dangle outside her door when she did not.

Once when he'd found her silent and morose, staring over the bow, he'd dared to ask if what was troubling her had to do with him. She'd shaken her head so hard that the tears flew from her cheeks. "Please," she'd said. "Please don't ask me about it. Not now. It's something I have to cipher out for myself, Leftrin. If I feel I can tell you about it, I will. But for now, I have to bear it alone."

And so she had.

He suspected it had something to do with Sedric. The man spent a lot of time in his cabin. When he was not there, he was likely to be up on the nose of the vessel, looking at his dragon as she plodded stolidly along. Recently he had taken to visiting her ashore every evening. Daily he made an effort at grooming the creature. He, too, seemed to be in the midst of puzzling something out. He reminded Leftrin of a man recovering his strength after a long convalescence. He no longer seemed to care so much if his boots got muddy or his hair was not combed. Leftrin had surprised Bellin and Sedric in the galley, drinking coffee at the table together. More startling had been finding Davvie showing him how he fastened hooks to a long line for the bottom fishing lines that he sometimes set at night. Once he had seen Carson leaning on the railing next to him, and he wondered if that alliance might not be the source of Alise's unhappiness. Carson, too, had been odd of late, and quiet in his watchful hunter way. Something was troubling him, but he hadn't divulged it to Leftrin. If that "something" was his relationship with Sedric, then the captain was content to remain ignorant of it. He had plenty to worry about as it was; there was no room left in his brain for minding other folks' business.

The expedition had changed, and no one was comfortable with the changes yet. There were not enough boats and paddles for the keepers to follow the dragons as they had before. Some of the keepers had to ride on board the barge each day. After one day of leaving them in idleness, Leftrin had recognized the danger to that and found tasks for all of them. When he had time, he supervised them in the shaping of new paddles for the remaining boats, and other mundane tasks. Tarman was not a large vessel; it was sometimes difficult to find enough chores to keep them all busy. Nonetheless, he kept the on board keepers busy with any tasks he or Hennesey could think of. In his experience, idle hands on a boat made for trouble all around.

He'd already seen signs of it. Bellin had come to him, uncomfortable and shy, to tell him that she'd had a talk with Skelly about Alum. "Neither one of them means any harm. But the attraction is there, they are young, and routine demands that they see each other almost every day. I've cautioned her. You'd be wise to speak to the young man before any hopes are raised or damage done."

He'd hated that task. But it had been his, both as captain and as her uncle. Skelly had avoided him for the last few days, and Alum, proud but respectful, had gone out every day since then in Greft's boat. Greft was grateful for Alum's help, but the older keeper would not have been Leftrin's choice of a companion for Alum. It was more and more clear to him that Greft did not respect his authority and was not above stirring rebellion. But there it was. Greft had reclaimed the boat that Carson and Sedric had brought back. Leftrin thought it was shortsighted of the keepers to let him assert ownership to it; surely all the boats had been owned in common when they set out. But he would not interfere in keeper matters. He had more than enough on his own plate to keep him busy. Greft had assumed Jess's mantle as a hunter, and everyone seemed content to let him do so.

Tarman had let him know about the major tributary before

he saw it. No change in the river took him unawares. Tarman had felt it early in the day, when he had tasted a change in the water and had informed him. Tarman always preferred a shallow channel, and as the river began to deepen, he had once more hugged the eastern bank. Hours before they reached the junction of the tributaries, long before he actually saw it, Leftrin began to hear it and feel it with Tarman's senses. When they finally arrived at the merging of the two rivers that fed the Rain Wild River, it was clear which one of them had been the source of both the acid and the wave that had nearly destroyed all of them. The western tributary presented a wide open channel that was littered with debris to either side. Down that chute had rushed the deadly wave, destroying all in its path and leaving the trees and vegetation on its banks festooned with all manner of torn and broken branches and grasses. Sunlight sparkled on the grayish river, and it presented a welcoming vista of straight open waterway.

A lush delta of tall reeds and bulrushes separated it from the more sedate eastern tributary, a meandering shallow river overhung with vines, the edges choked with coarse grasses and rushes. Without hesitation, the dragons had followed the open channel, staying as close to the shore as they could. They were well ahead of the barge, as always, but the straight river allowed Leftrin to see them, strung out in a long line as they paced on. The hunters had proceeded ahead of them. There in the open waters, the sunlight glittered on the dragons. Golden Mercor led, with immense Kalo right behind him. The other dragons, green and scarlet, lavender and orange and blue, trailed him in a brilliant parade. Relpda the copper dragon and the aptly named Spit brought up the tail end of the dragon's procession. The straight open channel was sunny and inviting. Easy sailing ahead, and Leftrin suddenly had the feeling that Kelsingra was not that far away. If an ancient Elderling city was to be found, surely it would be up that sunstruck waterway.

He was anticipating a long afternoon of easy travel when, with a sudden lurch, Tarman veered toward the delta and ran aground. Leftrin stumbled and caught at the railing to keep from falling. A chorus of startled shouts rose from the throats of everyone aboard. "Damn it, Swarge!" Leftrin shouted, and "Wasn't me!" the tillerman shouted back at him, a tinge of anger in his voice.

Leftrin leaned over the railing and looked down. There was almost always a sandbar whenever two bodies of moving water met—always a delta of some sort. Tarman knew that, as did every riverman aboard him. Tarman knew it, and Tarman never ran aground. Hadn't for years, even before Leftrin had had the opportunity to modify him. Yet there they were, stuck fast in mud, with the ship making no effort at all to free himself. It made no sense.

He leaned on the railing, growled deep in his throat. "Tarman. What are you doing?"

He felt no response from the ship that he could decipher. He was well and truly wedged on the muddy bottom.

"Captain?" It was Hennesey, confusion all over his face.

"I don't know," he replied quietly to the mate's unvoiced question. He gave an exasperated sigh. "Get the extra poles out. The keepers may as well earn their keep today. Let's get off this mudbank and back on our way."

"Aye, sir," Hennesey responded and began to shout his relay of the orders. Leftrin gave the ship's railing a brief squeeze. "We'll have you off this bar and under way again soon enough," he promised Tarman quietly. But as he lifted his hands away, he wondered if he felt assent or amusement from his ship.

THE KEEPERS GATHERED on the forward deck, summoned by Hennesey's shouted orders. Thymara had been working in the galley, trying to scrub ancient burned-on residue from the bottoms of the ship's pots, when the sudden lurch had tossed her against the galley table. She'd hurried out to see what the fuss was about and was shocked to find they were stuck. It had never happened before: they had passed numerous small tributaries feeding into the Rain Wild River. Some had been small streams wending through the trees and out to dump into the river. Others had been wide rivers cutting their own boggy paths through the forest before adding their waters to the river. Tarman never got stuck in any of their deltas. But this was different.

To the left was an immense river with a wide, free-running channel down its center. It was obvious that it had recently been a flood channel. Damaged trees with dangling limbs and mud-daubed debris lined the shores of it. The color of the water was definitely lighter as it fed into the main channel and dispersed. Up that river was the source of both the torrent that had nearly killed them all and the acid that colored the waters of the Rain Wild River white. The river and the forest that bound it to either side ran off into an unimaginable distance. A bluish shadow against the sky at the far horizon might have been mountains, or her imagination. The dragons were silhouettes against that horizon as they made their way upriver.

As Thymara watched, a flock of birds with yellow-barred tails rose as one from the trees, fluttered for a distance, and then resettled. The angry yowl of a frustrated hunting cat followed them. She smiled. The lush and untouched vista attracted her. She suspected both hunting and gathering would be easier there. She wished they were staying here for the night. If they were, she'd explore in that direction. With no weapons or fishing gear of her own left, fruit and vegetables had been the best she could offer her fellows. She longed to borrow gear from Greft's hoard, but he hadn't offered it to anyone and she would not ask.

Thymara had found a spot along the bow railing to survey the divergence of the waters. Now she turned back to look at the company assembling on the forward deck to look over the side. Hennesey and Swarge were bringing out the spare poles and passing them out to the stronger keepers. Tats received his grinning. She suddenly suspected he'd always wanted the chance to try his hand with one.

For an instant, she saw them all as strangers. There were ten keepers instead of the dozen they'd begun with. All of them were more ragged and weathered than they had been. The boys had all grown, and most had the shape and muscles of men now. They moved differently than when she'd first met them;

they moved like people who worked on water and land rather than as tree dwellers. Sylve, she realized, had grown and was acquiring the shape of a woman. Harrikin still was her shadow; they seemed content with each other's company despite the disparity in their ages. Thymara had never mustered the courage to ask Sylve if she knew that Greft had arranged the match. Over the last few days, she'd decided it didn't really matter. They seemed well suited to each other; what did it matter who had decreed it?

Jerd stood to one side, watching the activity. Her face was pale. Despite Jerd's frequent patting of her belly and posturing, she was not showing much of her pregnancy yet, save in her temperament. She had become unpleasantly bitchy to everyone of late. She had near-constant morning sickness and complained of the way the boat smelled and the food tasted and of the constant motion. It would have been easier to be sympathetic to her, Thymara thought, if she were not so insistent that everyone else's concerns should give way to her whining. If her pregnancy were typical of the state, Thymara wanted nothing to do with childbearing. Even Greft had begun to weary of Jerd's constant nipping at him. Twice she had heard him reply to her roughly, and each time Jerd had been both furious and tearful. Once he had turned on her almost savagely, asking her if she thought she was the only one in pain from a changing body. Alum had stood up and Thymara had thought he would interfere. But before it came to that, Jerd had run off wailing, to cower in the galley and weep while Greft had sourly declared he'd rather face a gallator than "that girl" right now.

The crew of the ship had changed almost as much as the keepers had. Thymara had become more aware of both Skelly and Davvie as people. It was often obvious that they longed to socialize more with the keepers; they were, after all, of an age with most of them. Captain Leftrin had tried to keep those boundaries intact, but there had been some breaches. She knew that Alum was infatuated with Skelly, and that both had been rebuked for fraternizing. Davvie's growing friendship with Lecter appeared to be tacitly ignored by all, which did not seem

fair to her. But then, she thought with a wry grin, Captain Leftrin rarely consulted with her on what she thought about how
he ran his ship.

Alise had come out on the deck. She stood on the roof of the
deckhouse with her sketchbook, capturing the moment. Thymara looked at her and scarcely recognized the fine Bingtown
lady she had first seen at Cassarick. She had abandoned her wide-
brimmed hats, and her smooth and gleaming hair was a thing of
the past. The sun and wind had tanned her skin and multiplied
her freckles. Her clothing showed plainly the hard use she had
put it to. There were patches on the knees of her trousers, and
the hems were frayed out. She wore the cuffs of her shirts rolled
back now, and her hands and arms had browned in the sun. For
all that, even during the days when she seemed quiet and sad,
she seemed more alive and real than when Thymara had first
met her. Her companion, Sedric, however, reminded Thymara
of a bright bird in a molt. All his lovely colors and fine manners
had dropped away from him. He said little to her anymore, but
he cared for his new dragon with a clumsy sincerity that Thymara found touching. The little copper was blossoming under
his care and had become something of a chatterbox when he
was not around to occupy her. Her language and thoughts came
clearer now, and cleansed of her parasites, she was growing as
rapidly as her limited diet allowed.

She was not the only dragon who had changed since the
big wave. The silver, Spit as he now called himself, was almost
dangerous. Quick-tempered and fully venomed, he had already
accidentally scalded Boxter. Boxter had not done anything to
provoke him, except to be in the area when Spit became angry
with one of the other dragons. Mercor had descended quickly,
roaring at Spit. Luckily for Boxter, he had only received a
drift rather than a direct spray of dragon venom. His arm was
burned, but he'd torn his shirt off quickly enough that he'd
avoided worse injury. Restraining his own dragon from going
after Spit had demanded most of his effort. It was only later
that the other keepers had treated and bound his arm for him.

If he had not already been scaled, the damage would have been much greater.

Some of the dragons were discontented and weary of traveling, others as determined as when they had begun. Their attitudes to the journey varied as much as their attitudes toward their keepers. Some seemed to have grown very close to their keepers. Mercor and Sylve reminded Thymara of an old married couple. They knew each other well and were very content with each other's company. She and Sintara had still not resolved their differences, and with every passing day, she wondered if they would. The dragon seemed angry with her, but she could not decide what the original basis for it was. Sintara still asserted the right to order her about, to command her to groom her or remove parasites from around her eyes. Thymara, true to her contract, cared for the dragon. Despite Sintara's annoyance with her, she felt their bond had grown stronger; she was much more aware of the dragon's needs, and when Sintara spoke to her, the meaning went far beyond words. Something stronger and deeper than affection bound them to each other. The linking was not always comfortable for either of them, but it was real. Why it existed was a conundrum. Alise still visited the dragon, but Sintara was even less attentive to her. Strange to say, Alise did not seem to take it to heart. Thymara sometimes wondered what had distracted her from the dragon, but most often took it to mean that Alise had realized, as she had, that she was simply not that important to the dragon.

Baliper was a lonely soul without Warken. The keepers took turns grooming him, but he spoke little to any of them and took small interest in any of the humans. Some of the other dragons seemed to understand his mourning; others seemed to find him weak because of it. Jerd's Veras was not pleased with her keeper's lack of attention to her and didn't care who knew. Greft tended Kalo still, but in a perfunctory way, and Kalo had been in a period of black temper for almost a week. Something, Thymara felt, was brewing among the dragons, something they had not shared with their keepers. She dreaded what it might be. When she let her thoughts wander, she considered every possibility from the dragons simply abandoning them to the dragons turning on them and eating them. By day, such imaginings seemed silly. Not so in the dead of night.

"You! Thymara! Think you're decorative? There's a pole left. Get on the end of it."

Hennesey's order jarred her from her daydreaming. She felt a blush rise as she hurried forward to pick up the last available pole. Jerd still stood to one side, a hand on her belly. Sylve stood near her, arms folded, mouth set in disapproval. Obviously she had expected to be part of the pole crew despite her diminutive size.

Hennesey was still barking orders. "I don't expect you to know what you're doing, but I expect you to help. It's pretty simple. Shove the pole down into the mud. When I yell, everyone pushes. It shouldn't take much to get us off. Once we're clear of the mud, bring your poles back on board without braining each other, and let the crew take over. Ready?"

Thymara had found a place alongside Skelly. The deckhand grinned at her. "Don't worry, sis. This ought to be easy. Then you can get back to those pots in the galley."

"Oh, yes, I'm longing to do that," Thymara assured her, returning her grin. She looked at Skelly's hands, copied her grip on the pole and her stance. The deckhand gave her an approving nod.

"Now push!" Hennesey shouted, and they all strained.

The boat rocked, shifted, rocked again as they grunted and strained.

And the *Tarman* settled in deeper.

THE LONG AFTERNOON passed very slowly.

The crew and the keepers manned their poles. They shoved, the barge moved slightly and dug in again. Long after it was apparent to Leftrin that Tarman was opposing their efforts to free him, he stubbornly kept his crew at work. First Hennesey called him aside, then Swarge and Bellin together approached him. Skelly read his humor and left him alone. His replies to each query were terse. Yes, he could see that the barge was deliberately digging in. Yes, he could tell it was not accidental. No, he didn't want to stop trying. And no, he had no idea what was upsetting the ship.

In all the family history of Tarman, Leftrin had never heard of him directly defying his captain's will. He couldn't quite believe this was happening. "Ship, what ails you?" he muttered as he clutched the aft railing. But there was too much going on around him. The clustered and chattering keepers, the anxious crew, and Leftrin's own frustration clouded his ability to read his ship. Tarman conveyed by turns agitation when they tried to move him and determination as he dug in deeper.

More than once that day, Leftrin had silently set his hands to the railing and tried to find out what was troubling his ship. Demanding to know what was wrong only brought an echo from his ship that *this is wrong*.

At one point, he bellowed aloud in frustration, "How is it wrong?"

All heads turned to him, Skelly gaping in shock. The only response he felt from Tarman made no sense. *Water wrong, river wrong*. It made no sense. So Leftrin dug his heels in as firmly as Tarman's claws were set in the bottom and kept crew and keepers busy at trying to rip the barge free. Twice the barge swung wide and almost came free, only to suddenly dig in at the other end. It was oil on the flames of his frustration to sense his ship's amusement at the humans' puny efforts.

He had given the pole handlers a break when Swarge and Hennesey came at him together. "Cap, we think it might have something to do with the new, uh, hull design."

That from Swarge, and then Hennesey added, "And if it does, we might be better off to find out what's troubling Tarman before we insist on having our own way."

He was still formulating an answer to that when someone shouted, "Keeper boats are coming back, hunters, too. And the dragons are headed back toward us."

He glanced up at the sky, and then at the approaching boats

and dragons. The dragons and hunters must have finally realized the barge wasn't following them. They were returning. They'd lose most of a day's travel at a time when supplies were running low. He wasn't pleased. He looked over at his crew. This was probably the hardest day they'd put in since the barge had been modified. They were exhausted and worried. The keepers looked weary. He gave in.

"Put the poles up. Even if we got free tonight, we'd just have to find a good place to overnight. So, we'll stay here. Keepers, you can go ashore, see what you can find for firewood, make a blaze. Let's all take a break, and I'll have a fresh look at things in the morning." He turned and walked away from their puzzled stares. It did not help that he sensed Tarman's profound satisfaction at getting his own way.

ALISE SAW THYMARA clambering over the railing and called out to her hastily, "May I go with you?"

Thymara stopped, startled. She had a bag slung over her shoulder and her hair, freshly fastened into long black braids, had been tied in a bundle at the back of her head. "I've already been to check on Sintara. I'm going to use what's left of the light to look at the other tributary."

"I'd guessed that. May I go with you, please?" Alise put a bit of emphasis on the last word. She'd already seen the girl's reluctance.

"If you wish." Thymara sounded more resigned than welcoming. She was still missing her friend, Alise supposed.

She followed the Rain Wild girl to the railing and climbed down after her to the muddy shore. The dragons had taken refuge for the evening on the delta between the two rivers and were rapidly trampling the vegetation into oblivion. Even so, it was the most pleasant place they had stopped at for a while. Scattered white trees with papery bark grew on almost dry land. Behind them a forest grew that looked almost familiar to Alise—a woodland of smaller trees with open spaces between them.

But she was following Thymara and the girl did not go that

way, but toward the other river. For a time, Alise followed her in silence, intent on keeping up with the younger woman. Thymara walked swiftly; Alise did not complain. But as they reached the bank of the gentler river and began to walk up its shore, Thymara slowed, knitting her brow and peering around at the trees and moss and grasses.

"It's so different here," she said at last.

"It's a more familiar kind of forest," Alise agreed and then added, "To me at least."

"The water is so clear."

It wasn't, to Alise's eyes. But she saw immediately what Thymara was referring to. "There's no white to it. No acid at all, or at least very little."

"I've never seen a river like this." Thymara made her way to the mossy bank and stooped down. After a moment of hesitation, she dipped her fingers into the water and let drops of it fall on her tongue. "I've never tasted water like this. It's alive."

Alise didn't laugh. "It looks like normal river water to me. But I haven't seen this much of it since I entered the Rain Wilds. Oh, we've passed some streams of clear water on our way here, but as you said, nothing like this."

"Shh."

Alise froze and followed the direction of Thymara's stare. Across the river, deer had come to drink. There was a buck with a substantial rack, two spike bucks, and several does. Only one had noticed the two women. The large buck stood, muzzle still dripping, and stared at them while the other deer came and drank.

"And me with no bow." Thymara sighed.

The buck's large ears flicked back and forth. He made a sound in his throat, a *whuff,* and his companions immediately lifted their heads. He made no sign that Alise saw, but the deer immediately retreated into the shelter of the trees and underbrush with the buck being the last to wheel and go. Privately, Alise was glad that Thymara was weaponless. She would not have enjoyed watching him die, nor helping with the butchering.

"If stupid Greft wasn't so selfish with the hunting tools, we'd all be having fresh venison tonight," Thymara grumbled.

"Perhaps the hunters will bring something back."

"And perhaps they won't," Thymara replied sourly. She set out again, following the riverbank, and Alise followed her. "Why did you want to come with me?" Thymara asked abruptly. Her voice was more puzzled than unfriendly.

"To see what you do, and how. To spend time with you."

Thymara glanced back at her, startled. "Me?"

"Sometimes it's pleasant to be in the company of another woman. Bellin is kind to me, but she has everything she needs in Swarge. When I spend time with her, I know she is making that time for me. Skelly is busy and her concern is the ship. Sylve is sweet but young. Jerd is . . ."

"Jerd is a nasty bitch," Thymara filled in when Alise paused to find tactful words.

"Exactly," Alise agreed and laughed guiltily. "At least right now. Before she was pregnant, she was too interested in the boys to speak to me. And now her life is focused on her belly. Poor thing. What a situation to be in."

"Perhaps she should have thought of that before she got into it," Thymara suggested.

"I'm sure she should have. But now, well, she is where she is, and it's up to all of us to be kind to her."

"Why?" Thymara paused in her speech as she climbed over a fallen log and then waited for Alise to join her on the other side. "Do you think she'd be kind to you or me if the situation was reversed?"

Alise thought about it. "Probably not. But that doesn't excuse us from doing what is right." Even to herself, her words sounded a bit self-righteous. She peered at Thymara to see how she would react. But the Rain Wild girl had her head cocked back, looking up at the trees.

"Do you smell something?"

Alise hadn't, but now she deliberately tested the air. "Maybe," she said cautiously. "Sort of sweet, almost rotten?"

Thymara nodded. "Do you mind if I leave you here and go up the tree? I think there might be fruit vines up there."

Alise looked at the tree trunk and realized for the first time that Thymara had probably been keeping to the ground for her sake. "No, of course not, go ahead. I'll be fine down here."

"I'll be back soon," Thymara promised. She chose a nearby tree trunk and went up it, digging her claws into the bark as she climbed. Alise stood on the ground and watched her go where she had no hope of following. She smiled, but her heart sank quietly inside her.

What was I thinking? she asked herself with a sigh as Thymara vanished up the tree. *That a girl like that could offer me friendship or an insight into my problems? Even if we were of an age, we're too different.* She wandered a few steps away from the tree, trying to see Thymara's world. It was hopeless. *I see deer and she sees meat. I'm here on the ground and she's up in the trees. I pity Jerd and she thinks we should hold her responsible.* She looked around herself. The forest here was different, more inviting somehow. It took her a short time to realize that it was a difference in smell. The acridity that she had become used to as they traveled was less here. When she looked up at the treetops, it seemed to her there were more birds, and more wildlife in general. *A gentler place,* she thought.

Thymara had said she'd be right back. Did that mean she was supposed to wait for her? She'd followed the Rain Wild girl thinking that perhaps a few hours with Thymara would help her put her own life in perspective. And here she was, standing and waiting for her.

She shook her head as she realized that perhaps that was the perspective. That Thymara did things while Alise stood and waited for things to happen. Wasn't that what she'd been doing over the last few days? Agonizing over Leftrin and what Sedric had told her. Agonizing over what Hest had done to her. Thinking and stewing and pondering, but doing nothing except wait for something to happen, wait for things to resolve themselves. Well, what was there she could do? What action could she take to spur events along? One option came immediately to mind, and she shook her head at herself. It still surprised her to be so interested in that! And running back to Leftrin's bed would not be a true resolution to anything.

As if it were a meaningful decision, she resumed her walk along the riverbank. She wouldn't wait for the girl. When Thymara came down, she'd either follow the river or go back to the boat. She knew where she was. If it started to get dark before she saw Thymara again, she'd simply follow the river back to the boat. She couldn't get lost.

At least, not any more lost than she was right now. She had no home now.

Ever since Sedric had revealed his secret, she'd felt cut off from her Bingtown past. She couldn't go back. Simply could not. Regardless of what happened with this expedition, she would not go home to Bingtown and Hest. She would never face him and their friends, never smile stupidly and look around a table of guests and wonder how many knew the secret of her empty marriage. She'd never confront Hest and watch his sneering smile widen as he enjoyed how he'd deceived her and trapped her. Well, she was trapped no longer. A marriage in Bingtown was, after all, like any other Trader contract. She could easily prove that Hest hadn't lived up to his end of the bargain. He had never been sexually faithful to her, never intended that she and she alone be his life partner. He'd broken his word and with it broken the marriage contract and freed her from her word. She did not have to remain faithful to him. She was free to turn to Leftrin.

But then Sedric had shared that other rumor with her—the one that had left her wondering if she should ever trust her own judgment again. He had been so certain, but all his information seemed to have come from the vanished hunter, Jess. She had felt paralyzed since then, unable to move in any direction. She wanted Leftrin as she had never wanted anything or anyone else in her life. But the thought that he might not be what she had believed him to be, the idea that perhaps the real man differed from her imaginary lover, had frozen her. She had seen the puzzlement and the patience in his eyes. He had not rebuked

her and had not pressured her. It was clear to her that he did not
think that their one night together gave him a claim upon her.
That should mean something, shouldn't it?

Or did it merely indicate that she was not as important to
him as he was to her? Was she merely a pleasure he would enjoy when it was offered to him, something that he could easily
forgo when it was not? A cruel part of her mind replayed that
night. She had been forward, aggressive even. Had all that had
transpired happened only because she had made it happen? Silly
to think that was so. Foolish to think it was not.

"Damn you, Sedric. You took everything else from me, my
dignity, and my faith in my judgment, my belief that no one
else in Bingtown knew what a sham my marriage was. Did you
have to take this from me, too? Did you have to take my belief
in Leftrin?"

Once taken, could anything restore her confidence in him?
Or was it all spoiled for her, her doubt the crack in the cup that
held happiness?

A streamlet crossed her path. She hopped over it and went on.
Slowly it dawned on her that she was following a game trail. She
ducked under an overhanging branch and realized the path she
was following was beaten earth. Not mud. Earth. The land here
was firmer. The forest was still too thick to allow a creature as
large as a dragon to move freely or to hunt. But humans could
move here easily. She stood still and looked around her in wonder. Solid land, in the Rain Wilds.

LEFTRIN HAD GONE to his bunk physically weary and sore of
heart. How could his ship do this to him?

When he had first sought his bed, he could still hear the
sounds of the keepers and the hunters around their campfire.
The dragons had fed earlier in the day when they'd disturbed a
herd of riverpigs from their slumbers. Carson had managed to
bag a pig as well, and he'd towed the carcass back to Tarman
for the crew and keepers to share. The roasted pork had been a
welcome feast for all. Alise and Thymara had returned with a

carry-sack full of fruit and a report of firmer land, while Harrikin and Sylve had found a bed of freshwater clams right where
Tarman had nosed up onto the delta. All in all, they'd had a
feast to make up for their days of scarcity. Their water barrels
were full again, and both keepers and crew were in good spirits
despite the ship's delay. It could have been a good day, but for
the ship's stubbornness.

He had gone to bed early in a fit of gloom. Alise was still
keeping him at arm's length, and Tarman's incomprehensible behavior was infuriating and frightening. All the keepers seemed
confident that tomorrow the expedition would continue as
planned. They all believed that he, the captain, would somehow
remedy the situation. His crew did not seem so sanguine. Hennesey and Swarge shared his concerns about the boat's decidedly
odd behavior. They had not discussed it with him, but the looks
and whispers his crewmen had exchanged let him know that
they were as troubled as he was. This was not like the Tarman
they all knew and loved. Was it a result of adding more wizardwood to his hull? And if it was, where might it lead?

Unlike all the other liveships, Tarman had no simulacrum
body with which to speak to his captain and crew. He had only
his eyes right at the waterline, and as large and expressive as they
might be, they could not communicate every thought in his
mind. Tarman always had been and continued to be private in
many of his thoughts. When Leftrin put his hands on Tarman's
railing, he could sense something of what the ship wanted. He'd
known from whence came the idea to use the chance-found
wizardwood to give Tarman a body that was a bit more independent of human will. It was odd, now that he thought of
it, that Tarman had never requested a figurehead, or arms and
hands. No. All he had wanted was independence of movement.

There were a hundred ways he could interpret that decision
by his ship, perhaps a thousand. He mulled all of them over in
his mind that night. Long after the voices from the beach had
quieted, and long after the reflected light from their bonfire had
faded from the roof of his cabin, he thought about them.

At some point, he slept.

They walked together through the streets of Kelsingra, arm in arm. Alise had a basket in her free hand and she swung it as they walked. She had the day planned out for them and was speaking, detailing it all. But he wasn't listening. He didn't need to hear her plans. He was enjoying the sound of her voice, and the sunlight warm on his shoulders. He wore his hat on the back of his head and sauntered along, her hand hooked so nicely in the crook of his arm. The streets were full of folk going about their business. They strolled past fine buildings made of silver-veined black stone. At the major intersections, fountains leaped and danced, playing a music that always changed but was ever harmonious. The music and smells of the market rode the air. Perhaps that was where she was taking him. It didn't matter to him if they were going to buy silk and spices and meat cooked on a skewer, or if the basket held a cloth and a picnic for them to share on the riverside. They were here together. The sound of her voice in his ears was sweet, her hand was warm on his arm, and all was well. All was well in Kelsingra.

LEFTRIN AWOKE TO darkness and stillness. The warmth and the sense of certainty he'd had while he was dreaming was gone. His heart yearned after those things. He'd so seldom had them in his waking life. "Kelsingra," he whispered into the quiet of his room, and for an instant he shared a dragon's certainty that once they reached that fabled city, all would be well. Was it possible that when they arrived there, that would be so? In his dream the city had been peopled and alive. He and Alise had belonged there, belonged together in that place where no one could ever separate them. That, he knew for certain, was only the stuff of dreams.

A sound softer than the scratch of Grigsby at his door came to him. "Cat?" he asked, puzzled.

"No," she spoke into the darkness. The white of her night-gown caught what little light came in his stateroom window as she eased open the door. He caught his breath. She shut the door more quietly than his beating heart. She ghosted silently to his bed and he lay still, wondering if his dream of completeness had returned, fearing that if he moved he might awaken himself. She did not sit down at the edge of his bed. Instead, she lifted the corner of his blankets and slid in beside him. His arm fell easily around her. She put the arches of her chilled bare feet on his ankles and perched there. Her breasts against his chest, her soft stomach against his belly, she faced him on the pillow.

"That's nice," he murmured. "Is this a dream?"

"Maybe," she said. Her breath was on his face. It was a wonderful sensation, so gentle and yet so arousing. "I was walking with you in Kelsingra. And I suddenly knew that when we arrive there, everything will be fine. And if everything is going to be fine, then everything is actually already fine. At least that makes sense to me."

A strange stillness filled him, welling up from inside him. He ventured toward it. Yes. It made sense to him, too. "We were walking in Kelsingra. You had a basket on your arm. Were we going shopping or for a picnic?"

A little shiver of tension went through her. She spoke near his mouth. "The basket was heavy. There was fresh bread, and a bottle of wine, and a little crock of soft cheese in it." She took a small breath. "I liked how you were wearing your hat."

"Tipped back, so I could feel the sun on my face."

"Yes." She shivered again and he pulled her closer, thinking at the same moment that they could scarcely be closer. "How can we dream the same dreams?"

"How can we not?" he said without thinking. Then he took a breath and added, "My ship likes you. You know Tarman is a liveship. Don't you?"

"Of course, but—"

He interrupted her. "No figurehead. I know. But a liveship all the same." He sighed and felt his breath warm the space between their faces. "A liveship learns his own family. I know you must know about that. Tarman can't speak, but he has other ways of communicating."

For a time, she did not reply. She moved her body slightly against his, a communication of her own. Then she asked a question. "That first time I dreamed of flying over Kelsingra. Looking down on it. Was that a dragon dream from Tarman?"

"Only he could say for certain. But I suspect it was."

"He remembers Kelsingra. He showed me things I couldn't have imagined, but they fit perfectly with what I knew of Kelsingra. And now I can't see the city any other way than how he showed it to me." She hesitated, then asked, "Why is he talking to me?"

"He's communicating with both of us. His talking to you is a message for me as well."

"What's the message?" she whispered against his mouth.

He kissed her, and her mouth was pliant under his. For a time, they both forgot the question he could not answer.

SHE DID NOT return to her own bed that night. Very early in the morning, he woke her, thinking it might be an oversight on her part. "Alise. It's dawn. Soon the crew will be stirring."

He didn't need to say any more than that. She had been sleeping with her back against his belly, her head tucked under his chin, his arms around her holding her there, safe and warm. She did not lift her head from the pillow. "I don't care who knows. Do you?"

He thought about it for a time. The only one who might look askance at the arrangement would be Skelly. If it became long term or permanent, it might lead to her losing her position as his heir. Now there was a strange thing to think about. A child of his own? He wondered if Skelly would be unhappy or angry about it. Perhaps. Regardless of that, he wasn't going to give Alise up. The sooner Skelly knew about it, the better.

"No problems from me. Sedric?"

"Am I asking whom he sleeps with these days?"

So she knew about him and Carson. Hmm. The two men had been discreet, but perhaps not discreet enough. There was more than a drop of bitterness in her question. Something else was there, something he didn't want to know about right now or perhaps ever. So he made no answer. He kissed her hair, clambered over her, and took his clothing from its hook. As he dressed he said, "I'll stir up the galley fire and put on coffee. What would you like for breakfast?"

"Um. I may sleep in a bit longer."

So. She truly didn't care who knew and might be going out of her way to be sure that everyone knew. He tried to think of the problems that might cause and again decided that it wouldn't change his mind. Was he captain on this ship or not? He'd deal with anyone sooner rather than later. She had already closed her eyes and pulled his blankets up to her chin. He looked at her for a long moment, at her red hair spilling across his pillow and the wonderful shape she made in his bunk. Then he pulled on his boots and left the room, quietly closing the door behind him.

He smelled the fresh coffee before he reached the galley. Skelly was there before him, sitting at the table, a white mug of thick black coffee in front of her. She looked up at him as he came in. He avoided her glance, fearing to see accusation there. *Coward.* He poured himself a mug of the coffee she'd made and sat down opposite her. "You used up a lot of our coffee to make this. Didn't I tell you we'd have to be careful of our supplies?"

She cocked her head at him. "Maybe I'm like you. Maybe I think it's better to make the best of what you have right now rather than giving yourself stingy bits of happiness." A crooked smile crawled across her face as she dared to ask him, "Don't you agree?"

He met her gaze. "Yes." There wasn't much treacle left. He scooped a big spoonful into his mug and then asked conversationally, "How did you know?"

"I saw you walking in the streets of Kelsingra. I was trapped in the crowd, trying to catch up with you. I called your name, but you didn't hear me."

"Our Tarman was a busy fellow last night." He took a sip of his coffee and weighed his thoughts. "If I were just your uncle and not your captain, what might you say to me about it?"

She looked down at her mug. "I'm happy for you. Happy you get to be with someone you choose."

Nice little jab there. "I'm not promised to anyone else."

"She's married."

"She was."

"And now she's not?"

He considered. "I trust her to know what she's free to do."

She thought about that and gave a slow nod. He was trying to be absolutely fair when he said to her, "This could change things for you, you know. A lot. If we have a child."

Her smiled widened. "I know that."

"Have you thought about what it might mean?"

"Since before dawn."

"And?"

"That boy back in Trehaug? The one my parents promised could marry me? He thinks he's been promised the heir to the *Tarman*. If he finds out that might not be so, he might look for a more promising bride."

That was so. For the first time he thought about how his decision might affect a wider circle of folk.

She hadn't finished. "The way I see it, I'm on this boat for life. It's what I know, and I'm not worth much to anyone anywhere else. Not to sound cold, Uncle, but even if you had a child tomorrow, chances are I'd still get in my years as captain on Tarman. That's all I want out of it. Not to own him. No one ever owns him. But my chance to be his captain. And maybe get my chance to be with whom I choose to be." She sipped her coffee and grinned at him. "It seems to agree with you."

"Don't be cheeky, girl." He fought the smile that tried to break out on his face.

"Captain or uncle speaking?"

"Captain."

"Yes, sir." She wiped the grin off her face so smoothly that he had to wonder how often she'd employed that talent to learn it so well. But there were other fish to fry right now.

"So Tarman sent you a little dream in the night, did he?"

"That he did. Kelsingra. Clear as I've ever seen any town. Nice place. Really made me want to be there."

"Me, too."

Skelly spoke more hesitantly. "I think Tarman remembers it. And that might be what he wants us to know."

"So what was yesterday all about?"

"I don't know. But I wager we'll find out today."

$\diamondsuit$ $\diamondsuit$ $\diamondsuit$

Day the 4th of the Gold Moon

Year the 6th of the Independent Alliance of Traders
From Erek, Keeper of the Birds, Bingtown
To Detozi, Keeper of the Birds, Trehaug

Enclosed, and sealed with official seal, a request from the
Building Committee of the Bingtown Traders' Council
for competing bids for timber in the quantities and types
specified, for the construction of an expanded hall for
the Bingtown Traders' Concourse in Bingtown. To be
considered, all bids must be submitted before the first
day of the Rain Moon, with a guarantee that the full
amount of timber could be transported to Bingtown
before the first day of the Change Moon.

Detozi,

*And yet they tell us that we do not have the funds to finish repairing
Circle Street that fronts our main market, while unrolling these
elaborate plans to expand the Traders' Concourse! I trust the
Council in Trehaug is a bit more careful with its coin!*

Erek

$\diamondsuit$ $\diamondsuit$ $\diamondsuit$

CHAPTER FIFTEEN

TARMAN

hymara came to her shortly after dawn. She had a line with two gleaming silver fish strung on it. They were fat and flopping still. Sintara was not enamored of fish; she'd had far too many of them in her life. Still, they were food and fresh.

"I made my own spear to get these for you," Thymara said as she unfastened the first fish from the line threaded through its gills. "I didn't have a spear point, but I hardened the wood in a fire, and it seemed to work very well."

"Commendable of you," Sintara said, waiting.

Thymara held the first one up and then asked suddenly, "What are you doing to me?"

"I'm waiting for my fish," the dragon pointed out acerbically.

Thymara didn't give it to her. "I'm changing faster than I ever have in my life. My skin itches with the scales. My back hurts all the time. Even my teeth feel sharper. Are you doing this to me?"

"The fish," Sintara insisted, and Thymara tossed the first one. Sintara caught it in her jaws, tossed it up, caught it again, and gulped it down.

"You're changing, too. You've grown. You're bigger and stronger, and you're not just blue anymore. You're sapphire and azure and every color of blue that there is. Your tail is longer. And yesterday, I saw you shake water off your wings. They're more beautiful than ever, with a silver web on them as if you'd embroidered them. They've grown, too."

"I'd grow even faster if I were offered more food and less talk," Sintara interjected, but she could not keep the pleasure out of her voice, despite her words. Sapphire and azure. One thing she had to say for humans, they had descriptive words. "Cobalt, cerulean, indigo," she said as Thymara unfastened the second fish.

The girl looked up. "Yes. All of those colors, too."

"And black. And silver, if you look carefully."

"Yes. And there are greens on your wings when you unfold them, like a pattern of lace over the silver. I noticed that your markings have become much sharper."

"The fish," Sintara reminded her, and with a sigh, Thymara complied.

"Are you doing something to me, or is this just happening?" she asked after the dragon had swallowed.

Sintara wasn't certain. She replied, "No human can be around dragons for long without experiencing some changes. Accept them."

"And no dragon can be around humans constantly without being changed by them." This was Mercor, strolling up to interrupt their conversation, and probably to see if any fish were left. There weren't any, so Sintara minded slightly less that he was intruding. But then he offended her gravely by lowering his head and carefully sniffing her keeper. "Are you in pain, girl?" he asked her quietly.

"A bit." She turned away, uncomfortable with his attention.

The gold dragon turned his gaze on Sintara. His eyes, black on black, spun accusingly. "It isn't something you can ignore," he warned her. "The bond goes both ways. What affects one affects all. You could cause great discontent among the keepers."

"What does he mean?" Thymara broke in anxiously.

"The concerns of dragons are the concerns of dragons," Sintara said crushingly.

Mercor did not reply to the girl. "It will be like your name, Sintara," he said flatly. "I will let it go so far, and then I will take charge of it. And perhaps I will take charge of your keeper as well."

Sintara opened her wings and stretched her neck. She felt what would one day be the frilled spines of her neck stand out. Even so, Mercor was still larger than she was. A glint of amusement in his black eyes only incensed her more. "You will never take charge of my keeper," she hissed. The barest threat of venom floated on her words. "What is mine, I keep." Thymara lifted her arms to shield her face and eyes and retreated a few steps.

"See that you do," Mercor replied affably. "Keep your keeper as you should, and you have nothing to fret about, little queen."

The diminutive infuriated her beyond reason. She shot her neck out, jaws wide. Mercor whirled, and a snap of his larger wing slammed the bony joint knob of it against her ribs. She slapped ineffectually at him with her smaller wings as she staggered back. Thymara let out a shriek. All around them on the muddy delta, dragons were lifting heads and opening wings, staring toward the altercation. Keepers darted about like ants in a disturbed nest, squawking at one another.

"Do you require help, Sintara?" Sestican asked. The large blue advanced a step toward them, his own wings lifting and the frill on his neck standing out in challenge.

"Sestican, no!" his keeper shouted, but the dragon paid no attention to Lecter. His spinning eyes were fixed only on Mercor. The two dragons, wings lifted, heads swaying, regarded one another balefully.

"I am a queen! I require no help from anyone," Sintara replied disdainfully. "Keeper! I wish to go to the freshwater river to be cleaned. Get your tools and follow me there."

It was not a retreat, she thought angrily as she stalked haughtily away. She was simply not interested in anything either of them might do or say. She would not allow the males to fight over her on the ground, as if such an earthbound battle could prove something or win favor with her. No. When the time came, she would soar in flight, and all the males, every one of them, would vie for her and beat one another bloody in an attempt to catch her eye. And when they were eliminated to one, then she would outfly and defy him. Mercor would never master her.

"Perhaps you could reason with him."

Leftrin glared at Skelly. She folded her lips and turned away. He wasn't angry with her, but the idea that Tarman could be reasoned with only irritated him. He'd gone out on deck in the morning to discover that the barge had only hunkered down deeper into the mud in the night. Leftrin had had every hand he could muster straining to shove the ship off for half the morning. It was impossible to ignore that the barge was deliberately resisting efforts to move him. Every member of the crew knew it; the confusion and worry were painted in their eyes.

The keepers were beginning to pick up on the uneasiness. It was strange for him to realize that every one of them must know that Tarman was a liveship, but so few of them seemed to grasp fully what that meant. They seemed to have forgotten that at his core, Tarman was kin to the dragons and just as capable of being cantankerous. Or dangerous.

Leftrin glanced over at Skelly, who was not looking at him. She had her pole over the side again, positioned and ready for when he might demand another effort from them. He pitched his voice for her ears alone. "I'll try. You come with me."

"Hold on to this for me, will you?" she asked Bellin, surrendering her pole to her crewmate. She followed her captain forward. "He showed us Kelsingra," she whispered. "Why would he do that, and then wedge himself in the mud here? Why would he make us want to go there, and then refuse to budge?"

"I don't know, but I do know we're wasting daylight. It won't be long before the dragons decide they're ready to go, and we have to be ready to follow them. Not stuck in the mud."

"What happened with the dragons earlier this morning?"

"No idea. Some sort of a dustup. Not too serious, I suspect, as it was over so fast. Probably just a bit of sorting out as to who's on top. Happens in any group of creatures, animal or humans. Or dragons."

He heard his own words and realized a truth he hadn't before. Dragons were not animals to him in the way that deer or birds were animals. But they weren't humans, either. It suddenly seemed a very large truth to him. When he had been a boy growing up, he had divided creatures that lived and moved into two groups: animals and humans. And now there were dragons in his life. When, he wondered, had that distinction formed in his mind? When they had begun this expedition, they had been animals to him. Oddly intelligent animals who spoke. But now they were dragons, not animals and not humans.

And what about Tarman, then?

He'd reached the bow and been on the point of putting his hands on the railing. Skin to wood, he'd always felt, was how he heard Tarman best. But now he folded his arms and stood, reordering his thoughts, wondering just how much of them he wanted his ship to know. Tarman reached right into his dreams with apparent ease. How much of his day-to-day thoughts was the ship aware of?

Skelly already had her hands on the railing. "Kelsingra was beautiful," she said quietly. "The best place I could imagine. I wanted to be there. I want to be traveling to Kelsingra now. So, Tarman, old friend, why are we stuck here in the mud? What's the problem?"

She didn't expect a direct answer to her query. Neither did Leftrin. Direct answers were not in a dragon's nature, and that, Leftrin suddenly knew, was what he was dealing with here. He was as much a keeper as any of the youngsters were. Only his dragon had the form of a barge. He was reaching for the railing to put his hands on it when Tarman answered. The whole ship lurched. With a surprised curse, Leftrin's reach for the railing became a grab. He hung on, hearing the confused shouts from the crew and the keepers aboard as Tarman lurched again. And again. The ship heaved up and settled, heaved up and settled. He could imagine those squat wizardwood legs and the finned feet shoving and shifting, not unlike a toad resettling itself in the mud. But with every heave and lurch, the Tarman was shifting his bow.

"What is going on?" Greft was grabbing at the railing as he came staggering down the deck. His teeth were bared behind his narrow silver lips as if he were in pain.

"Don't know. Hang on," Leftrin said sharply. Something was happening with his ship, and he wanted to focus his attention on Tarman, not some cocky young man.

Perhaps Greft picked up a hint of that, or perhaps the glare that Skelly shot him silenced him. He clung to the railing grimly as Tarman continued to heave and lurch along. When at last he settled, Leftrin waited a few minutes longer before he spoke. The ship had reoriented himself until his stern floated free. The merest push of the poles would now be enough to free the barge's bow from the muddy bank.

But the most important change was that the Tarman's bow now pointed up the freshwater river rather than toward the main channel. For a short time Captain Leftrin mulled over what he was seeing. He reached a conclusion and received the assent of his ship.

"Nothing's wrong!" He bellowed at the rising babble and clamor of voices from crew and keepers alike. In the shocked lull that followed his shout, he spoke clearly. "We were about to go the wrong way. That's all. Kelsingra is up this river, not that one."

"How can you possibly know that?" Greft demanded.

Leftrin gave him a chill smile. "My liveship just told me so."

Greft gestured to the dragons gathering on the shore. "And will they agree?" he asked him snidely. A dragon's sudden roar broke the relative quiet.

"Did you see that?"

Thymara had. She had been on her way back to the vessel,

having given Sintara a hasty scrubbing with cold river water. She was soaked and cold. She didn't believe the dragon had wanted or enjoyed the washing; she suspected that Sintara had used it as an excuse to flee the snorting males and their aggressive display. She had spoken very little to her keeper through the whole process, and Thymara had kept her questions to herself. Sylve, she decided, would be her best source of information. She had an uneasy feeling that there was something more to the increase in her scaling. Harrikin had dropped a careless remark about his scaling and his dragon, but he had become very quiet when she wanted to know what the connection was. And Sintara had been no help at all.

So, cold, wet, still half frightened, and with her injured back hurting more than it had in days, she had begun her dash back to the boat. She hoped to get on board and cozy up to the fire in the galley stove before the day's travel began. It was her turn to be in one of the remaining keeper boats, and she wanted to be warm again by then.

Instead, she had seen the boat suddenly heave itself up as if a wave had risen up under it. She had heard the cries of those on board. All the dragons had turned at the sound; she heard Mercor trumpet in surprise. Ranculos roared a response as he looked all around, seeking a source of the supposed danger. The ship suddenly settled again, sending a little wash of water out from his sides.

She had halted an arm's length away from Sedric. She hadn't realized he'd come ashore. He turned to her and said, "Did you see that?" His damp sleeves were rolled back to his elbows, and he carried a ship's bucket and a scrub brush. She suspected he had borrowed them without asking to aid in his grooming of his copper. She hoped Captain Leftrin would not be angry at him.

"I did," she replied. At that moment, the ship again lifted, lurched and rocked, and then resettled.

"Is one of the dragons behind the ship? Are they pushing it?"

"No." Mercor had overheard her question as the golden dragon arrived to stand near her. "Tarman is a liveship and a most unusual one at that. He moves himself."

"How?" she demanded, but in the next instant she had her answer. The ship rocked from side to side and then, with tremendous effort, heaved himself up. For a moment, she had a glimpse of squat front legs. Then they bent and the ship settled once more in the shallow water and mud. She stared in astonishment and then her gaze wandered to the ship's painted eyes. She had always thought they looked kind. Now they seemed determined to her. Water had splashed up over them in his latest effort. She stared at him, meeting his gaze and trying to decide if she looked at more than paint.

A moment later the ship gathered himself and again lifted, shifted, and dropped. He was unmistakably moving his bow.

"He's trying to free himself," Sedric suggested shakily. "That's all."

"I don't think that's all," Thymara muttered, staring.

"Nor I," Mercor added.

Ranculos had come closer. This time, as the ship lifted, he flared his nostrils and lifted the fringes on his neck. "I smell dragon!" he proclaimed loudly. He lifted his wings slightly and craned his head about.

"You smell the ship. You smell Tarman," Mercor corrected him.

Ranculos lowered his head and extended his neck. With his wings slightly lifted, he reminded Thymara of a courting bird as he approached the liveship, nostrils flared.

Mercor spoke in a voice that seemed resigned to foolishness. "Tarman is a liveship, Ranculos. His hull was made from a dragon's case, one that never hatched." He paused, watching the ship again gather himself, lift, and then shift the direction of his bow as he lowered himself again. "But that old case has a more recent overlay. Part of him comes from the case of a dragon who would have come to be from the same tangle of serpents we came from. Tarman is as much one of us as a being of his kind can be."

"A being of his kind? A 'being' of his 'kind'? And what is that, Mercor? A ghost trapped in the body of a slave?" The silver eyes of the scarlet dragon flashed as Ranculos raised his head high, rearing up briefly on his hind legs. Arbuc trumpeted shrilly, echoing his feelings while Fente lashed her tail and rumbled a growl.

Baliper spoke. "He is wrong. He smells wrong. He exists wrong. It is wrong for humans to ride on a dragon in any form, let alone for them to enslave the ghost of one. We should tear him apart and eat him. The memories trapped in his 'wood' should come back to us, for they belong to us." He snapped open his scarlet wings and reared back briefly in a show of size and aggression.

"I think *not*." This came in a roar from Kalo. The great blue-black dragon, largest of the drakes, waded forward through the gathered dragons, forcing the smaller ones to step aside or be trodden on. When Baliper did not give way, Kalo shouldered him roughly aside, sending him crashing against Fente. The little green queen screamed in fury and struck at Baliper, lightly scoring his shoulder with her teeth. In turn, the red clapped his wing at her, sending her sprawling into the mud. At this threat to Fente, a yell of outrage from Tats reached Thymara's ear. He stood on board the Tarman, eyes wild with panic as he stared down at the conflict that threatened to engulf all the dragons.

"Stop!" Mercor cried out, but the golden went unheeded.

"Stop or I'll kill you all!" Kalo roared.

A stillness froze them. The immense drake turned his head slowly, surveying the gathered dragons. A few of the keepers stood among them. Sedric had moved closer to Thymara. Sylve huddled by Mercor's front leg.

Fente began to get to her feet.

"Don't!" Kalo warned her. He opened his jaws wide and displayed to all of them the bright green poison sacs inside his throat. They were swollen and full, pulsing with his anger. "I am not Spit, to show my power before I need it. Oppose me now and I'll let you feel the strength of my venom."

The dragons were still. Kalo closed his jaws, but the spiny ruffs on his throat still stood out. He spoke slowly. "I do not recall all that a dragon should. And I recall much that a dragon should not. Kelaro I was, of Maulkin's Tangle. And I followed

Maulkin, a great golden serpent, without question." His silvery gaze suddenly fixed on Mercor. The golden dragon looked puzzled for a moment, then bowed his head in assent. "Kelaro I was, and Sessurea was a companion to me." He looked now at Tarman. "I was the stronger, but sometimes he was the wiser." His gaze moved over the gathered dragons. "If we tear that wisdom to pieces and share it amongst us, will any of us have the whole of it? Will any of us know what Tarman seems to know? Open your mouths and your nostrils, dragons. There is more than one way for a dragon to communicate. Or a serpent."

Thymara was shocked to discover that she had taken Sedric's arm and was holding it firmly. Something was happening here, something that frightened her. There were shrieks and shouts from the barge as he once more heaved himself high. For an instant, she clearly saw the squat powerful front legs and had a glimpse of the folded and flippered hind legs. A waft of stench, not unlike the smell she recalled from the day the dragons had emerged from their cases, enveloped her. Her eyes stung and she put her shirtsleeve over her mouth and nose, gasping for breath. Then, the barge wheeled, and Tarman's bow slapped down onto the river. As his powerful hind legs pushed him away from the delta of river mud, a wave of dirty water washed up onto the beach.

The barge moved out into the river. It nosed, not toward the swift-flowing acid river with the wide open channel but toward the long green tunnel of the fresh water that she had explored yesterday. She realized what was happening at the same moment Sedric did.

"Tarman is leaving without us!"

"Wait!" This came in a wild shriek from Sylve. Thymara glanced in her direction, but she could not tell if Sylve called to the ship or Mercor, for the dragons were in motion, moving to follow the barge. Tarman had wallowed out into deeper water. None of the polemen was at their posts, but he was moving determinedly against the current. Thymara saw a disturbance in the water behind him and guessed at the presence of a tail.

"We're being left behind. Come on!" She had been the one

clutching at Sedric. But now he shrugged free of her hold on his arm, caught her by the hand. Her free hand snagged the still-staring Sylve. "Run!" he told them. "Come on!"

They pelted down the beach toward the shore. Shouts of both anger and dismay from Tarman's deck told her that there was nothing that the crew or keepers could do to detain the barge. She wondered briefly about the hunters. As was their wont, they had set out before dawn to look for meat, and they had doubtless headed up the other tributary of the river. How long would it take them to realize that the barge and the dragons had gone off in a different direction?

They were not the only keepers left onshore. All of them were converging on the three small boats that remained on-shore. Kase and Boxter had claimed Greft's boat, but they stood by to see if they'd have to make room for another keeper. Alum was in one of the other boats, and as she watched, Harrikin spoke with him. The third boat was empty. "Go!" Thymara shouted at them. "We'll take the other boat."

"Right!" Alum shouted back to her, and in moments they were launched. The barge was moving with swift certainty up the waterway. The dragons split and went around the small boats, waded out into the water, and followed. They would soon pass the barge. Kase and Boxter had taken up their paddles and were moving out into the river.

By the time Thymara, Sylve, and Sedric reached the final boat, they were alone on the shore. Thymara glanced back at the campsite. No, nothing left behind. A fire smoldered on the wet muddy flat. Nothing remained to show they had been there but trampled ground and the rising smoke.

"Will it hold three?" Sedric asked worriedly.

"It won't be comfortable, but we'll be fine. Besides, there's no choice. You can turn your bucket upside down and perch on that. I suspect we'll come alongside Tarman before too long, and we can ask them to take you up then, if you'd like." She turned to a strangely quiet Sylve. The girl looked stricken. "What's the matter?"

Sylve shook her head slowly. "He just went with the others.

Mercor didn't even wait to see if I had a way to follow. He just left." She blinked her eyes and one pink-tinged tear trickled down her cheek.

"Oh, Sylve." Thymara felt sorry for her, but also impatient. Now was not the time for indulging in emotion. They had to catch up with the ship.

"MERCOR'S NO FOOL. He knew there were boats on the shore, and that you've taken care of yourself in the past. He had to get the dragons moving before any of them had second thoughts. He hasn't abandoned you; he just thinks you're capable. Let's prove he's right." Sedric spoke hastily, smoothing the quarrel before it could start. He was tired of conflict.

He upended his bucket to make a seat for himself in the middle of the boat, and it gave him a slightly higher perch and a different view of the river. Thymara pushed them off, and Sylve dug in her paddle with a will, and they devoted themselves to creating as much speed as they could. There was no discussion; all knew they'd make better time with the girls at the oars.

This was Sedric's first opportunity to observe the river and the surrounding jungle from this perspective. The last time he'd been in one of the small boats, he'd been so busy trying to keep up with Carson that he hadn't had time to look around. Now he stared at the lushest forest he'd ever seen. Trees, both deciduous and evergreen, leaned out over the water. Vines draped some of them. Undergrowth was thick, and reeds and rushes populated the mossy banks of the river.

"It's so alive," Sylve said in a voice full of wonder.

So he hadn't been imagining the difference.

"It even smells different. Just, well, green. Alise and I walked a short way up here yesterday, and we both noticed it. There's no acid in the water, no whiteness to it at all. And there's a lot more life. I saw frogs swimming in the water yesterday. Right in the water."

"Frogs usually swim in the water," Sedric suggested.

"Maybe near Bingtown they do. But in the Rain Wilds, we find frogs up in the trees. Not in the river."

He thought about that for a bit. Every time he thought he had grasped how much his life had changed, some new awareness doused him. He nodded quietly.

This tributary was completely unlike the main channel. It wound gently through the forest, and the trees leaned in over the water, seeking sunlight and blocking the view upstream. For a time, they pursued the dragons and the barge, but then the river rounded a gentle bend and they lost sight of everything except the other two small boats. They were at the tail end of the procession. If they capsized now, or if they came upon a pod of gallators on the riverbank . . . for a moment, tension tightened his gut. Then a peculiar thought came to him.

If anything befell him, Carson would come looking for him.

Carson.

A smile relaxed his face. It was true and he knew it. Carson would come for him.

He was still trying to reconcile the man with his concept of life. He'd never met a man like Carson, never known anyone who schooled his strength to such gentleness. He was not educated or cultured. He knew nothing of wines, had never traveled beyond the Rain Wilds, and had read fewer than a dozen books in his life. The framework that supported Sedric's self-respect was missing from Carson's life. Without an appreciation for such things, how could he appreciate who and what Sedric was? Why did the hunter like him? It mystified him.

Carson's life was framed by this forest-and-water world. He knew the ways of animals and spoke of them with great fondness and respect. But he killed them, too. Sedric had watched him butcher, seen his strength as he cut into an animal's hip joint and then used his hands to lever the bone out of the socket. "Once you know how an animal is put together, it's a lot easier to take it apart," Carson had explained to Sedric as he finished his bloody chore and made the meat ready for cooking.

Sedric had watched his hands, the blood on his wrists, the bits of flesh caught under his nails as he worked, and thought of those strong hands on his own body. It had put a shiver up his spine, a thrill of erotic dread. Yet Carson was gentle, almost tentative in his moments with Sedric, and several times Sedric had found himself moving into the role of aggressor. The sensation of being in control had been heady and in some ways freeing. He had watched Carson's eyes and mouth in the dim light of his small room and seen no fear in his face, no resentment that, for that time, Sedric was in charge. He contrasted it sometimes to how Hest would react to such a thing. "Don't try to tell me what you want," Hest had once commanded him disdainfully. "I'll tell you what you're getting."

He thought of Hest less frequently than he once had, and in the last few days when he had contrasted his old lover to Carson, Hest seemed like a fading ghost. Thoughts of him triggered regret, but not in the way they once had. Sedric regretted not that he had lost Hest, but that he had ever found him.

The two girls had fallen into a rhythm in their paddling, one that sped them along but was not closing the gap between them and the dragons, barge, and other keepers' boats. As they passed a low-hanging tree, an explosion of orange parrots startled them. The birds burst from the branches, shrieking and squawking before the flock re-formed and abruptly landed in a taller tree. All three of them startled, and then laughed. It broke a tension of silence that Sedric hadn't been aware of. Suddenly he didn't want to be alone and lost in his thoughts.

"I'll be happy to take a turn paddling," he offered.

"I'm fine," Sylve said, turning her head to shoot him a smile. The light caught briefly in her eyes as she did so, showing him a pale blue gleam. As she turned back, he could not help but note how the sunlight also moved on the pink scaling of her scalp. She had less hair than when they had started out. Her worn shirt was torn slightly at the shoulder seam and scaling flashed on the flesh that was revealed there with every stroke of her paddle.

"I may take you up on that, in a little while," Thymara admitted. That surprised him. He had thought her the tougher of the two girls.

Sylve spoke over her shoulder, keeping her eyes on the river. "Is your back still bothering you? Where you hurt it in the river that day?"

Thymara was quiet for a time and then admitted grudgingly, "Yes. It's never healed up all the way. The second dunking I got in that wave only made it worse."

The boat traveled on. They passed a backwater spattered with huge flat leaves and floating orange flowers. The fragrance, rich to the point of rottenness, reached Sedric.

Sylve spoke. "Have you ever asked your dragon about that?" Her voice was hesitant and yet determined.

"About what?" Thymara replied, equally determined.

"Your back. And the way your scaling is getting heavier."

Silence like a block of stone fell on the boat and filled it perfectly. Sedric felt as if he was unable to breathe for the heaviness of it.

When Thymara spoke, she could not hide the lie in her words. "I don't think my back has anything to do with my scaling."

Sylve kept on paddling. She didn't turn back to look at the other girl. She might have been speaking to the river when she said, "You forget. I saw it. I know what it is now."

"Because you are changing in the same way." Thymara flung the words back at her.

Sedric felt trapped between them. Why on earth would Sylve bring up such a topic, so private and specific to the keepers, while he was in the boat?

Then dread dropped the bottom out of his stomach.

Thymara wasn't the target of her words. He was. His hand shot up to the back of his neck and covered the line of scales that had started down his spine. Carson had assured him that they were barely noticeable yet. He'd said they didn't even seem to have a color yet, unlike the pink of Sylve's and the silvery glints on Carson's own scaling. Sedric didn't say a word.

"I am changing," Sylve admitted. "But I was given the choice, and I chose this. And I trust Mercor."

"But he left you today," Thymara pointed out. Sedric wondered if she were relentless or just tactless.

"I've thought it over, and what Sedric said, too. If, tonight, I were not there when we gathered, then Mercor would go back for me. I know that. But I will be there, and I will have got myself there. It is what he expects of me. I am neither a pet nor a child. He believes I am not only capable of taking care of myself, but that I am worthy of the attention of a dragon, and that I can survive without him."

When Thymara asked her question, she sounded half strangled. "Why does he believe that of you? How did you convince him?"

Sylve glanced back at them, and an otherworldly smile flitted across her face. "I am not sure. But he offered me a chance and I took it. I am not an Elderling yet. But I will be."

"What?" Thymara and Sedric chorused the word together.

Then Thymara added another one. "How?"

"A little bit of blood," Sylve said in a near whisper, and Sedric went cold. A little bit? How much was a little bit? He tried to remember how much blood he'd taken in that night, and wondered how much it took.

"Mercor gave you some of his blood?" Thymara was incredulous. "What did you do with it?"

Sylve's voice was very quiet, as if she spoke of something sacred. Or horrifying. "He told me to pull a small scale from his face. I did. A drop or two of blood welled out. He told me to catch it on the scale. And then to eat it." Her breath caught, and the rhythm of her paddling broke. "It was . . . delicious. No. It wasn't a taste. It was a feeling. It was magical. It changed me."

With two strong strokes of her paddle, Thymara drove them out of the current and into the shallows. She reached up and caught a branch and held them all in place.

"Why?" The question exploded out of her. It sounded as if she asked it of the universe in general, as if it were almost a cry of despair at an unfair fate, but it was Sylve who answered her.

"You know what we are, Thymara. You know why some of us are discarded at birth. Why those of us who change too much too soon are denied mates and children. If they discover us when we are born, we are denied any future at all. It's because we change in ways that make us monstrous. And make us die, sooner rather than later, after giving birth to monsters who cannot live. Mercor believes those changes happen to any humans who are around dragons for any length of time."

"That makes no sense! Rain Wilders were changing from the very first generation who settled here. Long before dragons came back into this world, children were developing scales, and pregnant women were giving birth to monsters!"

"Long before dragons came back, we were living where they had lived, and digging into the places where the Elderlings had dwelt. We were plundering their treasures, wearing their jewelry, making timber out of dragon cases. There may not have been dragons walking among us, but we were walking among them."

A silence held as Thymara digested those words. The water rushed past their canoe. Sedric felt cold and still inside. Blood. Blood from a dragon was changing Sylve. Two drops and one small scale was all it had taken. How much had he taken in? What changes had he triggered in himself? Monsters, they had said. Monsters who didn't live long, monsters denied any future. Something in the middle of him had gone tight and was twisting, twisting so hard it hurt. He bent forward slightly over his belly. Neither of them appeared to notice.

"But the blood he gave you will change you more?"

"It was his blood. He says he will shape my change. He warned me that it doesn't always work, and that he does not remember all of what a dragon should do to facilitate such a change. But he said the Elderlings did not just happen. Every Elderling who existed was once the companion of a dragon. Well, almost everyone. Sometimes humans started to change and even unguided, the changes didn't kill them. They noticed it in the humans who tended the dragons while they were in their cases and the ones who were present at the hatchings. Some became beautiful and lived a long time, but most didn't. But the ones the dragons chose as worthy and guided carefully, they became extraordinary and some lived for generations."

She ran out of words for a moment.

"I don't understand."

"Art, Thymara. Elderlings were a form of art for the dragons of that time. They found humans they thought had potential and developed them. That was why they cherished them. Everyone cherishes what they create. Even dragons."

"And my changes? I was born with the sort of changes one usually sees only in very old women. And since we left Trehaug, I've continued to change. The changes are progressing faster than they ever have before."

"I've noticed. That's why I asked Mercor if Sintara was changing you. He said he would ask her."

"I asked her already," Thymara admitted. "I suspected she had something to do with it. From something I heard Harrikin say. Is his dragon changing him, too?"

"Yes. And Sintara is changing you."

A silence. Then Thymara admitted. "No. She said she wasn't, and Mercor said that if she didn't take charge of my changes, he would."

"What?"

What was in that incredulous question from Sylve? A touch of jealousy? Disbelief?

Thymara seemed to hear it, too. Her reply was glum. "Don't worry. He won't. Sintara said she would never allow anyone to take over her keeper. I'm doomed to belong to her, even if she doesn't want me. And doomed to change however I change, for better or worse." She took a deep breath. "We'd better get moving. I can't even see the other boats now."

"You want me to paddle for a while?" Sedric offered.

"No. Thank you." Quietly she added, "I think I just want to work for a while."

Sedric cleared his throat, forced the difficult words out. "I'm changing, too."

A silence. Then Sylve said delicately, "Yes, we noticed."

He phrased his next statement a dozen ways before he found one that avoided the issue of blood and how he had tasted it. "Sometimes I'm afraid that Relpda doesn't know how to control the changes."

"I think we're all a bit afraid of that," Sylve commiserated. And he could think of no response.

Thymara's paddle dug in, pushing them out into the river. They moved on, battling the slow current.

Day the 9th of the Gold Moon

Year the 6th of the Independent Alliance of Traders

From Erek, Keeper of the Birds, Bingtown
To Detozi, Keeper of the Birds, Trehaug

Contents: a legally registered notice from Hest Finbok, to the merchants, inns, and suppliers of Trehaug and Cassarick, to be duplicated and distributed freely. Please be advised that as of the first day of the Gold Moon, Hest Finbok will not be responsible for any debts incurred by either Sedric Meldar or Alise Kincarron.

Detozi,

The swift pigeons arrived a full day and a half before the regular carriers. As the weather was both rainy with the wind against them, I am even more impressed with their speed. Clearly, the breeding program is working, and working well. I shall sit down and try to work out a system of bands for the birds that we can use to establish which of them are fastest, so that we may breed more accurately for this trait.

Erek

$$\diamond \quad \diamond \quad \diamond$$

Day the 10th of the Gold Moon

Year the 6th of the Independent Alliance of Traders

From Erek, Keeper of the Birds, Bingtown

To Detozi, Keeper of the Birds, Trehaug

Enclosed, a notice from Trader family Meldar and Trader
family Kincarron, offering a substantial reward for any
information as to the location and well-being of Sedric
Meldar and Alise Kincarron Finbok. To be duplicated
and distributed freely, and a copy sent on swiftly to the
Keeper of the Birds, Cassarick, all fees having been paid
in advance for such service.

Detozi,

*You are not alone in wishing that you could make a journey
between our cities as swiftly as our pigeons do. I have puzzled
for several hours over the markings I could use to designate
swiftness of flight on the birds I wish to band. Somehow I am
sure that if we could but spend an afternoon together, we could
devise such a marking system. I have been curious as to how you
manage your coops and flocks in such a dangerous place as the
Rain Wilds. I think it would be in the best interests of all the bird
keepers if I could take time to come for a visit to study your flock
management. As soon as Reyall is able to return to handle my
duties in my absence, I intend to apply for such a leave, if a visit
from me would not be too great an inconvenience to you.*

Erek

$\diamondsuit$ $\diamondsuit$ $\diamondsuit$

Day the 12th of the Gold Moon

Year the 6th of the Independent Alliance of Traders

From Erek, Keeper of the Birds, Bingtown

To Detozi, Keeper of the Birds, Trehaug

From Sophie Meldar Roxon, in the enclosed message, a letter of credit for the use of Sedric Meldar or Alise Kincarron, as they may have need. To be held for them at the Traders' Concourse in Trehaug, with a notice of it sent on to the Traders' Concourse in Cassarick.

Detozi,

I am very worried that perhaps I sounded too forward in my last small note to you. I only meant that I know we share a great interest in our birds, and that a conference between us might greatly benefit both our flocks. Such a meeting would only occur, of course, at your convenience and if you are so inclined.

Erek

$\diamondsuit$ $\diamondsuit$ $\diamondsuit$

CHAPTER SIXTEEN

REEDS

As evening closed in, the river still had no discernible banks. Leftrin stood on the bow of the barge, looking out over the wide spread of water before him. To the left and to the right, tall reeds and unnaturally thick cattails bounded the open channel that remained. The shallow channel itself was only about three times as wide as the barge itself. The dragons trudged slowly before them in a disconsolate bunch. Nothing even approaching solid land was in sight. Likely it would be their second night of standing in water all night. Dark was coming on. A single bright star already showed in the deepening blue of the sky. Soon the hunters and keepers would be bringing their boats back to the barge to reboard for the night. It felt strange to be on such flat water, on the deck of Tarman, and to have such a wide open sky overhead. The forested horizons were a distant circle surrounding his boat. A wide margin of vegetation-choked shallow water walled him off from them.

Overhead, flocks of waterfowl and small birds were wheeling and coming down to settle for the night. The waterfowl coasted in to land in sprays of water. The small birds found perches in the tassels and seedheads of the water plants. Small fish, frogs, and something that looked like swimming lizards were plentiful in the shallows. The dragons did not enjoy the effort of feeding on such small life-forms, but at least they were not going hungry. Yesterday, they had encountered an immense flock of long-legged wading birds. They were at least as tall as a man, and heavy-bodied. Their plumage had been stunningly brilliant, in every shade of blue. He'd only had a short time to marvel at them before the dragons charged them. Most of the birds fled, almost running on top of the water in their haste to take flight. The rest had become dragon fodder. He'd had Davvie pluck a few of the floating feathers from the water for Alise to record and collect. Life here was plentiful on this river, and in varieties that Leftrin had never seen or imagined.

"At least this is fresh water, with no acid." Alise spoke as she approached him. "There's that small mercy to be grateful for. Still, the dragons aren't going to be happy about standing in water all night." She came to stand beside him, and he watched her place her hands lightly on the bow railing. How long had she been doing that, he wondered, but did not ask her. Tarman accepted her touch, even acknowledged her. She smoothed her hand along the railing the same way she stroked Grigsby when the ship's cat honored her by leaping into her lap. It was a fingertip stroke, an awareness that he belonged to himself, and she was allowed to touch him but never own him.

Yes. That described Tarman for as long as Leftrin had known him, and even more since his modification. There was a stubborn streak to the ship that was familiar but more intense since they had entered the freshwater tributary. He sensed a certainty in his ship that neither the keepers nor the dragons shared. It pervaded his dreams at night; it was the only thing that let him rise and face each day with optimism.

Alise set her hand upon his.

Well, perhaps not the only thing. For how could any man

feel discouragement when every night a woman engulfed him in tenderness and sensuality? She woke in him appetites he had not known he had, and she sated them as well. He had been more surprised than she had at how quickly the crew and keepers accepted their new arrangement. He had expected difficulties with Sedric at least, for although Alise nominally kept her separate quarters, she openly came and went from his stateroom without apologies or explanations. When Sedric's silence on the matter had extended to two and then three days, he had asked Alise if she thought he had best directly tackle the subject with him.

"He knows," she said bluntly. "He doesn't approve. He thinks you are taking advantage of me and that I will one day greatly regret the trust I've put in you." Her eyes scanned his as she said this, as if she were trying to read his very soul. "I thought about that for a time. And I decided that if you were deceiving me, at least this is a deception that I have chosen." A strange little smile knotted her mouth. "And it is a deception that I will enjoy however long it lasts."

He'd folded her into his arms then. "It's not a deception," he promised her. "And what we have will last. Perhaps some days you will be disappointed by me; perhaps eventually you'll tire of me and seek someone cleverer or wealthier. But for now, sweet summer lady, I plan to enjoy my days with you wholeheartedly." They had been standing in his stateroom, face-to-face, as they spoke. And on his final words, he stooped and picked her up and deposited her on his bed. She gave a whoop of surprise as he scooped her off her feet, and then, as she landed safely on the bed, she had given a throaty chuckle that sent a flush of pleasure through him. There was a bit of the bawd in this Bingtown lady, he was discovering to his delight. He suspected that discovery was new to Alise also.

Now, as they stood and looked out over the water, quiet stretched out around them. When she finally spoke, she asked her question gently. "Are you sure Tarman was correct when he brought us this way?"

He lifted his hand from the railing, catching hers as he did so. The ship was irritable enough without him doubting it. "I'm as certain as he is," he said. More quietly he added, "What else do we have to go on, Alise? If the dragons had felt strongly that it was in the other direction, I think they would have objected."

"I just thought, well, it appeared to be more of a navigable waterway. And so I thought it likely that a large city, such as Kelsingra must have been, would be built on a navigable waterway."

"That would make sense." That idea had occurred to him, more than once. He consoled her as he did himself. "But everything has changed since the days of the Elderlings. This might have been a deep lake then. Or perhaps a lazy river wandered through low banks of farmland. We can't know. Trusting Tarman makes just as much sense as ignoring him and going the other way."

"So. We have an even chance of being right and finding Kelsingra."

He scratched at his beard. "As even as any other chance. Alise, we might have passed its sunken ruins days ago. Or the tributary that led there might have silted in and grown up as forest a hundred years ago. We don't know. Do you want to give up and go back?"

She thought for a long time. "I don't want to go back ever," she said quietly.

"Then we go on," he said. He squinted. "Look at that, over there. Something wrong with that patch of reeds?"

She leaned past him, pressing against his arm to do so. Boyish and silly to enjoy that so thoroughly, but he did. Then she shocked him by gripping the railing and saying, "Tarman, we need to go over there and see what that is! Right away!"

He didn't know whether to laugh aloud or feel affronted when he felt his ship heel over to obey her.

"It's a perfect rectangle. And look over there. Another, smaller one." Despite her efforts to be calm, Alise was grinning insanely and her voice shook. She leaned so far over the edge of the small boat as she peered down through the water that Leftrin leaned over to grip the back of her shirt. "I won't fall in," she responded to his touch, but did not straighten up.

"Do you think they're roofs of sunken buildings?"

"That could be, I suppose, but they're flat and from the tap- estries and preserved images from Elderling times, I know they seldom built plain, flat-roofed structures. Some cities, such as the sunken one at Trehaug, were more like interconnected war- rens rather than the freestanding buildings that we create in our cities. One of the difficulties in excavating Cassarick is that the structures are not all connected as they were at Trehaug. Why they built one way in one place and differently in another is something we don't know." Alise lifted her eyes and scanned the shallows. Plant life was thick on the surface of the river. The flat leaves of lilies barely moved in the sluggish current here, and ranks of reeds lifted tasseled heads. At the oars, Leftrin held the small boat in position over a perfect rectangle of shorter rushes. The uniformly stunted square of plant life was unmistakably unnatural. She eyed the shallow water beneath the boat and an- nounced, "I'm getting out."

"Alise!" Sedric objected before Leftrin could, but she was al- ready pulling off her shoes and rolling up her ragged trousers.

"It's clean water, remember? And so shallow here that not even reeds can take root and grow tall. That's what first attracted Leftrin's attention. Don't worry so much." She clambered out and was pleased that she hardly tipped the boat. Nonetheless she landed with a splash that flung water up to her thighs. Her feet sank into the muddy bottom.

"What about leeches? And rasp snakes?"

"I'll be fine," she repeated, but wished Sedric hadn't men- tioned them. She wasn't sure why he'd insisted on coming along in the small boat to explore the square of uniformly short reeds. She gritted her teeth and then scraped her bare foot, trying to discover what was beneath the mud. Sediment spun up to ob- scure her view. She rolled up her sleeves and reached in with both hands. The water over the sunken structure was shallow, barely knee-deep. But reaching to the bottom with her hands still meant nearly putting her face in the water. She dug at the mud and matted roots, and then ran her fingertips over what she'd exposed. Then she straightened up, dripping and grinning. "Mortar and stone. And the stone feels regular, as if it were cut and shaped and then put together."

"So what is it? What have we found?"

When Leftrin had halted the *Tarman* and then ventured out in the small boat to investigate the patch of reeds, the dragons had paused and then come back to watch the humans. Now Mercor and two of the other dragons lumbered up to investigate for themselves. Mercor lifted a foot, tested his weight on the concealed surface, and then surged up out of the water to stand beside Alise. "Be careful!" she cried, alarmed. "It may give way."

"It won't," he said shortly. "It was made to take a dragon's weight." He paced to the edge, turned, and then came back. "Somewhere here," he said, and then, "Ah. Here."

He hooked his claws into something, tugged, then grunted, "It's stuck."

"What is?" Alise demanded, and "What are you doing?" Leftrin demanded just as the dragon, with a roar of effort, pulled on something under the water.

The result was immediate. Alise gave a cry of fear as the mud and water under her feet suddenly warmed. A bluish light suffused the sunken rectangle unevenly, making the water clear as glass in some places but in others was blocked completely by straggling roots. Alise splashed hastily back toward the small boat as the water swiftly warmed around her. She seized the edge of it, and Leftrin, with no regard for her dignity, reached over the side and clutched her shirt collar and the waist of her trousers to haul her in. "Back away from it!" he shouted to Sedric, and the two men employed their paddles to move the boat away from the glowing and humming rectangle.

"Mercor, Mercor, be careful!" Alise shouted at him. But the dragon calmly lay down in the water. Ranculos and Sestican had already ventured to join him there, and the other dragons were moving slowly toward them.

Mercor stretched and spoke as if in a dream. "They're not supposed to be underwater. Once, they stood on the grounds of some of the finest lakeside cottages. They were built for dragons, to welcome them when they chose to visit here. On cool evenings or rainy days, they made a warm and comfortable place for a dragon to stretch out."

"Guest beds for dragons," Alise said faintly.

"Um. You might call them that. Delightfully warm. Even now, the heat feels good."

As Alise watched, Sestican lay down in the water. He heaved a sigh and stretched out. Around the dragons, the water had begun to shimmer with heat. Kalo clambered up onto the rectangle and found just enough space to join them. The other dragons drew closer, staring enviously and leaning as close to the warmth as they could. Streams of bubbles began to rise and break at the surface.

"Does this mean you know where we are? Are we close to Kelsingra? Was this place a part of it?" Alise shouted her questions to the blissful dragons.

Beside her, Sedric yawned suddenly. "You'll get no sense out of them," he said quietly. "The warmth is something they've been craving for a long time. They're nearly stupefied with it."

And indeed, they reminded Alise of cows more than dragons as they crowded together, leaning against one another. Even Sedric had begun to breathe more slowly and deeply. Alise stared at him in horrified fascination. His eyes were beginning to droop closed.

"What's the matter—" Leftrin began, but she placed a restraining hand on his arm. She leaned closer to Sedric. "Does Relpda remember this place?"

He sighed. "There were lots of places like this. Elderlings wanted to welcome the dragons. They competed for dragon favor, and to get the attention of the most powerful ones, wealthy Elderlings spared no efforts in accommodating their large guests."

"So there were many of these dragon beds?"

It took longer for him to respond. "Not in the city. Kelsingra had an entire plaza that remained warm. But at the country homes of wealthy Elderlings, or at the dwelling places of Elderlings who lived on the northern islands or even farther north, there would be places for dragons to be comfortable." He opened his eyes and tried to focus them. He took a deeper breath, and his voice changed slightly as he seemed to come back to them. "At Trehaug, there were chambers with glassed-in ceilings, places large enough for dragons to enter. They were kept warm for them when they visited. The Elderlings grew beautiful plants in them and had fountains."

"That makes sense," Alise said quietly, recalling what she had heard of an excavated room called the Crowned Rooster Chamber. "The place where Tintaglia hatched was a chamber with large doors and heavy glass panels. It would have admitted sunlight year-round, but been a shelter from the rains of winter. It has been speculated that there was a great earthquake or other disaster, and some of the dragon cases were dragged into the chamber for protection. Instead, when the city was buried, the dragons were interred with it."

"So." Leftrin's brow was furrowed. "What do we have here? The buried remains of a city? Kelsingra?"

"No." She was decisive. A thrill shot through her. She knew, really knew what this was. "The platform the dragons are warming themselves on is below water level, but I think it's plain that the water rose to cover it. And it isn't covered deeply at all. If we anchored here and searched, I daresay we'd find other signs of Elderling habitation—the remains of old stone foundations, and perhaps more dragon-warming spots. But this wasn't a city. Kelsingra was a place of many palatial stone buildings, fountains, courtyards, towers. If this were Kelsingra, or even the outskirts of it, we'd see the remains of those building still, for the dragon-warming spot is scarcely covered at all. No, Leftrin, we are at the site of an Elderling habitation, but not Kelsingra. Sedric! Wake up. We need to take measurements and make notes. Before the light is gone, we need to survey as much of the area as we can."

"I'll be making notes of my own on my charts," Leftrin observed. They were grinning at one another as Carson came alongside them in another small boat. The hunter's face was flushed with excitement.

"There are other ruins here. I pushed back into the reeds and looked around a bit. Just downstream from here, there's a long structure that might be the remains of a stone pier that ran out into a river or lake. It's underwater now, but you can feel the shape of it. Exciting, eh?"

Alise was surprised by the answering grin on Sedric's face. "This is why you wanted to come on this expedition, isn't it? To find something like this?"

"It's a start," the hunter replied. "But now that we've seen this, it makes the possibility of finding Kelsingra more real to me." He glanced up at the darkening skies, and Alise followed his gaze.

More stars were appearing. The simmering river water was giving off a ripe green smell. The unearthly bluish light limned the dragons against the gathering night and changed their colors. Eyes closed and heads drooping, they looked more like statuary than real creatures. "Are they going to cook themselves there all night?" she wondered aloud.

"Oh, yes," Sedric replied. "I think this is the warmest that Relpda has ever been. I never realized how chilled she always felt." He paused and then added, "It may be hard to get them to move on tomorrow."

"Perhaps we could take a day here," Alise suggested. "To chart what we've found and explore a bit more."

Everyone was startled when Mercor opened his eyes and lifted his head. "No. We have gone too slowly and been delayed too often already. Tomorrow we move on. Summer is gone. When the fall rains come down, the river will rise. We need to be in Kelsingra before the rains come again."

THYMARA CAUGHT HER breath and Tats's hand in the same instant. "No," she said. The word came out much more decisively than she actually felt about his touch. She sighed reluctantly as she pulled back from him. The sound he made was much more frustrated.

It was very late at night. The two of them were standing at the stern of the barge, in the relative privacy of the deserted deck and the night. The other keepers were sleeping, some on top of the deckhouse and others in the galley and on the foredeck. She'd agreed to meet him here to "talk," knowing that that was not at all what either one of them wanted to do. She tried to regret how she tormented both of them by allowing him to touch her, but her blood was still racing with the sensations that his kisses and touch could awaken in her. It was harder to say no to herself than it was to deny him. Their encounters always followed the same pattern. They would talk, and one or the other would give in to the impulse. There would be kisses, followed by touches. And it always ended the same way.

"Why?" he demanded abruptly. "Why do you let me touch you and then make me stop? Do you think it's funny?"

"No. I just . . ." She was flustered by the anger and hurt in his voice. She took a breath and opted for honesty. "I love how it feels. I know I shouldn't let you touch me at all, but . . ."

"You like it?"

"Of course I do. But—"

"Then let me be with you. Thymara, please. I want you so badly. I know you want me."

"I'm afraid—"

"I'll be gentle, I promise. You can trust me."

"Let me speak. You keep interrupting!"

He pulled back from her without letting go of her. "Fine. Talk then." His words were brusque, but he didn't release her from his embrace. He still pressed himself against her thigh, and she could feel the throbbing urgency there. She was the one who disentangled herself and took a step away from him.

"I'm not afraid of you, Tats, or of joining myself to you. I'm afraid of getting pregnant. Look at Jerd and how miserable she is, vomiting every morning. She's always weepy now, or angry, or both. She barely does any of her duties. I heard her dragon complaining. Sylve actually did some grooming for her the other day, around her eyes. I don't want to turn into that."

"You don't want children?" His words seemed almost accusing.

She bridled incredulously. "What? Now? Of course not! Do you?"

He moved one shoulder. "It wouldn't be so bad."

"Not for you, perhaps! But even if my pregnancy were easy, I can't imagine having a baby now, while we are still trying to find Kelsingra. Have you even thought about what you just said? About nursing a child, or finding something to use for its napkins, or a blanket for it? Where is Jerd going to sleep after the baby is born? Greft still claims her, but he spends less and less time with her since she turned him out of her bed. Oh, don't look at me like that. It's no secret! She sleeps badly and can scarcely keep food down. How would she be interested in sex with him?"

Tats had half turned from her. "It would be different with us. I care about you. If I got you pregnant, I wouldn't abandon you."

She spoke with sudden certainty. "You're only saying that because you know how unlikely it is for me to get pregnant. So you're willing to take a chance."

"Well, everyone was shocked when Jerd caught a child. All I've heard from everyone is how surprising that is."

"Well, if you talked to the girls about it, you'd hear how alarming it is." Thymara shook her head and made a sudden decision. "Tats. I'm not going to mate with you. Not while we are still journeying like this. I . . ." She wanted to tell him that she still wanted to be able to kiss him, to touch and be touched by him, but that seemed so unfair. Until he spoke.

"Then I don't see how we can go on at all." There was hurt in his voice but also a shadow of a threat. That angered her.

"Oh. I see." She bit the words off sharply. "If I let you mate with me and you get me pregnant, you care so much for me that you'll stay at my side through thick and thin. But apparently you don't care enough for me to stay with me if I'm not willing to mate with you! Does that makes sense to you?"

For a moment he was silent and uncomfortable. Then, "Yes," he blustered. "It does. Because it would show that you cared for me as much as I care for you. Right now, what we do, it's like teasing me. I feel like a fool when you suddenly stop me and say no as if I'm a child begging for another sweet. When people love each other, one doesn't say no to the other."

His absolute certainty took her breath away. "Married people say no to each other all the time!" she insisted, thinking of her parents' frequent quarrels. Then she stopped, wondering if that was so. Her father and mother had disagreed often, but was that true of other long-married folk?

"I'm tired of you making a fool of me, Thymara." Tats turned away from her.

"I'm not trying to make a fool of you," she hissed after him. "I just don't want to get pregnant! Can't you understand that?"

"I understand that you don't care enough about me to want to take a chance. We both know it's very unlikely I'd get you with child. But you don't care enough about me to risk even that small chance!"

She drew breath to speak, and then wondered what she could say. It was true. He was right. She liked Tats, even loved him a little, and his touch sent her heart racing and warmed every inch of her skin. But when she weighed that pleasure against the chance that she'd get pregnant, her blood cooled and her belly tightened with dread—as it did now. She tried to find something to say, some way to tell him what she felt.

At that moment, a dragon's roar of outrage pierced the night. Thymara felt the entire ship shudder under her, and she heard the querulous sounds of people jolted awake from a sound sleep.

Then the roar was followed by a man's yell of terror.

She heard the slam of a stateroom door, and Leftrin shouted, "Hennesey! Swarge! Eider! Lanterns! What's going on out there?"

There was another roar. This time she recognized the dragon's voice. It was Kalo's. She heard a high-pitched scream that wavered in the night, and then the sound of a loud splash not far from the ship. Kalo's outraged words shocked her. "You are no keeper of mine, Greft! Never again will I speak to you! Never again will you touch me!"

"Man overboard!" shouted Skelly.

"I'll get him!" That was Alum's voice. Both voices had come from amidships. Thymara shook her head. She wouldn't be the only one wondering how they both happened to be in the same place at the same time in the middle of the night. She heard a different sort of splash as Alum dove in. A moment later, the kindled lanterns were converging on that side of the ship. Without a word to each other, she and Tats joined the others gathering there.

Swarge lifted his lantern high. In the water, they saw Alum cover the last small distance between him and a floating body. She saw him turn the man over and heard him gasp out, "It's Greft! Lower a ladder over the side."

By the time Alum had towed Greft's limp body back to the side of the barge, Swarge was on the bottom rung of a rope ladder, waiting for him. Together they wrestled his body aboard the ship. "Bring him into the galley!" Leftrin barked. Tats stepped up to catch Greft's feet as they carried him. Halfway there, he began to struggle. They let him try to stand, and he stepped to the railing, coughing and spitting out water. Swarge waited patiently, lantern held high. Greft's shirt was torn and hanging loose in flaps of fabric. Thymara glimpsed two long scrapes on his chest and one on his back.

"I'm fine," he insisted abruptly. "I don't need help. I'm fine."

"You're bleeding," Thymara pointed out.

Greft rounded on Thymara, savagely angry, shouting in her face. "I'm FINE, I said. Leave me alone!"

Leftrin clapped a hand on his shoulder and abruptly spun him around. He let go of him and Greft nearly fell. Leftrin didn't care. He barked his words. "You're fine, and I'm captain. And that means you'll tell me just exactly what happened a few moments ago."

"It's none of your business. It didn't happen on your ship."

Leftrin stood absolutely stock-still and silent. Thymara wondered if he was shocked, if no one had ever spoken to him like that before. But he did not so much as blink when Eider seized Greft by his shoulders, lifted him off his feet, and walked to the railing. With no apparent effort, he held Greft out at arm's length over the side of the boat. Greft roared in wordless fury and clutched at the big man's thick wrists. Thymara noticed he didn't struggle. Like her, she suspected that Eider would simply drop him. Or perhaps he was too battered to offer any resistance.

Leftrin took a small breath and spoke conversationally. "You're not on my ship now. I suppose what happens to you now isn't my business either."

"I went to check on my dragon. He got angry at me and picked me up and threw me. And I am not Kalo's keeper anymore!" The last sentence he shouted defiantly into the night. In response, there was a roar of anger from the dragon. The other dragons echoed him, and a muttering of growls followed the exchange.

"That's half or less of the truth. What happened?" Leftrin demanded.

Thymara had never seen the captain look so angry. Alise had appeared, wearing the Elderling gown that Leftrin had given her. Her hair was loose on her shoulders, her eyes frightened. Others of the keepers and crew were gathering around them. The deck was getting crowded.

"I went to see my dragon." Greft was stubborn. His hands were tight on Eider's wrists. Thymara wondered if the big man was getting tired of holding him out there.

"In the middle of the night?" Leftrin queried.

"Yes." A flat answer.

"Why?" Leftrin wouldn't let it go.

Greft touched the scrapes on his chest and looked at the blood on his fingers. "To ask for blood," he admitted abruptly.

"Blood? Why?" Leftrin sounded shocked.

"Because I want to become an Elderling like the others!" The furious jealous words burst out of him. "I've heard the whispering. I know. The other dragons have given their keepers blood, to help them change. The other dragons are making their keepers into Elderlings. Yesterday I went to Kalo and I asked him when he would give me blood and take charge of my changes."

The captain's eyes had gone flinty. He spoke quietly. "Eider. Bring him aboard and set him down."

As if he were a derrick moving freight, Eider turned and dropped Greft on the deck. Greft staggered two steps, then straightened up. He glared around at all of them defiantly.

Sylve abruptly pushed her way into the ring of bystanders. "I was with Mercor. I heard you demand blood. And I heard Kalo refuse you."

She was pale and shaking, and for the first time Thymara saw how much Sylve feared Greft. She didn't want to wonder why. Harrikin ghosted up behind the girl and set his hands lightly on her shoulders. "It's all right," he said reassuringly.

"No. It's not." Her voice trembled, but she faced Greft squarely. "I heard what Kalo said. He said he wouldn't give you blood because he no longer trusted you. That you might not want the blood to change, but only to sell." Her hand darted out and seized the front of his torn shirt. She tore at his pocket, and a small glass bottle fell with a thunk and then rolled in a circle on the deck. It was empty. She pointed at it. "It doesn't take a bottle of blood to change someone, only a few drops. So what was that for, Greft? Do we have a traitor in our midst?"

Thymara gasped for air. For as Sylve spoke, Mercor abruptly loomed up alongside the ship. His dragon's voice and thought echoed his keeper's exactly: "Do we have a traitor in our midst?" he demanded.

Greft looked around at them wildly. The ring of humans who surrounded him was shocked, silent. Thymara saw Sedric turn his face away, pale and sick with horror. Alise's face was set like stone, and Leftrin's eyes hardened. They waited.

"I'm not the only one!" he shouted. "You liars! Liars one and all! Jess told me, he told me everything. He told me the whole expedition was just to get the dragons far enough away from Trehaug that no one would know of the slaughter, except for the men doing the buying. He told me Leftrin knew about it, that him getting the contract was rigged! The Rain Wild Traders' Council and even Cassarick's little Council know about it! Why do you think they agreed to this? It's all a farce! Even the 'expert' from Bingtown and her assistant are in on it. There is no Kelsingra, there's no final destination for any of us. The plan was to get the dragons away from Trehaug, then slaughter them and load the barge with the pieces. And set course for Chalced, to sell it all to the Duke of Chalced."

He glared around at all of them defiantly. A shocked silence followed his words. The pained smile he gave them mocked them all. "Don't you understand, you fools? Why do you think the Council chose you? To get rid of you! And have no one care that you were gone. Once you'd helped move the dragons far enough upriver, no one would need you anymore. And the dragons are supposed to die or be killed. And then the barge full of dragon parts heads straight to Chalced. And everyone is happy. The Rain Wild folk don't have to support the dragons anymore, Trehaug gets rid of a bunch of misfits, the Duke of Chalced is cured and allies with the Rain Wilds, and a lot of people get very, very rich very quietly! You liars! Don't look at me like that! You know I'm speaking the truth! Why are you all pretending?"

Boxter shouldered his way to the front of the huddle. Tears were starting to fall from his eyes. "But you said . . . you said all those things! About having our own city, and starting new rules and, and everything!" He sounded like a small confused boy. For a moment Thymara thought of Rapskal and his ingenuous questions. Grief scored her heart. But Boxter was not Rapskal, and anger began to dawn in his face, making it ugly. "You liar!" he cried out when Greft just looked at him. "You liar! Telling us we had to leave the girls alone, and then you went after them! Making all those rules about sharing and then keeping the best for yourself. We know what you done, Kase and me. We're not stupid."

"Aren't you?" Greft sneered, and Boxter swung. Greft snapped his head back, but Boxter's fist still grazed his chin, clacking his teeth together as it slammed his mouth shut.

"Enough!" Leftrin shouted, and Swarge suddenly had Boxter's arms clamped to his sides.

A thin line of blood trickled from the corner of Greft's mouth. He ignored it, instead looking disdainfully from one of them to another. When he realized the full hostility of those watching him, he took a breath. "At first, I believed in what we were doing. Then Jess set me straight." He looked at Leftrin, and his eyes were full of accusation. "What happened to Jess, Captain Leftrin? He told me you wanted to back out on his deal with you, told me that you wanted that woman in your bed, and that if you killed him, you'd bribe her with dragon blood to get what you wanted. Is that how it happened?" He swung his accusing glare to Alise. "Fancy Bingtown lady like you whores herself for dragon blood?"

"Leftrin!" Alise gasped, but the captain's fist had already connected solidly with Greft's mouth. The force of the blow slammed the keeper up against the deckhouse wall. His head wobbled on his neck, but he managed to pull himself straight and stand up. He glared at the staring bystanders, then deliberately spat blood on Tarman's deck. Skelly gasped in horror and leaped past him to wipe it up with her sleeve. Greft deliberately leaned closer to Leftrin. Alise had hold of his arm, trying to restrain him, but Thymara knew that it was the captain's own will that knotted the muscles in his jaw and swelled his chest tight.

"I'm tired of pretending!" Greft said. There was something so disillusioned and broken in his voice that for a moment pity for him swelled her heart. "I thought the Council was finally offering us a chance. I thought there was some sort of a future for me. That's why I signed up." He looked around at all of them, and his eyes were accusing.

"I tried to make you all see how it could be. I tried to make you see we could change all of it. But some of you didn't want any changes." He glared at Thymara. "And some of you just wanted someone to think for you and tell you what to do!" His accusing eyes came back to Boxter. Kase had stepped up behind his cousin. He'd put a hand on Boxter's shoulder, but Swarge still hadn't released him from his hug.

"Sa, how I tried!" Greft shouted the words up into the night. Then he glared at everyone again. "But none of you really listened to me. And then Jess told me why. Told me what a web of lies this whole thing was. Well, now he's dead and gone, and I don't think *that* was an accident. And I heard that some of the dragons were changing their keepers on purpose, had given them blood to make them change. But not Kalo, no. Not for Greft. Nothing ever for Greft. I took care of that monster. I hunted for him, I fed him, I groomed him, I scraped the filth off him. But would he give me one drop of blood, one scale? No. Not one drop to change me, not to put my body right, not to give me something I could sell to make a new life for myself." He looked around at them, self-righteous and angry. Blood was seeping from his scored flesh. Thymara guessed now that Kalo had seized him in his jaws and flung him, tearing his skin as he did so. It was only surprising that the dragon had not sheared him in two and eaten him.

Greft's voice was suddenly calm and level. "I've known all my life that I wouldn't get as much as anyone else did. Not respect. Not even time. People like me, like us, we die young. Unless a dragon takes us on and makes sure we don't. I know that now. I heard Sylve and Harrikin talking about it in the night, talking about waiting now because they'd have maybe hundreds of years together, after their dragons changed them. But not Greft. Not for me. So I went tonight to take what should have been given to me. All the times I groomed him, fed him, you think he'd give me just one scale, just a few drops of blood. But no. No."

He sighed out through his nose and looked all around at every one of them. He shook his head slowly as he did so, as if he could not believe his bad luck or the harshness of fate that had doomed him to be here.

"I'm going to die," he said finally. His tone made it their fault. "Things are starting to go wrong inside me. I can feel things going wrong. My gut hurts when I'm hungry and hurts worse when I eat. The shape of my mouth has changed so much that I can't chew or even close my mouth comfortably. My eyes are dry, but I can't close my eyelids all the way. Nothing simple is simple anymore. I can't get enough air through my nose when I try to breathe, and when I breathe through my mouth, my throat dries out until it cracks and I spit blood." He looked around at them again and his eyes came to rest on Thymara. "That's my life," he said quietly. "Or my death. The death of someone who is changing, without a dragon to guide it. The death of someone who was born so Rain Wild touched that I can't even live to be middle-aged, let alone old."

Suddenly he was standing alone in their midst, with no one touching him. When he walked away from them, people parted wordlessly to let him pass. Alise stooped down and picked up the small glass bottle that had been dropped. She looked at it, then glanced at Sedric in consternation. "It looks like an ink bottle," she said.

Sedric shrugged. His mouth was pinched and his face pale. He looked sick. Carson moved closer to him. Alise slowly turned her gaze on Leftrin. "It's not true, is it? The hunter lied to that boy, didn't he?"

Leftrin looked at her for a long, silent time. He glanced around at the watching keepers. "Someone thought they could force me to do something like that. Because they knew about Tarman, knew how much wizardwood was in him. But I never agreed to it, Alise. I never agreed to it, and I never planned to do it."

A small wrinkle had formed between her eyes. "That's what he was talking about that day, wasn't it? Jess, that day in the galley? He thought that Sedric and I were here to help you?"

"He had a lot of peculiar ideas. But he's gone now, Alise, and what I'm telling you is true. I never agreed to smuggle dragon blood or parts." He looked at her and then added very quietly, "This I swear on Tarman. I swear it on my liveship."

For a moment longer, Alise stood uncertain. Thymara watched her. She glanced from Leftrin to Sedric and back again. Then, Alise hooked her arm through Leftrin's and looked only at him. "I believe you," she said, as if she were making a choice. "I believe you, Leftrin."

Day the 12th of the Gold Moon

Year the 6th of the Independent Alliance of Traders

From Detozi, Keeper of the Birds, Trehaug

To Erek, Keeper of the Birds, Bingtown

From the Rain Wild Traders' Council in Trehaug to the Bingtown Traders' Council in Bingtown, a sealed message with a full accounting of the expenses for the rebuilding of the mutually owned docks at Trehaug, with the Bingtown Traders' share of the reconstruction carefully accounted. As always, swift payment is greatly appreciated.

Erek,

Reyall will be taking ship two days hence, on the 14th day of the Gold Moon, to return to Bingtown. Our family thanks all the bird keepers for their assistance in giving him time to return home for our days of mourning. I thank you especially for the understanding and kindnesses you have shown our family over the years. I will be sending with Reyall two fledglings that you may enjoy. Their parents are the most colorful in my flock, with feathers bordering on a true blue. They are healthy and while not as swift as some of the birds, they home to the coop without fail. I thought you might enjoy them.

Detozi

CHAPTER SEVENTEEN

CHANGES

Sedric padded barefoot out onto the deck and stood looking around him. The dawn sky was still streaked with colors to the east. Overhead, it was wide and blue, with a faint rippling of very white clouds in the distance. The sky had never seemed so large to him. All was quiet and serene. The water around the anchored ship was as smooth as a pond. A little distance away, the dragons were still dozing; steam rose around them from the heated water. As he looked at them, he felt Relpda give a twitch of acknowledgment. Gently he withdrew his scrutiny. Let her sleep in the warm water while she could. Soon enough, all of them would have to move on.

He lifted his hand and touched the back of his head, his fingers following a line of scales down to the nape of his neck. "Copper," Carson had told him last night. "Copper as a gleaming kettle, Sedric. I think that answers your question. If she were not guiding it or at least attempting to guide it, I don't think you'd have that sort of a color on your scales. Mine are nearly colorless."

"I've noticed," Sedric said. "Carson—" he began, but the hunter shook his head, his breath moving against the nape of Sedric's neck as he did so. "Enough questions," the hunter whispered. He'd kissed the top knob of Sedric's spine there. "I don't want to think of you changing into an Elderling. I don't want to think about you outgrowing me, outliving me. Not right now."

The memory of that kiss put a shiver up Sedric's spine. A moment later, arms enveloped him from behind and pulled him close. "Cold?" Carson asked by his ear.

"No. Not really," Sedric replied. But he put his hands on Carson's arms and pulled them more tightly around him as if he were putting a coat on. For a moment, they held that embrace. Then, with a sigh, Sedric released his grip and shook gently free of Carson's arms. "Everyone will be waking up soon," he apologized.

"I don't think anyone much cares," Carson said. His voice was so deep that Sedric had to listen carefully to catch the words. "Davvie and Lecter are not exactly subtle, you know. I've had to speak to Davvie twice about keeping private things private."

"I've noticed," Sedric said, but he did not lean back into Carson's embrace. Instead he asked, "What's to become of us?"

"I don't know. Well, I do, a bit. I suspect you will become an Elderling. I see some of the changes in you already. The speed with which you're scaling is increasing, Sedric. Your hands and feet seem longer and slimmer than they were. Have you asked Relpda directly if she is guiding your changes?"

"Not exactly," he admitted. He did not want to bring the subject up with her. Did she completely recall how he had taken her blood that night? Sometimes she seemed like a sweet, simpleminded child, forgiving a wrong she did not completely understand. Of late, however, there had been a time or two when she had clearly shown him that she was a dragon and not to be trifled with. Did her memories begin with him awakening her by consuming her blood? Had she been aware of him even then, had hers been the prompting that made him taste it? Or would the day come when she recalled how it had truly come about, and would she then turn on him?

"I've made such a mess of everything," he said aloud.

"Are you and I a 'mess'?" Carson asked him gently.

"No."

"You can be honest with me, Sedric. I know what I am, and that's a simple man. I know I'm not educated or sophisticated. I know I'm not—"

"It's what you are that matters, not what you're not." Sedric turned to him. He glanced around, and even as Carson grinned at his caution, he turned back and brushed a kiss across the hunter's mouth. It startled Carson as much as it delighted him. But when the hunter would have embraced him again, Sedric stepped free, shaking his head. "You are one of the few things in my life that is not a part of the mess I've made. I didn't deserve you, and I don't deserve you. Unfortunately for me, I do deserve to deal with most of the messes I've made."

"Such as?" Carson gave up his pursuit of him and folded his arms on his chest against the morning chill.

"Alise is angry with me, I think. She believes I lied to her about Leftrin."

"I think you might have," Carson pointed out affably.

"I only repeated what Jess had told me, things I had every reason to believe were true."

"Perhaps if you'd talked to me first, I could have cleared that up for you."

"I was just getting to know you then."

"Sedric, my dear, you are *still* getting to know me."

"Look. The dragons are waking."

"And you're changing the subject."

"Yes, I am." He didn't mind admitting it. There were too many messes he never wished to discuss with Carson. Let him go on thinking he was a good person. He knew he wasn't, and he knew Carson deserved better, but he could not bear to give him up. Not yet. Soon enough he'd be found out but not yet. He diverted his attention. "Sweet Sa, look at their colors. That warm water did something to them."

The dragons reminded him of geese or swans. Some were just waking. Others were stretching, opening their wings and shaking them. Droplets of water flew out from them, and the rising steam of the heated water made them look as if they were rising out of a dream. All of the dragons seemed larger this day, their wings stronger and longer. He felt a whisper of assent from Relpda. *Warmth to make us grow, warmth to make us strong.*

Suddenly she emerged from the throng of dragons, brighter than gleaming coins, shimmering with warmth.

You think pretty of me, she praised him. She opened her wings and held them wide so he could admire them. In the night, a tracery of black had developed on them. The patterns reminded him of ice spray on a cold windowpane. She suddenly beat them frantically. She did not lift off the water, but she "flew" over it to come to rest beside the barge looking up at him.

"I am so beautiful!"

"Oh, that you are, my lovely one."

"You were afraid in your dreams. Don't be. I shall make you as beautiful as I am."

He leaned over Tarman's railing, felt the presence of the ship against his belly as he did so. "Then you know how to shape an Elderling."

She preened the feathered scales of her wings. "It cannot be hard," she dismissed his concern. Then she looked over her shoulder. "Mercor comes, with Kalo. Kalo has a grievance. Changes will be made today. Do not fear. I will protect you."

THIS WAS NOT the behavior of dragons, Sintara thought. Each dragon always acted on her own behalf. They did not descend in a swarm and impose their wills.

Except when they did. As once they had when they dealt with Elderlings. A memory unfolded in her mind. There had been agreements. Rules about the taking of cattle. Agreements about rolling in grain fields. Necessary rules that benefited all. Rules that even dragons had gathered together to create. The thought filled her with wonder. And nostalgia for better times.

She had secured a place at the edge of the warming platform and stubbornly refused to be budged from it all night. She had leaned against its comforting, healing warmth and felt the effects of it spread throughout her body. Heat and sunlight were important to dragons, as important as fresh meat and clean water. Since they had entered this tributary, her life had changed. Water was not some grainy, murky stew sucked out of a small hole in a riverbank. She could drink as much as she wished of the cool, sweet stuff. She could roll and bathe with no caution about her eyes and nostrils. She had felt her flesh fill out just with water.

And food. There was food in this river, small but plentiful, and it required some effort to catch it. It demanded a quick eye to pluck a fish from the water or a monkey from a low-hanging vine. But that was good, too, that satisfaction of winning the meat and gulping it down fresh and warm. This river of clean water was changing her.

But last night's warmth had changed her most of all. Sintara had felt things happening to her body as the water heated it, mostly in her wings. There had been a spread of warmth and sensation, as if they were plants taking up moisture and standing upright after a time of wilting drought. She opened them now and rejoiced in how the sunlight touched and rebounded from their blueness. She could see now how her blood pumped more strongly through them. She flapped them, once, twice, thrice and with a lifting spirit felt how they raised her body out of the water. They would not lift her into the sky, not yet, but it now seemed possible that some day they might.

She did not want to leave the comforting warmth, but they had all agreed in their long night talk that when morning came, they would confront the keepers. What Greft had done was unacceptable. *Kalo should have killed him,* she thought again. *If he had killed him and eaten him, it would not have come to this.* That a human had dared come among them by night, by stealth, not to serve but to take blood and scales from them, as if they were cows to be milked or sheep to be shorn, demonstrated how deeply flawed the relationship had become. It was time to end it, once and for all.

When they had left Trehaug, there had been thirteen dragons, for she had not counted Relpda or Spit as dragons then. Now fourteen gathered here still, despite the loss of Heeby. Fourteen dragons, all stronger and more capable than when they had left Trehaug. Fourteen dragons who would not be considered as anything less than dragons ever again.

They waded purposefully out to the barge in the strengthening dawn. She smelled smoke; someone on board had started a cook fire. On deck, Carson and Sedric looked down on them. The Bingtown man's heart shone in his eyes as he smiled down on the beauty of his dragon. He, at least, had a proper attitude for a human to bear toward dragons.

"Awake and attend us!" Mercor trumpeted, shattering the quiet of the dawn. A flock of waterfowl, startled, flew up from a bank of reeds. Squawking, they fled upriver. Kalo set his shoulder to the barge and gave it a sudden shove. "Awake!" he roared. The humans inside shrieked louder than the ducks, while the two men on deck clutched at the railing in fear.

"Patience, Kalo," Mercor counseled him quietly. "You will frighten them witless and then we shall get no sense or satisfaction from them."

Perhaps that warning was too late, Sintara thought, for the humans came boiling out of the ship's interior like termites from a crushed mound. The variety of sounds they made impressed her; some cursed, one wept, several were shouting, and the captain came out roaring threats at anyone who endangered Tarman. Alise was at his side, equally incensed. Waves of concern for her mate and the ship flowed off her wordlessly. No, Sintara thought. No, she hadn't been mistaken. Despite the correctness of her attitude toward dragons, Alise was not a fit keeper or material for an Elderling. She had so quickly transferred all her loyalty to a human mate and a liveship. She watched the woman who had once professed to worship her as she ran her hands along the ship's silvery railing as if she were soothing a flustered cat.

"Silence!" Leftrin roared at the humans on his vessel. Then he leaned over the railing and glared at Mercor. "If you've a problem with me or any of my crew, then speak it to me and hold me responsible. Touch my ship again, any of you, and I'll put a harpoon in you."

"Have you a harpoon?" Mercor asked in such intense curiosity that Sintara heard someone, perhaps Thymara, give out a wildly nervous giggle before stifling herself.

The captain didn't answer his question. "What is your grievance, dragon?"

"Last night, one of your company came among us as we slept and sought to do harm to Kalo. Not just harm, but to take from him blood and scales, to sell to other humans."

Leftrin didn't dispute the truth. "It wasn't me or any member of my crew."

"Greft is no longer my keeper!" Kalo roared this out. Sintara was ashamed for him. He did not cover the anger and hurt he felt. How humiliating, to admit that the human and his loyalty had mattered to him.

"Very well." The captain's anger was actually helping him behave as if he were calm. Sintara could almost see it shimmering around him. "Greft is no longer your keeper. I've no problem with that. I do have a problem with your battering my ship!"

Kalo opened his mouth wide. For a moment, Sintara feared he would release a venom mist. Of late, all of the serpents had acquired enough venom to be dangerous, but Kalo was largest of all and had always had a bad temper. He probably could release enough venom to kill every human aboard the *Tarman* as well as do extreme damage to the liveship. On the deck, some of the keepers scrambled away in alarm. Leftrin crossed his arms on his chest and stood, legs splayed wide. Beside him, gritting her teeth so hard that they showed, Alise tucked her hand into his arm and stood beside him. As the keepers retreated to the stern of the ship, the crew moved forward to flank their captain. Even Tarman knew he was too ponderous to flee such an attack. She sensed one lash of his hidden tail, and then the liveship stood his ground, facing Kalo.

Just as Sintara gathered her muscles to slam into him and spoil his aim, Kalo tucked his head into his chest. She winced, imagining the burn of Kalo's swollen poison glands as he denied them release. Then he slowly lifted his head. "I demand a new keeper," he said harshly. "One of my own choosing."

Most of the keepers had mustered their courage and were creeping forward to watch the confrontation. She saw Thymara in the forefront. At her elbow, Sylve looked heartsick. Her eyes clung to Mercor, begging him not to make her choose between the dragons and her human companions. Foolish, foolish girl. If she did not stand by the dragon, she stood to lose everything.

Thymara showed no sign of such schism. She looked at Sintara, her mouth a flat line. She'd expected something like this, Sintara decided. She looked at the girl, at her defiant glare, and found that it pleased her. Yes. Thymara had long recognized what she was, and she had expected the dragons to behave as dragons.

Leftrin had glanced back over his shoulder at the keepers assembling on the deck behind him. "That's keeper business." He spoke flatly. "It has nothing to do with my boat or my crew. That's for you to discuss with the keepers."

"All the keepers are taken," Kalo responded. "There were never enough to begin with."

"I have no keeper!" the silver dragon suddenly bellowed. "Am I not a dragon? Where is the one who will serve me?"

"Silence!" Kalo roared at him. "This is my time, lump!"

In response, Spit flung his head back. Sintara knew what would come next and saw with absolute clarity that his venom would hit not just Kalo but that the drift would encompass the ship and keepers as well. Thymara had reached the railing and was staring in horror.

Sintara and Mercor hit Spit simultaneously, crashing into the smaller silver dragon from both sides. She feared the water would not be deep enough, but they both bore him down and succeeded in submerging him. His venom sprayed, silver-gray, into the water. All around them, dragons were trumpeting in anger and dismay as they moved hastily away from the spreading toxins. The current here was not swift. As it spread visibly in the water, Tarman raised himself on his stumpy legs and scuttled sideways to avoid it, dragging his anchor after him. On board the ship, Captain Leftrin was roaring threats of vengeance at Spit while the keepers and crew shouted in dismay and fear. For a time, noise and disorder prevailed. Then, as Spit struggled to his feet, Mercor clamped his jaws on the smaller dragon's throat. He dragged him upright and spoke through his teeth. "Will you keep the peace while we speak, or shall I kill you now?"

Spit rolled his eyes wildly. Mercor's threat was unprecedented. He had no right: this was no battle for a mate. But none of the other dragons offered Spit support in any way. Even so, Spit did not concede. His trumpeting was strangled, but his thoughts reached them all. "I've a right to a keeper! More right than Kalo! He did not teach his keeper proper respect and now he discards him and demands a new one. When I have not had one at all! Is this fair? Is this just?"

Mercor did not relax his grip. To the contrary, he lifted his head even higher, stretching Spit's silver throat. The smaller dragon made a noise, a sound that was pain but not surrender. Mercor growled through his teeth. "You have not been neglected. My own tender spent hours upon you, as did others, grooming you and bringing you meat at a time when you were scarcely better than a riverpig. No one owes you anything. I release you now. Keep silent until Kalo has finished. Then speak your words. But if you spit venom again, or try, I will kill you and eat your memories."

Disdainfully, he flung the smaller dragon aside. Spit splashed into the shallow water, righted himself, scrabbled away, and then turned back to face them all. He tucked his head tight to his neck, a threatening gesture as if he were filling his poison sacs. When Mercor turned slowly to stare at him, the smaller dragon rumbled quietly but lifted his head. There were angry glints of red in his spinning silver gaze. Trickles of blood ran down his neck, outlining his scales in scarlet.

Kalo slowly moved closer to the *Tarman*. The blue-black dragon had grown since they'd left Trehaug. He now looked down on the ship and the humans aboard it when he stood alongside it. "I require a keeper," he said quietly.

Leftrin stood his ground. "All the keepers are spoken for, unless you wish to take Greft back into your service."

From the stern of the boat, Greft shouted angrily, "I will serve no dragon!"

Jerd had been standing beside him. She gave him a look the dragon could not read, and then she walked away to join the cluster of keepers who stood at the railing looking anxiously at their dragons.

Sintara was shocked when Thymara lifted her hand. "Kalo! I will serve you, if it will mean no harm to this ship or the humans aboard him. Sintara has indicated her dissatisfaction with me more than once. Still, I have continued to hunt what meat I could and to groom her as she requests. This I will do for you, also, if it brings peace to us."

"And what about me?" Spit demanded furiously before Kalo could even reply. Several dragons turned to hiss at him warningly.

But before Kalo could speak further, Sintara surged forward. She lifted her head to pin Thymara with a glare. "I have not released you from my service, human." She turned to face Kalo, who had looked intrigued at the girl's offer. "This girl is not free for your choosing. She is of my blood and my shaping. You cannot have her."

"Of your blood!" Thymara sounded outraged. "You have not given blood to me, nor spoken to me of shaping."

"Nonetheless, you have had my blood and I am aware of your shaping. I do not need to speak to you if I do not choose to do so! This one is mine, Kalo. I keep her. Choose another."

"I have told you. There are no others!" Leftrin tried to put thunder in his voice and failed. Kalo's head was hovering over the ship, considering the bunched keepers as if he were selecting a ewe from a flock of terrified sheep. How clearly that ancient memory came to Sintara. Those had been good times, of easy feeding on the pasturelands outside Kelsingra. The sheep and cattle had been fattened for them, grained on oats that grew in abundance in the cultivated fields there. And higher up the slopes, in the surrounding hills and mountains, there had been goats, gamy and delicious. For a moment, her thoughts and life were abducted to that other time, to being a dragon who was tended and fed, not by one small human but by a city of Elderlings and the humans who served them.

In the context of those memories, she saw Kalo lower his head. She saw the keepers cringe, just as sheep had once cowered before a dragon. But Kalo swept past them, to Leftrin's crew and the hunters who stood on the roof of the deckhouse. With his muzzle, he nudged a boy, nearly sending him flying. "This one I will have."

"No," shouted Carson, but before the hunter could speak another word, the youngster shouted, "Yes!" Davvie turned to Carson and spoke quickly and clearly. "I want to do this, Uncle." He glanced down at the gathered keepers, caught the eye of one of them, and grinned. He turned back to Carson. "I'll be Kalo's keeper."

"Why is he choosing you, Davvie?" Carson demanded.

The dragon responded before the boy could. "I've seen him walking among us. He hunts well. He doesn't show fear. I'm taking him."

"It will be all right," Davvie responded. "You'll see, Uncle. I think it's the place in the world that I've been looking for. I'll be with friends."

"You had rather stay with the dragons and your friends than go where I go?"

Davvie looked at him. "I know you, Uncle. You will stay with them, also."

"Then he can be *my* keeper!" This announcement came from Spit. "If Kalo can claim a hunter as his own, then I can take one for myself as well. I take Carson the hunter as my keeper, to tend me and to be changed by me as I require. There, that's done."

"Nothing is done!" Leftrin roared again, and this time he did manage the thunder. "We are not your cattle!"

"Leftrin. It will be all right."

Sintara was surprised to hear Carson accede to Spit's demand. Was it because of the boy? She watched as the hunter glanced once at the boy, but twice at the man at his side, Sedric. Now why was a keeper standing with the hunter? Why was he not with the rest of the keepers? It was a curious thing but not one that she felt she had to decipher. Humans were, after all, only humans. Their intellect was limited by the short span of their years. Perhaps that was why Carson was willing to serve Spit. It was almost certain the dragon would shape him as an Elderling. The man had changed quite a bit already, and he was not as young as the other keepers. If Spit wished to have a servant for a reasonable number of years, he would have to change the man just to increase his life span.

Just as she would have to change Thymara. She swung her gaze to stare at her keeper. Yes. What was sensible for Spit was sensible for her as well. She would have to pay attention to the changes in the girl lest they become deadly. And if she was going to have her for longer than an ordinary human's brief span, then she might as well make her attractive as well as useful. She examined her more closely than she had for days and was almost startled at what she noted. Well, *that* was unusual, especially for an unguided change. She searched her memories and found no precedents for such an unusual development. Well, the changes had begun; she could shape them but not undo them. The girl would live or not, as humans always did. Thymara was returning her gaze with the same diffidence that she felt for her. That almost warmed her toward her. The human didn't wish to cling and hide in her shadow. Good. She had no desire to be encumbered that way.

"Mercor!" Leftrin began, but the dragons paid him no attention. It was settled: whatever the human had to say was of little importance.

"It's time to leave," Mercor announced.

Sintara was not the only dragon who cast a longing glance at the warming place; but once the platform had sensed the dragons' departure from it, it had ceased to create warmth. It was visible now only as an area of open water in the reed-choked slough. She lifted her head and scanned the area, trying to match it to her dragon memories of Elderlings and their habitations. But if any of her ancestors had been here, she either did not recall it, or the area had changed so much that it no longer stirred the recollection. A small dread unfolded inside her. What if Kelsingra was equally changed? What if the marvelous city and the rich farmlands that surrounded it were no more?

Mercor seemed to sense her apprehension. "Water flows from somewhere, and it always flows downhill. If we keep following the current, we will come to higher ground eventually. Somewhere in this world, there must be a place for dragons. We will find it."

Kalo trumpeted loudly and set out. The other dragons fell in behind him and followed. None of them looked back to see if the barge would follow. It had to. It must.

Day the 19th of the Gold Moon

Year the 6th of the Independent Alliance of Traders

From Detozi, Keeper of the Birds, Trehaug

To Erek, Keeper of the Birds, Bingtown

Enclosed, an invitation for Erek, Keeper of the Birds, Trehaug, from the Dushank Trader family, that he may at his earliest convenience come to visit our home in Trehaug.

Erek,

Please, never let my father or mother know that I have scribbled this message on the outside of their formal invitation to you. My parents have insisted that this must be "done right" as my father portentously puts it! And so he and my mother will hereby formally offer you an invitation to Trehaug and to visit our home. I hope you will not consider them pompous. Please (and I blush as I pen this) ignore their hints that the purpose of your visit is more to visit me than to see the coops and birds. I fear that my parents will embarrass both of us unless we are very firm with them as to the nature of your visit. I warn you also that my father has invented what he thinks is a very cunning door for our fly pens, ones that allow birds to enter and exit freely during the day, but, as evening comes on, he adjusts them so that they may come home but not leave again. He is very proud of this innovation. Please respond as soon as you possibly can. I suspect they will ask me hourly if you are able to come for a visit until we have a definite reply from you.

Detozi

$$\diamondsuit \ \ \diamondsuit \ \ \diamondsuit$$

Day the 22nd of the Gold Moon

Year the 6th of the Independent Alliance of Traders
From Detozi, Keeper of the Birds, Trehaug
To Erek, Keeper of the Birds, Bingtown

From Trader Elspin of the Rain Wild Traders to Trader
Kerwith of the Bingtown Traders. A sealed message
requesting immediate payment of several overdue
obligations. This message is sent as a final plea before
resorting to a formal request to ask the Bingtown
Traders' Council to enforce payment of your obligations.

Erek,

*Please, do not be silly. As my previous message must have
reached you now, you must know how delighted we all would be
if you are able to come for a visit. I hope you will be able to make
arrangements to stay long enough that I can give you a full tour
of Trehaug!*

Detozi

$$\diamondsuit \ \ \diamondsuit \ \ \diamondsuit$$

CHAPTER EIGHTEEN

GONE ASTRAY

hymara blinked her eyes, then squeezed them shut. Vertigo spun her. She had been sitting on Tarman's bow, dangling her legs over the side and considering how big the world had become. The dense cloud and steady rains of the last few days had finally ceased; overhead was an endless canopy of stars that stretched from horizon to horizon. She'd stared up at them too long and had suddenly felt as if she were falling off the deck of the boat and up into the sky. She opened her eyes again and stared out at the water.

The forest was gone. It had retreated, day by day, until now it was no more than a smudge on the horizon. The ship was lost in a flat slough of reeds and rushes. Short trees and bushes with stilt roots stuck up in isolated groves. They had learned these indicated not only the shallowest water but also areas where gallators enjoyed sunning themselves. The dragons did not fear the gallators; they regarded them as a larger meat source. But the larger gallators felt the same way about the keepers and their small boats. The keepers had learned to hang back and let the dragons feed off the gallators before coming close to the stilt bushes. The dragons liked to overnight near the groves. All of them were tired of standing in water, but at least it was shallower by the groves. Captain Leftrin accommodated them, but she knew that he feared grounding Tarman in water so shallow that not even he could scuttle out of the mud.

The retreating forests had taken all her familiar food sources with them. Now the keepers set nets for fish at night and pulled up reeds and rushes for their thick, starchy roots. A few days ago, they had been lucky when a flock of waterfowl had got entangled in Carson's fish nets. They'd had fresh meat, but they paid for it in long hours of attempting to mend the tattered nets. She didn't like the monotony of the food now and disliked even more her feeling of being useless. With her hunting gear lost in the wave, all she could do was gather. And the only things to gather were the starchy roots or the seedheads from the tall grasses.

At least Sintara had become more attentive to her, if not any kinder. The dragon demanded nightly grooming now. The water made it difficult, and she had had to submit to Thymara climbing on her back and neck in order to reach the parts of her that needed cleaning. Bundled handfuls of reeds and grasses made coarse brushes for dislodging insects and polishing the dragon's scales, but they were harsh to human hands. Thymara felt sorry for those whose hands were less scaly than her own.

Despite the difficulty of grooming her, Sintara insisted that Thymara be thorough. Thymara had spent most of her evening on the dragon's wings. Despite her differences with the creature, she had enjoyed it. When Sintara opened her wings now, the delicate traceries of the bone and cartilage and the panels and patterns of her coloring meant that it was like cleaning stained glass. The scales with their serrated edges reminded her of translucent feathers. As large as the dragon's wings had become, the skin of them remained thin and fine. The overlapping scales could scarcely be separated. Her wings folded so compactly that it seemed almost impossible that so large a spread of wing could fit so smoothly against the dragon's back. Insects were an irritant when they crept into the folds, and the constant moisture of the river invited wet sores. There was no question that her wings needed daily attention of a kind the dragon could not easily give them. Even so, it seemed to Thymara that Sintara made her spend a ridiculous amount of time on them. Over and over, Sintara demanded that she praise the color and patterns that were developing, that she note the delicate strength of the structure and the fine barbed claws at the tips of each wing rib.

As a result, despite the fact that she'd traveled aboard the barge today rather than paddling one of the boats, she was tired. Tired to the bones, and they ached, too. Her hands hurt, and her back ached around her never-healed injury. That was a pain she was growing accustomed to; she seldom thought about it until a chance touch woke a stab of agony. Furtively she glanced around, and when she was sure no one was looking at her, she slid her hand up under her shirt and cautiously touched the area between her shoulder blades. Hot. Swollen. And a nasty scabby valley down the middle that made her feel queasy. It was almost a relief that Tats wasn't currently speaking to her, let alone trying to kiss her or touch her. Keeping his wandering hands away from her back had been a challenge, and a behavior that completely confused him. She should have let him touch her there; that would have put a quick end to his heat.

She sighed. Rapskal came to her mind. Not for the first time, she missed him intensely. If he were alive, he'd be sitting here beside her tonight, nattering on about something inane, cheery, and optimistic. He had been her friend without any obligations or expectations. She hadn't worked for him to like her, and he'd always just assumed that she liked him. He'd made friendship so simple. She missed that. Tonight, she longed for it.

She turned and looked back amidships. All of the keepers were on board tonight. Some of them were sitting on the roof of the deckhouse. They'd been playing dice until it got too dark to see the gaming pieces. Now Boxter was tormenting everyone by talking about the spice rolls his mother used to make.

Sylve and Kase and Alum were huddled around a pile of rush roots, peeling the tough outer skin off the thick tubers and then passing them to Bellin who was chopping them into chunks for tomorrow's breakfast. Thymara knew she should go and help them.

"Greft. Can we have a word with you?"

She turned at the sound of Tats's voice. He and Harrikin were standing behind Greft. She hadn't noticed him leaning against the railing not far from her. Lately he'd been quiet, withdrawn, and hostile toward the other keepers, and it had seemed wise to avoid him. Trust Tats to think it would be best to prod him out.

"You've already had several. Why stop now?" Greft replied sarcastically. His words were badly formed. She wondered if his lips were stiffening. She'd heard of that happening to heavily scaled people. It had been days since Leftrin had hit him. His mouth should have healed by now.

"We noticed you didn't take the boat out today."

"Didn't feel well."

"Well, yes, that's what I thought. So Harrikin and I, we're going to take it out tomorrow and see if we can't get some fish or some of those water gophers that we saw a few days ago. Or even one of those gallators. The dragons seem to think they're tasty. Any kind of fresh meat for the keepers and crew would be welcome."

She noticed he wasn't asking Greft if he could take it. He was telling him that they were going to do it. Harrikin wasn't speaking, but he stood ready to back Tats up. Greft looked from one to the other. His voice was low and serious as he said, "Don't like loaning my gear. No."

"It's keeper gear," Tats said.

"And a keeper boat," Harrikin added.

Greft looked from one to the other. "Gear was issued to me. I took care of it, stowed it right. That's why I've still got it." She marked how he said only the words he needed, and she suspected that speaking was painful, or an effort.

"Luck," Tats insisted. "Just luck, Greft. You weren't the only keeper who stored his gear tight. You were just lucky enough that your boat washed up where it was found. That's all. It's not fair for you to hold it back from everyone."

"It's mine."

Tats lowered his voice slightly. "I seem to remember standing near an elk that Thymara had killed and hearing you sing a different tune about how things should be shared out."

Tarman was not a large vessel. Silence rippled out from Tats's words. The conversation on the roof of the deckhouse stilled. Heads turned.

"That was different." Greft tried to clear his throat. He leaned over the side and spat, but it didn't come off his mouth cleanly. He wiped his ragged sleeve across his mouth, looked from Tats to Harrikin. "No. Or fight now."

Tats and Harrikin exchanged glances. Tats spoke for them. "No fight, Greft. I know you're not a healthy man. And I don't want to cross Leftrin about fighting on his deck. I didn't come to you to start a fight. I came to let you know that tomorrow we're taking the boat and the gear out at first light, to try to get some serious hunting and fishing done. No insult intended, but you're not holding up that end of things anymore. So, for the good of us all, Harrikin and I are stepping up to it. And we need to use the boat and gear."

Greft turned away from them to look out over the water again. "No," he said in a neutral but factual voice. Did his back dare Tats to attack him? If so, Tats refused the bait.

"Just saying that's what is going to happen," Tats said quietly. He glanced again at Harrikin, who nodded. As one, they turned away from Greft and sauntered off down the deck. Whispers in the dark behind them turned into muted conversation. Thymara stayed where she was, staring out over the water and darkness. She did not care for Greft, but she felt heartsick it had come to this.

Greft seemed to feel her regard. "Funny?" he asked her in a voice gone harsh.

"No," she replied shortly. "Tragic. I'm sorry this happened to you, Greft. For what it's worth, you have my pity."

When he turned to face her, the blue in his eyes shone with anger. "Keep your pity for yourself. Useless, stupid whore."

The insult stunned her, not just for the seething vehemence in his voice but because it baffled her. Useless? Stupid? Whore? Greft had turned and was walking away before she realized that it wasn't intended to make sense, only to insult. He'd actually expected her to be enjoying his downfall. "You don't know me at all," she said into his absence. She glanced toward the other keepers. "I don't think anyone does anymore."

The other keepers had resumed their activities. Alum was trying to give Boxter a haircut, with helpful advice from Kase and Lecter. Davvie was watching and laughing. Tats was sitting with Harrikin; Sylve was leaning against Harrikin. All three were talking softly about something. "I miss you, Rapskal," she said to the night. "I miss having a friend."

An unexpected echo bounced back to her. *Stop being stupid. You have a dragon. You no longer need human companions. Go to sleep.*

"Good night, Sintara," she muttered and went to take the dragon's advice.

THE RIVER WAS GONE. It was time to admit that. Leftrin wasn't sure what to properly call this body of water that he was on, if it could be termed a body of water at all. For three days, Tarman had been making agonizingly slow progress. They followed the dragons, but he doubted that they had any sense of where they were going. Were they following the main channel? Was there a main channel? The current was barely a current anymore. He watched the dawning light reflected in the still surface of the water, broken only by the faint stirring of the reeds and rushes as the morning wind passed through them.

The walls of the world had retreated. For as far as he could see from Tarman's deck, they were in an immense slough filled with water plants. Even from the roof of the deckhouse, he gained no vantage or sense of it ever ending. Perhaps this had once been a river system or a lake. Now he wondered if it were not a wide drainage for distant hills, a place of water that was scarcely deeper than a man was tall. *Like a flat plate,* he thought. He tried not to wonder what might happen when the rains began in earnest. If a deluge started and the water began to rise, there was nowhere for the dragons to retreat. He shook the useless worry from his head, certain that Mercor was aware of it. Daily he led them on, to Kelsingra or death. They'd find out which when they reached there.

He scanned the wide circle of horizon and saw nothing promising. He had never felt he was such a tiny spark of life floating on a twig as he did now. The sky overhead was wide and gray with high clouds. He missed the shady riverbanks he'd known all his life. The light seemed relentless during the day, and on a clear night, the blanket of stars overhead reduced him to insignificance.

Somewhere in the distance a hunting bird, hawk or eagle, screamed a long, lonesome cry. Tats's dragon roused and lifted her head from where she dozed. She made a questioning sound, but when no response came, she once more tucked her head under her wing. The dragons stood in a huddle, like a flock of exhausted waterfowl, heads tucked to their breasts or resting on the back of an adjacent dragon. It could not have been relaxing sleep for them. They slept on their feet like sailors kept on watch too long. He pitied them but could do nothing for them.

Insects had become more plentiful, but at least on this river, bats abounded by night; and during the day, tiny darting swallows feasted on the mosquitoes and gnats. There was still no lack of stinging, buzzing insects, but watching them be devoured in turn gave him satisfaction.

Habit made him take his pipe out of his coat pocket. He looked at it, turning it in his hands, and then put it away. Not even a shred of tobacco remained anywhere on the boat. It wasn't the only supply that was exhausted. The sugar was gone, as was the coffee. The tea that remained was more powder than leaf. There were two more casks of ship's bread. When that was gone, their dependence on what they could hunt and gather as they traveled would be absolute. He scowled and then resolutely shook off his gathering worries.

Where there's clean water, there's food, he reminded himself. Fish there were in plenty, and some of the rushes had thick, starchy roots. For the last couple of nights, Carson had been deliberately setting out nets for waterfowl. He hadn't had much luck yet, but when he did, not if, there'd be roast duck on the menu. Or more likely boiled, he reminded himself, to use less firewood. Large pieces of wood had become scarce of late. They watched avidly for driftwood now, any snag deposited in days of higher water. Until then, all the keepers had the task every evening of gathering as much dried reed-grass as they could. It burned quickly; they gathered bushels every night and twisted it into bundles to try to make it burn longer. Thank Sa the nights had remained mild so far.

Everyone's clothing was showing the effects of hard use and too much exposure to the acid water of the Rain Wild River. Fabric was fraying away to nothing. Trousers had become shorter as cuffs became patches for knees. Alise had shared out her previously ample wardrobe among the female keepers, offering it even before she was asked. Sedric had followed her example; it was strange to see the keeper lads going about their duties in linen and silk shirts in bright colors. Even so, Leftrin knew it was only postponing the inevitable. For now, they were coping, but eventually a solution would have to be found.

Alise joined him, carrying two steaming mugs with her. She balanced hers on top of the railing and handed one to him. "Tea?" he asked her.

"Yes. Pretty much the last of it. And weak at that."

"But hot," he said, and they smiled at each other over the steaming mugs.

They surveyed the horizons of their domain. After a time, she spoke both their minds. "The water gets shallower every day. I have no faith that the dragons know where they are going. In the memories that Tarman showed us, Kelsingra was on the banks of a large river, not a lake like this."

She said no more. They both sipped their tea and wondered. Wondered if they had followed the wrong branch of the river, wondered what would happen if the water became too shallow for Tarman, wondered if the dragons would demand to turn back. Then Alise put her free hand on the top of Leftrin's shoulder and he bent his head to trap it between his shoulder and cheek. "I love you," he said quietly. He hadn't told her that. Hadn't thought to say it aloud.

"I love you, too." The words seemed to come easily to her, as if she had said them a thousand times before. That pleased him. It wasn't the saying of the words that mattered to her, then. It was just acknowledging what was.

He smiled, put his arm around her, and pulled her close. It was a good thing to know, on a day when he felt he knew nothing else for certain. "Looks like the clouds are breaking up over there. Perhaps we'll have another sunny day," Alise said, looking at the sky.

"More freckles for you!" Leftrin declared, and she shook her head with a mock frown.

"I don't understand why you like them! I spent years of my life trying to avoid getting them and fading the ones I had with lemon juice and buttermilk."

"Kissing you must have been delicious."

"Foolish man. No one kissed me then." A crooked smile.

"Seems to me the Bingtown men were the foolish ones."

She smiled still, but a small shadow crossed her eyes, and he knew he had reminded her of Hest, and humiliation and deceptions. It saddened him that no matter how he tried he could not erase that from her heart. He knew that it still colored her relationship with Sedric. The two circled each other at a distance, polite, almost kind to each other, but with the caution of people who had bruised each other badly. He felt sorry for both of them. She had spoken enough of Sedric that he knew her friendship with him was years older than her disastrous marriage to Hest. He wished she still had the security of Sedric's regard. Losing it had cracked her image of herself. He wished his own respect for her was enough to make her see her own worth, and he recognized the selfishness of that wish. He could not be her entire world. She needed to mend her bridges with her old friend before she would be whole. For all of their sakes, he hoped it would happen soon. Tarman was too small a world for strife and conflict.

Yet they had enough of that and to spare in the person of Greft. He moved about the ship, neither a keeper nor a member of the crew, rejected by the dragons; a failed leader with failing health. Leftrin would have pitied him if Greft had allowed it. He didn't. He had become as bitter and nasty a man as Leftrin had ever known. Many a time he had wished that Kalo had simply eaten his keeper that night.

"You've grown quiet. What are you thinking?"

"Greft," Leftrin said briefly, and she nodded.

"It's coming to a head, isn't it?"

"There was a bit of a tussle last night after you'd gone to bed. Greft stayed on board all day yesterday; I don't know if the physical changes are hurting him that bad or if he's just too discouraged to make the effort. Tats went to him and told him that if he didn't hunt today, he and Harrikin intended to take the boat and gear and 'do some good' with it." He sipped his tea and shook his head. "He made it sound like it was about the boat and the gear, but I think there was more to it than that."

"What happened?"

"Not a great deal. Nasty exchange of words. Greft seemed willing to fight, but Tats said he wouldn't hit a sick man and walked away. Ended there. I hope." He took another long sip of the cooling tea. "Tats and Harrikin told him they were going to take the boat and gear and go hunting this morning. I hope Greft is smart enough to not be there when they take the boat. If he is, and it comes to blows, I'll have to intervene."

"Perhaps they've already gone," Alise suggested hopefully.

"Perhaps, but it bears checking into. Care to talk a walk, my dear?"

"THANK YOU FOR the invitation, kind sir." She mocked a curtsy to him, and then set a rough hand on the ragged sleeve that he so grandly extended to her. As they started their promenade down the deck, she found herself smiling at the picture they must present. She no longer had a single garment that didn't show some sign of wear from sun and acid water. The exception was the Elderling gown he had given her, but the long skirt was not the most convenient style for life on a barge. Her hair had gone wild and curly. A Bingtown street vendor would have had a better complexion. She was barefoot; she now saved what was left of her boots for times when it was possible to walk on the shore; she had not put them on for days now. Never had she felt less beautiful.

Or more attractive. She glanced at Leftrin, and his eyes immediately met hers. And when she returned his gaze, his smile widened and his eyes lit with interest. Yes. Here on the deck of this ship, she was the most beautiful woman in his world. It was a wonderful sensation.

"The boat's gone," she told him, recalling him to the business at hand.

"So it is. Well, that's trouble avoided," he said, well pleased.

Then Tats spoke from behind him. "Where's the boat?"

GREFT HAD TAKEN the boat, and all the gear both for hunting and fishing. No one was sure when he had left. Bellin remembered seeing him in the galley after most of the others had gone to sleep. It didn't surprise Thymara. Greft's changes had meant he was not sleeping well, and he'd told them it was hard for him to eat. A quick inventory revealed that a large portion of their small supply of ship's bread was gone completely along with a small pot. This more than anything else convinced her that Greft had not gone out to fish or hunt. He'd left the barge to go his own way.

The reactions of the other keepers surprised Thymara. Some were angered to find the boat missing, and all expressed surprise. None seemed concerned for Greft's well-being. Boxter and Kase were stubbornly silent, and Jerd was bitterest about his selfishness in taking the boat, gear, and ship's bread "when he knows it is one of the few foods I can keep down."

"As if everything must center on her," Sylve, standing at Thymara's elbow, whispered. Not quietly enough, for Jerd shot them both an evil glance and said tragically, "It is nothing to either of you that he has abandoned me while I carry his child."

Thymara thought but did not say that perhaps it would have mattered more to Greft if he had been certain the child was his. She edged away from the keepers, to stand where she could eavesdrop as Leftrin discussed the matter with Hennesey. "If it was only the boat and the gear, I'd say it was a keeper matter. Even though losing that fishing and hunting gear is going to impact everyone; ever since Jess got himself dead, Carson's had a hard time keeping meat on the table. Dragons are mainly feeding themselves now or things would be even worse. But he stole the ship's bread. And that makes it a ship's matter and for the captain to decide.

"That's how I see it. So. Someone's got to go after him and bring him back. It's the last thing we need just now. But if we ignore it, it leaves the door wide open for the next keeper who decides to jump ship and take whatever with them."

"Can't let it go," Hennesey agreed. "But who do you send?"

"Carson." Leftrin was decided on that. "He's mine. Not a keeper, even if that dragon has claimed him. I'm not going to send a regular crewman off on this. I want to move on today, not sit here and wait."

"Carson, then. Alone?"

"I'll let him choose if he wants a companion. This is such a damn nuisance."

"WHY ME?" SEDRIC asked the question quietly.

Carson glanced back at him, a puzzled smile on his face. "I thought by now you'd realize that I like to spend time with you."

Despite his worries, Sedric found himself answering Carson's smile. That response seemed to be enough for the hunter. He faced front again and dug his paddle into the water. Sedric copied him and tried to keep pace with him. The physical strength he had developed since he'd begun keeping company with the hunter surprised him. As for Carson, he'd complimented Sedric more than once on the developing muscles in his arms and chest.

Sedric glanced back, a bit uneasily, to watch the barge shrinking behind them. The boat had become the one point of safety in his life. It ran counter to all his instincts to be moving away from it in this tiny vessel, even with Carson guiding their way. A flash of silver caught his eye. "Your dragon is following us, I think."

Carson lifted his head for a moment. Then, without turning to look, he gave a tight nod. "That he is."

"Why?"

"Who knows why a dragon does anything?" he muttered, but there was amusement in his voice. Spit was a difficult dragon, cantankerous and sometimes obtuse to the point of stupidity. Even knowing why the hunter had stepped forward to be Spit's keeper, Sedric still wondered at it. He and Carson had not made any promises to each other. Carson hadn't seemed to think they were necessary. Yet he held nothing back. He'd spoken only once of a concern that Sedric might "outgrow or outlive him." Sedric had dismissed it as pillow talk. Yet when the opportunity arose for the hunter to follow Sedric into a transformation that no human could control, he hadn't hesitated. He'd stepped forward to become Spit's keeper, a spontaneous offer to change his entire life for the sake of being with Sedric. Never had he imagined that any man would make such a concession to him. It reminded him shamefully of how quickly he had discarded his old life and even shredded his family ties to be with Hest. He suspected that Carson was far more aware of what he had done than Sedric had been when he gave up his world to be with his lover. Yet Carson had not once mentioned it as a sacrifice. When the man gave, he gave with an open heart. He watched the man in front of him, saw the shifting of his muscles as he used the paddle, and wondered what he would look like a year or a decade from now.

Spit hadn't yet offered blood to Carson, but Sedric did not doubt that he would. The hunter tended the unpredictable little dragon with not only devotion but a deep understanding of animals and their bodies. The first day that he'd been keeper to Spit, he'd gone over the small silver dragon with an attention to every detail of his health that had sent every other keeper scampering to be sure he hadn't neglected his own beast.

Not many of them had been as bold as Carson. He'd spent over an hour inside the dragon's mouth, removing a wad of sinew that had wrapped around one of his shearing teeth and was causing him a great deal of pain. "Not a waste of my time," he'd gently rebuked Sedric later. "Sooner or later, it would have rotted away. But by removing it now, I gave him one more reason to appreciate me. And one less reason to be irritable all the time."

"What are we going to do when we find Greft?" Sedric asked Carson after a while. It was an obvious question, one of the many that he hadn't had time to ask before they departed from the barge.

"We bring him and the boat back to the barge. That's our only task."

"What if he resists?"

Carson's shrug was minute. "We bring him back. One way or another. Leftrin can't let him get away with that theft. So far, despite the shortages, there hasn't been any pilferage or hoarding. Food that is gathered or hunted is shared. You and Alise set an example when you divvied out your extra clothing. You can't imagine how relieved Leftrin was when you did that. He was surprised you'd do that. I told him I wasn't." He turned his head and gifted Sedric with a grin that parted his ruddy lips and showed his teeth. Who smiled like that? Not the sophisticated and urbane Traders who had once been Sedric's companions. They muted their expressions, never laughing too loud, hiding smiles behind well-tended hands. Appearing to be disaffected or cynical was stylish. Why had he thought that was attractive and civilized? A ghost of Hest's sneering smile came to his mind. He banished it, and it went much more easily than it had a month ago.

"I love your smile." He spoke the honest compliment aloud.

It made him feel silly and giddy at the same time. He would never have dared to voice such a simple thing to Hest. The man would have ridiculed him for a month. He watched as Carson silently took two more strokes with his paddle and then carefully shipped it. The little boat rocked as the hunter turned on the seat and then slowly moved through the boat until he crouched in front of Sedric. He cupped the back of Sedric's head with one hand and kissed him deeply and thoroughly.

His voice was hoarse when he spoke. "I've never done this in a boat before. It might be tricky."

"Tricky can be good," Sedric responded breathlessly.

"SOMETHING IS WRONG." Jerd's voice was tight and scared, and her grip on Thymara's upper arm was painful. Thymara had been sitting on the deck, trying to untangle a long fishing line with multiple hooks when Jerd had sought her out.

"What?" Thymara demanded, trying to pull back from her. Jerd was uncomfortably close as she crouched over her, and the fear in her voice was unnerving.

"I'm bleeding. A little bit. And I keep feeling— OH." She leaned on Thymara abruptly, and her free hand went to her belly. To Thymara's horror, a few drops of blood-tinged liquid spattered onto Tarman's deck.

"Oh no!" Thymara gasped. All knew that blood should never be spilled on a liveship's deck. She felt Tarman's suddenly heightened awareness. An instant later, she heard Leftrin shout, "Swarge, is there a problem?"

"None I see, Cap!" the tillerman shouted back.

"Quickly. Stoop down and let me use the hem of your night-gown to wipe that up."

"That's disgusting." Jerd was wearing one of Alise's night-robes to accommodate her modestly swelling belly.

Her cramp must have passed, Thymara thought, grimacing with distaste, for her to be too fastidious to deal with the mess she had made. She stooped and used the ragged sleeve of her own shirt, but some of the bloody water had already soaked into the deck. Not good. "We need to take you down to the bunks, I think. Jerd, why did you come to me? Why didn't you talk to Bellin?"

"She's mean. And she doesn't like me."

"She's not mean. She's just a woman who has been trying to get with child for years, and here you do it within months of your first mating, without even intending to. She's bound to resent you a little. Come on. Walk."

Jerd leaned on her heavily. Despite her whispering and the furtive way she had come to find her, Thymara suspected she was enjoying the attention they attracted as they made their slow way to the deckhouse and entered it. Davvie and Lecter were in the galley. "Go get Bellin, please," Thymara said, and something in her voice sent them scrabbling to obey her.

"And Sylve," Jerd called faintly after them. "I need women to attend me."

Thymara shut her teeth sharply on a hard-hearted reply to that. Jerd was enjoying the drama now, but Thymara had a feeling that bad things were about to happen. She helped Jerd sit down on one of the lower bunks.

Bellin arrived with not only Sylve but Skelly also. The woman's voice was hard but not without sympathy. "I felt blood on the deck from Tarman. You're losing the baby, then?"

"What?" Jerd was astounded.

Thymara exchanged a disbelieving glance with Sylve, but neither girl said anything. Skelly merely looked baffled.

Bellin spoke heavily. "If you're seeping blood and having cramps, then you're having a miscarriage. The baby is likely already dead inside you, and your body is pushing it out. Or the poor little thing will emerge far too early and die. Worst will be if this stops in a little while. Because I can tell you from experience that it will just start up again, a day or a week or even a couple of months from now when you've convinced yourself that everything is fine even if you still haven't felt the child move."

"NO!" Jerd shrieked and then dissolved into wailing and tears. Bellin turned her back on her. At first Thymara thought her attitude was harsh. Then she saw a tear track down the woman's weathered cheek.

Alise suddenly appeared in the doorway of the bunk room. "What's going on?" she asked in alarm.

"Jerd's losing her baby," Bellin said. Thymara suddenly knew that the flatness of her voice was actually the woman's effort to keep her own emotions under control. "Shut the door, please. Skelly, find clean rags. There's still a bit of wood left. Use it to warm some water. She'll want to bathe afterward."

Skelly went running to do as she was told, and Sylve nudged Thymara and tilted her head toward the door. They had almost reached it when Bellin stepped in front of it. "No," she said sternly. "I want you girls here. Time to see the consequences of what you're doing."

"I'm not doing anything!" The words burst out of Thymara's mouth before she had considered how revealing they were. Everyone stared at her.

Bellin spoke heavily. "Maybe you haven't, girl. But you will. This girl here, she did what she wanted, with whom she wanted at the moment. And that's her business, as she told me pretty hot once, and you've probably heard, too. But here we are at the crossroads, and who is the work falling on? You see any boys or men in this room? You see any fellow pacing up and down outside, praying to Sa to give that little life a chance? I don't. And that's the message, girls. If you don't have a partner ready to put it on the line for you, to the last drop of blood in his body, well, then you're a fool if you spread your legs. That's it, plain as I can say it."

Thymara had never heard such blunt and harsh words. She and Sylve froze where they were.

"That's not . . . fair." Jerd gasped out the words, and then she gave a small shriek. She curled over her belly, panting. Thymara heard the small rush of fluid as it exited her body.

"It's not fair," Bellin agreed. "It's never fair, girl. So all you can do in this hard and unfair world is make sure you're giving yourself and your baby the best shot you can at having a life.

Get a true partner, one with guts. Or don't get a child. It's that simple."

Skelly was back with a folded stack of clean blood rags. Bellin took some from the top and mopped between Jerd's legs, her lips a flat line. Thymara turned away, feeling humiliated simply by virtue of being female. Her glance met Alise's. The Bingtown woman stood with her back pressed against the door, her face pale. Was she wondering what would become of her if she suddenly found herself pregnant? Well, she had Leftrin, and he seemed the steady sort.

Jerd lay back, breathing hard, and Bellin continued mercilessly, "When this is over, a week or two from now, every one of those boys is likely to come sniffing after you. The ones you already had will assume you'll still accept them, and the ones who haven't will still be waiting to take a turn. If you're smart, you'll hold out for something from them this time, other than a few jolly humps."

"I'm not . . . a whore," Jerd retorted indignantly.

"No, you're not," Bellin returned placidly. She dumped the handful of used rags into a bucket and took up a fresh one. "A whore has the sense to get something for what she gives—money or presents. Something she can use to take care of herself. You just gave it away, girl. That's fine if you want to shove a wax stopper up there so you don't conceive. Then it's just yourself you're risking, when you get the ooze or the scabs. But right now, you're risking not just yourself but some poor little baby who might drop down in the middle of this. And that means you're risking us, too. You die popping out a baby, who has to find something for it to eat? Who has to stop her life to wipe its ass and pack it around on the deck? Who has to watch it dwindle and die and then put it over the side for a dragon to eat? Most likely me, that's who. And I'm telling you right now, you aren't going to do that to me. You have a baby and live, well, it still falls on us to find food for you and the child. Just pregnant, you haven't been pulling your share of the load. You get a baby on your own, you become a weight on the rest of us. Something like that falls on me, it's going to be Swarge's child, not yours. He gives me a baby, well, I know that he and I both will give the last breath of our bodies to make sure it lives. So, I'm letting you know, every one of you here with no partner willing to stand up and admit he's your partner: keep your legs together. If anyone catches a baby in her belly on this ship, it's going to be me. Or Alise there. We got the men to back us up. You don't."

Alise looked so shocked at Bellin's words that Thymara wondered if the Bingtown woman had ever considered that she might get pregnant.

"You can't tell me what I can— aaaah!" Jerd's defiant words died away in a hoarse caw. Her breath caught, she panted, and then grunted hard. She expelled her breath in a long sigh. Bellin bent over Jerd's tented legs and her face darkened with sorrow. One-handed, she gave a rag a shake, and then floated it down over something. Skelly, silent as a ghost, handed Bellin a bit of string and a knife. Bellin's hidden hands worked efficiently as she cut the cord and tied it off. She wrapped the rag around something small. A strange tenderness shone in her eyes as she lifted the stillborn thing from the narrow bunk.

"She wouldn't have lived, even if you had carried her to term. Look at her, if you want. No legs. Just a partial tail, like a serpent."

Jerd was silent and white-faced, staring up at her.

Bellin faced her squarely. "Do you want to see your daughter before she goes over the side?"

"I . . . no. No, I don't." Jerd began to weep noisily.

Bellin looked at her for a moment. Then she gave her head a short shake. "You'll be fine. Lie there until the afterbirth comes out, and I'll stay here with you. Skelly. Take the child. You've helped me before. You know what has to be done."

"Yes, ma'am." Skelly didn't hesitate, even though she paled. She stepped forward and, as tenderly as if the child were alive, Bellin put the tiny thing into her hands. She caught the girl's wrists before she could turn away. "You remember this," she said roughly to the girl. The tears that had begun to trickle down the woman's cheeks put the lie to the harshness of her voice. "You remember, when you think we're just being cruel to you, that there's a reason for the rules. The rules are to keep you from hurting yourself. Every girl always thinks she's smarter than the rules, always thinks she can break them and get away with it. But you can't. And I can't. So you remember that, next time you're sneaking around and kissing that boy and letting him touch you. The rules aren't there to be mean. They're there to make life a bit less unfair to everyone."

Bellin's eyes slid to Thymara and Sylve. Somehow, she had taken Sylve's hand and was clutching it tightly. Sylve's grip was as tight as her own. She felt six years old as the older woman pierced her with a stare. "You two help Skelly. And you think about what I said. And know this. If I catch you opening your legs to a boy on this ship, keeper or crew, it's going to hurt. And humiliate. Because that's a lot better than what we just had to go through here today."

Thymara bobbed a small stiff nod. Skelly edged past them in the crowded bunk room floor space. They followed her out into the open air. As they came out on the deck, they formed a small procession. Skelly went first, bearing the tiny wrapped bundle. They passed Hennesey and Eider. The mate shook his head sadly, and Big Eider looked aside. As they approached the stern, a cluster of keeper boys rose and evaporated, scattering throughout the ship. No one spoke to them or asked them what they were about, but Thymara was sure that every one of them knew, and she wondered how many of them thought they might have fathered the child. Or had that thought left their minds when Greft had stepped in to say he'd be responsible?

Bellin's words rankled. She thought of how Greft had said he would establish a place where there were new rules. Had he thought about why the rules existed, and who they protected?

The girls reached the railing. To Thymara's surprise, Jerd's dragon, Veras, was there. Like all of the dragons, she had grown larger, and her colors were brighter. She did not speak to any of them. They all knew why she was there. A little shiver went up Thymara's spine, and then she accepted it. Jerd's stillborn baby would be eaten by her dragon. Was that any worse than letting the tiny body drop into the water for fish to find?

Swarge was on the tiller. He looked up at them with a grave expression and sad eyes. Thymara knew this would not be the first stillborn child he had seen tipped over the side. He lowered his eyes and his lips moved, perhaps in a silent prayer. Skelly began to extend her hands and the wrapped bundle over the railing. Veras lifted her head.

"Wait." Sylve spoke abruptly. "I want to see it . . . her. I want to see the baby before she's gone forever. One of us at least should look at her."

"Are you sure?" Skelly asked.

"I am," Sylve replied. Thymara couldn't find words but gave a single stiff nod.

Sylve rested the small body on the railing as she folded the concealing rag back. Thymara found herself looking at a tiny creature who would have fitted in her cupped hands with room to spare. The little round head was tucked in toward her chest, and the tiny arms were folded tight to her chest. As Bellin had said, she had no legs, only a finned tail. Another partially formed fin was on her back. "She couldn't have lived," Sylve confirmed, and Thymara nodded.

Veras stretched her neck and Sylve reached out and, as gently as she could, rolled the child into the dragon's mouth. Veras closed her jaws and immediately turned her head aside and wheeled away from the ship. It was done.

CARSON HAD DECIDED to act on the assumption that Greft was attempting to head back to Trehaug. "Where else could he go?" he asked Sedric. "He's a man in failing health, alone. He doesn't have a lot of choice. One of his options was to remain with us. He decided against that. He must have felt there was too much hostility for him to endure. That makes me wonder why he'd try to get back to Trehaug. I doubt he'd be treated any better there. He's looking at traveling a long, hard way alone, to die among the people who rejected him in the first place."

Sedric nodded silently. He had a guilty theory of his own, one he kept to himself. He hoped he was wrong.

They had been backtracking through the reeds and shallow water, though how Carson knew where to go, Sedric could not have said. For days, the scenery had seemed unendingly the same to him. From time to time, Carson would say something like, "See, the dragons trampled that area flat when they came through here," or, "Remember that stand of rushes with the three blackbird nests in a row? We passed that late yesterday."

They had come to an area of scrubby brush on stilt roots. There was no solid ground anywhere, but the feeble current pushed floating branches and twigs and reeds up around the stilt roots where they formed soggy mattresses of plant material. This seemed to be the favorite bedding spots for gallators. The immense, toothy salamanders dozed in clusters in such places, the pallid bodies marked with brilliant stripes of blue and red. The wet-skinned creatures had proven especially vulnerable to dragon venom. Just touching the moist skin of a gallator was death for most creatures, but the dragons ate them with no apparent ill effects.

This area Sedric did remember clearly. Yesterday, the dragons had preceded them, devouring a number of gallators and sending the rest into hiding. But today the dozing creatures did not flee; instead, they lifted their heads and regarded the small boat with hungry interest. Sedric glanced around for Spit, only to discover that this was the time when the dragon had chosen to lag behind. "Carson?" he hissed in quiet warning as two of the gallators launched silently into the water and vanished from sight beneath the surface.

"I saw them," Carson replied as quietly. He lifted his paddle from the water, and Sedric did the same. "Hold tight. They may try to overturn us, but these boats don't flip too easily." He glanced back at the lagging Spit and shook his head ruefully. "Little bastard is using us as chum, to lure the gallators away from cover. That's nice, Spit, real nice." He took a slow, steady breath. "Hold tight to the seat, not the sides. You don't want any part of your body outside the boat. Move as little as you can. The less alive and meaty we look, the better."

Sedric quickly shifted his grip. They sat still, waiting. There was a tentative bump against the bottom of the boat. Sedric tightened his grip on the seat, felt his nails press against the hard wood. Carson was turned on his seat, watching him, a tense grin on his face. A short fishing spear was in his hand. Sedric moistened his lips and felt a second, harder bump, followed by a sideways push. Carson mouthed the words "Be still" at him. That wasn't a problem. He felt too scared to move.

Then came an impact that lifted Sedric's end of the boat out of the water. It settled with a splash and at the same moment, a gallator struck it from the side. The boat tipped far enough to ship some water, but righted itself. The gallator surged at the boat again but could not get its squat-necked head into it. Carson reared back and, with a huff of effort, sank the fishing spear into the thing's neck. It gave a gurgled squeal and fell back into the water. The slime it had left on the side of the boat stank.

"Hang on TIGHT!" Carson's terse warning came just in time. Sedric tightened his grip just as the boat was struck from the other side. His body whipped with the impact, and nearly slammed him against the toxic slime oozing down the side of the boat. A buffet of wind hit them, and then a tremendous splash of water. It soaked Sedric and added more water to what was already in the boat.

It took a few seconds for him to understand that Spit had been briefly airborne. The little silver dragon had actually managed a moment of flight before splashing down beside the boat and nearly swamping it. The cold water had driven the breath from Sedric's lungs. He was still shuddering and gasping when Spit lifted a struggling gallator from the water and joyously sheared it in half. As the two bloody halves fell from his jaws, the dragon darted his head under the water and came up with a second gallator. This one he gripped by its head, and it thrashed wildly, showering water and toxins in a spray. Both Carson and Sedric cowered in the boat, covering their faces until Spit clamped his jaws and the creature stilled in death.

As they sat up cautiously, Spit wolfed down the body of the gallator and then nosed in the water until he came up with the severed halves of the first one. These he ate with evident enjoyment.

"You're welcome," Carson said sarcastically. "I always enjoy being the bait on a hook." But despite his words, Sedric could tell that the hunter was mildly amused by the dragon's strategy and respected him for it. He was still shaking his head over this when Carson said in a low voice, "Oh, sweet Sa, no. I didn't want to find him like that."

Sedric's eyes snapped to his face, then he followed his gaze. There was Greft's boat. It was not quite overturned, but it was tipped up against a tangle of brush. As one, they dug their paddles in and left Spit to his feeding.

Greft was in the boat still. He'd wedged himself in, and the gallators hadn't managed to dislodge him. Some of the venom from a gallator's skin had hit him. His arm was a swollen sausage flung across his chest. Sedric judged that he had tried to ward off a gallator attack and got the venom on his skin.

Carson gingerly grabbed the thwart and pulled the boat so it righted itself. "What a way to die," he observed quietly.

As the boat rocked upright, Greft's eyes slowly opened, seeming to fight an awful lethargy as he slowly turned his gaze on them. His face had puffed around his eyes, and he looked out at them from under a swollen brow.

Sedric stared in horror as Greft's mouth moved. Words drawled out. "St-ole em frm 'er rm." The hand at the end of the sausage arm moved in a slight flipping motion, as if it would gesture at something. "S'all . . . gon naw. Din' mek no-awn rich."

"It's all right, Greft. It's all right." Sedric kept his eyes on Greft's face.

"Greft. You want some water?" Carson had opened his waterskin. Spit had appeared alongside the two boats. Sedric didn't know if the dragon was keeping watch for gallators or hoping to eat Greft's body.

Greft seemed to consider Carson's question for a long time. Then, "Yeah," he managed. Carson leaned across from one boat to the other and directed a tiny stream of water toward Greft's mouth. Greft sucked at the water; then as abruptly as a falling leaf, his head slumped slightly. His eyes didn't close, but Carson abruptly stopped the flow of water, stoppered the skin, and carefully restored it to its place in the boat. "He's dead. The venom causes paralysis. Took a while to stop his whole body, but it did. Horrible way to die."

"Horrible," Sedric agreed faintly.

"Well. Time to clean it up," Carson said grimly.

He lashed the two small boats together and poured water over the sides of both until he'd washed away as much of the gallator's venomous slime as he could. Then he clambered over into Greft's boat and straddling the body, matter-of-factly patted Greft's pockets. He unbuckled the keeper's belt and kept it and the sheathed knife on it. He hadn't carried anything else that Carson considered worth keeping. "Help me with the body," the hunter said, and Sedric didn't ask questions. He took the feet and Carson took the shoulders. They lifted Greft up. Sedric gritted his teeth as the small boat rocked beneath them. The gallators had fled Spit, he hoped, but he still didn't want to fall in.

They didn't even have to put Greft over the side. Spit reached over and took the body in his mouth, then turned and stalked off with him. For a moment, Sedric watched the dragon wade through the shallow water. Greft's head and feet stuck out either side of the dragon's mouth. Greft's head bobbed with every step that Spit took, almost as if he were nodding farewell to them.

When he looked back, Carson was crouched in the bottom of Greft's boat. Like their own, it has shipped some water and he was bailing it out. As items scattered in the bottom of the boat emerged, he picked them up and set them on the seat to drain. There was a broken fishing spear. Carson looked at the snapped shaft and shook his head ruefully. "The head's probably in a gallator on the bottom by now."

There wasn't much to tidy. Greft had been a precise fellow. The same organization and stowing habits that had saved his gear during the wave had preserved it now. Carson opened his canvas pack, glanced inside, and said, "The ship's bread is there, and mostly dry."

In the bottom of the boat was a sturdy cloth sack, drenched. When Carson picked it up, the chink of glass sounded inside it. "What on earth?" Carson muttered, and he untied the draw-string. Sedric's heart sank. Greft's last words had been clear to him. *I stole it from your room. It's gone now. Didn't make anyone rich.* He'd known immediately what the keeper was talking about. He hadn't looked at his dragon parts in days, hadn't wanted to gaze on the vials of blood or the scales he'd taken. He had hoped that Greft's last words had meant he'd thrown them over the side or otherwise lost them. But as Carson pulled the glass ink bottles and the specimen pots out of the sack and set them in a row on the seat, Sedric saw what Greft had meant. They were empty. The bottle that had held the blood had a swirl of scarlet left in the bottom. When Carson tipped it, it was still liq-uid. The color in it still swirled, scarlet on red. "What was this about?" Carson asked no one.

Sedric sat very still. If Carson was aware of how he crouched like a rabbit hoping a hawk would not see him, he gave no sign of it. Sedric looked at the emptied bottles. He was the last one to know what they meant. If he never spoke, then Carson need never know what kind of man he had been and the sort of deceptions he'd practiced. No one need know the full account of how he had deceived those who had trusted him. Deceived those who loved him.

But if he never spoke, then he'd continue being that man. He'd continue deceiving those who trusted and loved him. In-cluding Carson.

His voice sounded rusty when he spoke. "Those were mine, Carson. Greft took them from my room." He cleared his throat, tried to speak, couldn't, and croaked the words out anyway. "They had dragon parts in them. Bits of flesh cut from a dirty wound that Thymara was bandaging. A few scales. And that one held blood." He was choking again, his throat closing with shame. He didn't look at Carson's face. "That was my plan when I came on this trip with Alise. I was going to stay just long enough to get dragon parts to sell, and then I was going back to Bingtown. *I* was going to sell it all to the Duke of Chalced. And then I was going to be rich and I was going to run off with Hest, so we could live as we pleased."

When the words were out, he sat still, staring at the little flasks. He felt as if he had vomited up something foul and it lay, stinking and steaming, between them. He saw Carson's hand touch one of the glass containers and then draw back from it. His voice was always deep. Sometimes, when he was holding Sedric in his arms and he spoke to him, Sedric felt the words vibrate in him, chest to chest, as much as he heard them. But now his voice was the deepest Sedric had ever heard it, and confusion weighted it.

"I don't understand . . . Isn't that what you accused Leftrin of doing? Of using Alise so he could harvest dragon parts? And Jess . . . oh." For two quiet breaths, Carson thought it through. "I see, now. That's why Jess assumed that you'd help him kill Relpda, isn't it? He knew. He thought that you and he could collect parts from her, and then take the boat and head back to Trehaug. Or Chalced. Had you been working together then?"

"Sweet Sa, no! Never!" He looked at Carson's face now and what he saw there clove his heart in two. Carson's face was closed, his eyes unreadable. Waiting. Waiting to hear how he'd been deceived, how he'd been played for a fool. Wondering if even now Sedric had a plan. Sedric had to look down. "Jess knew what I'd done. He saw me come back to the ship one night, saw me throw my bloody clothes away. But I'd . . . I don't know why. I'll never know why. I drank some of Relpda's blood that same night. You thought I'd been poisoned. I hadn't, but the way it affected me, I might as well have been."

He reached back to those days. They seemed distant now, unreal. "A couple of times, I woke up to find Jess in my room. I thought he'd come to check on me, the same way that you and Davvie did. But now I know that he was just there to search. He knew I had this stuff. That day, that day that I . . . I killed him, he'd shown me the red scale from Rapskal's dragon. Alise had given it to me to draw for her journals. But afterward, she forgot about it, and I kept it. Jess knew about it and he found it. He said he hadn't found the other stuff. But I think he'd talked to Greft, and Greft found what Jess couldn't. I think that's why Greft took the boat last night. Not to try to get back to Trehaug. Not even to try to take the stuff to Chalced and sell it. But to try to cure himself with it. To fix what was going wrong inside him."

A long silence followed. When Carson spoke, his voice was slow and careful, as if he were slowly building something, one word at a time. "But it didn't work for him. He drank the blood and ate the scales, but it didn't cure him."

"Maybe it only works when a dragon guides it," Sedric suggested hesitantly. "Or maybe it would have cured him with time. Or maybe it did cure him, but the gallator venom killed him all the same."

"I guess it doesn't matter now," Carson said quietly.

"I'm sorry I didn't trust you. Sorry I didn't tell the whole truth to you from the beginning."

"You didn't know me," Carson conceded. The words were forgiving, but the wall in his voice was still there.

"It's more than that," Sedric said stubbornly. "I was treating Alise exactly as I was accusing Leftrin. I was using her to get close to the dragons, so I could harvest what I wanted, for my own ends. But somehow, when I thought about it, they seemed like two different things. I thought I could use her that way and keep it from her, so she'd never be hurt by it. And in my mind, I thought Leftrin would do that to her and just not care."

He glanced up at Carson. His face was still and closed. "I was stupid, Carson. You know that at first I couldn't even hear the dragons. I thought they were like, well, like clever cows. Why shouldn't I slaughter one and sell off the meat? We slaughter cows all the time. It was only after I had some of Relpda's blood that I could begin to hear her. And to understand what she was, what they all were. If I'd known from the start, if I'd understood, I'd have abandoned the plan immediately."

"Alise."

"What about her?"

"Did you ever think what would become of her after you

took Hest and ran away?" Carson spoke heavily. His hands, strong, calloused, competent, continued the work of tidying up the boat. He shipped the oars neatly, and restowed all of Greft's gear. The little glass bottles remained in an accusing row on the seat.

"A little bit," Sedric conceded. "Not much. I thought that perhaps we could make it look like we were lost at sea. Then she'd be Hest's widow. Part of his money and estate would stay with her, enough for her to live comfortably." He sighed and felt ashamed. "Once I even imagined that if she were pregnant when I left, it would be best of all for everyone. She'd have a child for company, to be an heir for the Finboks, and she'd control his inheritance for him until he came of age."

Carson had finished every conceivable task in the other boat. He remained crouched in it. His dark eyes under his heavy brow wandered over their surroundings. They were hunter's eyes, always seeking, always wary. There were still several gallators watching them, but the creatures were keeping their keenest watch on Spit. He had finished eating and was splashily cleaning himself as he watched the other gallators. Evidently not even two gallators and a human had filled his belly. The noises of the silver's ablutions were the only sounds for a time.

Sedric found himself meeting Carson's dark stare. The hunter spoke carefully. "I know you finally told Alise about you and Hest. Did you ever tell her this part? About coming here to butcher dragons and sell the meat to Chalced?"

"No. I didn't." By an effort, he didn't look away. "I didn't have the courage."

Carson took in a deep breath through his nose and slowly let it out. He gathered the little bottles into his hands and held them out to Sedric. Sedric received them in his cupped hands. Carson settled himself on the rowing bench, untied the rope that had bound the two boats together, and then took up a paddle. "You can't really begin something new until you've finished with the old, Sedric."

He dug the paddle into the water and moved his boat clear of Sedric's. Spit, sensing they were returning to the barge, made a futile charge at the gallators. They retreated into the sunken roots of the brush where the dragon could not get at them. He gave a roar of frustration and then gave it up to follow Carson's boat. Sedric watched them go. Neither one looked back at him.

Sedric dropped the little bottles into the bottom of the boat. They floated in the water that he had not bailed out. With his feet, he pushed them aside. Then he settled himself on the seat, took up a paddle, and followed Carson. Rain began to fall.

$\diamond \quad \diamond \quad \diamond$

Day the 27th of the Gold Moon

Year the 6th of the Independent Alliance of Traders

From Erek, Keeper of the Birds, Bingtown
To Detozi, Keeper of the Birds, Trehaug

From the Bingtown Traders' Council to the Rain
Wild Traders' Councils at Trehaug and Cassarick,
being a formal request, at the behest of the Meldar
and Kincarron families, to inquire into the fate of the
Tarman expedition, especially as to the well-being of
Sedric Meldar and Alise Kincarron.

Detozi,

*I am delighted with your family's invitation and will speedily
make arrangements for my duties to be taken on temporarily
by one of the other keepers for the length of my visit. I am sure
that you know your family assured me I was welcome to call
"on any date, for so long as I wished to stay," but I thought
to ask your advice in this matter. The weather here has been
unseasonably warm and fair, but we all know that cannot last
forever! I know that the rainy season will soon be upon all of us.
Am I too forward in suggesting that I would like to visit while
our fine weather holds? What would your preference be for the
timing of my visit?*

Erek

$\diamond \quad \diamond \quad \diamond$

CHAPTER NINETEEN

MUD AND WINGS

Toward midmorning, Tarman wedged and could go no farther. Leftrin was not surprised. He'd been expecting it to happen for some time. All of yesterday, Tarman's feet had been firmly planted on the bed of the slough. A few of the keepers had become seasick from the rocking motion that Tarman's walk contributed to his movement. As the day had progressed and the water grew ever shallower, Leftrin's concern had increased. He'd sounded the horn to call all of the small boats back to the barge, and then sent them out again in varying directions, in search of deeper water.

When they'd returned that evening, no one had good tidings to report. No detectible current, and the water seemed uniformly shallow in all directions. A straw dropped into the open water beside the boat did float away, but almost immediately got lost in the beds of standing reeds that had encroached ever closer, even as the bluish foothills remained ever distant against a gray backdrop of thick clouds.

The barge stopped of his own accord. For a time, Leftrin sensed the ship standing and thinking. Tarman groped toward him, perhaps seeking an idea that Leftrin didn't have. Then, with a very small lurch, Tarman folded his legs and settled in the mud. The barge he had carried on his back floated slightly now. A wave of sadness and resignation flowed up Leftrin's chest and settled around his heart. They'd come to their stopping place. It wasn't Kelsingra.

"Cap?" This from Swarge at the tiller. It had been weeks since anyone had kept up the illusion that Tarman needed to be poled through the water. Tarman usually appreciated the humans' efforts to speed him along, but in water this shallow, the poling only threw him off stride.

"Take a break, Swarge," Leftrin confirmed. He made a sound like a low growl in the back of his throat and gripped the bow rail tighter. He more felt than saw Alise coming down the deck to join him. When she reached his side, she halted and put her hands alongside his on the railing. Her eyes swept the scene before them.

There was no channel. Reeds, rushes, and those plants that loved swamps surrounded them. The dragons were bright-scaled giants who moved through the wrong landscape. Even yesterday, the dragons had still ostensibly led the way. For most of this morning, they had moved more slowly and uncertainly. No one was comfortable about venturing deeper into this borderless wet land. Yet there was no where else to go. Except . . .

"Do we go back?" Alise asked softly.

Leftrin didn't reply. Two scarlet darning needles flew past them, their wings making a tiny whickering sound. They danced around a nearby bed of reeds before settling, one upon the other, on a seedhead. In the distance, he heard very faintly the cry of a hawk. He glanced up, but the overcast blocked even a glimpse of the sky. The dragons wandered disconsolately around the barge. He wondered what they were hunting. Frogs? Small fish? As the water had grown shallower, the food sources had become smaller and swifter to elude predators. Everyone was hungry, and the keepers felt the hunger of the dragons as well as their own.

"To what?" he asked.

"Perhaps to the other tributary?" Alise ventured the suggestion cautiously.

"I don't know," he admitted. "I wish Tarman could speak to me more clearly. I don't think the other tributary is the answer. But I just don't know anymore."

"Then . . . what will we do?"

He shook his head unhappily. All he had were questions and no answers. Yet every life in his care depended on him having answers, or at least making good guesses. Right now he had no confidence in his ability to do either. Had he guessed wrong when he'd brought them this way? But he hadn't guessed at all. He'd listened to his ship, and Tarman had seemed so confident. But now, here they were. They'd run out of river. They still had plenty of water, but it sheeted over the saturated land, and he could no longer guess where it came from. Perhaps a million tiny streams fed it. Perhaps it just welled to the surface in this immense basin. It didn't matter.

In addition, in the last few days the mood of the expedition had soured. Perhaps all of them had just spent too much time in one another's company. Perhaps the battering wave and the losses they'd endured had demoralized them to the point at which they could not recover. Perhaps it was the lowering weather. He didn't know what had affected their spirits so, but it showed, in both keepers and crew. He thought it had begun the evening when Carson and Sedric had returned with the boat to report Greft's death. Carson had delivered the news to all of them as they sat on the deck with their meager rations of food. Carson had reported it flatly, and not apologized or explained that he'd fed the body to his dragon. No one challenged that; perhaps, for keepers, that was what they now expected. Sedric had looked drained and beaten; perhaps he had finally seen too much. Maybe his Bingtown shell had cracked, and some humanity was seeping in. Carson had made his report, formally returned the stolen ship's bread to him, and then announced he was going to get some sleep. But the weariness on his old friend's face did not look like the kind of tiredness that would yield to sleep.

Leftrin had looked from Carson's weary face to Sedric's hangdog expression and formed his own impression. Well, that was too damn bad. The Bingtown dandy had finished with him, and the hunter was taking it hard. Carson deserved better fortune.

But then, didn't they all?

The news of Greft's death had dampened the spirits of all. None of the keepers, not even Tats or Harrikin, seemed to take any satisfaction in it. Tats had looked almost guilty. And Jerd had spent the rest of the evening sitting near the port railing, weeping quietly. After a time, Nortel had gone and sat beside her and spoken to her in a low voice until she leaned her head on his shoulder and allowed him to comfort her.

And that was another thing he had his own thoughts on. Bellin had told Swarge she was going to speak to the girls, and Swarge had passed it on to him. He hoped she had. He'd been relieved that the girl had been all right after her miscarriage and saddened at the loss of the little one. He refused even to guess how hard that had been for Bellin and Swarge. He'd lost track of how often Bellin had been pregnant. Not a one had come to term.

Greft's boat had sat idle on the deck for two days after that until he'd brusquely ordered Boxter and Kase to divvy out the hunting supplies and then take it out and make themselves useful. It wasn't his place to do so, but they'd obeyed him. And having at least some of the keepers out hunting was much better than the whole crew of them idle and brooding on his decks.

"We've lost heart," Alise said, as if replying to his thoughts. "All of us."

"Even the dragons?"

"The dragons have changed. Or maybe how I see them has changed. They've become far more independent since they survived the wave. Maybe it was because they were instrumental in saving most of us. Once the roles were reversed, it was like the severing of a tie that had worn thin. Some are more arrogant, and others almost ignore their keepers. Of course the most shocking changes are in Relpda and Spit."

"I'll say. They've gone from being lumpish creatures who the keepers could barely push along each day to being, most definitely, dragons. That little bastard Spit is a danger to himself and everyone else since he discovered he could spit toxins. His accuracy leaves a lot to be desired, and he doesn't take kindly to correction from anyone. I preferred him the way he was. I appreciate Carson stepping up to try to manage him; he's the man for a job like that, if there is one. But even he can't keep a lid on that steam-pot forever. Sooner or later he's going to hurt someone."

A hawk cried in the distance. Several of the dragons turned their heads toward it. He wondered if they envied the bird's flight and wondered if he turned the barge back, seeking for deeper water, would they follow him? Or would they stalk off into the bog, seeking a way to drier land? He glanced at the sky again and wondered if he should hope for rain. Enough rain would lift the barge so they could push on. It would also raise the water that surrounded the dragons. How long could they last with no dry land to rest on? He pushed away his doubts and fears. "I'll make a decision tomorrow morning," he told her.

"Until then?" She looked up into his face, and he saw how he had changed her. It wasn't the roughened hair that mattered to him, nor how her freckles had spread and darkened. For him, it was all in her eyes. There was a question there, but there was no fear. None at all.

"Until then, my dear, we live."

THYMARA SAT IN the dimness of Alise's room. She had asked earlier if she might borrow it for an hour or so, and the Bingtown woman had readily agreed, assuming that Thymara wished to bathe in warm water in privacy. But that was not her mission. Instead she had begged Sylve to come with her.

"I don't see how I'm going to be a help, Thymara. It's almost as dark as night in here."

"We're out of candles completely. Bellin said that if the hunters bring in any sort of an animal with fat, she'll make some rushlights. But until then . . ." Thymara heard her voice, how quickly she spoke and how it was pitched higher than normal. Perhaps Sylve heard the fear, too.

"Let me look at your back, Thymara, and see how bad it is. I know you don't like people to fuss over you, but if it's infected, and has been for this long, well, you need to have someone open up the injury and clean it out. You can't just let it keep festering."

Sylve kept talking as Thymara pulled off her shirt and then unknotted the strips of rags she'd tied at her chest. Experience had taught her that this part was best done quickly. She took a deep breath and then snatched the rag free, gasping as she did so. The ooze from the injury on her back never seemed to cease and always glued the bandaging to her skin. Sylve made an exclamation of sympathy and then asked pragmatically, "What have you been doing for this?"

"I try to wash it every couple of days. Sometimes it's hard to find a place that's private."

"Are you heating the water or just standing in the river?"

"Usually just standing in the river. I wash out the rags and then use them to sponge a trickle of water over it. Then I bandage it up again."

"I can't see a thing in here. Turn this way, so the light from that little window . . . Oh." Sylve's hands were cool on her bare shoulders as she turned Thymara in the small space of Alise's chamber.

The sudden silence that followed her exclamation chilled Thymara even more. "How bad is it?" she asked roughly. "Just tell me."

"Well." Sylve took a ragged breath. "This isn't an injury, Thymara. Maybe it started out as one, but it isn't now. It's a change. Mercor told me that sometimes, when a human's skin and blood are open, a dragon's influence can be stronger. Stronger than intended, even. He told me about it because I cut my hand and when I came to tend him that day, he said I should stay away from him for a day or two."

Thymara tried to settle her breath and couldn't. "What kind of a change?"

"I don't know, exactly. I'm going to poke at you a bit. I hope I don't hurt you, but I have to do it."

"Just do it and get it over with, Sylve." An edge of anger crept into her voice despite her effort to sound resigned.

It didn't rattle Sylve. "I know you're not angry at me. Stand still, now."

She felt one of Sylve's cool, scaled hands track down her spine from the nape of her neck to the middle of her back.

"That didn't hurt? Good. It looks like it's all sound flesh, but it's scaled heavily and it's . . . I don't know . . . it's different from how a human's back should be. It stands up like it's more muscled or something. Now, to either side of that space . . ." Thymara hissed and flinched wildly and Sylve took her hands away. "Um, there are these two, uh, slashes. They match. Each is about the span of my hand long, and the edges are all ridged. And— please, stand still again."

She felt Sylve's cold hands again, and then, as Sylve picked at something, Thymara gave a sudden yelp and curled forward, clenching her teeth and eyes. A burning pain spread out from whatever Sylve had done. When Sylve spoke, it sounded as if her own teeth were clenched. "Sorry, Thymara. So sorry. I shouldn't have done that; it looks like you're bleeding a bit now. But there's— there's something inside each of the slashes."

"Something what? Dirt? Infection?"

Sylve took a deep shaking breath. "No. Something growing. Something bony like, well, like fingers or something. Thymara, you should go to Bellin or Alise. Or even Mercor. Someone who knows more than me has to look at this and tell you what to do. It's bad. It's really bad."

Thymara didn't bother with her rag bandage. She snatched up her shirt and pulled it on, heedless of how much pain the sudden movement cost her. "Don't tell!" she insisted hoarsely. "Please, Sylve, don't tell. Don't tell anyone until I have a chance to think about this." *And talk to that damn dragon.* "Promise me you won't tell anyone."

"Thymara, you have to tell. Something has to be done."

"Don't tell, Sylve. Please. Don't tell."

Sylve ground her teeth. "All right. I won't tell."

But just as Thymara began to relax, Sylve added, "I won't tell *yet*. I'll wait one day. One day only. Then I go to Bellin. You can't ignore this, Thymara. It won't go away on its own."

"I won't ignore it. I promise. Just give me a day, Sylve. Just give me a day."

"ALISE, I HAVE to talk to you. Do you have time for me?"

Sedric's request was oddly formal. Alise looked up from her work on the galley table. It was twofold. Boxter had snared half a dozen small waterfowl in the dawn and brought them back to the barge. She had prepared most of them for the pot, and they were already simmering. The final two, a male and a female, were carefully spread out on the table. She was sketching them into her journal and making notes on size, coloring, and what had been in their diminutive stomachs. She'd never seen ducks like these. The males sported a crest of bright blue feathers. She lacked any colored ink so she'd noted the colors adjacent to her sketch. As she looked up questioningly at Sedric, he added abruptly, "I'd have sketched those for you. All you had to do was ask."

"Well. Sometimes asking someone to do something is harder than doing it myself," she observed stiffly. She looked at him and desperately tried to see her old friend. A dozen times, she'd forgiven him. And a dozen times, she'd awakened in the night or looked up from some task to realize that she was gritting her teeth as she relived some incident from the past, now colored with the knowledge that Sedric had given her.

She now believed she knew which of her friends and acquaintances had been aware of Hest's true preferences. And which ones had not only known about Hest but about his relationship with Sedric. It all seemed so obvious now. The chance remarks that had once been mystifying were now barbed. The social slights now made sense. She remembered Trader Feldon chok-

ing on his wine when his young wife had sympathetically asked
Alise about her efforts to get pregnant. She had thought he was
embarrassed. Now she was certain he'd been trying to drown a
chuckle at the prospect of her bedding Hest. The memory and
her new interpretation of it blasted into her mind as she looked
at Sedric. He'd been at that dinner party, seated on Hest's left.

As she looked at him, he seemed to feel the same chill she
did. He pinched his lips together for a moment, and then shook
his head, denying something. "Alise, I need to talk to you," he
repeated.

She sighed. "I'm here." She set down her pencil.

Sedric's nose twitched as he looked at the stiff little bodies.
She heard a shushing noise; rain was falling, peppering the face
of the surrounding waters. Sedric stepped to the galley door
and shut it firmly. Then he sat down at the table across from her
and set a worn canvas bag on the table. He folded his hands together and then announced, "When I'm finished, you're going
to think even less of me than you do now. But you'll also have
every explanation that is owed to you for the ways I've behaved.
And it will be done. I'll have nothing else left to apologize for,
no more dirty secrets that I'll have to dread you discovering
some day."

She clasped her own hands. "That's not a reassuring way to
begin a conversation." Dread was already rising inside her.

"No. It's not. Here it is, Alise. When Hest told me I had to
accompany you here, I was furious. And hurt, because he was
doing it to punish me for taking your part. I'd insisted it was
only fair that you be allowed to travel up the Rain Wild River. I
reminded him, once too often, that he had agreed to it as part of
your marriage agreement." He paused very slightly, but she gave
him no sign that this swayed her in any way. "When I knew
it was inevitable that I must go with you to see your 'damned
dragons,' I recalled a Chalcedean merchant who had approached
Hest and me months before. He very cautiously approached the
idea that Hest might have connections to Rain Wild Traders
who might be able to procure dragon parts." He glanced up
at her and met her eyes. "You know that since the Duke of

Chalced began to age and fail, he has sought for remedies to prolong his life and restore his health."

She replied quietly. "I know all about his offers to buy such things."

He looked down again. "I contacted the merchant. I told him where I was going. He supplied me with what he thought I would need. Specimen bottles and preservatives. A list of the most desirable parts." He lifted his chin suddenly and said stubbornly, "I accompanied you on this expedition determined to harvest those parts. With them, I intended to make my fortune, and then to persuade Hest to leave you and come away with me."

She sat very still, waiting for the rest of it.

"What I accused Leftrin of planning, I actually did. I used you to get close to the dragons. I took scales and blood, even small pieces of flesh from when Thymara cleaned the wound on the copper dragon. I hid them in my room." As he spoke, he reached into the canvas bag. One at a time, he took out several small glass bottles and set them on the table. One had a tinge of red stain down it. "I intended to take them back to Bingtown, to meet up with the Chalcedean merchant, and make a fortune."

He stopped there.

After a moment, she realized he was waiting for her. She took up one of the empty bottles and turned it in her hands. "What did you do with them?"

"Greft stole them from me. When he fled with the boat. They're gone forever, now." He gestured at the glass vials. She suppressed a shudder and set the one in her hand back on the table with a small *clink*.

"Why are you telling me this now?"

He paused, then said unwillingly, "Carson. He said I needed to finish old things before I could start something new. This is part of that."

"You're finishing with me."

"No. No, that's not it at all. I don't want to lose you, Alise. I know that it's probably not possible, but somehow I'd like to go back to being the sort of friend I once was to you. Being that person from my side, if you see what I mean, even if you can't feel about me as you once did. Somehow I went from being your friend to someone who could participate in deceiving you, could even exploit you just to get close to the dragons. I don't want to be that person anymore. Telling you is a way of destroying him. Telling you about someone like him is something the old Sedric would have done, back when he was really your friend."

"You mean before Hest got to him. Before Hest got to either of us." She lifted a hand and rubbed her brow. It gave her a moment to cover her eyes, a brief time of being alone with her own thoughts. It wasn't really fair to blame it all on Hest. Was it? She and Sedric had gone their own ways before he came along and joined their lives again in such a bizarre fashion. She tried to remember how she had once thought of Sedric. In those years when their lives had taken separate paths, she'd recalled him fondly and smiled over her girlhood infatuation with him. Whenever she chanced to see him, in the market or visiting mutual friends, she'd always felt a leap of pleasure at the sight of him and always greeted him warmly.

His presence, she slowly realized, had been the only pleasant part of her marriage to Hest. She tried to imagine the past few years without him. What if she had been marooned in her marriage to Hest without Sedric's presence in the house, without his thoughtfulness and conversation at meals? He had, she recalled, been Hest's adviser in the gifts chosen for her, in her access to the scrolls and books that had made her life tolerable. In some ways, they had been two animals in the same trap. If he had some responsibility for her falling into Hest's power, he at least had done what he could to ameliorate her misery.

And he had helped to win this journey for her. At what must have seemed a terrible price to him.

It had been a chain of events that led to her finding Leftrin. That led to her finding both love and a life.

With a fingertip, she touched the red-stained bottle. Then she frowned, leaned forward, and picked up the one next to it. It was slightly larger than the others. Something winked at her from inside it. She held it up to the light from the galley window and peered at it. She shook it. It didn't move, but there was no mistaking what it was.

Then, with a strength that surprised him, she smashed it on the edge of the galley table. Shards of glass went flying, and Sedric instinctively put up his hands to shield his face. "Sorry," she muttered, shocked at her own impulsiveness. With cautious fingers, she separated the shattered glass until the bottle bottom was revealed. Carefully she plucked out the single small copper-edged scale that had remained stuck inside the bottle. She held it to the light. It was almost transparent.

"A scale," he said.

"Yes."

With a table rag, she wiped the shards of glass off the planks and into the waste bucket that held the guts and feathers of the birds she'd cleaned. Then, from her trouser pocket, she took the locket.

"You kept it?" He was stunned.

"I did. I didn't know why. Perhaps to remind me of how stupid I had been." She glanced at him from under lowered lashes. "But perhaps you need the reminder even more than I do."

She opened the locket, and Hest peered out at both of them, his supercilious smile no longer handsome at all, only mocking. She lifted the tiny bundle of silk-secured black hair and set it aside as she had earlier set aside the guts she'd pulled out of the dead birds. Then she picked up the knife she'd used to disjoint the fowls, slid it under Hest's portrait and popped the little image free. She carefully placed the copper-edged scale inside the locket case and snapped it shut. ALWAYS said the small case. She held it up on its chain. "Always," she said to Sedric, holding it out.

After a brief hesitation, he took it from her. For a moment, he held the trinket in his hand. Then he looped the chain over his neck and slid the locket inside his shirt. "Always," he agreed.

She rose so he wouldn't see her eyes filling up. Could it be that simple to be done with the old and finally begin clean with the new? She lifted the lid off the kettle and gave the soup a stir.

It was barely simmering. She'd have to ask the keepers to go out and bring her back anything that might burn if they wanted cooked food tonight. She opened the front of the little stove and scowled at the dying coals. "We need fuel," she said, to be saying anything.

"Here's something we can burn," Sedric said and flipped the tiny portrait into the fire. She hadn't seen him pick it up and look at it. It landed in the fire, and a single flame flared up briefly before the image curled and blackened. "And here's something else." The lock of Hest's black hair landed on the dying coals and singed. Smoke rose from it and she hastily slammed the door of the stove.

"Oh, that stinks!" she exclaimed.

Sedric sniffed. "He does, doesn't he?"

She covered her mouth and nose, and then she laughed around her hand. To her surprise, Sedric joined her, and suddenly they were both laughing together as they had not in Sa knew how long. Then somehow, he was crying instead, and her arms were around him, and she found she was crying, too. "It's going to be all right," she managed to say to him. "It's going to be all right. I've got you, my friend. We'll be fine."

AFTER SYLVE HAD left the room, Thymara had spent some time alone in the darkness crying. It was stupid and useless. She'd done it anyway. And when she was sure that all her tears had been used, that all of her sorrow had been converted to anger, she left the little room and went in search of Sintara.

She went to the bow rail and located the dragons. They were not far from the barge. Some of them were lying down next to one another, each one's chin cradled on the next dragon's back. It looked sociable and peaceful, but she knew the truth. It was the only way the dragons could rest their legs and sleep without their heads dipping into the water. Sintara was not sleeping. She was moving slowly through a reed bed, peering down into the water. Probably hoping for a frog or a fish. Or anything made of meat. The recent rainfall had washed the dragons clean. The

afternoon sun had broken through the overcast and glittered on
Sintara. Despite her anger, Thymara could not help but see the
beauty of her dragon.

Light ran and shivered along her blue scales. When she moved
her head, there was grace and danger in every ripple of muscle.
Despite her size, despite the fact that she was not a creature
made for the water, she edged through it soundlessly. *Beautiful
death-dealer,* she thought, and the now-familiar sensation of the
dragon's effortless glamour washed through her. She was the
loveliest creature Thymara had ever seen.

Thymara groped frantically and then angrily for her sense of
self. Yes. Sintara was the most beautiful creature in the world.
And the most thoughtless, selfish, and cruel! She shook herself
free of the dragon's charm, seized Tarman's railing, and clambered over it.

The keeper boats were tethered to Tarman's ladder. She didn't
bother with any of them. The *Tarman* was aground, and here the
water varied from waist- to knee-deep. *Just enough water to make
everyone perfectly miserable,* she told herself, and jumped down
into it. Her feet sank more deeply into silt than she'd expected
and she knew a moment's panic. But the water was not even
waist-deep, and she used the instant of fear to fuel her anger.
She wasn't going to cry or whine. Not this time. Maybe not
ever again.

She looked around, saw that Sintara was still hunting, and
made her purposeful way toward her. When she reached the
reed bed, she pushed her way through it, not caring how she
splashed or that she was most likely ruining what little hunting there was for the hungry dragon. Had Sintara ever thought
about what she was ruining for Thymara? She doubted it. She
doubted that Sintara had ever considered what any of her actions
might mean to Thymara or any other human.

"Stop being so noisy!" the dragon hissed at her as she drew
nearer.

Deliberately Thymara splashed through the water until she
stood directly in front of the incensed dragon. Sintara drew her
head up to her full height, looked down on the girl, and slightly

opened her wings. "What is wrong with you? There is little enough hunting here, and you have chased away every fish or frog in this reed bed!"

"You are what is wrong with me! What have you done to me?"

"I? I've done nothing to you!"

"Then what is this? What is this change in me?" Thymara stripped off her shirt angrily and presented her back to Sintara.

"Those. Oh. They're not finished."

"What is not finished? Sylve said it looked like I had fingers growing in gashes inside my back!"

"Fingers!" The dragon trumpeted her amusement. "Fingers? No. Wings. Here, let me see."

Thymara was too shocked to move. Wings. Wings. The word was suddenly nonsense. It meant nothing to her. Wings. Wings on her back. "But I'm a human," she said stupidly. She could feel the dragon's breath on her bared skin.

"You are, for now. But when you have finished changing, you'll be an Elderling. With wings. The first one ever, if my recollections are correct. They are still not mature, but . . . can you move them? Have you tried to move them at all?"

"Move them? I didn't even know I had them!" She had cried herself out earlier; shed every tear she had over her sorrow at her disfigurement. What had it meant to her earlier this afternoon? That she was a freak and a monster. That she would never dare bare her body to any man; no, not before any person at all. Fingers growing on her back. But they weren't fingers. They were wings. And the stupid dragon who had caused them to grow there without even asking her was now wondering if she could *move* them.

Tears threatened again, and she couldn't say what kind they were. Fear? Anger? Her heart was leaping against her ribs.

"Try to move them," Sintara insisted, and her voice was full not of concern but only curiosity. Thymara felt a puff of breath against her bare back and shivered, and suddenly felt the twitch of something on her back.

"What is that?" she cried, hunching away from her own body.

But now it hurt, as if she had wrenched her back or sprained a finger joint. Something connected to her spine was cramped, jammed, and painful. She writhed, and with horror felt a trickle of warm fluid run down her back, and then a damp weight hung limply against her back.

"What is it?" she cried out. She dared not and yet she must. She reached over her shoulder and touched something that felt like sticks bundled in wet cloth. "NO!" she cried, and as her body jerked with shock, she felt the other wing break free of its concealment. "No!" she said more faintly. She started to cover her face with her hands and found herself staring at a coating of thin blood on her fingers. She shuddered. That was a mistake. The things on her back twitched and shook. They were part of her. Foreign and monstrous and part of her. She could feel the summer air on them, feel Sintara's snort of amusement as she said, "Well. I'd expected better than that."

"I didn't expect them at all!" Thymara shouted at her. "How can you do this to me? *Why* would you do this to me?"

"I didn't intend to!" the dragon admitted. For that moment, she sounded almost flustered. Then anger won as she said, "You did it to yourself, if you must know. You were careless. When you pulled the rasp snakes from me, my blood spattered on you. Some must have gone in your mouth. From that time on, I felt you more intensely. You must have felt that our shared awareness grew! How could you not?"

"I thought it was just . . . just what keepers and dragons felt. But why did you do this to me?"

"I didn't. I didn't want to change you then; I hadn't planned to. Usually, a dragon is very selective in who she chooses to accept as an Elderling. Such a change is an honor reserved for the most devoted, the most loyal and intelligent of humans. In ancient times, humans vied for such attention granted by a dragon. They didn't just fall into it by virtue of being given the care of a dragon as if it were a menial chore!"

"Then why did you do it? Why?" Tears were running down her face. Their voices had carried. She heard keeper voices lifted querulously, heard the rumble of dragons. She didn't care, didn't care if the others were watching from the deck of the *Tarman,* didn't care if the other dragons were disturbed and drawing near to see what the fuss was. This was between her and Sintara, and she intended to have it out, once and for all.

"You began changing yourself! You dreamed of flying more than I did! I was not even thinking of changing you. When Mercor pointed out to me that you were changing, I took pity on you. That's all. You should be grateful! They will be quite beautiful when they are finished, almost a mirror to my own. And I, I will have the first winged Elderling! No other dragon has ever created such a creature."

Thymara craned her neck to try to look over her shoulder. The dragon sounded so pleased with herself. Were the wings actually beautiful? Should she feel herself honored rather than made monstrous? No matter how she twisted her head, all she could see was the wet tip of something that reminded her of a rain-soaked parasol. Timidly she reached back with both hands. Wings. She felt skin stretched over bone and cartilage, but strangest of all, when she touched them, she felt herself, just as she did when she touched her own hands.

She dared herself, took hold of them, and tried to stretch them out. No. No, that was like bending her fingers the wrong way. She twitched a shoulder and instinctively folded her wings back in tight to her back. Tight to her back, yes, but not concealed as they had been. Folded smooth to her body, even as Sintara's wings or a bird's wings fit flush to her back. "Will they . . . will they grow more?" She dared herself and then asked boldly, "Will I be able to fly some day?"

"Fly? Don't be ridiculous. No. They're much too small. But they will be lovely, as lovely as mine. All will envy you."

"Why can't they grow larger? Why couldn't they grow large enough for me to fly? I want to fly!"

"Why are you daring to ask for more than you've been given?" The dragon had gone from being bemused at what she had created to being angry again. Thymara thought that perhaps the truth slipped out when Sintara demanded, "Why do you think you should be able to fly when I cannot?"

"Perhaps because it would only make sense to me that any changes you made in me would be useful to me!"

"You will be pretty! And interesting to other dragons. And that is enough for any Elderling, let alone a human!"

"Perhaps 'pretty' wings are enough for you, but if I must bear their weight and the inconvenience of having something growing out of my backbone, perhaps they should be useful. I have never understood why you don't even try to use your wings. I see the other dragons stretching and working theirs. I've seen the silver almost lift himself from the water with his, and he began with a much more ungainly body and smaller wings than yours! You don't try! I groom your wings and keep them clean. They've grown larger and stronger and you could try, but you don't. All you do is tell me how lovely they are. And lovely they may be, but have you never considered trying to use them for what they are intended?"

She could see the dragon's fury build. She'd dared to criticize her, and Sintara could not tolerate even the implication that she was lazy or self-pitying or perhaps even just a bit . . . "Stupid."

Thymara said the word aloud. She had no idea what prompted her to do it. Perhaps simply to show Sintara that she'd gone too far and that her keeper would no longer be terrorized by her. How dare she put wings on her back when she could not even master the ones that had grown naturally on her own?

The murmur of voices from the barge was growing louder. Thymara refused even to glance in that direction. She stood, her bunched shirt clutched over her breasts, and faced the furiously spinning eyes of her dragon. Sintara was magnificent in her wrath. She lifted her head and opened her jaws wide, displaying the brightly colored poison sacs in her throat. She opened her wings wide, a reflexive display of size that the dragons often used in an attempt to remind one another of their relative sizes and strengths, and they spread like magnificent stained-glass panels unfolding. For a moment, Thymara was dizzied by her glory and her glamour. She nearly fell to her knees before her dragon.

Then she took a grip on herself and stood up to the blast

of pure charisma that Sintara was radiating at her. "Yes. They are beautiful!" she shouted. "Beautiful and useless! As you are beautiful and useless!" A shudder passed over Thymara. She felt suddenly queasy and then realized what she had done. In a bizarre reaction to Sintara's display, Thymara had spread her own wings. There were shouts of amazement from the keepers on the boat.

Sintara was drawing breath. Her jaws were still wide, and Thymara stood rooted before her, watching her poison sacs swell. If the dragon chose to breathe venom on her, there would be no escape. She stood her ground, frozen with terror and fury.

"Sintara!" The bellow came from Mercor. "Close your jaws and fold your wings! Do not harm your keeper for speaking truth to you!"

"Fight! Fight! Fight!" Spit was trumpeting joyously.

"Quiet, pest!" Ranculos roared at him.

"Do not spray here! The drift will burn me! Blast your own keeper if you wish, Sintara, but spray me and I swear I will burn your wings as full of holes as rotting canvas!" This from small green Fente. The dragon reared onto her hind legs and spread her own wings in challenge.

"Stop this madness!" Mercor bellowed again. "Sintara, hurt not your keeper!"

"She is mine, and I'll do as I wish!" Sintara's trumpet was a shrill whistle of anger.

Despite herself, Thymara clapped her hands over her ears. Terror made her reckless. "I don't care what you do to me! Look what you've already done! You want to kill me? Go ahead, you stupid lizard. Someone else can clear the sucking insects from your eyes, take the leeches off your useless, beautiful wings. Go ahead, kill me!"

Sintara reared up, her wings spread wide, glorious, and potentially deadly. The gleaming spikes that tipped each rib of her wing could, if the dragon willed it, ooze toxins with which she could slash a rival in sky battle. Thymara had a brief moment in which to wonder how she suddenly knew such a thing. Then Sintara screamed like a storm wind. She swept her wings closed, and then as she opened them again, she turned slightly. The wing struck Thymara and sent her flying.

She hit the hard, hard water on her back, felt the agonizing pain as her new wings absorbed that slap. She sank, breathed water, and then her feet found the bottom. She stood up, choking and gasping, her eyes running with silty water and tears. She heard screams from the barge, and Tats shouting, deep, hoarse, and angry, "Thymara! Thymara! Damn you, dragon! Damn you!"

His words did not stall Sintara. She came stalking toward Thymara, her head low now and weaving. "Is that what you wanted, worthless girl? Shall I make you fly again?"

"I warn you, Sintara!" Mercor was bearing down on her. His golden wings were spread, and the light bouncing from them seemed brighter than the sun. Their false eyes seemed to glare.

Choking and coughing, Thymara was backing up as fast as the deepening water would let her, while the angry dragon came on. Sintara's eyes spun with relentless fury.

Overhead, a hunting hawk screamed. And screamed again. Every dragon looked skyward. The hawk was diving down at them, blasting through the air.

"Tintaglia?" Mercor spoke the name in wonder.

"It's red!" someone shouted.

The dragons froze, looking at the sky. Thymara seized her shirt, floating on the water near her. She wiped grit and silt from her eyes and stared upward. A bird had broken free of the clouds. The red hawk was growing larger, larger, larger.

"HEEBY!" she screamed suddenly. "RAPSKAL!"

The scarlet dragon trumpeted a triumphant response. Her folded wings suddenly cracked wide, braking her wild dive. She made three tight, impossible circles over the gawking dragons and the grounded barge. Then, with a beat, beat, beat of her wings, Heeby cut in the other direction, enlarged her orbit, and flew a loop around Tarman and the excited dragons. Her ruby wings seemed as wide as a ship's sails as she slowed gracefully. She flew low, the tips of her wings stirring the standing reeds and rushes. And on her back, a slender scarlet man laughed joyously.

"I've found you!" he shouted, and it was Rapskal's voice, gone a bit deeper but no less wild with optimism. "I've found you, and Heeby found Kelsingra! Come on. Follow us! It's not far! No more than half a day's flight east of here. Follow us! Follow us to Kelsingra!"

✧ ✧ ✧

Day the 10th of the Browning Moon

Year the 6th of the Independent Alliance of Traders

From Erek, Keeper of the Birds, Bingtown

To Detozi, Keeper of the Birds, Trehaug

A message from the parents of Erek Dunwarrow, Keeper of the Birds, Bingtown, to the parents of Detozi Dushank, sealed in wax and marked with the seal of the Dunwarrow Trader family.

Detozi,

Obliterate this note before you deliver this scroll to your parents. I fear I know what is in it. I have spoken of you perhaps too often to my family, and they have listened to many stories about you from your nephew Reyall, my apprentice. Their proposal may be precipitate, when we have not even met yet, but as Trader for our family, my father still has the authority to act independently in such negotiations. I fear this may offend you and your parents. In truth, I fear even more that it will lead you to refuse an offer that I had hoped to make myself, in person, when perhaps you had had the chance to meet and know me better.

My travel arrangements have been made. Before the moon turns again, I will finally meet you. Until I have a chance to speak for myself, I beg you: do not refuse my parents' inopportune offer. Remember, you can always turn me away. At least let me make my own plea before you do so.

Erek

✧ ✧ ✧

CHAPTER TWENTY

KELSINGRA

So why are you writing it all down?"

In some ways, Alise thought, Rapskal had not changed at all. He fidgeted like the restless boy he had been, anxious to stop sitting still and be off doing things. In other ways, it was difficult to look at the tall, slender scarlet creature he had become and see the keeper boy at all. And getting coherent information out of him was like trying to talk to a dragon. Or a small, impatient child.

She sat on the doorstep of what had most likely been a shepherd's hut. Below them, a wide rolling green went down to the edge of a rushing river. She was only slowly adapting to the idea that they had finally arrived. To sit on a hillside, to look across a vista of sloping green meadow down to a swiftly flowing river was strange enough. To stare across the wide breadth of that river and study the ancient buildings of Kelsingra in the distance was surreal.

"HALF A DAY'S flight for a dragon" had proved to be over six days of slow travel for the barge. None of it had been easy. For the first day, Heeby had appeared at intervals, looping over the ship and then flying off in the direction they were to follow. Unfortunately, that route led them to even shallower water. The dragons trudged ahead of them, laboriously plodding through standing water and sticky mud. Tarman lurched after them, scraping along with a terrible teetering gait.

On their second day of travel, the rain had returned in relentless sheets. The insistent drops patterned the still surface of the slough with ever-widening circles that negated one another as they overlapped. When the rain stopped, mists rose and cloaked the world in gray. The fog remained until the rain returned to banish it in a deluge. Dragons and ship groped their way forward through a cloud of wet. Life on the barge became more miserable. The keepers crowded into the galley and crew quarters in an attempt to stay dry, but the damp invaded every cranny of the ship. What food they had was eaten cold; they could find no dry fuel for even a small fire in the ship's stove. Although no outright quarrels broke out, frustration simmered. The sole topic of conversation was Kelsingra, and where Rapskal and Heeby had been, and why they had not come down to the ship and why they had not returned. Speculation chewed all the theories ragged, with no satisfaction for anyone.

"How long can this go on?" Alise had asked Leftrin when they woke to rain for a third morning. He had looked at her oddly.

"Alise, did you never stop to think why this place is called the Rain Wilds? This is our weather for the winter season. It's come a bit early, and we may yet have another spate of sunny days. But we may not. The good side of it is that the water is rising and lifting the barge. But that's also the bad side."

She had grasped it immediately. "The deeper water may make it easier for Tarman to move. But harder for the dragons."

Leftrin had nodded grimly. "The dragons need to get out of the water, but we've seen no sign of even a muddy beach." He rolled from their bed and went to the small window and stared up at the sky. "And I think this downpour is why we didn't see Heeby and Rapskal yesterday. Even if they could fly through this storm, I wonder if they could find us down here."

It had rained all night and half the next day. Once, she thought she heard Heeby give a cry overhead, a sound like a distant hawk. But by the time she reached the deck, there was nothing to be seen in the swirling mist. The dragons were looming shapes alongside the barge. Tarman crept along, moving in the general direction of where Heeby had flown. It was hard to keep their bearings in the rain and the fog. The water was slowly becoming deeper, for both barge and dragons, but was it the rain or had they found a hidden channel? Alise was not certain if Tarman followed the dragons, or if the dragons lingered near him, following his lead. She thought she would go mad from the endless pattering of the rain and the uncertainty.

On the fourth night, she awakened to find Leftrin gone. She'd risen swiftly and found her Elderling gown by touch in the dark. A shivering sense of urgency and excitement trembled through her, though she could not name a reason for it. She left the cabin and found a single rushlight burning on a saucer on the galley table. Bellin had just lit it and was standing near it, blinking sleep from her eyes. "Do you know what's going on?" Alise had asked her.

Bellin shook her head. "Tarman woke me up," she said quietly. "I'm not sure why."

Alise pushed the galley door open against the wind's resistance. The rain struck her full force, a pelting of icy drops that nearly drove her back inside. But Bellin was on her heels, and she would not lose face in front of her. She folded her arms across her chest, bent her head to the driving rain, and felt her way along the deckhouse until she stood on the bow of the ship. Leftrin was there before her. On the deck by his feet, a lone lantern burned the last of their precious oil. Swarge leaned on the railing beside his captain, peering into black night and rain. The skinny shadow clutching herself and shivering proved to be Skelly. As soon as Alise joined the group, Leftrin put a protective arm around her. It was no shelter from the rain, but it was good to share the warmth of his body.

"What is going on?" she asked. "Why did Tarman wake us?"

He pulled her closer in a happy hug. "There's a current. A definite current flowing and we're making our way upriver again. It's getting deeper and stronger by the moment, but it's definitely more than the rainfall. This will connect us to another waterway."

"And the dragons?"

"They're moving along with us."

"In the dark?"

"We've little choice. At the rate at which the water is rising, we need to find where the bank will be and hug it. If we stand still, chances are we'll all be swept away."

She heard what he didn't say. That if the water rose too rapidly, they might still be swept away. Excitement and tension thrummed through the group. Even before dawn rose, the keepers drifted out to join them. Rain drenched them as they huddled on the bow, peering forward into a future too black to see.

Somewhere, the sun rose. The dragons became silhouettes and then, as the rain lessened and the fog returned, moving shapes. When the rain ceased, Alise realized that she could now hear the moving water. It came from all around them, and that terrified her. What if they could not find the bank? What if they were not venturing toward the side of the flow but toward the middle?

When Leftrin grimly ordered his crew to their poles and told the keepers gruffly to get out of the way, her heart sank. The sun rose higher and more light penetrated the mist. The dragons were silvery shades of their colors as they moved majestically beside and behind the ship. Tarman was clearly leading the way now. Alise retreated to the top of the deckhouse, knowing that however much she wished to be at Leftrin's side, his ship needed his complete attention now. Some of the keepers had retreated to the galley and crew quarters to be out of the chill, but Thymara sat cross-legged and staring, while a shivering Sylve stared anxiously at her dragon. The dragons were communicating with one another in low rumbles and occasional whuffs of sound.

Slowly the mist began to rise from the river's face. It was, unmistakably, a river again. The current was visible as dry leaves and broken stalks were borne swiftly away on its flow. As she watched, the water rose higher and then higher on a bank of reeds, and then suddenly the last tips of the plants vanished under the flow. She could hear Thymara breathing next to her, an anxious quaver in each intake. The clouds must have given way overhead, for suddenly a blast of light diffused in the fog. For six breaths, they moved in a world of silver shimmering droplets. The reflected light dazzled her eyes; she could barely make out the dragons.

"TREES!" The cry was a triumphant trumpeting from Mercor. "Bear left! I see trees again."

THYMARA STARED, TRYING to make her gaze penetrate the mist. She was cold. She'd wrapped a blanket around her shoulders, but ever since her wings had moved to the outside of her body, she'd felt chilled. She pulled her blanket-cloak tighter, but it only hugged the frigid framework closer to her back. Would she ever become accustomed to them, ever think of them as her own rather than as something Sintara had attached to her body? She wasn't sure.

She came to her feet at Mercor's announcement of trees. Silent and yearning, she stared with the others. She felt the barge change course and knew a moment of terror as a strange vibration thrummed through the ship. Her leaping heart identified it; Tarman's claws were slipping on the bottom as he lost traction. The barge slewed and Swarge yelled, "Doing my best, Cap!" even before Leftrin bellowed his name. There was a spate of loud splashes, and the barge lurched suddenly as Veras brushed past them, scrambling for shallower water. Tarman's claws caught again and the ship suddenly surged forward so vigorously that Alise sat down hard next to Thymara, who had sunk back down to the top of the deckhouse. The Bingtown woman didn't make a sound, only grabbed Thymara's arm in a painful clench to keep from falling off the deckhouse. An instant later, the motion of the ship suddenly steadied.

The mist burned off as if it had never been. A landscape appeared around them, a place so different that at first Thymara wondered if somehow they'd made a mystical passage to another world. To their right was a river rushing past them, tossing up and carrying off the debris of what had been still swamp but an hour before. The rush of its passage was a loud and joyous noise. To their left, there was a narrower strip of river, rapidly closing as Tarman worked his way closer to the bank. The dragons were moving hastily now, stringing out in a glittering line as they hurried upstream.

But it was the riverbank that Thymara stared at. The land rose. It was not just the trees that towered. The land rose in a way that Thymara had never seen before. She had heard of hills and even mountains and thought she had imagined how they must be. But to stare at land that hummocked upward, higher and higher, was almost more than she could grasp. "Dry land!" Alise breathed beside her. "Tonight we'll camp on dry land. And build a fire! And walk about without getting muddy! Oh, Thymara, have you ever seen anything so beautiful?"

"I've never seen anything so strange," Thymara whispered in awe.

A wild shrill cry startled everyone aboard the ship. Thymara looked up. Heeby's scarlet wings were stretched wide against a blue crack in the cloudy sky. She swooped lower and ever closer. Rapskal's thin shout reached them. "This way! This way!"

"I have never seen anything so beautiful as that," she whispered, and Alise leaned closer to hug her.

"We're nearly there. We're nearly home," she said, and it did not seem at all a strange thing for her to say.

AT LEAST SIX times that day, Rapskal and Heeby flew with them, urging them on and tantalizing them with shouts of "It's not far now! A pity you can't fly!" and other useful bits of information.

As they followed, the land to either side became firmer. The reed beds gave way slowly to ferns and grasses, to boggy meadows and then to low, rolling grasslands that met forested foothills in the distance. The river became wider, and stronger, fed by streams and rivulets as the land rose up around it. The young Rain Wilders had looked out in wonder at vistas and hilly horizons they had heard of in old tales but never seen. They had exclaimed over rocky cliffs seen in the distance, and then shores with sand and rock along the edges. A different sort of forest edged closer to the river, one of small deciduous trees with random groves of evergreen. On one sunny day, a row of toothy mountains had appeared in the distance. And that afternoon they had come to the outskirts of Kelsingra.

Leftrin had nosed Tarman up to the sandy bank. The barge crawled, exhausted, to rest half on the shore and half on the water. The dragons had emerged from the shallows, clambering out and looking around as if they could not believe their good fortune. Most of them promptly found sunning spots and stretched out to rest. Mercor had not paused but had left the water behind, climbing ever higher up the grassy slopes. Sylve had run after him, barely keeping pace with her dragon. The other keepers had climbed down from the barge almost hesistantly and stared around at a landscape completely foreign to them. High up the slope behind them, Mercor had suddenly reared up on his hind legs and trumpeted out his triumph. On the riverbanks below him, the other dragons had lifted their heads and wearily returned his challenge. And Alise had stared, torn between triumph and heartbreak, at the towering ruins of Kelsingra . . .

On the other side of the swift-flowing river.

"I'm writing it down for posterity. Just as we know from the journals and letters of the time how Trehaug was founded, so will my journal one day tell our descendants how Kelsingra was rediscovered. By you and Heeby. You want your descendants to know that, don't you?"

She'd had a night and part of a day to recover from her initial disappointment. The city was not that far away. As soon as he could, Leftrin would find a way to get her there. In the meanwhile, he had other duties to his ship, his crew, and the keepers. And so did she. She'd practically had to strong-arm Rapskal to pull him away from the other keepers, but she had insisted. "It has to be recorded, while it is still fresh in your mind. There are so many things that we think we'll remember clearly, or we think that everyone will 'always' know. It won't take long, Rapskal, I promise. And then whoever comes after us will always know the tale about what you did."

Now she waited while the boy shifted restlessly and tried to order his thoughts. He had changed so much, and yet so little. His skin was scarlet, scaled fine as a brook trout, and he seemed to have grown. He was leaner and more muscled and completely unaware of how his tattered clothes scarcely covered his flesh.

Rapskal's uplifted eyes followed Heeby's flight. The dragon was hunting the hills and cliffs across the river. Alise followed his gaze with longing. It was all there, just as she had seen it in the Elderling tapestry on the walls of the Traders' Concourse. The sun touched the glittering stone of the map tower and glinted off the domes of the majestic buildings. She longed to be there, to walk the wide streets, to ascend the steps and see what wondrous artifacts the Elderlings had left for them to discover. Leftrin had explained to her a dozen times that the current swept deep and wild along that shore. On this side of the river, it had been easy to nose Tarman ashore. Over there, the current ran swift and deep, and there was nothing to tie the barge to. They'd found the remains of the stone piers that had once run out into the river, but time had worn them and the river had eaten them. Tarman did not trust them, and Leftrin would not ignore his ship's uneasiness. He had promised Alise that once the ancient docks of Kelsingra had been restored, it would be a fine place to tie up a boat. But for now, for a short time, she was doomed to look on the Elderlings' side of Kelsingra with longing.

"Well, I guess I've told you everything, right?" Rapskal was standing up again. He was looking down the hillside now to where the other keepers were walking along the shore or exploring the stony, skeletal remains of the town. Hundreds of foundations were scattered along the shore; a few standing structures remained, enough for the keepers to take shelter in by night. Leftrin had climbed up the hill and discovered the intact shepherd's hut and insisted it was perfect for them. She tended to agree with him. It was the most privacy they had ever had. The first night, he'd built a crackling fire in the old hearth and discovered that, once he removed an old bird's nest from it, the chimney drew as well as ever. Golden firelight had filled the single room of the cottage. They'd spread their bedding on the floor in front of it and hung a blanket where once a wooden door had swung. She'd felt, for the first time in her life, that she was truly mistress of this tiny home. The very next morning, she'd brought her journals and notes up from the barge. Now she sat on the stone doorstep of the little house and surveyed her domain. From here, she had a wide view of the sweep of the river's bend and Leftrin's ship. She had the vista of all of old Kelsingra to tempt and taunt her.

She called her thoughts back to the moment at hand. Her four remaining sheets of good paper rested on her battered lap desk. "You haven't really told me anything, Rapskal."

He took a breath that lifted his narrow shoulders. He smiled at her, his white teeth showing strangely in his red-scaled face. "Well. Here's how it was. I was talking to Tats and he was mad at me for telling Thymara that I'd like to do to her what Jerd had taught me to do with her . . . Why aren't you writing?"

"Because, well, that's not the important part," Alise replied and heard her Bingtown primness come to the fore as a blush heated her face.

"Well, after that, then. Then that wave hit. And I got washed away by it."

"Yes."

"And then, I was trying to swim and I felt that Heeby was near, so I shouted for her, and she came to me. And we swam together for a while. Then a really big tangle of wood floated by. Maybe it had been part of the bonfire, I don't know. But it hit us and we sort of got tangled in it. Well, I didn't. I climbed up on top, but Heeby got tangled. She wasn't drowning, but she couldn't break free. So I told her, 'Don't fight it, let's just ride it out.' And we did, all that night, and the next morning we found we were way out in the middle of the river and could hardly see the shores. I didn't think we could swim to the shore so I thought, well, just stay with the floating wood tangle until we can see the shore. And that was a bad time for both of us, because she was stuck and we just got pushed on and on by the river. No food or water for either of us."

"How long was that?"

"Don't remember. More than two days, anyway." His claws were black. He scratched under his chin, gave a happy wriggle, and then settled again. "By and by, anyway, the river washed us up on the place where there was a big low meadow. Must have been on the other side of the river from the side we kept to when we were following the *Tarman,* because it didn't look to me like anywhere we had passed. And the river was on the wrong side of us, if you get what I mean. Well, there I could help Heeby get untangled and we went ashore. And we didn't have much, but I still had my fire-starting stuff, because I always keep it in this pouch. See?"

"I see," she replied. Her pen flew, but she glanced up briefly as he held up the pouch he wore on a string around his neck.

"So I built a fire to warm up my dragon and waited for some-one to see it and find us. But no one did. But there was pretty good hunting in the meadow place. There were these animals, maybe goats, maybe sheep I think, from what my dad used to tell me. They weren't deer or riverpig, anyway. They weren't very fast, and at first they weren't very scared of us. By the sec-ond or third day, they started to be scared because they figured out that Heeby liked to kill them and eat them. So we were eating those, and then we found this place back near some trees. It had a get-warm place for Heeby that she knew how to make work. And a stone building, mostly fallen down, but two rooms of it had good roofs, so that was plenty big enough for us. And Heeby hunted a lot and ate a lot, and so did I. And sometimes we slept on the get-warm place, and sometimes we slept in the old building. Heeby started to grow and get brighter colors, and her wings were growing, and her tail, and even her teeth! And we kept doing her flying lessons, you know what I mean. You used to see us doing them, right?"

"Yes. I used to see you trying to get her to fly."

"Yes. Well, her wings just got bigger and stronger, and one day she flew, just a little bit. And the next day, she could fly more, and then more. But she couldn't fly for a long time then, not for a whole day. But she could fly long enough that it got so she could hunt really good. And that girl of mine, all she wanted to do was hunt and eat and sleep on the get-warm place and hunt and sleep some more, and she just kept getting bigger and stronger all the time."

He shook his head, smiling indulgently. Then he stood up again and looked longingly down at the riverbank. Some of the keepers and their dragons were splashing one another and shouting and laughing. Tats had Fente on the bank and seemed to be scratching her with sand. The dragon looked stupefied with pleasure. Alise looked at her wet letters. She sprinkled sand over her page to dry the ink, waited a breath, and shook it clean. She set out a fresh page. "And then?"

He paced a turn, restless as a tethered dog. "Oh, you know. Ate more, slept more, and got even bigger. We both got lonely, and Heeby said one day, 'So, let's go to Kelsingra.' And I said, 'Can you find it?' and she said she thought she could. And I said, 'Can you fly that far?' and she said she thought she could, as long as she could find places to land and rest at night. And no landing in the river because she knows she can't fly up from water, and after being stuck in the tangle of wood and in water for days, she hates it now. So I said, 'Well, then, let's go,' and we did. And we found Kelsingra, but no one was here. And I was really sad thinking you all must be dead, but she said, 'No, I can feel some of the dragons, but they don't or can't hear me.' So we just started flying around every day, looking and looking and calling and calling. And then one day we heard dragons trumpeting, and it sounded like a big fight starting. So we went to see and found out it was just Sintara having a fuss. But we found you all up in that slough and told you to come here and here we are."

He was silent until her pen stopped moving. Then he asked with a trace of impatience, "So. It's done now, right? Posterity will know."

"It will indeed, Rapskal. And your name and Heeby's name will be remembered, generation after generation after generation."

That seemed, finally, to give him pause. He looked at her and smiled. "Good, then. That's nice. Heeby will like that. She wasn't sure about her name at first. And maybe I should have thought of something longer and grander, but I'd never named a dragon before." He lifted one shoulder in a shrug. "She got used to it. She likes her name, now."

"Well, she will be remembered by many, many people as the dragon who gave Kelsingra and its history back to us." Alise once more stared at the gleaming city on the other side of the swiftly flowing river. "It's a torment to see it and not be able to get over there. I cannot wait until the day I can walk those streets and enter those buildings and find what is left to us of them. I dare to hope for their city records, for scrolls and perhaps even a library . . ."

"Not much there, really." Rapskal dismissed her dreams with a shrug. "Most of the wood is gone rotten. I didn't see any scrolls or books in the places where I slept. Heeby and I walked around over there for a couple of days. Just an empty city."

"You've been over there!" Why had it never occurred to her before? He and his dragon would not be inconvenienced by a dangerous current. Of course they had gone first to the main part of the ancient Elderling city. "Rapskal, wait, come back. Sit down. I need to know what you've seen."

He turned and gave an impatient wriggle that made him a boy again. "Please, Alise, ma'am, not now! Later today, after Heeby hunts and kills and eats and sleeps, when she wakes up, I'll ask her to take you over there. Then you can see it for yourself and write it down and draw it or whatever. But it's been so long since I had time with my friends, and I've been lonely."

"What?"

"I've been by myself for so long! I really missed having people to talk to and . . ."

"No. No, not that! Heeby would take me across to Kelsingra? She would fly me there?"

He cocked his head at her. "Well, yes. She doesn't swim that good, you know, so she'd have to fly you there. She doesn't like to swim at all anymore. Doesn't even like to wade out in the water since we got stuck in the river like that."

"No, no, of course she doesn't! Who could blame her? But—but she'd let me ride on her back? I could fly on a dragon's back?"

"Yes, fly you to Kelsingra. And then you could see it all yourself and write it down as much as you want. I'm going to go down there now, with my friends. If you don't mind, please, ma'am."

"Oh, of course I don't mind. Thank you, Rapskal. Thank you so much."

"You're welcome, ma'am, I'm sure."

Then, as if fearing she would delay him again, he spun and ran. She watched him go, watched his long red-scaled legs flash in the sunlight. His clothing looked ridiculous on him now; the ragged trousers were too short for his Elderling legs, and the tattered shirt that had long ago lost its buttons flapped as he ran. His stride ate up the distance, and he shouted to his friends as he went. They turned and called to him in return, motioning to him to hurry and join them.

"Well, he has changed," Leftrin observed, watching Rapskal run down the grassy hillside toward the river.

"NOT AS MUCH as you might think," Alise replied as she turned to him. She was smiling, unaware of the ink smear by the side of her nose. He went to her, turned her face up to his and kissed her, and then tried to thumb the smear away but only succeeded in spreading it across her cheek. He laughed and showed her his inky thumb.

"Oh, no!" she cried and pulled a tattered kerchief from her pocket. She dabbed at her face. "Is it gone now?"

"Most of it," he told her, taking her hand. Still such a fine lady she was, to worry about something as trivial as a bit of ink smeared on her face. He loved it. "I see you've added some more pages to your stack. Did you get his entire story, then?"

"I got a summary of what happened to him, and how they found us again." She smiled and shook her head in wonder. "These youngsters take so much in stride. He sees nothing extraordinary in that he found a place where sheep or goats were running wild, near what had to have been an ancient Elderling dwelling. He doesn't even consider what it means that he found land, dry land suitable for pasturing livestock, right there on the Rain Wild River. Do you know what that would mean to Trehaug or Cassarick? The possibility of raising meat! Perhaps even sheep for wool. And he shrugs it off as an interesting spot with a 'get-warm' place for his dragon."

"Well. I'll agree that is a big discovery, one that is likely to remain undiscovered again for almost as long as it has been."

"Not when the dragons start flying," she said, and then, to his shock, sprang at him and trapped him in a hug. "Leftrin, you'll never guess what Rapskal told me! He said he'd ask Heeby to carry me across to the main part of Kelsingra, so I can walk the streets there as long as I want!"

He felt almost hurt at her excitement. "But I told you I'd get you there! There's just no safe place for Tarman to put in along the bank right now. But maybe tomorrow, the barge could take us most of the way across, and then we could cover the rest of the distance in a small boat. And Tarman could come fetch us back in the afternoon. There's just no way for him to stay there. Water's too deep for the poles, and while he can move the barge against a slow current in shallow water, deep swift water is too hard for him."

"Tomorrow! We could do that tomorrow? Together?"

Had she heard a word he'd said? "Yes, my dear. Of course we

could. It's only the barge that can't safely put in on that shore. And in the future, when the docks there are restored, that won't be a problem."

She looked down at her remaining sheets of paper, and then lifted her last bottle of ink to the light. "Oh, Leftrin, what a fool I was! I documented every little thing all along the way, and now that we are here, on the outskirts of a major intact Elderling city, I'm down to a few sheets of paper and a few drops of ink!"

He shook his head at her fondly. "Well, when we get back to Trehaug, I shall have to buy you a crate of paper and a hogshead of ink." He reached over and playfully twitched the abused handkerchief from her fingertips. "And perhaps a few of these, too."

"What?" she asked him. All life, all merriment faded suddenly from her face. "Trehaug? Go back to Trehaug?"

He cocked his head at her. "Well, I think we'll have to before winter, or we're going to have keepers running around here in the cold in next to nothing. And while meat and fish and wild greens are fine things, I for one am starting to miss even such bread as ship's biscuit. And a dozen other things we've been doing without." He grinned at the prospect.

She just stared at him. "Go back to Trehaug?"

"Well, of course. You must have known that we'd have to go back eventually."

"I, well, no. I hadn't thought about it. I never want to go back, not to Trehaug, not to Bingtown."

He looked at the distress in her face and then carefully folded her into his arms. "Alise, Alise. You don't think I'd let you get away from me? Yes, we'll go back to Trehaug. We'll go back together, just as we came here. Tarman will show you what he can do, downriver in the current, when we know where we're going, without a herd of slogging dragons setting the pace for us. We'll go down to Cassarick and put in our order for provisions. You'll report to the Council there, and I'll collect my money. Yes, and you'll report to Malta the Elderling, too."

She was looking up at him, and the life had come back to her face. Her eyes had begun to shine. He had to continue the tale for her.

"And then we'll go down to Trehaug, pick up our cargo, and be back here before the worst of winter, with blankets and knives and tea and coffee and bread and whatnot. Now I've never so much as seen a herd of sheep or an apple tree, but from what I've heard tell, I think they'd go here. So we'll make that an order, too, and next spring, we'll make another run, and we'll pick up whatever it was we sent for. Seeds and animals and such things from Bingtown and beyond. Look around us, Alise. You see that old city over there, and it's a very fine thing, I'm sure. But I see the one thing that the Rain Wilds has never had, and that's arable land. What if, after all these generations, the Rain Wilders could feed themselves without having to dig for Elderling artifacts to do it?

"We're going to change everything, Alise. Everything."

COPPER AND SILVER they gleamed, side by side on the sandy riverbank. They were both stretched out in utter repose. Sedric's back ached and his hands felt raw from the scrubbing, but Relpda shimmered as if she were a newly minted coin. She was growing again, he was sure of it. Both her neck and tail seemed longer and more graceful, and her wings were getting stronger all the time. Beside her, Spit's ribs rose and fell in the slow cadence of deep sleep. Sedric glanced up at Heeby's distant circling silhouette just in time to see the red dragon clap her wings tight to her body and dive on something; he knew a moment of purest jealousy. Then he looked at Relpda, and it all ebbed away. In time. Soon enough, the sun would catch on her copper wings in flight. For now, the deep sleep of her repose was satisfaction enough for him.

"I've never seen anything as beautiful as she is when she's clean. Nothing gleams like she does."

Sedric was perched on the riverbank. A short distance away from him at the water's edge, Carson straightened slowly, shaking water from his hands and arms. Both men had spent most of the afternoon grooming their dragons. Carson had gone hunting in the dawn and brought back a deer. The dragons had not been happy about having to share a kill, but he'd insisted. In the process of eating it, they'd managed to get blood all over themselves, and Sedric had insisted it was time they both had a good grooming. That task finished, Carson had discarded his shirt while he'd sluiced his hands and arms in the river.

He toweled himself with the discarded garment as he walked back to Sedric. There was silvery scaling on his arms now, and sparkling drops of water clung to the black hairs on his forearms and chest. The hunter was grinning. "Oh, I think I've seen a thing or two as pretty as she is, copper man." He tossed his shirt to the ground and then sat down on the sand beside Sedric. He ran a finger up the line of scaling on Sedric's bare back. Sedric gave a delighted shiver and in response, Carson put his arm around him and pulled him over to lean against him. The hunter rested his chin on Sedric's head and said quietly, "Let's nap while they do. And when we wake up, I'll take you hunting."

"I don't know how to hunt," Sedric admitted.

"That's why I'll be teaching you," Carson explained. When he spoke, Sedric felt the words thrum through his chest.

"Sounds like work," Sedric complained. "Messy, bloody work. What if I don't want to learn it?"

"Oh, these lazy Bingtown boys," Carson lamented. He lay back on the sun-warmed sand, pulling Sedric over with him. The hunter put one arm over his face to shade his eyes. His free hand found the hair on the back on Sedric's head and his fingers twined gently through it. He sighed. "I guess I'll just have to think of something else to teach you, then."

Sedric sighed. He caught the hunter's hand, brought it to his mouth, and kissed the palm of it. "I might be open to that," he agreed.

THYMARA SAT ON the edge of the grassy sward, right where it met the riverbank. It was a peculiar sort of place. Behind her was gently sloping, open, dry meadow, carpeted in tall green grass. And then the meadow stopped suddenly, and there was a sudden drop in the land, and then the sandy, rocky edge of the river. She had never even imagined such a place before. It pleased her to be sitting on the edge of that meadow world, dangling her legs. The sun was warm on her skin, and it eased the deep ache in her back. She closed her eyes and turned her face up to the sunlight. Warmth. Light and warmth felt so good to her now. She knew that the light and warmth were accelerating her changes. She could feel it now, the way she had once felt her teeth growing in. A pleasant, achy pain. She rolled her shoulders and felt her folded wings rub against the shirt that confined them. Sylve had helped her cut and hem slits in her shirt back, but it still felt odd to have them exposed. For most of the time, she kept them covered. Everyone, she told herself, knew she had them. Sometimes it felt silly to cover them.

On the other hand, she thought, everyone knew she had breasts. She covered those, too. She smiled slightly at the comparison. The boys seemed as intrigued by either.

She heard the swish of the grasses against his legs a moment before he sat down beside her.

"So. What are you smiling about?"

"Nothing, really." She opened her eyes and turned toward Tats. "What have you been up to?"

"Helping Davvie learn how to care for Kalo. That is one big dragon."

"Does Fente mind your grooming Kalo?"

He smiled ruefully. "Not as much as Lecter does. Finally, I took him aside and told him plainly there was nothing to be jealous about. I was just helping Davvie with his dragon. I'm not interested in Davvie that way at all."

She found herself smiling back at him. Things had become a bit easier between them of late. It felt almost to her as if they had gone back to being the friends they had been back in Trehaug. She studied him now, unabashedly considering how his scaling was progressing. "Fente is changing you fast," she observed. The dragon had not echoed her green in him, but had chosen instead bronzes and blacks. His scaling was fine, almost undetectable. Fente had outlined Tats's eyes in black and bronzed his skin. She was keeping his hair and brows as they were. Thymara found herself nodding in approval of her choice. It seemed to her that most of the other dragons were changing their keepers in their own images. Fente had chosen to keep Tats as he was, right down to giving color to the fading slave tattoos on his face.

"She says it's the warmth of the sun here, and the light. How about you? Has Sintara continued to change you?"

"I continue to change," she said simply. Despite their confrontation in the river that day, nothing had been resolved. Sometimes that seemed the most surprising thing of all. The other keepers never quarreled with their dragons. Their dragons seldom spoke harshly to them; they didn't have to. The keepers knew they were harnessed with glamour and didn't care. But she and Sintara were not like that. They spoke their minds to each other, and she found that didn't displease her. After their last crisis, their relationship had resumed as it had been before. Thymara tended the dragon and brought her food when her hunting went well. She enjoyed Sintara's beauty, just as she would have enjoyed living in a fine house, just as she had once enjoyed the art and music of her neighbors in the Cricket Cages. She didn't confuse that beauty with Sintara herself.

"You're quiet," Tats spoke carefully.

"I'm thinking. That's all."

"You think a lot lately."

"That's true. I don't think it's a bad thing."

"I didn't mean that it was."

"I know."

He shifted unhappily and then sighed. "Thymara. Did I ruin everything between us?"

She turned to look at him and gave him a genuine smile. "No. Of course you didn't. You just, well, actually, we just pushed it to a point where we had to talk about what would happen next. It wasn't bad that we reached that point."

"But *nothing* happened next," Tats grumbled softly and looked away from her.

It made her smile. "Oh, something happened. It just wasn't what you expected. I said no and I meant it. I still mean it, Tats. But it's not about you. It's about me dealing with what I'm becoming, and dealing with it one change at a time."

He glanced over at her. His lashes were long and thick as they had always been. "Then it isn't . . . forever. It's just a decision for now."

"Tats," she began, but she was interrupted when Rapskal flung himself down beside her. She jumped; she still wasn't accustomed to him being back. A smile spread across her face of her own accord. It was incredibly good to have him back. Tats made a small sound in the back of his throat, but the smile he gave their friend was genuine.

"So, let's see them!" Rapskal greeted her.

"See what?"

"Your wings, of course! Everyone else has seen them but me. Take them out, I want to see them."

"Rapskal, they're not, well, they're not finished yet." She couldn't think of what else to say. She wasn't sure how to express what she meant to say, and then it came to her. "I'm not ready for people to see them yet."

He turned his head to one side. Sunlight ran down the scaling along his jaw, and she had to suppress the impulse to trace the same line with her fingers. He gave a confused shrug. "But people already saw them, in the river that day. Even I saw them, if only for a minute as we flew over. So it's only fair I get to see them now, because everyone else got a chance to see them then."

"That doesn't make sense."

"Please."

She tried to think if he'd ever said please to her before. If he had, it hadn't sounded like that. She didn't answer, but only reached over her shoulder to where the openings were cut in the back of her shirt. She began to grope for the tips of her wings.

"Oh, I'll help," he offered, and before she could refuse, she felt his fingers on her wingtips as he gently guided first one and then the other out of her shirt. His gentle touch put a shiver up her back and when she shook, she felt her wings suddenly quiver in response.

"Ohhh," he said. "Open them. Let me see the pattern."

She glanced at him. The expression on his face was rapt. She looked shyly at Tats. He was staring at her wings as if trying to grasp the concept that they were part of her now. "I'm still learning how to move them," she said quietly. Suddenly she wanted both of them to see her wings. She closed her eyes and focused on feeling the sunlight touching her wings. Sylve had been right, she suddenly decided. They were like fingers coming out of her back. Fingers, long fingers on hands . . . she opened her eyes and looked down at her hands. She closed her fingers together and then, very slowly, aware of every muscle, every movement, she opened them.

She knew it had worked when she heard Rapskal catch his breath. "Oh, they're lovely. Can I touch them?"

"Rapskal, I don't think . . ." she began, but he wasn't listening.

"They're like Heeby's wings were at first. The skin is as fine as parchment, and the light shines right through the colors. I'm going to hold them open all the way so I can see them." He crawled around behind her, and she felt him take the outermost tip of each wing in each of his hands. Then, as carefully as if she were a butterfly, he opened her wings fully to the light. She could feel the difference, could feel the light and then the warmth of the sun touch them. Warmth spread through them as if it were water flowing.

"The colors just got brighter," Tats said quietly.

"You should do this every day," Rapskal said decisively. "And you should practice moving them, too, to make them stronger and help them grow. Otherwise, you'll never be able to fly."

"Oh, she won't be able to fly with them," Tats told him quickly, as if fearing that Rapskal had hurt her feelings. "I heard Sintara tell her that. The dragon said she should just be grateful to have such beautiful wings. She won't be able to fly with them."

Rapskal laughed merrily. "Oh, that's what everyone said to me about Heeby, too. Don't be silly. Of course she'll be able to

fly. She just has to try every day." He leaned forward and spoke
by her ear. "Don't worry, Thymara. I'll help you practice every
day, just like I did with Heeby. You'll fly."

SINTARA HAD MOVED far up the hillside. From her vantage, she
could look out over the wide, sloping meadow before her. Kelsingra. They had returned. The tall spire of the map tower and
the gleaming stone roofs of the city beckoned to her from the
other side of the deep, swift river.

Earlier today, she had watched Heeby hunting. She'd seen the
red dragon open her wings and spring almost effortlessly into
the air. Her wings had beat hard for a moment, and then she'd
caught the motion of the air over the river and lifted. In a few
moments she had dwindled to the size of a crow, and then to a
hunting hawk. Heeby had circled high over the city, and Sintara
had watched her and remembered in agony exactly how it felt,
how you cupped your wings just so to capture a rising wall of
warmer air, and how you spilled wind from your wings to go
sliding down the sky.

She remembered. She knew. She was a dragon, a ruler of the
Three Realms, a queen of earth and sky and water. Kelsingra
with its wells of sweet silver was just across the river. A real
dragon would simply open her wings and fly there.

She had opened her wings and felt the sun on them, felt them
warming in the kiss of light. She moved them slightly and felt
the wind they made. She recalled how Thymara had mocked
and defied her, calling her lazy, even stupid. She recalled all of
Heeby's foolish early efforts at flights. How ungainly she had
looked, how clumsy as over and over again she had tried to fly
and failed. She'd had no pride, no dignity at all.

She heard a distant cry, the shrill whistle of a hunting dragon.
Her keen eyes picked out Heeby as she suddenly folded her
wings and stooped on something. Something large, Sintara was
suddenly certain. Something large and meaty, something hot
with blood.

She shook out her wings to the summer sunlight. The hillside was wide and green before her. And across the river was Kelsin-gra, city of Elderlings and dragons.

She ran half a dozen steps before she had the courage to beat her wings. Her feet left the ground briefly, and then she crashed down again. But she didn't fall. Her wings were open and wide and they caught her and cushioned her fall.

"Sintara!" she heard someone shout in awe. "Look at Sin-tara!"

Another dozen running steps and this time she beat her wings more slowly and powerfully.

And when she leaped, she left the ground behind.

✦ ✦ ✦

Day the 17th of the Rain Moon

Year the 6th of the Independent Alliance of Traders

From Detozi, Keeper of the Birds, Trehaug

To Reyall, Acting Keeper of the Birds, Bingtown

Enclosed, a formal announcement from the Dushank Trader Family of the Rain Wild Traders, Trehaug, to be publicly posted in the Bingtown Traders' Concourse, being an announcement of the intention of the Trader family of Dushank of the Rain Wild Traders to accept a marriage offer from the Dunwarrow Trader family to join their offspring in marriage.

Reyall!

And so you are the first to know of the official announcement.

Erek and Detozi

✦ ✦ ✦